REASONS
WE BREAK

REASONS WE BREAK

JESMEEN KAUR DEO

HYPERION

Los Angeles New York

To Jen, who always believed in this book

First Edition, November 2025
10 9 8 7 6 5 4 3 2 1
FAC-004510-25233
Printed in the United States of America

This book is set in Baskerville/Monotype
Stock image: Grunge texture 310639790/Shutterstock
Designed by Zareen Johnson

Library of Congress Cataloging-in-Publication Data

Names: Deo, Jesmeen Kaur author
Title: Reasons we break / by Jesmeen Kaur Deo.
Description: First edition. • Los Angeles : Hyperion, 2025. • Audience
  term: Teenagers • Audience: Ages 13–18 • Audience: Grades 10–12 •
  Summary: "To keep Rajan out of prison, Simran agrees to handle his
  former gang's books, but when a gang war erupts, they must decide how
  much they will sacrifice for each other"—Provided by publisher.
Identifiers: LCCN 2024055867 • ISBN 9781368113748 (hardcover)
Subjects: CYAC: Gangs—Fiction • Bookkeeping—Fiction • East
  Indians—British Columbia—Fiction • British Columbia—Fiction • Romance
  stories • LCGFT: Romance fiction • Novels
Classification: LCC PZ7.1.D46836 Re 2025 • DDC [Fic]—dc23/eng/20250320
LC record available at https://lccn.loc.gov/2024055867

Reinforced binding

The authorized representative in the EU for product safety and compliance is Disney Trading
B.V., Asterweg 15S, 1031 HL, Amsterdam, The Netherlands
email: DCP.DL-EU.bookscontact@disney.com

Visit www.HyperionTeens.com

Content warnings: on-page parental cancer (treated and improves); off-page parental death (prior to book's events); drugs/alcohol use and addiction; gang-related violence; mentions of sex trafficking

SUSTAINABLE FORESTRY INITIATIVE
Certified Sourcing
www.forests.org
SFI-01681

Logo Applies to Text Stock Only

PROLOGUE

FOUR YEARS AGO

WHEN RAJAN RANDHAWA failed eighth-grade math, the school forced him to get a tutor.

Northridge Secondary offered smart kids money to do one-on-one sessions with "struggling students." Rajan wasn't a fan. His first tutor got frustrated with his slowness and quit. His second tutor sat down on day one, turned Rajan's homework toward herself, and did it for him. His third commented *Aren't Indian people supposed to be good at math?* then reported Rajan to the admin when he cussed him out. His fourth smelled weed on him and also reported him to admin. His fifth tutor apparently wanted in on this trend because he reported him too, although to this day Rajan didn't understand why. He and the Northridge admin were pretty tight by then. And not in a good way.

So, when his sixth tutor came around in grade nine, Rajan wasn't impressed. He'd already accepted that he sucked at math and wished Northridge would do the same. Instead, they seemed to be doubling down by sending him Simran Aujla.

Rajan had cringed automatically at her name. It was practically a

Pavlovian response, since every kid in Kelowna's Punjabi community grew up unwillingly hearing it. *That Aujla girl has perfect grades and perfect manners*, went the parental refrain. *Why can't you be more like her?*

Since they were in the same grade and school, he had witnessed her perfection firsthand. She collected awards like baseball cards—top student, volunteerism, debate, science fair, spelling bee, math contests— plus, she had extracurriculars coming out of her ass. This tutoring gig was probably just another line item to beef up her résumé. He hoped she expected it to go smoothly.

Because he had no intention of letting it go smoothly for any of these pretentious fuckers anymore.

Rajan sat in the library, his knee bouncing under the table as he waited for Simran. The librarian hissed at him to take his hat off. He blew her a kiss but obeyed. Once her back was turned, he put it on again. The cycle would repeat the next time she looked his way. The inevitability of that was nice.

He waited ten, then fifteen minutes. He got told to remove his hat thrice in that time. His mind wandered. Maybe he should leave. Simran clearly didn't give a shit about this tutoring thing, which made two of them. But the moment he stood, the library doors burst open.

A breathless, bushy-browed girl with wire-frame glasses and a long braid scanned the otherwise abandoned library and spotted him. Reluctantly, he sank back into his seat.

She sat in the chair next to his, tossing her gigantic backpack on the table. "Hi, I'm Simran." Pause. "But I guess we've gone to school together for a while."

"Really?" He popped a toothpick between his teeth. "Never noticed."

She frowned slightly. Rajan wondered if she could tell he was screwing with her. But she seemed to shake it off and opened her backpack, kara sliding down her wrist as she did so. His eyes wandered to the collar of her baggy T-shirt, where a black kirpan strap peeked out. So the rumours were true—she was *Sikh* Sikh.

"We're doing . . . Math 8, right?" Simran asked. Rajan pulled his gaze back to her face. From the grapevine he knew this girl was in Math 10 this semester. Behind that innocent facade, she was probably judging him *hard*.

He winked. "Yup. Round three."

"What's your assignment today?" He slid it over, and she read it eagerly, like all the other tutors had before they realized how stupid he was. "'Fractions, ratios, and percents.' Do you have an approach?"

"Yeah, it's usually"—he crumpled the assignment into a ball, and tossed it into the garbage several feet away—"that."

Simran stared at the bin her hour's wages had just disappeared into. When she looked back at him, her jaw was tight. He gave her a mocking grin. *Just give up*, he thought. *Walk away*.

Instead, she reached into her backpack and tugged a fresh piece of loose-leaf free from underneath the binders. She wrote a fraction problem on it, then pushed it his way. "Why don't you try again."

Her voice was soft, but this time her hand stayed on the corner, pinning it to the table.

He gazed at the paper and thought about how bored he already was.

"Are you thinking?" Simran asked eventually. "I can show you."

He shrugged, pulling the strings of his oversize hoodie. He always wore a few sizes up. Having yet to hit a growth spurt, it made him look bigger than he was—which was a survival skill, in his life. "Nah, I'm trying."

Time crawled by painfully slowly. Eventually, she picked up the pencil and showed him the steps. He nodded along and then, when she passed the pencil back, did nothing. She tried to show him again. Same thing. *Give up*.

She didn't. She glanced at the clock and said, "We'll keep at it next week."

"Got it, Auntie." He swiped his textbook off the table and left without looking back.

The following week, the same thing happened. And then the week after. The next time, he deliberately smoked right before, but she didn't report him even though he smelled like a fucking grow op. She just kept explaining fractions, and although he was too stoned to pay attention, he liked listening to her voice. It was soothing, like some kind of ASMR.

When he told her that (he didn't have much of a filter right then), she looked surprised for a split second. Then she giggled. Slightly. She tamped down on it real quick, but he heard it. Until that point, Rajan hadn't known she was even capable of giggling. He was sort of pleased he'd made her do it.

That freaked him out. He decided not to get high before tutoring anymore.

The next day, Friday, he was summoned to the office. He'd just been caught dealing to some dude in his class. It was Jake's fault for being so obvious with the baggie when the teacher walked by. Of course, that white kid was on the soccer team, so he got off with a slap on the wrist. Meanwhile, Rajan had already been threatened with suspension.

A school counsellor, Ms. Fernandez, was now here playing good cop. Somewhere between the lectures about how he needed to *stop whatever dangerous things you're involved in outside of school*, how he still had *a chance not to become a statistic*, blah blah, she finally said something interesting. "How's math tutoring going?"

"It's fucked," he said.

"Language, Rajan."

"Golly gee, it's fucked."

Ms. Fernandez pursed her lips. "Simran's the best junior tutor we've ever had. She's helped many students. Never failed, actually."

"First time for everyone."

She sighed. "You're never going to convince me you're a lost cause, Rajan. Why don't you tell me how I can help you, instead?"

He winked. "Give me my weed back."

She sighed again, clearly not getting that he'd answered honestly. Thanks to his stash being confiscated, he was going to fall short with the cash handover tonight. And he was short last time, too.

The office released him after sentencing him to a week's worth of detentions. By that time, he'd missed art class, which sucked since he actually liked that one, and it was lunch hour. Restless, he wandered to his usual hangout—the smoke pit, on the corner of the school property facing the woods.

His mood soured further when he saw Zach Singer among the people there, smoking a cigarette and flicking his pretentious brand-name lighter. Zach was one year older and kind of a dick. He was also a business competitor of Rajan's, in a manner of speaking. But the smoke pit was neutral turf, so they tolerated each other here. Mostly.

As Rajan passed him, Zach punched his shoulder slightly harder than could be considered friendly. "Where've you been?"

"The circus." That was the common name for the admin office in his social circle. Rajan leaned against the chain-link fence and wished he had a joint.

Zach wasn't done. "What about yesterday after school?"

"Math tutoring." He considered asking Zach for a drag off his cigarette. But he wasn't about to stoop that low just to soothe his nerves.

"Oh, right. What's that bitch's name again? Susan?"

"Simran," Rajan said shortly. Zach noticed.

"What's the matter? You hot for teacher?"

Rajan rolled his eyes. Zach was always trying to get a rise out of him. "Dude, come on."

"Yeah, you're right," Zach chuckled, blowing a smoke ring at him. "She's the last teacher anyone would be hot for."

Rajan said nothing.

"You think she could be hot if she tried? If she got rid of that moustache, or something?" Zach looked around at the group. He seemed to mull it over, cigarette stuck in the corner of his mouth. "Nah. Not even a hot librarian type. She's ugly as f—"

Rajan ripped the cigarette out of Zach's mouth with one hand and punched him in the face with the other.

Zach staggered back several steps, then looked up, eyes screaming bloody murder. He was bigger than Rajan, but most people were. That never stopped Rajan when his blood ran hot.

Zach lunged. Rajan took a drag of the cigarette, then waited until Zach crashed into him to press the smoking point into his arm.

Zach swore, momentarily distracted enough for Rajan to get another hit in. Blood spurted from Zach's nose. That was the last satisfying punch he threw, because then Zach tackled him to the ground. Things sort of devolved after that.

Later, Rajan was back in the office for the second time that day. This time, the principal's office.

Mr. Kerr sat at his desk, two files open in front of him, as he droned on about responsibility. Rajan nodded along while sneak-reading Zach's file upside down. *Long detention record*, yeah, obviously. *Suspected gang affiliation*, no shit. *Family on income assistance . . . that* was interesting, considering Zach made being rich half his personality. He'd probably stolen that fucking lighter.

"Rajan, you *burned* Zach with a cigarette," Mr. Kerr said, pulling Rajan's attention back to him. "That's a very serious assault." Rajan rolled his eyes. He hadn't even pressed it long enough to cause any lasting damage, but clearly Zach was going to milk it for all it was worth. "We can only move forward if you help us. Did Zach threaten you?"

So that's what this was about. Kerr just wanted dirt on Zach. Zach, who was even more of a pain in his ass than Rajan. Rajan shifted in his seat, wincing slightly at his aching ribs. That dickhead hit like a truck.

"Rajan?" Kerr prodded. "Why'd you hit Zach? I don't buy that it was about cigarettes."

Now that was something Rajan was choosing not to examine. It was nobody's business, anyway. He and Zach had been long overdue for a fight. He half glanced at the poster on the wall, which said *Zero tolerance policy for inappropriate language.*

He chose his words carefully. "I hit Zach because he's a—"

Rajan then let loose a string of words so foul that the principal's pen fell out of his grasp and rolled off the table before he managed a response.

And what a response it was. Needless to say, the conversation was over. Rajan was sent home with two weeks' suspension, and that was that.

When Rajan returned to school, he was even more screwed. For one, he had no clue what was going on in *any* of his classes anymore. And secondly: Zach was back, too.

A friend informed Rajan at lunch that Zach was planning some revenge after school with his buddies. Rajan knew instinctively that these "buddies" weren't the school variety. He'd stirred up an already tense turf war, and now, he had exactly three hours to figure out a survival strategy.

Rajan skipped next period to make a plan. Perry was his supplier lately, so he called him first. He explained the situation, that he needed a safe ride home. But instead, Perry promised to be there to *fight*.

"Be ready tonight," he said, sounding gleeful, and hung up. Of course. Perry was probably ecstatic to have a reason to get rid of Zach—he was taking half the customers at Northridge. Just the other day, a popular girl in his class, Chandani, had chosen Zach's cheaper product over his. Rajan leaned his head against the wall and cursed.

He needed a weapon. Otherwise he'd be dead meat as soon as he left school grounds. He used to drag around a baseball bat for occasions like this, but that was confiscated several fights ago . . .

Wait.

A teacher poked her head through a doorway and told him to go to class. He pushed off the wall and obeyed. But his mind was elsewhere— coming up with a plan.

Picking the lock of the storage room was easy, with the help of a twisted paper clip. Security at Northridge was a joke. Or maybe they didn't think anyone would have the balls to break in there, since it was across from the admin office. Rajan stole a glance that way before slipping inside.

The tiny room was littered with random shit. Magazine boxes, plastic tubs of gym equipment, Hula Hoops, and rolled-up posters lined the shelves. A Swiss Army Knife, on a shelf beside a lockbox, caught his eye, and he pocketed it immediately. The bat had to be here. This place wasn't cleared out often—

He spotted it leaning against the farthest corner at the same time the doorknob turned.

Rajan backed away immediately, toward the wall. Nowhere to hide. He was caught. He pulled the knife out of his hoodie, not wanting it on him when they inevitably demanded he turn out his pockets.

But when the door swung open, it wasn't a teacher. It was Simran.

Instead of putting the knife down, he froze. She blinked. And then they were staring at each other, him holding a knife, her a stack of papers.

From somewhere beyond her, Mr. Kerr's voice sounded. "Simran, did you find the cashbox?"

Kerr's heavy footsteps drew closer. Rajan tensed. Of course Miss Goody-Two-Shoes was running errands for the *principal*. He was screwed.

But Simran turned away, letting the door fall nearly closed. "I just realized, I left it in Mrs. Scott's classroom."

"Really?" Mr. Kerr stopped in his tracks. "But you were here with it last. I was with you. Did you look?" His voice grew louder, as if he were trying to peek inside. Rajan stepped out of the sliver of light and nearly bumped into a shelf—the shelf with the *lockbox*, the one school council used for money collection.

"That's what I thought, too," Simran said. "But I just remembered. When you left for your meeting, I went to Mrs. Scott's room to get some uncounted envelopes. I think I left the cashbox on her desk."

She sounded so sincere Rajan found himself glancing at the cashbox again to confirm it was there.

Kerr seemed convinced as well. "Oh, well, if you're sure . . ."

"I am," Simran said. "Sorry. Let's go."

And she closed the door firmly behind her. *Click.* Two pairs of footsteps faded away, and a dazed Rajan counted to thirty before picking up his bat and making his escape.

The next day, though, he was furious.

He burst into the library, the door banging against the wall so loud the librarian hissed, "Careful!" He ignored her, scanning the room. Simran sat at one of the study tables as usual.

As he made a beeline for her, Simran noticed him, too. Her eyes flicked down to his bruised jaw—the only visible evidence of what went down the night before.

He planted his hands on the table. "What the fuck do you want?"

Her eyes widened. He realized belatedly that he'd never lost his cool with her before. But he'd been thinking about this all night, and there was only one reason she would've done it. And it pissed him off.

"What?" Simran said. "I don't want anything from you."

"Bullshit. You let me leave with a *knife* yesterday. You could've let Kerr see me. There's no way they'd make you tutor me after that." He was frustrated. She'd lasted longer than all the others, and for what? They weren't making progress. It was a stalemate. Why wasn't she giving up? "What do you want? Me to be grateful? Let you talk fractions so you can get a reference letter? Or"—he laughed as the possibility occurred to him—"you want some free product, is that it?"

She just stared. It pissed him off even worse. And confused him, too, honestly. Most people would have their favour ready to ask. "Spit it out," he snapped, "or I swear I'm going to the office right now to fess up."

Her eyes flashed with alarm. "They'll expel you."

He knew that. With all his infractions lately, this'd be the last straw. But right now, it felt like the better option. He didn't need to add her to the list of people he owed. "So?"

She looked down at the table, her expression a mask. Finally, she said, "Fine. You're right. I do want something."

"Which is?"

"I want you to try in our tutoring sessions. Or I'll turn you in, and it'll be your word versus mine."

The knot of tension in him loosened. He sank into his seat. Threats, he understood.

Still, he was a negotiator. "I'll try until the end of this semester. That's it. No one will expel me for something from a semester ago, especially if they know you held on to it that long."

Simran shook her head. "You're underestimating Mr. Kerr's dislike of you. We'll go until June."

Rajan narrowed his eyes. This fucking nerd was driving a hard bargain suddenly, for someone who only appeared to have come up with it five seconds ago. But maybe that was her game.

"I *could* be bluffing," Simran added, as if guessing his thoughts. "But would it be *so* bad to just . . . try, in our sessions?"

She sounded almost hopeful. Rajan had a feeling he knew why. "Ms. Fernandez said you've never failed at what you do," he said conversationally. "Guess you have that sort of rep. Don't want me ruining it, huh?"

"That's not true. I haven't always succeeded."

"Yeah? Then why's Fernandez so up your ass?"

He didn't really expect Simran to give an answer—it was rhetorical, really, since *all* the teachers were up her ass—but she did. "Once, I overheard her saying some very unflattering things about the principal. She's been kind to me ever since. Because she's afraid I'll tell him otherwise."

Rajan stared. Simran folded her hands neatly in front of her. In the ensuing silence, it felt like she was daring him to ask, *Would you?* And the fact that he was wondering it at all made his view of her shift slightly.

He'd thought he was in a unique position to learn the gossip in this school, like what he'd learned about Zach's family situation recently, because he was always here after hours and between classes, doing detention and running teachers' errands as punishment. So naturally he overheard their casual conversations, saw the shit they left out on their desks. But Simran did, too. Just for different reasons.

The idea of them having any similarity was disturbing. He leaned back. "Say we do it. How do I know you'll be satisfied with my 'trying'? Because teachers usually aren't."

"If you're trying and not doing well, that's the teacher failing, not you."

He didn't know what to say to that, so he ignored it entirely. "You're being optimistic as hell, but fine. End of June it is."

"And longer if you like it."

"Longer if I—" He gaped. "You've got a lot of balls, you know that?"

Simran merely smiled. "Give me a pen."

Reluctantly, he did. She opened her notebook and started writing.

Wow, they were actually doing this. She was about to find out how stupid he was. A familiar sense of dread rose in him, but he was distracted from it when she glanced at his bruised jaw again. "Did you win the fight?"

Her voice was hesitant. She had, after all, seen him steal a knife. And maybe she'd heard some rumours, too.

Just the thought of what he'd witnessed last night made his stomach curdle. And Zach, well . . . Rajan suspected he wasn't going to be a problem for a while. Not after Perry had threatened him at needlepoint. Not gunpoint. *Needlepoint.* Rajan really had to hand it to Perry for that one. At least with a gun, you knew what kind of pain you were in for.

Of course, he didn't say any of that. "Simran Sahiba, if I lost, I wouldn't be here."

She smiled again, this time a little sadly. "Well," she said, "I'm glad you are."

She bent back over the paper. And Rajan had the strangest feeling that, despite his efforts, he'd been manipulated anyway.

That evening, he went home earlier than usual. He had a lot to think about.

At first, he'd only listened to Simran out of obligation. To show her it was a lost cause. But something else had happened, instead.

Sure, Rajan needed things explained repeatedly and was embarrassingly slow. But Simran was *so* patient. He felt like he could get it wrong, and wrong, and wrong again, and she'd just point back to the right path without comment. And that made him want to get it right the first time, if only to surprise her.

He told himself he was developing Stockholm syndrome.

Surprisingly, his mother was up when he got home. Nobody was usually around to greet him. But there she was, in a patio chair on the porch, a Korean mink blanket warding off the October chill. A stack of envelopes dangled from her hand. As he came up the gravel driveway, she jolted awake, quickly dropping them into her lap. As if Rajan didn't know what they were. The bills, the mortgage, the debt.

He climbed the porch stairs and kissed her clammy forehead in greeting.

"Sweetheart," she said. "You're home early."

It was a soft observation. The sun was setting, but he was usually out much later with his friends. He wished she'd be angrier about it. About *something*.

"I got in a fight yesterday," he told her, sinking into the other ornate chair on the beautiful porch they couldn't afford, attached to the house they couldn't afford.

"That's okay."

He stared out at the driveway, at the car they couldn't afford. The SUV they couldn't afford wasn't there; his father must not be home yet. "I stole my bat back. The one they confiscated."

His mother made a noise of sympathy, expression half glazed over. Was it dialysis day tomorrow?

"I failed a test," he told her.

She merely closed her eyes.

"I killed a dude," he said, to test the waters. Her eyes remained closed. He willed her to open them. To care. She did not. And he knew that wasn't her fault—she never had the energy—but it still sucked. Nobody cared when he did well, and now, nobody cared when he screwed up either.

Her breathing evened out. Asleep. He tipped his head back and sighed. Distantly, he heard his brothers running around inside the house. He wished he were like them. Completely stupid, that was. And unable to understand their mother was dying.

He'd offered to donate a kidney multiple times, even though he wasn't old enough yet. His mother laughed each time. *Don't be silly, sweetheart. You need your kidney.*

But he didn't need his kidney. He needed his mom.

Since there was nobody else to talk to, he spoke to the sky. "My math tutor saw me steal the bat. She's blackmailing me into tutoring now. But I feel like she only did it because she knew I expected her to. Isn't that fucked up?"

His mother thwacked his arm. He was so surprised she was awake, he jumped.

"*Language,*" she scolded. "There was a letter from your school about this tutor. The Aujla girl? The one who gets all the awards?"

Rajan was so relieved she was talking again, so happy she'd had the energy to read Northridge's shit-talking letters, that he couldn't even be annoyed she was fixated on how great Simran was. "I guess so. She's *perfect*, isn't she." No response. His mother's eyes were sliding closed again. He poked her arm. "Nobody can be that perfect. She'll crack one of these days."

"Well," his mother murmured. "That happens when people have a lot of pressure on them." Her voice lost its playfulness. "They crack. They bend. And eventually, they break."

Rajan's heart faltered. "Mom—"

"Don't make her life difficult, then," she said, voice fading now. "Don't be the reason she breaks."

"I won't," he said immediately. It was an easy vow to make, and he was desperate to keep her talking. Desperate to keep her hopeful that he could do something she'd be proud of. "I won't, I promise. Okay?"

No answer. Her eyes were fully closed, chest rising and falling steadily. Rajan sat back in his chair, alone again. He knew she wouldn't remember this conversation in the morning. But he would. For a very, very long time.

ONE

PRESENT DAY

"I CANNOT BELIEVE this," Simran's mother exclaims in rapid-fire Punjabi. She clutches the phone closer. "How my sister can show her face, I don't know."

She paces by the living room couch, where Simran is pretending to be absorbed in her calculus assignment. Simran can't quite make out what the auntie on the other end is saying, only that she's talking just as fast. As her mom paces out of the room again, taking the gossip with her, Simran refocuses on her laptop screen. Or rather, the email displayed on it.

Dear Simran,

I heard from our department head that you're applying to transfer to UBC Vancouver! I'd be thrilled if you joined us. I was so impressed when we met during the Euclid luncheon last year. If I remember right, you were interested in my research—I'd be happy to have you in my lab, should you decide to come.

Hoping to see you in September!

Warmly,

Dr. Emily Maxfield

The sign-off is followed by the professor's long list of titles and degrees. Simran's eyes track over each and every one.

"Just *shocking*," Simran's mother exclaims in Punjabi. Simran jumps slightly; she hadn't realized her mom had paced back into the living room. She hastily switches back to her calculus assignment, but her mother doesn't notice. One hand is clutching the phone, the other raking through her grey hair—normally tucked under a turban, but currently curling down her back. Then she glances at the clock and does a double take, as if unable to believe how long she's been gossiping. "We'll have to talk later. See you Sunday?"

She hangs up and is silent. Simran feigns busyness by typing the same equation into the mathematics software repeatedly. It's running into three lines by the time her mother speaks. "Why didn't you tell me about this?"

For a split second, Simran thinks she's talking about the email from Dr. Maxfield. "About—what?"

Her mother snorts. "Simran, don't pretend you didn't hear. You must've known your cousin had a boyfriend? A *white* boyfriend?"

Oh. Simran relaxes slightly and starts backspacing the gibberish she typed. "No," she says, like a liar.

Her mother squints at her suspiciously. "TJ didn't tell you? Aren't you two always on the phone?"

As if Simran's going to admit to playing secret-keeper for her cousin's relationship. "We don't talk about that stuff. What did you hear?"

"Kamaljot's daughter saw a photo of them on the internet." Her mother sits next to her, plunking a bowl of sliced fruit on the coffee table. "Going behind her parents' backs for so long— You know what your masi'll do, right? She'll pretend she always knew. To save face." She giggles. Simran's long given up trying to unpack whatever's going on between her mom and her aunt. "If you have a secret boyfriend, tell me now so I don't find out from someone else like a fool." She jabs Simran's side teasingly.

As if such a thing wouldn't absolutely end her life. However, Simran *is* keeping other secrets. Enough is enough.

She clicks back to her email and tilts her laptop screen. "Mom."

Her mother starts turning her head. "Yes?"

And . . . Simran loses her courage. A millisecond before her mother's gaze hits the screen, Simran minimizes her email, revealing the math software again. "See this assignment? I need to finish it before class."

It's not her best segue. But her mother immediately gets up. "Oh. Sorry. Of course we can talk later. Focus on your homework." The abruptness of it has Simran feeling guilty; but before she can say anything, her mother's peeking out the window and tsking. "Your windshield looks horrendous. Do you have any wiper fluid in there? This spring slush is terrible for visibility. I'll top it up for your drive to the university." She kisses Simran's forehead and heads for the door.

Simran returns her gaze to her blinking cursor, listening to her mom's feet crunch around the gravel driveway. The math software keeps spewing error messages, but she can't focus. Just as TJ probably should've gotten ahead of her secret coming out, Simran should do the same. Especially if she wants her parents to be happy about her transferring to a different university.

She never even planned to apply—truly. She likes Kelowna, and the university here. She got several scholarships, and adjusting to her first postsecondary year while living at home was smart. Plus, her parents love having her around—Simran could've gone anywhere, but she knew they were relieved she chose to stay.

Maybe that was even *why* she stayed.

But in this second semester, Simran has found herself restless. Bored, even. Her cousin always has debate tournament stories that make Simran miss their high school club. And each time she attends guest lectures from the Vancouver campus profs, she wonders if their regular classes are just as fascinating. Not to mention the research being done there that she'd love to participate in. So she applied, on a whim. Her application was haphazard. She hadn't expected a response, let alone a personal email from a UBC prof she knew from her high school math contest days.

Simran pulls up the email once again to reread it. And again, just like every other time, her mind races with the possibilities of a far more interesting next three years. She doesn't *need* that for her math degree. But she wants it.

The only thing left is to mention it to her parents. It should be easy. They wouldn't discourage this choice, especially if Simran framed it as having more opportunities for the future. And yet, every time Simran tries to bring it up, the words get stuck in her throat.

Frustrated with herself, Simran picks up her phone instead.

She texts TJ: My mom heard about you and Charlie.

The reply is instant: WHAT

Before Simran can type out an explanation, TJ's name lights up her screen.

When Simran picks up, TJ says, "I knew the secret was out, but I didn't know it was *that* out. Was your mom judging me?"

"Of course." Simran gets up to stretch. Dealing with someone else's problems is always a refreshing change. "I said no when she asked if I knew, by the way. Sorry."

"Don't be. We agreed on that already." They'd discussed it around the third time Simran acted as TJ's alibi. In the same grim way governments decide their plan in the event of nuclear war, TJ insisted she go down alone in the lie.

But it still doesn't feel great. "I thought you were careful about what you post."

"It wasn't me. It was someone at a party months ago, when we were in Kelowna for Christmas!" TJ sounds irritated; she goes to university in Ontario, across the country, and comes home a couple times a year. "Okay, but seriously, who posts a selfie with people kissing in the background? What the hell?"

Simran winces. Being caught holding hands is one thing, but . . . *kissing*? That's nuclear.

She pauses while picking up the fruit bowl her mother left. Come to think of it, this might actually be the *best* timing to tell her parents about transferring to Vancouver. In comparison to TJ's news, it's nothing. They'll be so relieved that the most deviant Simran's ever been is going a few hours away for school, they won't even think to be sad.

TJ, meanwhile, sighs. She sounds like she's walking somewhere. Simran envisions her tottering around campus in impractical heels, long hair blowing into her face. "My mom's called four times already. God, my *secret boyfriend*. She's going to kill me."

Simran pops a grape in her mouth. Tonight, she decides. She'll tell her parents tonight. "What she's *really* going to kill you for is avoiding her calls four times."

"Whatever," TJ says. "I'll figure it out. Maybe I'll ask your sister for help. She's the expert in parental blowups, right?"

Simran glances up at the childhood photo of herself and her older sister on the mantel. She hasn't seen Kiran in ages. "She's the opposite of an expert," she mutters. A clattering noise from outside draws her attention to the window.

Simran's not the only one socializing. Her mother has her cell to her ear as she bends to pick up the jug of wiper fluid she dropped. It's spilling on the ground. All so Simran can finish her homework. Yet here she is gossiping with her cousin instead.

Guilt creeps up on her. She turns to the couch. "I'll call you later. After I get back from Hillway, maybe."

TJ doesn't get the hint. "Ooh, Hillway. How *is* that girl you're mentoring? Did she try to punch you again?"

Simran pulls her computer back into her lap. Hillway House is an organization for troubled youth to help them integrate back into the community, usually via volunteer service. Since Simran started there a year ago, she's mentored her fair share of interesting people, including her latest, a girl who took a swing at her in their first week together. "Laura graduated from the program. I'm meeting my new mentee today."

"Is it too much to hope they're *not* an asshole?"

"None of them are." Simran checks her email inbox, but the Hillway coordinator, Paul, still hasn't sent the new mentee matchups. "They're just struggling."

"That doesn't mean it's okay for them to hurt you." TJ's voice softens. "I know you like helping strays, but be careful, okay?"

"All right, Mom," Simran says, exasperated. "I really have to finish this assignment, so—"

"You're starting homework an hour before the deadline again, aren't you?" Simran doesn't reply, just starts scrolling through her code. "Look, I get it. This is your version of an extreme sport. But is the adrenaline worth—"

The front door opens—her mom has returned. Simran lowers her phone. TJ's still rambling on the other end, but Simran smoothly hits end call before her mother can notice.

However, her mom doesn't even look up. She's a little pale, actually.

"Everything okay?" Simran asks.

"Of course." Her mother straightens. "Your wiper fluid was empty, by the way. If you're going to have your own vehicle, you need to keep an eye on these things." Although she's scolding Simran, she sounds half distracted as she heads for the stairs.

"Are you sure you're okay?" Simran calls.

Her mother mutters something unintelligible before yelling, "Your class starts in twenty-five minutes! Do you ever look at the clock? I swear you'll be late to your own wedding."

Well, that sounds more like her. Simran gets up.

Dr. Chen smiles at Simran when she speed-walks into his chemistry class. Simran returns it before finding a seat near the back of the lecture hall. She prefers sitting far away so she can answer emails, study for other classes, or, as in this case, finish assignments that are five minutes from being due.

She pulls her tea mug and laptop from her backpack. A notification pings in the corner of her screen. Paul—the Hillway coordinator—has finally emailed. She ignores it. The math homework takes priority. On her way here, she even triple-checked her calculations by hand at the traffic lights. It should work. So why isn't it?

Sweat gathers on her back. She shouldn't have wasted so much time rereading Dr. Maxfield's email today, or gossiping with TJ. Now she's only got three hundred seconds to hand in this assignment. Most people would just submit as is. But Simran can't. She needs the perfect score. The thought of her grades being tarnished, Dr. Maxfield finding out and rescinding her offer as she realizes Simran isn't as smart as she thought, is almost too much to—

"Hey."

The voice comes from behind her. She jumps, barely managing to catch her mug before it tips into the aisle. Once she's righted it on her lap, she turns. The Punjabi guy in the row behind her is leaning forward, blinking his green eyes slowly. He's got a scruffy beard, and a short black turban.

He whispers, "Your program isn't working because you're using the letter e instead of the number ϵ. You see how it's not italicized?"

Simran glances back at her screen. He's—he's *right*. She hasn't been using the symbol the program would understand. "How do you—"

"Took a class with Garcia last semester." He shrugs. "Same problem."

Simran swaps in the right symbol. Her code goes from red to green, generating her output instantly. How did she not see something so simple?

She submits her assignment with a hundred and eighty seconds to spare. Dr. Chen starts class right then, and Simran twists in her seat. The boy is now studying his laptop.

She swallows her pride to whisper, "Thanks."

"No problem, Simran," he replies without looking up, voice quiet. Simran turns back around, cringing internally. Of course it had to be *Jassa Singh* helping her. She likes him fine, but she beat him for the academic award last semester, so he's probably wondering how she accomplished that when she apparently needs him to do her homework for her. He's not even a math major; he's *premed*. Embarrassing.

Simran sinks farther into her seat, sipping from her tea mug. Dr. Chen's on his fifth slide. She ignores it and checks her email. The unread ones this time.

Her inbox is full of meeting minutes and class reminders and one passive-aggressive email about how whoever broke the lab's ten-thousand-dollar computer should come forward. The unread Hillway email catches her eye. Paul's sent out the new schedule with his usual message: You all know the drill. Let me know of any conflicts with your new mentees and I'll re-match you in a jiffy!

Simran clicks on the attachment. Half-heartedly scans it.

And drops her mug into the aisle with a loud, class-stopping *clang*.

TWO

RAJAN'S NEW PROBATION officer is creeping him out.

Her smile hasn't wavered since he walked in, even when he propped his muddy shoes on her desk and took a candy from her jar without asking. She doesn't even *look* like a probation officer; in that ankle-length, baby-blue dress and long blond hair tied in a low ponytail, she could be in a preschooler show with stuffed animals, singing songs about sharing. Instead, she's threatening him.

The most unnerving part is that she's smiling so widely while doing it. Like they're picnicking, instead of discussing how he can be dragged back to court, and then jail, if he breaches any of his probation conditions. Of which there are many. She's reading the list in her Eastern European accent, and he gets the sense she's learning it along with him. His case was passed off to her when he returned to Kelowna.

Report as directed to your youth probation officer.
Do not have or use weapons.
Do not use any drugs or alcohol.
Do not operate a motor vehicle.

Rajan reclines his chair onto the rear legs, looking out the window at the downtown skyline. Part of him can't believe he's back here. The town he left at the end of high school.

Have no contact with the people the court has specified.
Attend community service as the court has specified.
Be on good behaviour and keep up the peace—

Rajan removes the toothpick from his mouth. "A lot of conditions," he drawls, interrupting her and basically violating the last condition in the process. "I have some follow-up questions. Like, who're you again?"

She beams, unfazed though he's asked this question twice already. "Katarzyna Mackewicz. But call me Kat." She extends her hand for him to shake. Rajan looks back to the window.

"Next question. Why'd you have to bring alcohol into this? I wasn't even drunk when I was arrested."

"I did not set these conditions. The judge did." Kat lowers her hand and flips through her notes package, presumably still digesting all the messed-up details of his history. Bored, Rajan flicks his toothpick in the trash (he always keeps a supply on him) and reaches for another piece of Kat's candy instead. The jar is next to a framed photo of a younger Kat with a small boy. He shares her creepy smile. Must be a relation.

"I have some questions, too," Kat says. "Any drug use lately?"

He rolls his eyes. "Obviously not, dude." When Rajan was arrested, he apparently had THC, coke, *and* fentanyl in his system. He couldn't claim surprise about the first two, but that last one had been a shock. Or at least, Rajan told himself it was a shock. Part of him knew the high that day was different—clearly, the friend who'd been raving about the "purity" of his supply was talking out of his ass. Anyway, the judge wasn't impressed either, so on top of everything else, Rajan isn't allowed to have any fun for the next four months.

"And how's the job?" Kat asks.

It's no coincidence Kat went from drugs to his new job at a local roofing company. She definitely knows what happens there. Rajan shrugs, repressing a wince from the pain in his shoulder. Swinging a hammer for hours can do that. Even the foreman noticed; Rajan thought he was going to tell him to take more breaks, but instead he offered to pay him under the table for overtime work. Rajan wasn't about to say no.

"Well," Kat says after a pause, "I'm glad we got a chance to talk." She closes his file. "You can go after we sign those papers at Hillway."

That's the *Attend community service* probation condition. Rajan was given several options, and Hillway seemed the least mind-numbing. But apparently, he has to sign something before he starts that basically says he promises to be nice to his mentor. The honour system for criminals? He finds it funny, but sure.

Rajan follows Kat out of the office. There are three others in the waiting room. She waves to them. "I'll be back in twenty minutes. Sit tight!"

Nobody responds; they're riveted by the TV. Rajan gets the surprise of a lifetime when he sees his old drug dealer's mug shot on-screen. *Perry?* No way. But there he is, with his ratty beard, massive eyebags, and the scar above the left side of his scowling mouth.

Rajan hangs back to listen to the news anchor.

". . . seizure of illicit drugs including several kilograms each of fentanyl, methamphetamines, cocaine, and numerous firearms. Five people with suspected ties to the gang known as the Lion's Share face charges of drug trafficking and firearms offenses. Among them: a car dealership owner and an accountant from a well-respected Kelowna firm. Police say this was the result of an extended investigation and is a huge win against the drug trade in the Okanagan region of BC."

They show all the mug shots side by side, and Rajan laughs under his breath. The fact that he recognizes every single one probably doesn't say much good about him.

"Come along, Rajan!" Kat trills from the elevator. He finally makes himself move.

The car is crowded. People eye him warily, seeing that he's coming from the corrections floor of this government building. Rajan offers a smile he hopes looks off-kilter, and stands with Kat. As the doors close, he notices a Punjabi auntie leaning against the opposite wall. He vaguely recognizes her. Probably from his childhood, a time when his family actually participated in their community.

The auntie makes eye contact with him. Manners his mother drilled into him spring out without conscious thought. "Sat Sri Akaal, Auntie ji."

People look his way, then away when they realize he's not speaking English. The auntie blinks. But then she smiles tentatively. "Sat Sri Akaal, putt. I'm trying to remember your name . . . Rajan, right?"

"Yes, Auntie."

"Oh, you're all grown up now," she coos in that way aunties do. "So tall, so handsome. You must be in university."

Why do people always think *more* school must be the next step after high school? He barely got out of that hellhole. "No, Auntie. I've just been living in Surrey."

"Ah. Down south. But why not school? Are you taking time off?"

Something in him sours, right then. The smile is a lie. The warm voice, the compliments, all lies. She knows he's not going to school. Of *course* she knows about him—there's enough gossip. And she saw him come from the corrections floor. She's trying to get more details, to give her something else to gossip about.

Well, fine.

Rajan looks around the crowded elevator before switching to English. "I was in jail for the last six months, if that counts. I ran over a guy and killed him. But, I'm happy to be back."

He finishes with a wink. The auntie's expression is priceless. As is the dead silence of the whole elevator.

Kat's the only one still grinning. "What a nice purse! Where'd you get it?" she asks the lady beside her, who is not-so-discreetly shielding her handbag with both arms. No response, but Kat seems unfazed. When they reach the main floor, she's the first out, whistling out of tune. "Off we go, Rajan!"

He follows without looking back.

Hillway House is across the street. The sidewalk is slushy, the last late snowfall of the year melting in the light April rain. They wait at the curb for a vehicle to pass.

It's an ice-cream truck. Kat's whistling is drowned out somewhat, thankfully, by its music. Who's getting ice cream in this shit weather, anyway? Rajan glances through the windshield. Does a double take.

The driver is staring at him.

He's just some random white guy. Rajan doesn't know him, and their eye contact lasts only a moment before he looks back at the road. But something feels . . . off.

The truck passes, splashing slush onto the curb. Its song fades. The entire encounter lasts less than two seconds, but Rajan's suddenly hit with the urge to run.

Kat doesn't notice. She's already crossing the street. Reluctantly, Rajan follows.

Hillway House is crammed between a bakery and a fabrics shop. A middle-aged, brown-haired dude waves from the door, then ushers them into his office. It's only slightly bigger than the elevator, and plastered with inspirational posters. "I'm Paul," he says. "Your new mentor isn't here yet, but that's okay. We can get started on the paperwork . . . You must be Kat!"

Rajan tunes out the introductions. They all sink into hard-backed chairs, and he only jolts back to alertness when he hears the ice-cream truck's music again. He sits upright and looks out the window. Within seconds the truck passes again.

Most people wouldn't get antsy when an ice-cream truck starts circling the block, but Rajan has only survived this long because he's paranoid. It can't be a coincidence. Right? He didn't expect them to find him so fast. He's only been back in Kelowna a week and a half.

There's a knock on the office door. Paul and Kat stop talking.

"There she is," Paul says. "Come in, Simran!"

Because Rajan's staring out the window, it takes him a second to process the name. By the time he does, the door's already opening. No. Surely that's not—

He turns to look. And it is.

The way his heart rate skyrockets, you'd think someone just pulled a gun on him.

Simran Kaur Aujla looks almost exactly the same as the last time he saw her, the end of high school nine months ago. Right down to the wire frames of her glasses. Dressed in her usual way: a shapeless maroon turtleneck, straight-leg jeans stuffed into laced boots. And of course, that glossy, thick braid that falls to her knees. He looks back at her face and finds her brown eyes locked on his.

"Rajan, Kat, this is Ms. Aujla," Paul announces, oblivious. "Simran, this is Rajan, our newest volunteer, and his PO, Kat."

Rajan didn't read Hillway's welcome brochure, but he's pretty sure having history with your mentor would be frowned upon. He waits for Simran to say something.

But she doesn't. "Hi, Rajan."

Interesting. Well, two can play this game. "Hey, *Ms. Aujla.*"

"Call me Simran." Her tone is completely neutral, and she greets Kat next before perching in the chair next to her. "Sorry I'm late, Paul."

"No problem," Paul says merrily, sorting through the files on his desk. "Let me find the papers to sign and we can get you out of here . . ."

Kat engages Simran in friendly, aimless conversation, while Rajan silently wills Simran to look his way. But she looks everywhere in the room *but* at him.

Maybe she saw his file. Maybe not. For him to even be here means he majorly screwed up. And the idea that she knows that, that that's the reason she won't look him in the eye . . .

"Here it is!" Paul slides a piece of paper in Rajan's direction. "I need both your signatures on this mentor-mentee agreement. By signing, you're agreeing to be kind and respect each other's boundaries."

Rajan hesitates. He *could* confess they know each other. Sure, the next mentor Paul pairs him with will probably be a pain in the ass, but at least Rajan won't have the overwhelming sense he's disappointed them before even starting.

He opens his mouth, and that's when Simran finally looks at him.

Her expression gives nothing away. But, the same sixth sense that warned him off from an ice-cream truck whispers something now.

He shuts his mouth and signs.

Rajan wonders throughout the next ten minutes if she'll ever mention it. He wonders if she'll hesitate when she signs the agreement (she doesn't). He wonders if she'll break when they're told their first volunteering day is Saturday at a breakfast kitchen. Or when Kat jots down Simran's number before bouncing across the street to see her next client. But Simran appears fully committed to acting like they've never met.

So, he's actually a little surprised when she follows him out to the bus stop afterward. He says nothing; she'll talk when she's ready, he figures. When the coast is clear. But they stand in silence so long he starts genuinely wondering if she's just waiting for the bus.

Then, finally:

"Why didn't you say anything?"

Rajan scoffs. Of course that's the first thing she says. "Why didn't *you?*"

Simran doesn't respond. He suspects she doesn't have an answer to that. Good to know they're on the same page.

"What happens if they figure it out?" he asks instead. "Do I get kicked out? Do you?"

That shakes her out of her funk. "There's nothing to figure out. Hillway rules prohibit conflicts of interest. That would require us to have a significant relationship of some kind, which we don't."

Okay, *that's* kind of fucking rude. "You don't call four years of tutoring a significant relationship?"

She meets his gaze squarely. "It wasn't if we decide it wasn't."

Her voice is firm. After a second, it clicks, and he finds he's no longer offended. In fact, he has the urge to laugh.

"Okay, so," he says, "what's the story? You tutored half the school and don't even remember me?"

"We never had classes together either," Simran confirms. "You definitely never promised free edibles to people who donated to my fundraisers."

Damn, he'd forgotten about that. "Right," he says, enjoying this game now, "and we never stayed late trying to connect the dots of teachers' affairs with each other."

"You never rehearsed my speeches with me before my debate tournaments."

"And you never stole my earbuds to listen to my music. You never liked my music taste."

"That's right," Simran says. "None of those things. So what kind of significant relationship was there, Rajan?"

He shakes his head, grinning. "Beats me, dude." He should've known Simran would do this. Lie, and invite him to lie with her. "You haven't changed at all."

"*You* have."

His amusement vanishes at her somber tone. Fine. She's going to ask about it, then. About what happened to get him to the point of probation. There was never any way they *really* could've picked up where they—

Simran blurts, "Your hair's different."

His hand automatically comes up to run through his hair, now closer-cropped than it was in high school. Gone are the waves he once kept shoved under a hat. He'd had it buzzed in juvie.

It's hilarious (and a relief) that *this* was her first thought. "You like it?" He flashes her a grin, loving the way she goes a little pink. Yeah, he's still got it.

Simran dodges his question. "It's just, I haven't seen you in a long time. You . . . left."

Now *that* sounds loaded. He dodges, too. "And you didn't. Thought you'd be out of this town by now, Sahiba."

She purses her lips, but before she can respond, a phone rings. Not his. Hers. She fishes it from her coat pocket. "Sorry, I have to take this."

Rajan nods and that's when a vehicle passes by, splashing slush onto the curb yet again. He jerks his head up to see the ice-cream truck driver looking at him once more before passing. This time, no music. No warning at all.

Rajan watches it disappear around the curb.

"What's going on?" Simran asks, and he looks back to her, only to find she's not talking to him. Her head is ducked, phone pressed to her ear. He realizes how close they've drifted, and he takes a large step back. Screw the bus. He's getting out of here *now*.

Simran doesn't call after him when he takes off down the street. He turns a corner and cuts between two buildings. The narrow alley is littered with trash and storage containers and, at the end, a chain-link fence between buildings. He goes for it, jumping onto a storage container and scaling the fence. The metal bites into his palms, but the pain barely registers.

He's just crossing the next street when the truck screeches into his path. *Shit.* He barely halts in time to avoid being run over. Either someone really wants to sell him a Popsicle, or he's completely screwed.

A few pedestrians look up at the sound of the tires squealing. Rajan feels slightly reassured by their presence. He won't be killed in front of a bunch of witnesses. Right?

That becomes his last concern once the back doors fling open.

"Well, well, well. Look who's back from kiddie jail," says a familiar voice. "Get in. We have a lot to talk about."

THREE

IT'S NOT A suggestion. Rajan knows this because he knows Nick Dewan.

He gets in, and Nick closes the doors. The truck lurches into motion; a quick glance confirms the driver is the same guy he saw earlier. He doesn't even look Rajan's way.

Rajan scans his surroundings. He's never been in an ice-cream truck before, but he's pretty sure the serving window wouldn't normally be covered by aluminum foil. Also, the freezer next to him wouldn't contain paper-covered bricks instead of ice cream.

"Popsicle?" Nick's voice cuts through his thoughts. He's rummaging through the freezer on his side of the truck, which, Rajan now notes, actually does contain frozen treats. Nick offers him one. Rajan's gaze is drawn to his LS tattoo instead, very visible over the collar of his designer tee. Rajan's is mostly hidden by his hoodie, and he likes it that way. But Nick is completely at ease with who he is. A piece of shit with a goatee, freshly faded hair, artfully ripped jeans, and blindingly white Air Jordans. The guy's never been discreet about his wealth.

When Rajan's silent, Nick tears the Popsicle wrapper. "So? How was Weenie Hut Junior jail?"

"Juvie was fantastic, thanks for asking." Rajan leans casually against the other freezer, mirroring Nick.

"Yeah?" Nick takes a bite of Popsicle. With his teeth. Rajan wonders if it's supposed to be some kind of power move. "What'd you do in there all day?"

"Played basketball and finger-painted. It was like kindergarten." Enough small talk. "Why're you here?"

Nick doesn't miss a beat. "Getting you back to work. Or have you forgotten how much money you owe?"

Rajan rolls his eyes to mask his pounding heart. "I know *that*, dipshit. But why *you*?" Nick's from Surrey, where Rajan met him last summer. He never imagined he'd see him here. That was partially why he requested probation in Kelowna, rather than down south. The Lions are based in Vancouver; Kelowna's just an extension of their operations. He figured the farther away he went, the easier it would be for them to forget him.

Apparently not.

"Orders from Manny." Nick tosses out the name of one of the LS godfathers as carelessly as he does the wrapper.

"Why does *he* care about me?" Rajan's met him exactly once, during high school, at some party at his mansion. If you could even call it a meeting; Manny barely spared him a glance, just gave him and a few others free lines of coke like it was Halloween. He did not, of course, mention what it would cost them down the road.

"It's not about you, specifically." Nick finishes his Popsicle and drops the stick on the freezer. "It's about numbers. The godfathers asked me to help clean up some messes. We've been in deep shit around these parts. Cops picking us off like flies, haven't you heard?"

So he's recruiting. Rajan remembers the mugshots on TV and shakes his head. He made a promise to himself when he left juvie. "I don't care. I'm not going back."

He starts toward the door.

"What, you're gonna jump out? Brilliant plan." Nick, looking amused, glances at the driver. "How fast are we going?"

"How fast do you wanna go?" the driver responds.

"Floor it," Nick says. The truck lurches beneath their feet, gaining speed. Rajan nearly loses his balance. "Jump out now. Seriously. I wanna see."

Jesus, that guy is driving fast. Rajan glares. "I'm breaching probation just being here. Fuck off."

"No," Nick says simply. No other explanation needed. The Lions do not simply fuck off. They linger like blood under fingernails. And they definitely don't give a shit if you're on probation. "We missed you, you know. *I* missed you."

He almost sounds earnest. Because Nick is good at this. Making you think he likes you—as a person. That you're unique. Rajan's fallen for it before, but never again. "Right."

"I'm serious. Nothing makes people cough up money faster than your left hook. My business suffered without you, man."

"Maybe it's because your supply is laced with fentanyl."

"Still sore about that?" Nick laughs. "We've got a new supplier. It's a great time to come back. At least this time, you'd get to be home." He pauses. "How're your brothers, anyway?"

That gets Rajan's attention. He pushes off the freezer. "Are you threatening them?"

"No." Nick shrugs. "I'm just saying, once your debts are paid, you can make big money with me. Enough to buy them nice things."

"And if I decide no? Then what?"

"Then imagine this." Nick smiles brazenly. "Your brothers finding you bleeding out on their doorstep. Like their mom dying all over again, except this time they actually see the body—"

Rajan punches him across the face. Nick staggers back. Rajan takes the opportunity to shove him against the freezer and pulls back for another hit.

But then cold metal presses against his temple.

"Hit me again." Nick's not smiling anymore. "See what happens."

Rajan seriously debates hitting him anyway. But eventually, he steps back. Nick lowers his gun. Slightly. Meanwhile, the driver hasn't slowed during this entire altercation, just looked in the rearview mirror with detached interest, like this is a TV show he's watching alongside dinner. "Don't talk about her."

"Why not?" Nick mocks him. "It's not like her dying was a *surprise.*"

Nick's clearly trying to piss him off. When Rajan doesn't reply, Nick produces a paper with an address on it. "This guy owes three grand. Squeeze it out of him. Smash his teeth in if you have to."

"Or I could smash *your* teeth in," Rajan suggests, and Nick chuckles as the truck slows to a stop. Out the windshield, Rajan can tell they're in his neighbourhood by the squatting, fifty-year-old houses made of peeling paint and bound by rust. Of course Nick knows where he lives. The Lions know everything.

"I really did miss you, man." Nick slaps the paper in his palm. "I'm sure your family will, too. You've got one week."

FOUR

SIMRAN'S STOMACH IS full of knots as she enters the doctor's office. The reception area smells like rubbing alcohol, pressing against her nose, making it difficult to breathe.

It doesn't help that her dad was so cryptic on the phone when he asked her to come. It's almost four o'clock—the office should be closing soon.

The only people in the waiting room are her parents. Her father waves unnecessarily. His turban is speckled with sawdust from the mill. He must've just come. Her mother, meanwhile, is buried in a pocket copy of Sukhmani Sahib, which she often reads when she's stressed.

She doesn't acknowledge Simran, so Simran sits beside her father. "What's going on?"

"Dr. Tran has some results for your mother today," her father replies, running his fingers through his greying beard. "She asked us to come, too."

He sounds casual. Too casual. "Dad," Simran says slowly. "What're the results about?"

Just then, the secretary calls Simran's mother's name. "Tarleen?"

Automatically, all three of them stand. They follow the secretary into an examination room. The secretary gives them a careful look as she leaves. "Dr. Tran will be along in a minute, okay?"

Her voice is very kind. *Too* kind. Simran rubs her eyes as if that might also rub away the horrific thoughts forming behind them. She refuses to even entertain them, because . . . that can't happen to *her*. This must be about something else—

The door opens. They all straighten.

Dr. Tran sits at her computer. "Nice day, isn't it." No one responds. She swivels to look at Simran's mother, who's finally closed the Sukhmani Sahib. "The endometrial biopsy results came back."

Simran's mother grips the book tighter. "And?"

"I'm very sorry to tell you this. You have cancer."

There's a long silence. Simran stares at the anatomy poster on the wall. The colours seem too bright. Perhaps she's dreaming; she's had nightmares like this. When did she fall asleep?

Her mother speaks first. "How is this possible? There's no cancer in my family. I—I eat right and exercise. This shouldn't be happening." Her voice is flat. It's hard to tell what she's thinking.

"You can do everything right and still get this," Dr. Tran says, with the weary tone of someone who knows every beat of this conversation. "But there's always a small chance the biopsy could be wrong. That's why we'll do more tests."

It feels placating. The anatomy poster blurs in front of Simran's eyes. She leans forward, bracing her elbows on her knees. *Breathe.*

Her father asks, "How bad is it?"

"We don't know yet. The scans will show if it's . . . spread." Her voice is regretful. "I'll refer you to an oncologist. There'll be a surgery later. Other things, too."

And as she launches into all the possible procedures and treatments, medications and outcomes, Simran wills Dr. Tran to stop. *Stop talking. Please.*

But Dr. Tran goes on relentlessly. Simran barely hears a word. She only jars back into reality when Dr. Tran sends them off, promising to get in touch with next steps.

Simran's the last to file out, but Dr. Tran stops her. "You're a smart girl, Simran. You can help your parents read through this." She presses a stack of brochures into Simran's hands. "I know it's a lot to take in. I know your life will never be the same again. Trust me, I know." A shadow passes over her face. "But you'll get through it. Your mom has everything going for her. A prompt diagnosis. No systemic symptoms. A healthy lifestyle." She pats Simran's shoulder. "And, of course, you."

If someone asked Simran how the next few hours passed, she wouldn't be able to say. All she knows is they got home and suddenly it was dark outside.

Her mother sat on the couch and stared into space. Her father sat beside her, holding her hand. Simran couldn't bring herself to do the same.

Instead, she memorized Dr. Tran's brochures, reading the important bits aloud. Her mother didn't acknowledge any of it. Her dad nodded encouragingly as she read out the good prognosis statistics. She finally understood he wasn't listening when she asked him what he thought, and he only nodded.

Now that she's read all the brochures, she feels useless. "It'll be okay," she says to the silence. "We just have to get through this." Her own words feel empty.

But her father looks up and strokes her cheek. "You're right, sher putt."

Sher putt. Lion daughter. Brave daughter. He says it admiringly.

Simran straightens. That, she can do. She can be brave for them. "I'll make dinner," she announces, and when her father smiles again, it bolsters her to do more, be above all this. After all, someone has to function.

Newly determined, Simran heads into the kitchen. She takes out an onion, garlic, ginger, and chilies. While chopping, she calls her sister. Three times. She finally leaves a message. "This is *Simran*. Call me back, okay?"

She can't keep the annoyance from her voice. Kiran rarely picks up.

She turns on the kitchen fan as she works. It's loud, but she finds herself glad for the noise. Anything to drive the thoughts from her head. How strange to think how the day began—worrying about assignments, gossiping with her cousin, and Rajan—*Rajan*, but she can't even digest that encounter yet. She has no right, with her mother in the next room reeling from a cancer diagnosis, to think about her old friend or her grades or . . . or . . . her transfer to Vancouver . . .

She nearly drops her wooden spoon. She'd totally forgotten her resolution to tell her parents about it tonight.

Her hopeful self from six hours ago seems stupidly naive now. Of course Simran can't go to Vancouver. Her family needs her. Staying in Kelowna will be fine—more than fine, actually. Moving to a new city would be tedious.

Decided, Simran pulls out her phone and finds Dr. Maxfield's email. Standing in the kitchen, she composes a reply.

Dear Dr. Maxfield, thank you for your email, but I've decided not to transfer . . .

She writes a few lines about how she appreciates the opportunity and maybe they can work together later. After proofreading, it's ready to send. Her thumb hovers over the button.

But she can't seem to bring it down. Her brain keeps whispering: *What if? What if you did go?*

The frying onions on the stovetop sizzle distractingly loud, stinging at her eyes. She blinks the tears away, but they're unrelenting. She hates it. No crying allowed today. Not even from onions.

Frustrated, she turns the heat off and heads to the bathroom to wash her face. As the loud kitchen fan fades behind her, she faintly hears a conversation taking place in the living room. She slows. Her parents are murmuring to each other. What could they be talking about after hours of silence?

Simran creeps closer. The first thing she catches is her sister's name.

". . . Kiran's made it a point to do the opposite of everything I wish for her. I think I've lost her forever."

"That's just Kiran being Kiran," her father replies. "Let her be."

"But Simran . . ." Simran freezes at the sound of her own name. Her mom sighs. "I've always had hope for her. I've lost every one of my dreams, except her."

Why are they talking about this? About her, and Kiran, after the day they've had?

"I've kept myself going, hoping I'd at least see *one* thing I wanted for Simran. I hope she can get a stable career, on this path she's on now. Of course it would've been better if— Well, it doesn't matter. If nothing else, I thought, I'd get to see her grow up." She grows quieter, so Simran has to lean in. "I'd get to see her become an adult, get married, have children, and be settled. And now I'm learning I won't even get that."

"You can't say that," her father says. But his voice is rough, too. "No one knows what will happen."

"But we do know this. I'm *old*." Her voice is bitter. "We both are. We knew it when we had Simran. That we wouldn't be like the younger parents. *They* didn't have to try for ten years. *They* didn't have to learn a new country before they could even get started with their lives. Sometimes I wonder if we ever should've left home."

"Hush, Tarleen. We did it to give our family a better life."

"Maybe." Her voice cracks. "But I don't think I made a better life for anyone. I think I just wasted mine."

And then, Simran hears the most dreadful thing she's ever heard: her mother crying.

FIVE

TEN MINUTES BEFORE his alarm, Rajan cracks his eyes open to the sounds of a scuffle in the hallway. He stares at the ceiling of his storage-closet-turned-bedroom. He could ignore it. His brothers aren't actually going to kill each other, right?

"I'm gonna kill you!"

Rajan flings the covers off. His mattress takes up most of the floor, so he stands on it, wood creaking under him, and opens the door. At least, he tries. Damn thing's hinges are stuck.

He hates this shitty house. It's objectively not the *worst*; it may be one floor, cramped, falling apart, and shared with the city of rodents in the crawl space, but it's way more livable than certain places he crashed in after his mom died. It's more about what it represents. Or rather, what it doesn't represent: a home.

He shoulders the door open and is rewarded with a sharp pain down his arm. He makes a note to pick up some Tylenol. That freaky probation officer will be so smug if Rajan has to cut down on work.

In the hallway, two young boys are on the floor, locked in a very unfriendly wrestling match. Rajan strides forward to grab the back of the bigger one's shirt, since he's currently hitting the younger one. "Sukha, what the hell? You're gonna be late for school."

Sukha's barely fourteen, but Rajan's surprised by the force with which he shoves him away. "This asshole finished my last box of Oreos!"

"So? Let go of Yash right now." This time Rajan hauls him away like he means it, catching a few elbows in the process.

Sukha staggers back, dark eyes flashing. As usual, Rajan is startled each time they make eye contact; he came back home and suddenly his brother was the spitting image of him at that age. Stockier, maybe, but the same straight nose, heavy brows, wavy hair, and sharply angled face. Not to mention the constant anger in his eyes.

Sukha's voice is just as venomous. "This is none of your fucking business."

"Stop fucking swearing so much," Rajan snaps. "You're fighting your eleven-year-old brother in your pajamas. Go cool off and get ready for school."

Sukha looks half ready to fight him, too. Rajan braces himself. It wouldn't be their first physical altercation recently. But Sukha storms off, knocking into him as he goes. Rajan watches him slam his bedroom door hard enough to make the frame rattle, before squatting next to his youngest brother, Yash.

Yash is also in his pajamas, breathing hard. Rajan studies him. The fringe of his hair is plastered to his forehead. He doesn't look like Rajan much at all. More like their mother: softer features, wide eyes, a rounder chin. He's pale, holding his arm awkwardly.

"What's wrong? Does it hurt?"

"No," Yash whispers. His lower lip is trembling, though. "I'm okay."

"Then why do you look like you're gonna cry?"

Yash blinks rapidly. "I'm not."

Yash used to cry freely around him all the time. He used to say a lot in general. Sukha might be angry all the time now, but Yash is just quiet. Has a year changed that much?

Rajan flounders for words in the silence that stretches between them. He has a feeling Yash wouldn't let him look at his arm, and he's too much of a coward to find out. "Why'd you eat his cookies, anyway?"

That gets a reaction. "He doesn't own them," Yash says hotly. "Besides, I was hungry."

And there wasn't any food, is the unsaid part. "I'll make something. Get ready for school." With a last pat to Yash's hair, Rajan ducks under the doorframe to the kitchen, kicking the crate of glass bottles in the corner as he goes. Their father must still be asleep. A small mercy on mornings like these.

Rajan pops bread into the toaster, then leans against the grimy counter, staring out the window at the decrepit swing set next door. It's been five days since Nick's visit. Five quiet days. But he's hyperaware he has forty-eight hours left. Less, actually, because he's spending the next couple with Hillway.

He's gone over his options countless times. None are good, although he knows what his probation officer would say. That he should tell her. Or the cops. He laughs under his breath at that thought. As if half the department hasn't picked him up in a cruiser at some point. They'd probably say he breached probation just getting in the truck with Nick. And what's Kat gonna do, anyway? Smile the Lions into submission?

Yeah, no. As always, he's on his own.

Rajan cracks open the Hillway pamphlet on his bus over. Hillway has apparently partnered with several local organizations in the last year to provide "more rewarding community service opportunities" for juvenile offenders. It was, of course, Simran Kaur Aujla's idea. The only catch is the volunteers have to be on their best behaviour. One strike, and he'll be out with a garbage-picker-upper instead.

Today's location is a breakfast kitchen downtown; it was founded by a local gurdwara, funded collectively by the Sikh community. Rajan feels odd taking off his cap and donning a rumal, tying it bandana-style over his hair. He hasn't put one on since he was a kid.

When he enters the kitchen, an elderly Punjabi auntie in a white salwar kameez spots him and lights up. She ushers him over to write name plates for the dining tables. While Rajan helps her decorate the cards for their sponsors, she engages him in conversation about his parents' ancestral villages. Someone's grandma clearly didn't get the message about Rajan Randhawa, but he's relieved to be spoken to normally for once. And she's clearly just happy to find a volunteer who speaks Punjabi.

Their conversation is interrupted by a young woman with curly hair under her chunni and an amused smile. "Okay, Nani ji. I have to actually give him a task now. I'm Neetu," she introduces herself. "You must be . . . Rajan?" He nods, and Neetu checks something off on her clipboard, the big-ass rock on her finger catching the light and practically blinding him. "You can help bring groceries from the truck."

Ah, manual labour. His usual job. Rajan drops his Sharpie and turns to the exit door, just in time to see Simran emerge from the management office, a rumal tied over her head. And he can't help himself—he veers in her direction instead.

"Kiddan, Simran Sahiba?" He jokingly reaches to touch her feet like she's a respected elder.

However, Simran doesn't do her usual funny dance-away-from-his-hands routine. In fact, she doesn't even look at him, but rather off behind him. "Did Neetu assign you yet?"

"Yeah. But don't worry, I'll still do whatever you tell me to."

He grins at her, but she doesn't return it. "No, that's fine."

And she brushes by him to the kitchen.

Rajan stares after her. What was that? Was she irritated by him acting familiar? But she seemed so *normal* during that conversation at the bus stop a few days ago.

Confused, he joins the chain of people hauling supplies into the building. During one of his many trips back and forth, he notices someone in the management office watching him from the doorway.

Not just anybody. It's that auntie he spoke to in the elevator a few days ago. The one he told about his arrest.

He winks at her, and she instantly turns away.

By the time he's set his last bag of flour down, cooking is well underway and patrons are lining up at the door. He spots Simran wiping down tables in the seating area, stiff-backed. Wait. Wasn't she in the management office earlier, too?

It all clicks. That auntie *told her*.

Of course she did; really, he'd counted on her to tell people. It was satisfying at the time, but now, with Simran ignoring him . . . his stomach sinks. The same way it did when he was fourteen and his best friends admitted their parents told them to stop hanging out with him. Or when he was sixteen and his mom stopped reading Northridge's shit-talking letters. Or when he was seventeen, at her funeral, and his dad suggested it would be better for his brothers if he didn't come back home.

He should be used to it by now, but he's not. He swallows and turns away, to join the serving line.

His task is easy—just slapping a ladleful of oatmeal into each bowl that slides by. It's uneventful for several minutes. He's starting to think this whole volunteering thing might be a breeze when a familiar hand puts a pristine bowl on the counter. A vintage watch on the wrist. Leather jacket.

Rajan looks up.

At Nick's smirking face.

"I want some food," Nick says loudly.

A couple other volunteers glance his way. Fantastic. Rajan matches Nick's grin and speaks through gritted teeth.

"I still have two days."

"Not even. I'm here to remind you not to . . . procrastinate." Nick raises his voice. "I just want some help. That's what you do here, right? Selfless service?" He points to the slogan on the wall.

Rajan pours steaming-hot oatmeal onto Nick's hand. "Whoops."

Nick's only sign of discomfort is a twitch of his jaw. His hand slides off the counter. "You're not safe, Rajan. Not if you keep doing shit like this."

"That a threat?"

"Of course it's a threat." Nick glares, apparently done with games now that he's got a first-degree burn developing. "And *not* from me. This is serious. The godfathers—"

That's the *last* word Rajan wants said here. Next thing he knows Nick will be mentioning the LS by name. "Shut the fuck up."

Unfortunately, there's a lull in the surrounding conversation at the exact time he says that. His words echo, and instantly, someone calls from behind him. "Step away from the counter!"

Rajan turns. One of the admin people is approaching with an accusatory finger pointed at him. And everyone's watching, that elderly Punjabi auntie included.

Rajan holds his hands up. "I didn't do anything."

"You spoke rudely to our guest. I think it's time for you to go."

"What?" That seems a slight overreaction.

"You heard me. We have a zero-tolerance policy toward misbehaviour."

Damn, he's actually serious. The other volunteers' expressions mirror his shock. It dawns on Rajan that he's being made into an example.

Which is fucking unfair. His desperation pushes him to look back at Nick, who's smirking again. "I'm sorry, okay? Want me to grovel?"

The admin person is unmoved. "You can leave, or you can be escorted."

Rajan eyes the security guys now pushing off the wall. He backs away from the counter. "Is this— Is this going to mess with my probation?"

"That's between you and your probation officer when they get the report."

Great. He's already on thin ice, due to the many times he failed to follow restrictions for community sentences in high school. The judge had warned him this meant that now, even one breach would land his ass in hot water.

And Nick—Nick stands there grinning, like this was his intention all along. To show Rajan just how pointless this whole going-straight thing was.

And once he realized that, of course, he'd come crawling back.

Severely pissed off, Rajan heads for the exit. He's hurling his rumal into the used basket when someone catches his arm.

"Wait," Simran says.

Startled, he looks at her. For the first time today, she's showing emotion. Her eyes are wide. *God*, those big brown doe eyes should be registered as a weapon.

"Who was he?" she asks quietly.

Does she want to ban Nick from the kitchen? If so, he'll gladly help. He puts his cap on. "I know him from before. He's a filthy-rich prick. You should definitely not let him come back."

Her brow furrows, clearly with more questions. But then someone from the admin office calls, "Simran! Come here!"

Simran looks over her shoulder. Rajan reaches for his shoes. "You should go."

She turns back to him instead. "Is everything okay?"

Why does she care suddenly? "Yeah. Why wouldn't it be?" He looks down at her sharply, because it occurs to him that he could call her out on it. "And what about you?"

She blinks. "What about me?"

He stares her down. "Everything cool with *you*? Because you're acting fucking weird today."

"I'm acting—weird?"

"Did you not notice? Because I did. A lot. If you have something to say, say it." He nearly spits this last part out. He wants her to bring it out in the open.

And yet . . . he's terrified in the silence that follows.

Eventually, Simran's gaze slides away from his. "I don't. Everything's fine."

He stares at her another moment, then laughs. Because of course Simran is avoiding the elephant in the room. If she addressed it, she'd have to give him a chance to explain. And clearly she doesn't want to. Clearly, she's heard enough.

That sinking feeling comes back, times a hundred. He pushes out the door. The last thing he hears is people calling Simran's name.

SIX

AS THE DOOR swings shut behind Rajan, Simran makes her way to the admin office, still shaken. What happened back there? How did Rajan notice she was acting off? For the last few days, she's been going to class and her volunteer shifts and everywhere else pretending she's fine, and it's worked. Just because she thinks about her mom's diagnosis twenty-four seven—researching it when she's supposed to be studying, scheduling her mom's scans, constantly ruminating over the conversation she overheard—doesn't mean it's written on her face. Which feels surreal. How is it, really, that Simran can walk around carrying all this heaviness and nobody sees it?

But Rajan did.

Although he seemed different, too. More vigilant, somehow. He scanned the street every time he went out for groceries. She's not sure he even realized he was doing it.

She glances back at the food line, only to find the guy who provoked Rajan studying her. Before she can react, he turns to leave.

She shakes her head and enters the admin office. Inside, she's surprised to find the whole team crowded around the desk. "What is it? Did something happen?"

Kamaljot Uncle waves this away. "We're concerned about you."

Her hackles immediately go up. Did they notice she's been off, too?

"You shouldn't go anywhere with that boy alone," Kamaljot Uncle adds. "What were you thinking, grabbing his arm? He might've hurt you."

Oh. They're talking about *Rajan*. She relaxes slightly. "It's fine. There was just someone in here antagonizing him." She doesn't know that for sure, of course, but the man who was grinning as Rajan got kicked out likely didn't have the best intentions. "There's no need to inform Hillway."

Rupi Auntie snorts, already filling out the paperwork. "Of course there is. Don't fall for his charm, Simran. Have you not heard? What that boy did?"

Simran pauses. She doesn't know, and it hasn't occurred to her until right now that she almost . . . doesn't want to.

She's heard the rumours about his incarceration. But the thing about Rajan is that it's very difficult to reconcile those rumours with the boy who gossiped with her in school and pretends to bow at her feet when she walks by. "It's not my business."

Rupi Auntie scoffs. "It *is*, because he told me."

"I don't know anything about this boy," another auntie complains. "Who is he?"

And then it's a flurry of voices.

"Arshdeep's eldest son."

"Arshdeep Gill?"

"Randhawa. She died last year."

Everyone makes sympathetic *tut-tut-tut* sounds.

"She moved to Surrey last summer with her eldest," Rupi Auntie explains. "To be closer to her family and the specialist doctors. They said it was her kidneys, but in the end it was her heart."

"Those poor boys of hers," says Kamaljot Uncle. "Her sons were so sweet, so cute."

"*Not* the oldest," Rupi Auntie says with a huff. "I taught in his school. He was involved in the gang stuff. Always doing drugs or in detention. And the other day! I saw him in the government building. He told me— no shame—that he went to jail for killing someone. Like he was *proud*."

All eyes swivel to Simran for her reaction.

She forces stillness into her expression. "Everyone at Hillway has made mistakes."

"Putting your shirt on backward is a *mistake*," Kamaljot Uncle says. "This is *murder*. Don't you know what men in gangs do?"

"My in-law's friend's son went that way in Surrey," adds another. "Apparently, he always carried a gun. Beat people for money. Now he's in prison. Simran, you're a sweet girl, but you can't give everyone the benefit of the doubt."

Neetu's grandma, who's been sitting quietly on the couch in the corner, speaks up. "Are we sure about all this? I spoke to him this morning. He was very well-mannered. And he added some beautiful designs to the table plates. Far better at it than that fool you brought me to help later."

"Look, he's even charmed *you*," Kamaljot Uncle scoffs, and turns back to Simran. "Simran, you must request a new mentee. We'll worry about you otherwise."

Everyone makes noises of agreement. Simran bites her lip, overwhelmed at their concern for her. She wonders if something's wrong with her that she's not concerned herself.

Just then, Neetu pokes her head inside. "Simran, I need a hand."

Relieved, Simran follows her out with an abashed shrug at the others.

"They were absolutely going in on you in there," Neetu comments once they're out of earshot. "Was it about Rajan?"

From the way she says his name, Simran can tell Neetu shares the admin team's opinion. "He wasn't being violent. Someone came in trying to get a rise out of him."

"If they succeeded, that means he hasn't gotten ahold of his anger," Neetu says matter-of-factly. "So he's not well suited to working here.

Hey, you're still coming for the catering testing for the engagement party, right? It's in two weeks."

Simran's relieved for the change in topic. "Wouldn't miss it." Neetu, who's seven years Simran's senior, is getting married this summer in Abbotsford. But they're throwing an engagement party in Kelowna first, in early July, before she moves away with her soon-to-be husband. Simran tries not to dwell on that part. Neetu's the one who taught Simran the harmonium growing up; Simran can't imagine the gurdwara without her. Ever since high school ended, it feels like all her friends are slowly leaving Kelowna. Eventually she'll be the only one left.

Unless, of course, she accepts that UBC transfer offer. The deadline is today. Not that she's thinking about it or anything.

Good, because you aren't taking it, she reminds herself firmly, and busies herself filling Rajan's position in the serving line.

Two hours later, when breakfast's done, the dishes washed, floors swept, and volunteers filtering out, Kamaljot Uncle shoos her out despite her protests, insisting he'll lock up. Simran finally relents and gets in her truck. She does, after all, have a student association meeting at the university to get to. But she doesn't leave just yet.

Instead, she studies the sponsor card she plucked off one of the tables. It *is* beautifully decorated—neat cursive, with detailed, geometric designs around the edges one might think were printed professionally. At least until she flips it over, to see that ink has bled through the cardstock. She runs her thumb over the stain.

When Kamaljot Uncle finally exits the building, Simran pretends to be texting. It's only when he drives away that she hops out and lets herself back in using her own spare key.

She goes to the management office, where the Hillway reports are in the outbox, ready to be sent off tomorrow morning. She plucks out the complaint against Rajan.

On her drive to the university, she glances at it in the passenger seat and feels the first seeds of doubt. She doesn't actually *know* what happened. Why is it so hard for her to accept Rajan might be in the wrong?

Because of his card-decorating skills? She needs to get it together. Nine months could've changed him. After all, Simran feels like a different person now than she was a week ago. Maybe she's the cliché she's been warned against becoming: the inexperienced good girl getting played by a guy who knows his exact effect on her.

She shakes her head and crumples the paper in her fist. *Next time,* she tells herself. Next time, she won't interfere.

As she speed-walks into the meeting half an hour late, the long table of undergraduate society members give her looks. Jassa Singh, who's vice president, doesn't even pause his spiel about leftover council tasks to be done before summer. Simran takes her seat and scans the agenda. As treasurer, all she cares about is the budget, which is the next item. She opens her laptop to retrieve her spreadsheet, but instead, her screen wakes to the email from Dr. Maxfield.

Okay, so *maybe* she's been thinking about it more than she should. But it won't matter after today. There's no harm in imagining

"Simran."

Simran jolts to find Jassa staring at her. "I— What?"

"The budget. That's the next item."

Although he's clearly repeated this several times, he doesn't sound annoyed. He never does; he's just trying to run the meeting efficiently, as he always does when the president is absent. The least Simran can do is match it.

Quickly, she closes the tab and ends up on the last Google search she made: endometrial cancer. She switches it again to find an assignment due tonight that she completely forgot about. She switches the tab several more times, fully aware of Jassa's eyebrows rising with every passing second, until she finds the spreadsheet. Clears her throat. "We're in—"

"A deficit, I know. I saw the numbers, too. I just don't understand why."

A prickle of irritation goes through her. Here Jassa is again, violating her area of expertise. She feels the strong urge to one-up him. "It's because we're still missing a significant portion of member fees."

A quiet. Jassa twiddles his pen casually, then speaks to the room. "If I remember correctly, we delegated who would collect those months ago. Anyone remember who that was?"

Everyone remembers, given it's the student services representative's job, but before any of them can speak up, the offender shrugs. "Me."

Simran sighs inwardly. Chandani Sharma lounges in her seat a few chairs away. Simran went to high school with her, but she was TJ's friend. Now Chandani has glommed onto Simran. Mostly for help with classes. And, apparently, to apply for vacant student council positions only to do *none* of the tasks she's assigned.

"It'll get done," Chandani says now. "Stop riding my dick about it."

Simran can practically see Jassa weighing the pros and cons of berating her. Chandani is infamously a drama queen. Simran kind of feels bad for him, so she clears her throat. "I have the list too, Chandani. I can send the emails."

"Okay," Chandani says, but Jassa cuts her off.

"No, Simran." His voice is sharp. "Chandani can handle it."

Chandani merely yawns, unimpressed, as Jassa abruptly switches topic to the next agenda item. Simran flattens her expression to hide her annoyance.

Maybe Jassa can tell anyway, because once the meeting is over and everyone's filing out, he drops into the chair next to her. It's too low for him, but he's somehow graceful about it. "I didn't mean to undermine you back there. I just didn't want you to take on yet another thing."

"I can handle it."

Jassa arches one brow. "Can you? Because sometimes I think you seriously don't know when to stop. You're constantly behind. Like that assignment that—"

"That was an off day," she interrupts, somewhat shaken that he's noticed. "That's not how I . . . normally am."

He blinks at her. She stares back resolutely. She rarely does this, because the truth is, he's uncomfortably handsome. But what unsettles her more than his sharp, scruffy jawline or long-lashed eyes is that she cannot figure out his intentions with this conversation.

He misinterprets her silence. "I'm not trying to boss you around. I just think we both need a reminder sometimes to take a breather. Feel free to do the same for me."

"I'd rather watch you crash and burn," Simran replies straight-faced, and he chuckles a little.

"Yeah," he says. "I bet you would."

And she has the feeling they're both only half joking.

When Simran arrives home, she finds her dad and an uncle she knows well sitting on rocking chairs on the porch.

Toor Uncle lights up when she hops out of her truck. "There's our little birdie!"

Birdie is his affectionate nickname for her after years of her singing at the gurdwara. "Sat Sri Akaal, Uncle ji," she greets him automatically, accepting his hug.

"How's your truck running?" he asks when he releases her. "Those new brakes working okay?"

Toor Uncle is a mechanic, and therefore the family's go-to for anything that needs a handyman. "Perfectly, Uncle ji. How're you?"

"Good, good. Now, I have another question for you. A while ago your mother asked me to fix her bike. The shop's getting busy, so I thought I'd come pick it up. But your useless father"—he winks—"doesn't know where it is. Where's your mom?"

Simran glances at her father, but he doesn't give any direction on how to respond. He just remains in his seat, eyes unfocused, stroking his beard. He's been like this more and more lately. For days, both of Simran's parents have.

Toor Uncle frowns in the silence. He glances up at the house—specifically, the upstairs window of her parents' bedroom, currently with the shades drawn. He must be wondering why he hasn't been invited inside. Simran can practically see his confusion morphing into true curiosity, and she can't have that.

"I'm sorry, Uncle ji, we'll get the bike to you later. I have to go to class soon. Dad, can you help me find my bag?"

There's no bag to find, nor any more class. But her dad nods jerkily, finally coming to life. "One minute," he says to Toor Uncle, and follows Simran into the house.

Usually, on an afternoon like this, the smell of fresh food would greet them. Her mother would be cooking away, humming along with kirtan on the speaker. But today, like the last five days, Simran hears nothing.

She faces her father once he's closed the door. "He doesn't know?"

"Of course not." He looks exhausted. "Your mother doesn't want anyone to know. She thinks people would see her differently."

Simran nods slowly. She'd suspected as much. "She's still in bed, isn't she?"

He says nothing. Simran feels a headache building. Her mother is *always* in bed. The last few times Simran tried to get her up, she simply moved to the couch and continued staring into space. It's baffling. She's never been one to sit still.

"Nikka putt," her father says quietly. "Let her grieve."

Simran's breakfast pushes up her throat. "What's there to grieve? We don't even know how bad it is yet."

He's silent a moment. "I misspoke. Come, have food."

He did not misspeak. Simran is certain of that as she follows him to the kitchen and accepts a plate of his karelé. As she tries to eat it—it's too bitter for her taste, not as well-cooked as her mom's—she can't stop her thoughts from turning to the conversation she overheard a few days ago between her parents.

Simran has always known their lives didn't go as planned. When her father immigrated, neither his engineering experience nor his various academic degrees meant anything. And her mom . . . Her parents died unexpectedly, leaving her to drop out of school to look after her younger sister. Her dreams of being a doctor went unfulfilled, but her sister did it instead. Simran always wondered if her mother felt bitter about that.

But of course, all that sacrifice was supposed to be worth it for their *children*.

Kiran clearly didn't get the memo that she was supposed to be a balm to their parents, not a new source of heartache. And when she moved out after high school, it was just Simran, ten years younger and acutely aware that she was their parents' last chance at that happy immigrant ending.

She thought she was doing okay at that. She thought, when she chose math instead of premed last year, that their agreement meant approval. But no. They were simply digesting another hope of theirs flying away.

She cannot do that to them ever again.

Simran pushes the plate away. "I'm not that hungry."

"Why didn't you say? More for me." He takes a bite with gusto. "Perhaps I'll offer some to Toor Uncle."

She smiles, appreciating his attempt at normalcy. "If the plan is to make him avoid our house in the future, that could work."

He chuckles, then strokes her cheek. "You're the best thing that ever happened to us, you know that, right?"

Her smile drops. She knows that a little too well. "I'll help with dinner, okay? I'm just going to my room for a bit."

She kisses him on the cheek and leaves. She feels calmer, now that she's made her decision.

In her bedroom, she opens her laptop and Dr. Maxfield's email again. Downstairs, the front door opens and closes. Her father must be sending Toor Uncle on his way.

Simran barely pays attention, though. She just reads the email until it's burned onto her retinas—so that when she closes her eyes, it's still there.

And her mind drifts. She imagines typing back, *I am planning to come to Vancouver, and I would love to work in your lab!* She imagines moving schools and taking all the niche classes she can and rejoining debate and meeting high school friends at tournaments and and *and* . . .

Leaving her parents all alone to deal with this.

Simran opens her eyes. This time, when she opens the email she'd drafted to decline the offer, she doesn't hesitate. She hits send.

And it goes. Without fanfare. When she sees it in her sent folder, she feels very little. Relief, maybe. That she doesn't have to make this decision anymore. Now she can focus on the real task—showing her parents all their sacrifices were worth it. She can still fulfill some of their hopes. She doesn't know how yet, but she'll do it. After the struggles of her mom and dad's lives, the least Simran can do is make them happy.

There's a knock on her door. Simran swivels around immediately. If it's her mother, Simran will be ready to offer to make chah, to do the laundry, or just sit and listen to her cry. If it's her father, she'll be ready to sound upbeat, to share her mother's upcoming appointments and the research she's done, to act as strong as he thinks she is.

But when the door creaks open, it's not either of her parents.

Instead, a tall young woman leans against the doorframe, running her fingers through pixie-cut black hair. Her eyes land on Simran. A lopsided smile curves her mouth, achingly familiar. And yet not familiar at all—because Simran hasn't seen it in over a year.

"Kiran?" Simran manages.

"Nice to see you, too, Simmi," her sister replies.

SEVEN

THE MORNING AFTER his disastrous Hillway volunteering, Rajan takes the bus to work.

Today they're starting a big project: redoing the roofs of buildings at the university. His bus is filled with UBCO students hoisting laptop bags and Starbucks cups. With his hood up, as he listens to them complain about exams and deadlines, he can almost pretend he's one of them. Yeah, Rajan knows a thing or two about deadlines. He's got thirty-two hours until his.

Nick's words swirl through his head as the bus screeches to a stop. The UBCO students head to campus, while he alone walks toward the dorms and the construction site. He nods at Trevor, one of the friendlier roofers who handled his orientation, before joining their task of ripping out the old roof. He works quickly, all the while scanning the ground far below. As if Nick might show up here, too, as another *reminder*.

He wants to believe Nick's threats were bluffs. They've spent a lot of time together—collecting debts and, in between, shooting the shit. But did Rajan ever really know him?

The first time they met, Rajan was wasted. It was July, high school had just ended, and he was in Surrey with his mom. Except, he wasn't *with* his mom right then. He was at a party, trying to forget the latest doctor's grim news: His mom's body was rejecting the transplant.

While he was staring into space, some dude sat next to him. He tapped the empty bottles next to Rajan.

"Want something better than this?"

The guy wore a leather jacket, diamond studs in his ears. An LS tattoo crawled up his neck. Rajan looked down to see he was being offered a bag of white powder. "I don't have money."

"This one's on the house. You look like you need it." He patted Rajan's shoulder. "I'm Nick."

Rajan took it without further questions and did a line right there. His face instantly went pleasantly numb. Nick watched, and then: "What would you say if I told you that you could make money to buy more?"

Despite the euphoric feeling now spreading to his mind, Rajan shook his head. Dealing lost its appeal in high school. "Not interested."

"You sure?" Nick pulled a wad of cash from his pocket. "I made this in one night. *One* night."

Rajan stared at the cash helplessly. It was a *lot*.

Nick went on. "I collect debts. Take a little interest, too." A flash of white teeth. "Call it my commission."

"And they just hand it over if you ask nicely, huh?"

"I ask *really* nicely."

Rajan knew what that meant, but right then, he didn't care. He *could* use the money. Looking back, he wishes he could say he was thinking selfless things when he considered it. Like, he could buy stuff for his brothers, or give it to his aunt as a thank-you for hosting him and his mom, or help with the mortgage. But he wasn't. He thought about one thing only.

"Give me another line and I'm in," he said.

Nick leaned sideways to address someone behind him. "Zohra! Get my man Rajan some more chitta."

"Sure thing," said a husky, feminine voice. Slender arms slid around

Rajan's shoulders and made him feel drunk in an entirely different way.

Later, Rajan would wonder how Nick knew his name. He'd learn that Nick and Zohra had him marked the minute he'd used his LS connections to find that party. Before he even walked in, they knew exactly who he was, how he couldn't afford his own taste in drugs, and what he used to do for the Lions in Kelowna. And they'd decided he could be put to work here, too.

And if Nick was *that* cutthroat then . . . their brief friendship doesn't matter. He won't hesitate to put a bullet between Rajan's eyes at all.

Rajan wipes the sweat off his brow. Holy hell. Is this how sober people feel all the time? High-strung and scattered, like the world could fall on their heads at any moment? The smoke floating over from his coworkers has never been so tempting. If he were just *relaxed* enough, maybe he'd be able to think through a solution.

Or maybe somebody would narc on him and he'd go to jail over a joint. Nick would probably die laughing.

Trevor yells up at him. "Kid! You gonna spend all night up there?"

He looks up. The sun is lower in the sky. Somehow, he spent all day working. He didn't even take a break. Time passes fast on a deadline.

He slides down his ladder, and when he gets to the bottom, a girl's voice sounds from behind him.

"Rajan Randhawa, is that you?"

The voice is familiar, and when he turns, so is the face. A gorgeous Indian girl with long straight hair, a wicked smile, and a fashion sense for weather at least ten degrees warmer than this. She draws closer, and his coworkers give her second looks. Chandani Sharma has that effect.

Although she's one of those popular girls who probably hit her peak in high school, she's not actually a total bitch. He knows this because Simran's cool with her. And if Simran is, so is he. Even if she used to buy weed from Zach Singer instead of him. "Chandani, I thought you'd be on a runway by now."

"And I thought you'd be in prison."

He flashes her a grin. "I think your guess was closer than mine."

She doesn't ask for an explanation. She's too busy looking him over—eyes skating over his orange hoodie, his dusty cargo pants with caulking on the knees, his work boots, and then back up. "Are you . . . a construction worker?"

"Roofer. You go to UBCO?" She nods. Figures. Everybody he knew in high school has gone on to bigger and better things. "What do *you* study?"

"Wish I knew. Then I wouldn't have flunked that exam I just took." Chandani flips her hair. "Selling anything fun these days?"

She's standing a little too close, but he doesn't move away. He's starting to get some interesting signals. "I don't do that anymore."

"That's too bad." Chandani casually brushes dust off his shoulder. He can practically feel the other roofers' eyes on them. "Guess I have to find some healthy coping strategies now."

"Let me know if you do. I wanna try smoking them in a pipe." Chandani snickers, but it doesn't quite reach her eyes. His curiosity overpowers him. "What do *you* need coping strategies for?"

She shrugs. "Do you ever feel like you're in over your head?"

Twenty-three hours left. "Nah. I'm a chill dude."

She leans against the ladder. "Lately I've realized I don't know what I'm doing here. At university. It feels like everyone knows except me."

It's unsettling, how much he's relating suddenly to Chandani Sharma. "Maybe university just isn't your thing."

"What else would I do? Work in construction?" She snorts. "Is that your life's calling?"

"Is flunking out of school *your* life's calling?"

She glares. "You're such an asshole." Rajan grins and turns to go, but her voice stops him. "You're off now, right? Wanna hang out?"

He turns back. He's got a meeting with Kat in, like, two hours, but . . . "Why?"

She sighs. "God, boys are so brainless. Do you wanna have sex or not?"

Subtlety's never been Chandani's strong suit. But he wanted to be sure. And, well, he has a feeling she needs a distraction just as much as he does.

He faces her fully. "You know, I went to juvie." Chandani says nothing. "For drug trafficking. Weapons possession. And . . . murder."

He waits for her alarm, for her to step away, to make excuses and leave. But Chandani's expression doesn't change. "So? I already knew all this."

He stares. "You . . . don't care?"

"Why would I? Let's go." Her nails sink into his hoodie like claws. His coworkers hoot in the background. "And *definitely* bring the hard hat."

Two hours later, Rajan's back in the elevator up to the corrections department. He leans his head against the wall, watching the numbers go up and wanting to kick something. Why did Kat set their meeting so late on a Friday, anyway? According to the judge, he has to come running whenever Kat calls—and she's scheduled these to happen once a week. Which feels like a waste of time. Of which he already has very little.

And no, that didn't bother him with Chandani earlier. She got his mind off things for a while. But after she kicked him out of her house, saying he was the *last* person she wanted to be caught with, it felt like he'd wasted an hour he could've spent figuring out his dilemma with the Lions.

Less than a day left. He's completely screwed.

As Rajan walks through the waiting room, another guy emerges from the hallway on his way out. Rajan remembers him from last time. He's bigger than Rajan, older too, with gothic-font tattoos running down his arms: *REIGN IN HELL*, the motto of the Silver Aces, wrapped in serpents. Unsubtle *and* unoriginal. But the Lions' main rivals have always been that way.

No words are exchanged as they pass each other, but Rajan sees the *fuck you* in Snake Tattoo's glare loud and clear. He hopes he radiates it, too.

Damn, maybe this gang psychology thing they talked about in juvie was legit.

Kat's waiting in her office with her usual batshit smile. Her dress today is checkered, her long blond hair pulled back into that same low ponytail. "Welcome, Rajan. Any plans for the weekend?"

"Just counting down the hours."

She chuckles. "I'm sure. How was Hillway yesterday?"

Rajan tenses. Shit. He totally forgot about that. If he apologizes first, maybe they'll let him stay? He doesn't want a mark on his record *already*.

"Listen, I—" he says at the same time Kat says, "I heard nothing, so I assume it went smoothly. What were you saying?"

"Nothing." Rajan glues his jaw shut. He'd thought they were writing him up, but maybe not.

Kat studies him. "How's your mentor? Simran?"

His mood sours instantly. He plucks a toothpick from his pocket and sticks it between his teeth. "She's all right."

"Did you get along?"

"I wouldn't know," he mutters. "She barely spoke to me." It hurts to even say. But he'd better get used to it. This is how it's going to be from now on.

"If she's treating you poorly—"

"I said she's *all right*," he says forcefully. "Can we talk about something else?"

After a long pause, Kat flips a page in her file. "Have you heard from the Lion's Share?"

Rajan stops chewing on his toothpick. Yes, he asked for a topic change, but where did *this* come from? "How would you know if I did?"

"We rely on you to tell us."

She doesn't look up, and he resumes rolling the toothpick between his teeth. This is clearly a routine question. And a stupid one. "You think I'd *tell* you if I breached probation?"

"Yes." Kat offers another unnerving smile. "Because you wouldn't want me to find out some other way. Such as upon your arrest. I'd rather be able to help before that."

He scoffs. "And how would you help?"

"Well, for example, we could relocate you again."

"Relocate?"

"Yes. Just like how you were relocated to Kelowna for probation. Move you somewhere you can avoid negative influences and instead be surrounded by positive reinforcements." At his blank look, she clarifies, "Social supports, family. Can you think of another place like that?"

He finds himself considering the question seriously. When he was younger and doing stupid shit constantly, his parents debated moving him across the country, to live with his father's side of the family in Halifax. He doesn't know them well, though. "I dunno. Maybe."

Kat tilts her head, eyes glinting. "If you need that, I could do the paperwork in a day."

Rajan sits back. He moved back to Kelowna because Vancouver was crawling with Lions. But the Lions just found him again. And even if Halifax *was* too far for them, who's to say they wouldn't retaliate some other way?

Nick's not-threats toward his brothers ring through his head again.

"Rajan?" He looks up to find Kat watching him intently. "Do you think you're in danger here?"

Of course he's in danger. Either the system or the Lions will screw him over.

But . . . the system will only punish *him*, not his family. He can't guarantee the same for the Lions.

And suddenly the choice seems very clear indeed.

"No." Rajan tosses the toothpick in the trash. "No, there's no danger anymore."

EIGHT

"YOU'RE ALL BEING so dramatic," Kiran says on Saturday morning. "I talked with Dr. Tran. She's optimistic. Mom can probably just get a hysterectomy and move on."

Simran watches the pot of chah on the stove and tries not to show her irritation. "We don't know that yet. And either way . . . I don't think she can just move on."

"Oh, I know." Kiran rolls her eyes and fluffs her short hair. Once, her hair was longer than Simran's, brushing past her knees. But at eighteen, she cut it all off, then cut ties too and left home. The rift has never quite healed in the years since. "She's the most dramatic of all of you. I bet she was going on about how her life is over, blah blah."

She *had* been going on about her life being over, but Simran isn't about to tell Kiran that. Kiran seems to know anyway. She nods sagely.

"That's what I can't stand about her. The smallest inconvenience will happen, you'll get one bad grade, and she'll start talking about how hard it was to move to Canada for you and give up her whole life. Guilt-tripping much?"

Simran's irritation grows, partly because Kiran's analysis is not entirely untrue. Partly because it's just like Kiran to parachute in and make judgments after a year of barely any contact.

Apparently, Kiran had finally gotten in touch with their father a few days ago. When she showed up last night, their mom actually came downstairs. She'd even washed her face and put on semi-nice clothes. Her dad opened their expensive box of biscuits. They hosted her in the living room like a guest—which she is, in a way.

"That's irrelevant." Simran twirls her kara. "We're talking about her being sick. The scans this week are to see how much it's . . . spread."

On the word *spread*, Kiran stands, her chair scraping back from the kitchen table. "Oh my god. She'll be *fine*. She's booked to see a surgeon! Stop looking so miserable. We'll be laughing about this by Christmas. Here, your chah's about to overboil." She hurries to the stove, where the chah is barely simmering.

Simran watches Kiran fumble around the cupboards, as disoriented as a houseguest. "Mom and Dad are really sad. I've been thinking about what we could do to make them happier."

Kiran snorts, tossing a cinnamon stick into the chah. "Simmi, you'll never make them happy. Unless you completely shape your life according to what they want." She tosses a glance over her shoulder. "Which I guess you're kind of doing."

Simran's forgotten how talented Kiran is at getting on her nerves. Back in the day, when it came to their parents, Kiran never picked her battles. She fought all of them. By the time she moved out, everyone was tired of the never-ending conflict. Simran the most of all. "It takes less than you think to make them happy."

"Not our job. They need to learn to have a life outside of their children."

"I know it's not my *job*," Simran snaps. "I just want to. What's wrong with that?"

Before Kiran can respond, their dad comes down the stairs, still in his nightclothes. His eyes fall on them—tired, but affectionate. "It's so nice seeing you two together again."

Kiran and Simran look at each other and then away. Probably best not to mention they were arguing.

He doesn't notice, extending his arms for a hug. Simran goes over immediately, and as always, his embrace is tight and safe and welcoming. When they pull apart, he glances at Kiran, who rather deliberately turns away. He lowers his arms, a trace of sadness in his eyes.

Sometimes Simran wants to shake her sister. Instead, she busies herself pouring chah for them all. Her father takes a biscuit from the box on the table. Kiran takes one, too, and so does Simran. They stand around the table munching their cold biscuit breakfast silently.

Just then, there's a creak of the staircase as footsteps come down. They all stop to stare as Simran's mom appears in the doorway. "Mom," Simran says, trying not to sound too hopeful. "You're up."

Her mom's freshly showered, eyes red-rimmed. "Of course I'm up," she says, voice feather soft. "I wanted to see my daughters. For as long as I'm able."

And just like that, any possible normalcy for the day goes out the window.

Kiran turns her eyes to the ceiling. "*Mom*. Seriously?"

Their mother sinks into a chair at the table. Simran rubs her shoulders. Her dad busies himself at the fridge, but Simran suspects he's turned his back for other reasons. Kiran doesn't move, just stands in the middle of everything with her arms crossed and lips thin. She seems immune to the anguish in the room, but Simran can feel it. Suffocating her.

She's guiltily glad she has a reason to leave the house today. She steps away from her mother. "I'm going to the university this morning. Jassa and I are cleaning things up at the student society office."

Kiran whips around to her, earlier frustration gone. "Ooh, 'Jassa and I'?" Her eyes twinkle. "A *boooy*?"

Simran sends her a flat look. This is *not* the time.

"Is he good-looking?" Kiran teases, but her mother cuts her off.

"Kiran, that's enough. Jassa is a respectable boy. I won't hear any more of these jokes." She leans her head back. "Let Simran go with him in peace."

Kiran raises her eyebrows at Simran, and for a moment, they share mutual surprise. Usually, if Kiran were to make a joke like this, their mom would take the opportunity to remind Simran to avoid romantic entanglements. But not today, apparently. Today it's Kiran getting berated.

Of course, Kiran's used to getting berated, and simply mutters, "Whatever," before grabbing her chah mug. Simran studies her mom curiously. Why is she not giving the usual lecture about boys whose brains are only half developed? Does graduating high school mean her mom is suddenly okay with dating? Or is it because it's Jassa Singh and her mom adores him?

While she's musing, Simran's phone rings. She fishes it from her pocket. "It's TJ." Right. She'd forgotten to call back after hanging up last week. "Let me——"

"Don't tell her," her mother says. Her eyes are fixed on Simran's phone. "Don't tell anyone *anything*. But especially not her. I don't want her mom to know. Accha?"

Her voice is firm. Simran nods hesitantly, but . . .

"Couldn't Masi ji be helpful?" TJ's mom is a doctor—an orthopedic surgeon, but still. And she has connections in the medical community. "Maybe she could get us in faster——"

"No."

"But why not ask——"

"I said *no*." Her mother glares. "Promise me you won't breathe a word of this to TJ. I don't care if you think she can keep a secret. *I don't want her to know.*"

Simran sighs. The rift between her mother and masi is out of her hands. "I promise." She glances at her phone, suddenly unsure she can act *completely* normal on the call. She needs to mentally prepare.

So, she lets TJ's name fade from her screen.

During her drive to UBCO, TJ leaves a voicemail, then sends three texts, the last of which is *ARE YOU EVEN ALIVE*. When Simran parks, she puts her phone on silent.

In the student services building, Jassa is already hard at work clearing out filing cabinets. It's a dull job, but one of those end-of-year tasks that need doing. She'd offered to help at the end of their conversation yesterday, just to skate over what felt like a supremely awkward moment.

They wordlessly sort through files until Jassa says, "How's your mom doing with her new thing?"

For a moment, Simran panics. "I— What?"

He doesn't seem to notice. "Last time I saw her at the gurdwara, she said she was learning to play the tabla."

Simran exhales. Slowly. "She did?" Her mom plays sometimes, but usually it's her dad who accompanies Simran at home.

"Yeah. She said the way I played made her want to learn."

He sounds vaguely surprised, but Simran's not. Jassa's a tabla expert. Despite herself, Simran enjoys performing at the gurdwara with him. When he first moved to Kelowna for university, Simran deliberately sang shabads in uncommon taals to test his drumming skills. But he never faltered. He's always matched her flawlessly.

Her mom probably noticed that, too. Simran swallows, suddenly looking at Jassa in a new light. Her mother not even *mentioning* that Simran should stay professional with him suddenly feels like a flashing neon sign screaming at her to pursue him instead.

Jassa doesn't seem to notice her staring. He pulls something out of the filing cabinet. "Huh. Look where all those 'missing' votes for the student fees referendum went."

Simran glances at them. "Chandani?"

"Yeah. I get the sentiment, but hiding votes is, how do I put this? Oh yeah. Illegal." He rolls his eyes. "You know she never did send those emails after the meeting? She said she was 'too busy getting laid.'" He uses air quotes. "Why do some people act like getting drunk and laid is the pinnacle of enjoyment?"

Simran represses a smile at his uncharacteristic grumbling. He's always so diplomatic in meetings. "Are you going to report her?"

"No. I don't want to pay higher student fees, do you?" He starts feeding the stolen votes into the shredder. Simran laughs, and he grins, too. And she realizes this is the most at ease they've ever been with each other. Sitting on the floor between desks with files scattered around them. No hesitation, no wariness. This is real.

Simran's treacherous brain goes back, as it has many times recently, to that conversation she overheard. *I'd get to see her become an adult, get married, have children, and be settled. And now I'm learning I won't even get that.*

And it comes out of her mouth without any further thought.

"Do you want to get coffee after this?"

Jassa blinks. Once. Twice. His hesitation lasts maybe a second, but in that time Simran has eons to regret every word she said. "Never mind—"

Then he looks into her eyes. "No, it's just, I've got an errand to run after this."

"I understand." What was she thinking? She doesn't even *drink* coffee. Desperate to change the topic, she says, "So—" at the same time he says, "Hey, wait."

She does.

"You didn't let me finish." His voice is light as he shreds the last stolen votes. "I'm free later. How about six?"

She *really* regrets it now. Based on his hesitation, he definitely caught the . . . flavour . . . of her question. There's no backing out. "Six sounds great."

And then they go back to their task like nothing happened.

By five o'clock, though, Simran is in full panic mode.

Is this a date? She can't decide. On one hand, this could be an olive branch after a year of passive-aggressive rivalry. And maybe it would've felt casual if they got coffee after they finished filing, but to come back *specifically* for that feels . . . definitely something extra. But he's the one who asked her to come back. So was *he* the one who made it a date?

This is so confusing.

Simran opens her closet. An avalanche of clothes falls from the top shelf—she didn't fold her laundry last night—but once the coast is clear, she pushes aside her T-shirts to reveal the part of her closet TJ has stocked.

It's the only neat section of her closet, mainly because Simran hardly touches it. These clothes are *nice*. Intimidatingly so. Simran's always too groggy in the mornings to bother with such clothing decisions. She generally regrets wearing a baggy shirt and jeans by midafternoon, resolves by evening to wear something cute the next day, stays up too late, and . . . the cycle renews each morning. But right now, she feels the compulsion to try them.

No particular reason, of course.

After agonizing for several minutes, Simran selects a blue paisley-patterned shirtdress. The silky material cuts closer to her body than usual, flaring at the waist and ending mid-thigh. After tugging on some leggings, she digs through her drawers, looking for the "makeup essentials" TJ stocked her with. After ten minutes she finally spots the bag behind a backpack in the corner.

She sets it on her dresser. There's no time to watch tutorials on all the various products, so she selects a tube of lipstick and turns to the dresser mirror. This, at least, should be simple.

She realizes she's wrong in approximately sixty seconds. In the past, she's only used tinted lip gloss. This is too bold. It's garishly striking and makes her look like a clown. She immediately heads to the washroom across the hall to scrub it off.

Except, as soon as she leaves her room, she collides with someone.

"Watch where you're—" Kiran's eyes fall to her mouth and then bug out. "What is *that*?"

Simran immediately backs away into her bedroom. "Just—trying something out."

But Kiran follows her in, her expression a mix of curiosity and glee.

She grabs Simran's chin. "Pretty colour, but you're using too much, Miss 'Trying It Out.' Nice outfit, too. What're you dressing up for?" Her voice becomes sly. "Or who?"

Simran wrenches herself out of Kiran's grasp and sits at her dresser again. Kiran's grin widens.

"I'm impressed. You're actually putting it on for someone, aren't you?"

"Leave," Simran says evenly.

Kiran picks through the clutter on her bedroom floor to come closer. "You're going to stab yourself in the eye with that."

Simran looks down at the eyeliner pen she's holding. This is probably true. She doesn't have any artistic skill. But Kiran's watching, so she removes her glasses and attempts it. Her hand trembles. The line emerges uneven, above the edge of her eyelid by a hair.

Kiran says, "You look stupid."

Simran immediately sets the eyeliner down. Kiran's right. She should just focus on her strengths, which have never included looking pretty. She fumbles for a Kleenex, but can't find the box.

Kiran sighs and brings the box over from the other side of the room. Simran takes it wordlessly and dabs at her eye. The makeup smears and makes her look like she's been punched in the face. Jassa will be swooning, she's sure.

Kiran picks up the makeup bag and starts taking products out to examine them. "TJ got you these? They're nice brands, you know."

Simran had no idea. Which reminds her she should probably return her cousin's calls. Maybe by tonight she'll feel normal enough.

Then Kiran comes at her with a brush. Simran jerks away.

"What're you *doing*?"

"Do you want your makeup done or not?" Kiran grips her chin. "I'm not as good as TJ, but I can make it halfway decent. Better than you, anyway."

"If you're going to insult me the whole time——"

Kiran rolls her eyes and lifts the brush again. "Okay, Simmi. I'll shut up. Now close your eyes."

And true to her word, when Simran's eyes slide shut, it's a ceasefire. At least until Kiran knocks something over. Simran squints to see her Hillway schedule on the floor.

"You need to stop being such a slob, I can hardly work—" Kiran scoops it up. Her eyes go big. "You're paired up with the *Randhawa* kid? Didn't he do some screwed-up stuff? I heard about him."

Who hasn't, apparently? Simran snatches the schedule and tosses it behind the dresser. "The program is full of people who've done stuff like that. That's the point."

"Well, you should be careful." Kiran lightly dabs lipstick on her mouth. "Who're you going to see tonight, anyway?"

"Jassa."

A pause. Kiran stares at her.

"Wait, the guy Mom bit my head off about this morning?" Kiran sighs. "*Simran*. What. The. Hell."

In those words, Simran can tell her older sister has seen right through her.

"Do you even like him?" Kiran tosses the lipstick back into the bag. "Or are you going out with him because *Mom* does?"

"I'm not going out with him," Simran snaps, sliding her glasses on. "And of course I like him. That has nothing to do with Mom."

"But the reason you're doing this *now* is . . ." Kiran half laughs, shaking her head. "This is so screwed up I don't even know what to say."

"Then don't say anything."

"You've never been on a date before, Simmi." It's a statement, not a question, even though Kiran hasn't lived at home for nearly ten years. "You're too inexperienced to be going in like . . . this. You should be doing the whole thing. Play the field. For yourself, not them."

Kiran is making Simran feel about five years old, and she doesn't like it. "Just because that's the way you do it doesn't mean I have to. Breaking Mom and Dad's hearts isn't my hobby like it is yours."

A silence. So long, it's more than enough time to remember the reason for Kiran's long absence from the household. Kiran announced last year she wasn't ever planning to get married. Her parents wanted to see her *settled*. Kiran shouted back that she was *ace*. Their parents didn't know what that meant, and Kiran refused to explain. That was what led to The Fight.

Simran draws breath to apologize. But then Kiran stands to leave with a soft, condescending laugh.

"Stop worrying about our parents' hearts. If you're going to start dating boys, you need to start worrying about *yours*."

NINE

JASSA'S LATE.

Which is a shame, because Simran is quite proud of herself for being *only* five minutes late to the university café they agreed on. She texts him and claims a table.

But twenty minutes pass, and he's still not here. She wishes she'd brought some study material. To occupy herself, she buys a black tea instead.

Thirty minutes in, she calls him, but it goes straight to voicemail. Have his errands gone longer than expected? Did she even get the time right?

The sun is lowering, peeking through the window and into her eyes, when her phone pings. She nearly drops her cup in her eagerness to pick up.

But it's not Jassa. It's her dad, asking her to pick up groceries on her way home from her "meeting." Simran sends an affirmatory text back, then glances at the time. She told her parents the imaginary meeting ended . . . now. Which means she should leave, if she's committing to this lie.

It's been an hour since she got here. Her mind runs through possibilities. Maybe Jassa showed up before her, got irritated she was late, and left. Maybe his phone's dead. Or . . . maybe she read this all wrong. Maybe he left her hanging deliberately? But why would he do that?

She feels silly suddenly, sitting here all dolled up. This was a ridiculous idea. There are more useful things she could be doing, like getting those groceries. Numbly, she tosses her cup and heads back to the parking lot.

The sun is getting lower on the horizon by the time she approaches the abandoned lot. It's Saturday night during summer, so there's barely anyone around. Her pickup is in a far corner.

But—her steps slow—it isn't alone.

There's someone leaning against the pole two spaces away from it. She recognizes him: the guy from the lunch kitchen. The one Rajan swore at. He's dressed in an unassuming green jacket, arms crossed, diamond studs sparkling in his ears. And he's looking straight at her.

This can't be a coincidence.

Keep calm, she tells herself, and runs through her options. Turning back seems too obvious. She could call security for an escort. But that's quite a wait, and for what? It's still light out; it would feel like overkill. She has to get going for those groceries.

While she's waffling, another girl crosses her path right ahead of her, turning toward the parking lot, too. Simran relaxes slightly and resumes her regular pace.

The other girl glances behind her, clearly sensing Simran. Simran nods to her, and she slows a bit to let Simran catch up.

She's South Asian, with blond-dyed hair; very skinny, in a crop top and joggers that hang off her bony hips. She clutches a law textbook to her chest and leans over to whisper. "Do you know that guy?"

"No. That's my truck, though."

"I'm getting real creep vibes." The girl makes a face. "Want me to walk you to your truck?"

Simran smiles, relieved. "Sure. I can give you a ride to wherever you're going, then?"

The girl sends her a similar surprised smile. "That'd be nice. I'm parked the next lot over."

Feeling more confident, Simran approaches her vehicle.

The guy only watches them lazily; he doesn't move or say a word as Simran unlocks her car. Simran slides into the driver's seat and closes the door behind her.

Then the girl beside her sighs. "I'm sorry about this."

Simran finally tears her eyes away from the boy, just in time to see the gun glinting in the dying sunlight.

TEN

RAJAN DOESN'T LIKE who he becomes when he picks up his baseball bat.

His parents enrolled him in the sport in grade five. It was expensive, but they weren't drowning in mortgage debt back then. Rajan's dad even used to attend games. But baseball fell to the wayside when the money troubles started, and most of his equipment was sold. Rajan only kept the bat. Eventually, he found another use for that swing of his.

He absentmindedly rubs at a rust-coloured stain as he stares up at the house he's been called to. Before he got arrested last fall, he wouldn't have thought twice about what he's about to do. It was a simple role. Nick played good cop; Rajan was indisputably bad cop. They were good collectors.

He can do that again.

A sedan pulls into the driveway. Rajan pushes off the tree he's leaning against and crosses the street. It's an unassuming house; you'd never suspect it's occupied by a guy who supports his OxyContin habit by gambling in underground casinos. The dude works in an *insurance office*.

His target doesn't even notice him, standing at his door, fumbling with his keys. Rajan waits until he finally turns the lock. "Took you enough tries, Oliver."

The guy whips around and immediately flattens against the door. His eyes are huge. He's middle-aged, balding, and looks ready to wet his pants. "I don't have the money!"

He clearly already knows what this is. "Relax." Rajan nods at the door. "Let's talk inside."

Oliver doesn't move. Rajan lets his bat tap against the front walk once. Oliver's eyes drop to it. "I'll call the police."

Rajan yawns pointedly. "Inside, I said."

When Rajan doesn't immediately attempt to hit a home run on his face, Oliver relaxes. Turns and opens the door.

Rajan's ready. When Oliver reaches inside and tries to swing around with a gun, Rajan grabs his wrist immediately, bringing it down and twisting his arm behind his back.

"Don't be an asshole," he says in Oliver's ear, kind of pissed off now. "Is this piece even registered? Or are the cops you're supposedly calling gonna be real interested in it?"

"Fuck . . . off," Oliver grits out. Sweat glints from his temple. Rajan doesn't let go of his wrist. He pushes until Oliver's backed up inside his house and then kicks the door closed behind them.

The inside looks like it's already been ransacked; there's a TV wall mount, cables coming out of the wall, even an Xbox, but no TV. A rectangular patch of carpet, lighter than the rest, indicates recently removed furniture. A desk with a mouse but no computer sits in the corner. Rajan would be willing to bet Oliver pawned all of it. Anything for his next hit.

Oliver makes a break for it right then, lunging to the desk where he's undoubtedly got another weapon stashed. Rajan hauls him back and punches him in the jaw.

Oliver wails and clutches his face, sinking to the floor. Rajan opens and closes his fist discreetly. Damn, his technique is rusty.

Once he's certain he hasn't broken anything, he grabs Oliver's shaggy hair. "Dude, shut up. I didn't even hit you that hard. Cough up the money and we're done."

"I don't *have* any!"

Fine, then. Rajan shoves him down and picks up his bat. The metal is comfortingly solid against his palm.

But, he can't bring himself to raise it yet. He vaguely recalls something they said in the gang violence risk group in juvie: *In every organization, there's grunt work no one wants to do. And in every organization, those dirty jobs go to the disadvantaged. Gangs are no different. You will have all the gore and none of the glory.*

Rajan attempts to shake off the memory. Oliver still hasn't moved. This grown-ass adult, curled up sniveling on the carpet. Eyes screwed shut, as if having given up.

Or . . . as if steeling himself for a job he has to do, like Rajan is.

Rajan pauses. Something about this doesn't feel right. Why wasn't Oliver vigilant at the door? Anyone who owes the Lions money should constantly be on edge. Rajan knows that intimately.

He backs up and picks up the discarded gun. He wasn't paying attention before, but now he weighs it in his hand. It's obvious now. The gun's not even loaded.

Rajan drops it. "You knew I was coming, didn't you?"

Oliver stiffens—momentarily—but that's all Rajan needs. Suddenly, he's examining the room, looking at everything differently. That Xbox in the corner. If Oliver's so in debt, why didn't he pawn it, too? Why does he even have one without a TV?

Rajan marches over to pick it up. Oliver says, "Wait," in a panicked voice, but Rajan ignores him. He tilts the reflective black surface up to the light.

And there. A tiny pinhole camera.

Shit. He hurls the whole thing at the wall. It shatters, and he kicks one of the pieces, feeling ill. This was a setup.

He rounds on Oliver. "They paid you to get your shit kicked." Even as he's saying it, he can't believe it. Do the Lions care *this much* about

Rajan's loyalty? "*Why* would you do that? How would you know I wouldn't kill you?"

"They said they'd clear my debts," Oliver says simply, and Rajan recognizes the feverish glint in his eyes. So one thing is true. The dude is an Oxy fan. But how desperate do you have to be?

Maybe, as desperate as a broke kid hooked on cocaine, a voice in his head points out.

Up until this moment, Rajan didn't think much about the fact that juvie forced him to get clean. Sure, he's a lot more clearheaded most days than he used to be, but he didn't exactly appreciate that until right now watching Oliver. God, is this what he looked like back then? Did people pity him? Were they disgusted?

Feeling even more ill now, he turns for the door.

"Wait," Oliver calls again. Rajan pauses. "Can you hit me a few more times? So it looks like it happened for real?"

He sounds *hopeful*. Rajan sighs. "Get help, dude."

Without waiting for a response, he leaves the house.

ELEVEN

THIS HAS TO be a dream, Simran thinks for the umpteenth time. It *has* to be.

It doesn't feel real that she's sitting in this ice-cream truck—it had sailed into the parking lot out of nowhere, as the blond girl ordered Simran out of her pickup. There was an ice-cream truck just like it the day she met Rajan at Hillway. It'd set him on edge. Now she knows why.

But what they want from *her* is a mystery. No one's spoken to her since they corralled her into the back of the truck and took her phone, her purse, and even her kirpan. All the worst, most nightmarish possibilities have circulated through her head a million times.

She can't believe she let herself get *kidnapped*. Just obediently got out of her truck and into theirs. It feels so silly, at least until she looks up and sees the gun still trained on her. She can see into the barrel a little, before black swallows it up. Her imagination does the rest.

The girl holding it has seemed half distracted, though, watching the guy take a call for the past few minutes. It seemed serious, because he climbed into the front to take it. Is it too much to hope they kidnapped the wrong person? Or maybe that would actually be a bad thing. They'd have no need for her anymore.

She forces herself to refocus. *Look around you. Listen. Find anything that might be helpful.*

She peeks into the freezer next to her. No frozen treats—just stacks of brick-size packages, wrapped in brown paper. She'd wager those aren't ice-cream sandwiches.

Then there's the blond girl with the gun. She looked so harmless back at the university with that law textbook. Now she's restless, listening to the guy with the goatee in the front. His voice is low, but she catches bits: ". . . are you *serious*? . . . tell him if . . . fine, we'll handle it . . ."

The truck screeches to a stop. The guy hangs up and comes to the back again. He heaves a sigh, then looks at the girl. "He'll be here soon."

She arches a brow. "Is that a good idea?"

"Better deal with him now than later. You know how he gets." He turns to Simran. "All right, well, I'm Nick."

Simran blinks. They're doing introductions now?

Nick points to the girl. "And this is Zohra. You're Simran, right?" When Simran says nothing, he says, "We have a mutual friend, you know. Rajan."

Simran already knew this was about Rajan, but she doesn't have to confirm it for them. What if they want information about him? Her mind runs in all sorts of scattered directions. Is she going to be interrogated, like in the movies?

Zohra stands next to Nick, mirroring his crossed arms. They study her together. "I *told* you that carjacking thing was too traumatizing to pull with girls, but you wouldn't listen."

"She doesn't have to talk. We just have to show our boy we mean business." Nick steps closer to Simran and speaks almost conversationally. "You might've seen on the news, five of our guys got arrested in one go?

Do you know how much product we lost?" He doesn't wait for an answer. "A lot. Do you know how much *money* we've lost lately? I can't even tell you, because our accountant got himself arrested, too. You see the shit I have to deal with?" He sighs and pokes his head into the other freezer, reemerging with a Drumstick. "We have to get our territory under control, before the Aces start getting ideas. That's why we need your help convincing Rajan to stay. He owes us."

Simran's stomach sinks further the more he talks. The tattoo peeking from Nick's collar confirms it. This is about Rajan's *gang*.

She's always known, on some level, that he was involved in something dangerous. She saw it firsthand in grade nine. She could even guess, based on who he frequently clashed with, which gang he was linked to. The Lion's Share—she's seen the name on the news often enough. Associated with drug busts. Trafficking. Murders.

But, on a *real*, everyday level, she was never able to associate that with *Rajan*. He was just . . . Rajan Randhawa, the class troublemaker, strolling Northridge's halls with a mischievous grin, taking naps on foyer benches instead of attending class, and celebrating School Spirit Day by popping the principal's tires. He was real, and the concept of the Lions was otherworldly.

Nick gives her a longer look, up and down. "I'll admit, you're not his usual type."

He glances at Zohra, and Simran catches up to what he said.

"Wait, what?" she blurts. "You— I'm—his *type*?"

Nick and Zohra stare as she sputters, and it occurs to her that her kidnappers are *confused*. Without meaning to, a laugh escapes her.

Up until now, Simran hasn't had time to dwell on her old feelings for Rajan. Her family issues took precedence. But now that she's being confronted with it . . . Now that she's been kidnapped because Rajan's gang thinks she's his *girlfriend*? Oh, it's taking her back to humiliating places.

Like the time at the end of grade nine when Rajan's hand touched hers to take her pen and she sucked in a breath so hard it startled him. Or in grade ten when he caught her staring while he flipped a tooth-pick with his tongue. Or in grade eleven, when he returned from sum-mer break *tall* and *adult-looking* and Simran had to avoid eye contact for days. Or just last week . . . when he smiled, and it was like no time had passed.

And each time it happens, he *knows*; she can tell he does, but he never mentions it. She's grateful for that. She's grateful he doesn't share her feelings, because then her crush can never become something dangerous. Unlike her kidnappers, she's always known her fantasies exist only in her head.

She stops laughing when the gun pushes against her temple.

"What's so funny?" Zohra says.

"Nothing." Simran sobers. Rajan's in trouble. "He can't work for you. He's on probation."

"Just like half our crew." Nick sounds bored. "So what?"

"But that's unfair." She knows she should shut up, but she can't help herself. "He's trying so hard to start over. Can't you forget about this one person?"

Nick looks at her like she's being deliberately slow. "Rajan owes us big money. If it's not me today, it'll be someone else tomorrow. And the day after, it'll be a bullet in his head."

His voice is resolute—clearly, there's no reasoning with these people. Rajan has no choice but to rejoin, until the day they decide his debts are paid. Or more likely, until he becomes another statistic on TV. It's tragic. It's futile. She wants to cry, not because she's being held at gunpoint, but because here's yet *another* person she cares about having horrible, inevita-ble things happen to them, and all she can do is watch—

An idea strikes her, all at once.

Nick notices. "What?"

It leaves her reeling for a second, the absurdity of it . . . yet, before she can stop herself, she asks, "His debts just need to be repaid?"

"What, you planning to give him a loan?" Nick laughs. "You don't have that kind of money. Trust me."

Simran glances down at the brown-papered bricks in the freezer again. This idea is bad. It's not logical. And yet . . . it's perfectly logical, in a way.

She takes a deep breath. "I have a proposal for you."

TWELVE

RAJAN MAKES IT a block from Oliver's house before he spots an ice-cream truck at the curb. No surprise. Whoever was watching that feed would've dialed Nick as soon as Rajan discovered it.

Outside the truck are two white LS guys, passing a cigarette back and forth on the sidewalk. When they notice him, casually tapping his bat against the pavement as he approaches, they drop the cigarette and face him. Like that's going to stop him. Rajan cracks his neck.

Just then, the back door of the truck cracks open. A girl saunters out and closes it behind her.

Not just any girl. *"Zohra?"*

She looks nearly the same as the last time he saw her—dressed in a crop top and sweatpants that sag on her hips, although that choker at her neck hints at her expensive taste. Her hair is bottle blond and stick straight, instead of black and wavy like he remembers. But. She's unmistakable.

Zohra smirks at his speechlessness. "Hi, Rajan. Long time no see."

"What're *you* doing here?" If anything could have defused his mission to personally beat Nick's ass, it was her.

Zohra is LS, too, but informally. Girls in the LS are valuable; they get away with more. Cops are less likely to frisk them. Less likely to suspect the pretty girl in the passenger seat. Hell, she's carried Rajan's gun multiple times when they were together, in her Guess purse. As long as she keeps squeaky clean, no one's the wiser; and Zohra's so clean, she's on track for law school. Where she'll inevitably come out the other end defending Lions in court. She is, after all, really good at convincing people to do things.

Zohra draws closer. His hackles rise with every step. "Would you believe it if I said I missed you, and I came with Nick to make sure you were okay?"

"No." With her standing a foot away, Rajan can now see the shadows under her eyes are gone, as are the purple-yellow bruises on her arms. Even the way she carries herself—different.

"I like the haircut," Zohra announces, and he realizes she's been studying him, too. "Jail was *good* to you."

Her flirtatious tone snaps him out of it. "Stop stalling, Z. Where's Nick?"

As if on cue, the truck's back doors open again.

Nick looks bored. He's dressed incognito in an unassuming getup, which can only mean he's been off suckering somebody. "Leave your pieces with our boys. I mean it."

"I don't have guns, I'm on *probation*." But the two goons pat him down anyway and take his bat. "Fine. As if I'm the untrustworthy one here."

"You never get over anything, do you? Come on." Nick disappears into the van, but Rajan hesitates. Are the Lions about to cut their losses with him?

Nick's head pops back out. "You still passed the test, you know. Everyone could tell where things were going if you didn't find the camera."

"That was fucked up," Rajan snaps. "That guy—"

"*Begged* for a chance to get his shit kicked. His debts are cleared. Yours, not so much."

Rajan grinds his teeth together and steps up to the truck. Zohra follows; the doors shut behind them. Nick flicks a light on. Finally, the inside of the truck is illuminated and . . . and . . .

Rajan goes very still.

"Not another step," Nick says. Rajan barely hears. He can't take his eyes off Simran.

Simran, leaning against the wall, like she's on the bus instead of in the lion's den.

He takes a step forward without realizing, only stopping when Nick cocks his gun. "Did you not hear me?"

"Don't do this." He can't keep the pleading note from his voice. There are zero coherent thoughts in his head right now; his nightmares are playing out in front of him. "Why—why is *she* here—"

Simran shakes her head infinitesimally. He falls silent. Somehow, she doesn't look panicked. She looks . . . Actually, she looks . . .

His brain blanks out, tuning out the danger of the situation and instead picking up completely irrelevant things about her appearance. Her lined eyes, appearing even bigger than usual. Her lips are fuller, too—no, it's the colour, a deep maroon. And that fancy blue-patterned top, where'd she get that? It clings to her, and the V-collar goes nearly to her sternum, although she's wearing something underneath that covers any cleavage—wait, why in the fuck is he looking *there*?

"Look at him," Nick says to Zohra. "He's found religion."

That shakes him out of it. He tries again to step forward, but the gun pointed to his head is the more pressing concern. Rocking on his heels, he finally decides to stay put. "Are you okay?" he asks Simran urgently. She nods once, slowly.

Rajan forces a steady exhale even as his anger ignites again. First the setup, now this? They've crossed a line. But he can't act like it. He's already shown too much of his hand.

So he swallows every emotion he's feeling and turns to Nick. "Want to explain what the fuck this is?"

"Just having a little chat with your girlfriend."

"Girlfriend?" Rajan repeats. "Jesus Christ." He should've thought of this possibility. Nick has seen him with Simran twice. They took her to try to throw him for a loop. Well, they definitely succeeded. Just not the way they probably thought.

Girlfriend. Simran . . . his girlfriend. Two ideas he's never allowed himself to put together before. Now, they won't get out of his head.

"Your intel sucks," he says blandly. "This is my probation volunteering buddy."

Nick looks unimpressed. "Yeah? Because the guys at your construction job say otherwise."

Rajan blinks. His job . . . his probation officer set it up, saying a spot had just opened for a roofer and his timing couldn't be better. But Rajan has a feeling it wouldn't have mattered when he got out of juvie; his timing would've been spot-on no matter what.

Okay. So he works with Lions. And they saw him leave with Chandani that day. They put two and two together . . . and got five. "You know there are more than two brown girls in Kelowna, right? It's not her. Let her go."

Nick and Zohra exchange looks. Then they glance at Simran, who stares back unblinkingly. Rajan has a feeling he's missing something as Nick says, "Okay, fine."

Rajan waits for the *but*. The next assignment. It doesn't come. Instead, Zohra reaches into the freezer and hands Simran her kirpan, purse, and phone. Then she and Nick step out of their way.

It's all too easy. Rajan stares at Nick, then at Zohra, hoping he can see through her facade again, but nope. She's closed off, too. Fine. They'll tell him the *but* later. For now, he has to get Simran out. The rest he'll figure out on his own.

Rajan and Simran step into the cool night. Nick's goons clamber into the back of the van, and Nick reaches for the doors to close them.

"Good night." He grins at Rajan. "Talk soon."

At the end of that statement, though, his eyes have slid to Simran's.

THIRTEEN

SIMRAN WATCHES THE truck rumble down the street, leaving them in the dust. The night seems too quiet suddenly. The only evidence that anything happened is the baseball bat in the gutter.

Based on what she just heard, Simran has some idea what Rajan might've done with that bat. She waits for horror to rise in her. But instead, she feels . . . nothing. At all.

Probably for the best. She busies herself sliding her kirpan back into its sheath. Her fingers fumble under the hem of her shirtdress. It's not usually a problem, but her coordination is strangely shot right now.

Fingers wrap around her wrist, stopping her trembling. Rajan is silent as he guides the blade to its sheath. She stops breathing when his knuckles skim the skin of her waist, scalding her in the seconds before her shirtdress falls back into place.

Rajan drops her wrist. "I," he says lowly, "am so fucking sorry."

"It's not your fault."

"Yeah, it is. I should explain—"

"I need to go to the store," she interrupts. He falters, and she takes advantage of it, brushing past him and marching into the night. She recognizes where they are from the IHOP sign across the road. There's a Save-On-Foods two blocks over. She's lost—an hour? two?—but she still needs those groceries.

She glances down at her silent phone. Normally she'd be peppered with texts from her parents if she was gone this long, but not tonight. "I'll get a cab from there back to my car," she tells Rajan, who's keeping pace. "I can give you a ride home, too."

"I don't need a ride." He grabs her arm. "*Stop* for a second."

That's the last thing she wants to do. Simran wrenches her arm away. "Then I'll see you next time at Hillway."

He catches up to her. "Where did they take you from?"

Her footsteps slow and stop. The street fades away. Suddenly, she's at UBCO with a gun pressed against her head. Obeying orders to get out of her pickup. Flinching as they yank her phone from her pocket. Being led into the back of a van, wishing that anyone on campus was watching, that someone would *help*—

"I'm quitting Hillway," Rajan says quietly, and she realizes, with a start, that he's been watching her reaction closely.

She attempts to smooth her expression. "You don't have to."

"The hell I don't. You can't even tell me what happened to you." He sounds shaken. "I'm not putting you in more danger."

For some reason, the thought of him leaving finally makes her feel something—panic. She faces him. "If you leave, it'll just confirm what Nick thinks about . . . us." Their eyes meet. Both look away quickly. "If you *really* want to throw him off, act like this didn't bother you at all. He'll realize he made a mistake."

It's funny how when her own lies gain steam, she starts believing them herself. And she can tell, from Rajan's silence, that he's considering them, too. Good. She marches on.

They don't speak as they cross into the grocery store parking lot, or when Simran grabs a shopping basket, or when she picks through the scarce amount of okra in the produce section. Rajan wordlessly leans against a display of avocados to watch, and she starts to think maybe they can avoid talking about it altogether.

But when she drops her okra into the basket, he finally speaks. "Do you always go grocery shopping on Saturday nights, or just after near-death experiences?"

His voice carries. An old couple gives him side-eye and a wide berth. He doesn't seem to notice, his eyes fixated on Simran.

She sets off for the spices aisle. "I needed groceries."

He falls into step with her. "Let me get this straight. You escape a kidnapping from your perfect little life, and your first reaction is: 'Well, time to go make bhindi now'?"

She stops in the middle of the spices aisle and spins to look at him. "Rajan. Either leave me alone while I shop, or go home."

A pause. Then his brown eyes widen. "Holy shit. Are you mad at me right now?"

She shoves her glasses up her nose and scans the shelf for garam masala. "No."

"You sound kinda mad, dude." He steps closer. Simran can feel his heat at her back. "What'd I say that got you worked up?"

"Nothing. I'm just trying to be efficient here." She turns to tell him to back off, but he's not as close as she thought. He's taken his cap off, his closely cropped hair making an appearance. It suits him, she finds herself thinking, absurdly; it shows off the sharp contours of his face and throat—

Rajan reaches for her.

Simran's heart jumps. She flattens against the shelf, spine digging against the price tags, unsure what she'll do if he touches her, wanting and not wanting to find out—

He reaches behind her head and plucks out a packet of garam masala. "Last one." He drops it in her basket and braces his hand against the shelf beside her head. *Now* he's too close. "Are you gonna tell me what I said that pissed you off?"

"You didn't." It's a struggle to think. "I'm fine."

His eyes bore into her for a moment before he scoffs, pushing back a healthy distance. He puts his cap back on. "Yeah, tell that to someone who'll believe it."

Everyone else does. "If you want to help, get me a bag of onions."

Rajan mock-salutes. "Yes, Simran Auntie."

"And don't call me that," she adds, but he's gone. To fetch her *onions.* As if this night could get more surreal.

She heads to the next aisle. They need flour for roti, but the shelves are sparse here, too. She scans the tags for her mom's regular flour. None left.

She spots a store employee and waves them down. "Do you have any more of these?"

"No, I'm sorry, ma'am. We're getting restocked tomorrow, though."

"Oh, okay. Thanks."

The employee walks away. Simran stares at the empty shelf, not entirely certain what to do. She squats to make sure there aren't any bags in the back. But there aren't; there will be no roti tonight. And her parents don't like the store-bought ones. Dinner is ruined.

And just like that, Simran is *crying.*

Real, hot tears, streaming down her cheeks. A violent shudder rips through her as she sinks to her knees. Full-on *sobbing.* She tries to wipe the tears away, but each time her eyes fixate on the empty shelf, they surge again, and she can't seem to control her breathing, can't claw back the sobs, can't *stop.*

"Honey, you all right?" someone says behind her. She nods into her hands, and she hears them walk away.

Get a grip. She drags a breath into her lungs. Someone she knows could be here, and if they see her like this, she'll have to explain herself. But she wouldn't know how to. It's just *flour*—

A bag of onions hits the ground beside her. And then Rajan's there, hand on her shoulder. "What happened?"

She shakes her head. Tries to stand up. But as she's rising, another uncontrolled sob rips through her. He presses down on her shoulders, gently guiding her back to the floor.

"Okay." His voice is soft at her ear. "Okay. Take a break."

This time, she doesn't resist. Her face falls back into her hands, and he kneels with her, rubbing her shoulders, hands big enough to span her shoulder blades. He's uncharacteristically quiet. She feels like she could cry past closing and he wouldn't lose patience, wouldn't leave her, wouldn't tell her to be strong and hold it together. No; instead it's like he's silently saying it's okay to fall apart.

It's so soothing she finds herself able to take her first steady breath. She wipes her eyes under her glasses, although she can't lift her face out of her hands yet. What must he think of her, breaking down in a grocery store? She has to explain.

What comes out of her mouth is: "They're out of my mom's favourite atta."

Rajan takes this in stride. "What about a different brand?"

"My mom doesn't like the other brands." She sounds so whiny, she can't blame him for not responding. But when she lowers her hands, she sees him jerk back slightly in surprise.

She looks down at her fingers. Smudged black and brown with all Kiran's makeup efforts. "Oh. This." She laughs absurdly and reaches into her purse for a tissue. Again, she feels the need to explain. It comes out unfiltered: "I was on a date."

"The *fuck*?"

His voice rings loud enough to attract stares from people shopping around them. They drift away quite quickly.

Rajan lowers his voice. "You're joking. Right?"

Simran finishes wiping her face and puts her glasses back on. Rajan's staring at her like she grew another head. Why'd she even tell him? They hardly know each other anymore.

"I mean, it wasn't really a date. We were just meeting up." Heat blossoms on her cheeks. "He didn't even show."

She shuts her mouth. Rajan stares at her another second before accurately summarizing. "Holy shit. You actually want to date this guy." He rubs his jaw. "I have so many questions I don't even know where to start."

"He's—a friend from school." Rajan's staring so dubiously, her self-confidence withers. Is the idea of her dating so ridiculous? Probably. She should count herself lucky he isn't laughing himself to stitches right now. She gets to her feet. "Never mind."

He rises, too. "Wait, no, I'm only surprised because—he *stood you up.* Talk about fumbling the bag. What, you're too perfect for him?"

"I'm not perfect." He scoffs, and she says it louder. "I'm *not.*"

An understanding gleam enters his eye. "So *that's* what I said that pissed you off."

She bites her lip, furious she gave it away.

But that's what people think of her. *Perfect Simran, so well-mannered and intelligent and disciplined and talented.* She didn't ask for that. She didn't ask to become the standard for perfection, so high up she can't even climb down herself.

"I don't want people to see me that way," she whispers. "As perfect. I have flaws. And limits."

He studies her. "I don't *really* think you're perfect, you know."

"I know." And she does. He's always being sarcastic. Rajan has known, since the day she let him sneak out of the Northridge supply room with a knife, that she is not perfect. But in the wake of everything happening in her life now, this joke is starting to sting.

Rajan nods slowly, and Simran has the feeling she'll never hear it from him again. "So this guy—"

"Let's just get out of here. Please," she adds, because he looks ready to argue. "I just . . . Today was hard."

His eyes become soft, and wide, and earnest. "Yeah, and I'm sorry. I'm going to murder Nick for what he pulled tonight."

He says it so sweetly she almost wants to laugh. "No, not that—" She sighs and pushes her glasses up. The lenses are horribly smudged after her crying. "My mom has cancer."

As soon as the words leave her lips, she feels an aftershock ripple through her body. *Cancer.*

"Shit," Rajan mutters, and that's when she remembers one crucial fact: *She wasn't supposed to tell anyone.*

Horrified, she says, "Never mind—"

"When'd you find out?"

She hesitates. She already broke her promise. What's a little more? She's bursting to talk about it. She needs someone to listen and care, and he's right *there*, and she can't stop herself, no matter how bad of a daughter that makes her.

"You can't tell anyone," she says in a rush. He nods. "I found out the day we met at Hillway."

Understanding dawns on his face. "*That's* why you've been acting so weird." He sighs again. "That's . . . Yeah, that's . . . Shit."

Somehow, his incoherent response is affirming. It's exactly how she feels on the inside. "She needs surgery," she whispers, "and I'm afraid of what her scans will show. I don't want to lose my—" Her throat clogs. She switches tack. "I want to cheer her up somehow. And she likes this guy for me, so I was going to meet him. I know it's stupid," she rushes to add. "I know I'm not supposed to care what my parents think, I shouldn't want to make them happy—"

"I don't think it's stupid," he says quietly. "Trust me, I get feeling guilty about your parents."

She shuts her mouth. How could she forget? If anyone knows this pain, it's him. Rajan was much younger when his mom got sick. He didn't talk about it much, but she knew through the grapevine, just as he knew things about *her* through the grapevine. Her high school problems must've seemed so silly in comparison.

"How'd you get through it?" she whispers. "How did you deal with everything happening?"

A self-deprecating smile twists his lips. "As everybody knows, I didn't."

Well, that wasn't the answer she wanted to hear. She never used to get why he did the things he did, but now she can see what broke him. It's breaking her, too.

The conversation lulls once they reach the cashier. As they're leaving the store, someone calls Simran's name. She turns, and there's Kamaljot Uncle, putting away his cart. She'd forgotten he lived in this neighbourhood. As he approaches, she and Rajan both bend to their manners, greeting him in Punjabi.

He only acknowledges Simran. "Simran, putt, out shopping so late? Is this a volunteering errand?" His eyes flick to Rajan at her side.

This is not a volunteering errand, and they all know it. "We ran into each other."

"Ah. Well, I'll take it from here. Let me walk you out.'

He thinks Rajan was *harassing* her. She opens her mouth to correct him, but Rajan subtly nudges her foot with his.

"See you at volunteering," he says, with a look. *Not worth it.*

And so, helplessly, she lets him go. He disappears into the night while she watches, and she keeps watching until Kamaljot Uncle turns to her. "Simran, you need to be more careful. I don't like the way that boy looked at you. Remember what he did?"

"Yes," she murmurs, but she finds it hard to make herself care, even now. Especially when she was offering Nick—

She shuts down her thought process right there. She doesn't want to think about what she offered. It's ridiculous. Born out of desperation. It no longer makes any sense.

Kamaljot Uncle, meanwhile, is oblivious. "Just be careful, Simran. You know what boys like him do to nice girls like you." He takes her grocery bags from her. "Don't do anything you'll regret."

FOURTEEN

THE NEXT DAY, Simran wakes to multiple texts and a voicemail from Jassa. He's extremely apologetic about leaving her hanging. A family emergency came up—his grandfather died—and he'd hopped in his car, heading for Quesnel immediately, not remembering to charge his phone. He'll be taking the remainder of his exams remotely. Both a disappointment and a relief.

But after the night she just had, it's the least of Simran's concerns. She spends the next few days going through the motions. Halfheartedly studying for and then writing her finals. Attending her mother's appointments and scans. Researching everything she can, trying to boost her parents' morale. Mostly, trying to forget that night.

Kiran must notice something's off, because a week later when they're in the kitchen together, she says, "Listen, I know you're bummed about Jassa, but cheer up, okay? You can go out with him another time. When you actually *want to*."

"I'm not bummed. He had a good reason."

"Even so, you got stood up on your first date. Not exactly a confidence booster."

Simran says nothing. It's true that she gave up dating after only one day, but in her defense, it's mostly because her experience was soured by a kidnapping. Also, Jassa never asked to reschedule.

She refocuses on the cake she's icing. She and Kiran just baked it: a lemon-vanilla concoction for the special occasion that happens to be their mom's birthday. Simran's determined to make it good. For once, Kiran seems to be on the same page. She's spreading sliced strawberries over it when Simran's phone rings.

Kiran, being nosy, glances at it first. "'Charlie Rosencrantz.' Isn't that TJ's infamous white boyfriend?"

"He's my friend, too." From years of high school student council together. And he only ever calls if it's important, so Simran hurriedly rinses her hands to pick up. "Hello?"

The voice on the other end is decidedly *not* Charlie.

"Ha!" TJ sounds triumphant. "I *knew* you were avoicing me. Charlie, didn't I say?"

There's the sound of a distant voice Simran can't make out. Then a door closing. While she's debating hanging up, TJ comes back to the phone, her voice clearer now.

"Charlie wants you to know I stole his phone, it wasn't given willingly." Simran can practically hear the eye roll. "But I was desperate. Kiran said you were fine, but I needed to hear it myself. You've been ignoring me for two weeks."

"I'm sorry." Simran leaves the kitchen, lowering her voice. "I've been busy with exams."

"Is that all? Jeez, Simran. I was scared I pissed you off or something."

"There's still time."

"*Ha.*" Pause. "Well, if there's anything else . . . You can tell me, you know that, right?"

Simran bites her tongue. Hard. "Was that all you called about? I've still got studying to do."

"Oh, okay." TJ pauses. "One more thing. I have a favour to ask."

Simran turns her eyes heavenward. "What is it?"

"Nothing big." TJ sounds casual. Too casual. "The thing is, I'm taking spring semester classes, so I'm not coming back home till the middle of June."

That's good to know. Two extra months for Simran to figure out how to act normal around her. "And?"

"Charlie's coming back, too. And my parents . . ."

She trails off, but Simran sees where this is going. "Your parents want to meet him."

"Yep." TJ sounds glum. "It's stupid. They've met him so many times in high school. But they're not budging. It doesn't help that Charlie actually *wants* to meet them. He doesn't know what he's asking for."

No, he probably doesn't. The extremely charged nature of TJ keeping him a secret probably eludes him. "Where do I come into this?"

"I need you to come run interference."

Simran rubs her forehead. "Run *what?*"

"Look," TJ says hurriedly, as if she'd expected pushback. "Mom and Dad are still kind of pissed. I've been avoiding talking about it, and I don't want to get lectured on my first night home, okay? Here's what I'm proposing. The dinner's the night I come home. You *coincidentally* swing by the same time Charlie's there, you end up sleeping over like you used to. Mom and Dad can't say anything to me. I'll owe you."

"But . . . won't they lecture you as soon as I leave?"

"You're the buffer. It won't be as bad after they've had a day to simmer down." She sighs. "You know what I mean, right? They'll make it so serious for no reason."

Simran tries to picture herself keeping a secret boyfriend from her own mother. "They'll act like you've decided to marry him."

"*Exactly.*" TJ groans. "And there'll be all these hypothetical questions about our future together. I don't want to deal with that on my first night back."

Simran wonders whether TJ has *thought* about those things; if the reason she wants to avoid the questions is because she doesn't like her own answers. But before she can ask anything further, her parents shuffle down the stairs. Her mom's combed her hair and is wearing a pretty floral T-shirt. Her dad's wrapped his nicest black turban. Time for the cake cutting. "Okay, I'll do it."

"Really?" TJ's voice lifts. "I owe you one, seriously. Call me when you're done with exams, okay?"

"Sure," Simran says, and hangs up. "The cake's—"

"Ready!" Kiran appears at the doorway with their frosted dessert, now decorated with berries. "Simmi, get the camera."

Simran obliges, while everyone sits at the dining table. Her mom doesn't smile when Simran presses the cake-cutting knife into her hand. She stares woodenly while Simran lights the candles.

Simran tries to ignore the dead silence and sings "Happy Birthday." Kiran joins in, off-key, but their dad just sits there, unusually somber. Today's supposed to be happy, and it's like her parents aren't even trying.

Frustrated, Simran lifts her camera. "Mom, make a wish and blow out the candles."

Her mother finally speaks. "This is such a nice cake.'

"It's lemon-vanilla," Simran says eagerly. "We wanted to make it special."

"Why?"

The question rings through the room. Her mom is suddenly looking directly at her. Simran begins to sweat. "Because—"

"Because what, you think I'll be dead next year?"

Complete. Silence.

Simran's throat is dry. "No, I— You'll *have* more birthdays, Mom. I just wanted a nice memory."

But she can tell that was the wrong thing to say, too. Her mother actually looks like Simran slapped her. *A memory.*

Her father excuses himself somewhat jerkily, chair scraping back, muttering something about going to the washroom. Her mother pushes the cake away. She looks so frail; the last few weeks have aged her.

"Mom?" Simran asks, voice soft, and to her horror, her mother's face crumples. Abruptly, she pushes away from the table too and disappears down the hall.

"Where're you going?" Kiran shouts, but their mother's already gone. Kiran shakes her head as if irritated. "Come on, let's eat. I'm starving." She pulls the cake toward herself.

"*Kiran,*" Simran snaps. "Are you serious? That's for Mom."

"And she's not eating it," Kiran hisses back. There's tension in her jaw, like she's holding something back, too. "Someone should. We went to all that effort, and she's being dramatic again."

"We'll eat it when they get back."

Kiran huffs. "You're *all* being ridiculous." And with that, she shoves away from the table too, storming upstairs. A minute later, Simran hears her bedroom door slam shut.

Simran waits. Long enough that the candles begin dripping wax onto the icing. Once they've melted by half and nobody's returned, she snuffs them out and puts the cake in the fridge.

It's as she's sliding the camera back into its case that her dad's familiar footsteps come down the stairs. She wheels around, full of hope, but one look at his face and it's extinguished again.

"Sher putt." His eyes are red-rimmed. "Will you play a shabad for me?"

Simran practically leaps to get her rabab and drag it into the living room. She sits cross-legged on the carpet, and her dad brings out the tabla. She plays a simple shabad, one her mother loves, and sings it loud enough that she should be able to hear from upstairs. Maybe it will even draw her out.

But when the last note fades, it's still just her and her dad.

He leans back. "We need to talk."

Simran's chest tightens. "Can we do it later?"

"I don't think so, nikka putt. Your mom and I have been thinking," he says, and as soon as he started with *your mom*, Simran's shaking her head. "No, listen. Listen. You've been so strong during all this. Keeping us together. But this whole thing has made us think about . . . the future."

"The future," Simran repeats.

"Well." He pauses, as if thinking of the best way to put this. "You know me and your mom will die one day, right?"

No. Simran wants to run away rather than hear this. *Anything* but this. Yet she also feels compelled to stay. To listen, because how can she deny her father what sounds horribly like *his dying wishes*? "Mom's going to be okay," she says weakly. "And, Dad, you're fine. You're completely fine."

"For now. But we both have health problems, and."—he shrugs— "everyone is orphaned eventually. We should have that talk."

Simran turns away from the effect of his words, setting her rabab against the wall. "Dad." Her voice wavers. No, not now—she's been so good about keeping her composure until now. "Please stop."

He doesn't.

"You need to live your life, too, Simran," he says gently to her back. "When I'm gone one day, you'll need support from other people. Do you understand?"

Simran can't speak. If she does, she'll break.

"You and Kiran aren't very close, and it worries me. You *are* strong, but you still need a family." Silence. "Please say something."

She stands up instead.

"Simran—"

And that's it. She walks away in the middle of his sentence, striding to the staircase with forcibly measured steps. She ignores him calling her name and, halfway up the stairs, breaks into a jog.

On her way to her room, she passes Kiran's. Her sister stands in the middle of the carpet, throwing clothes into her suitcase. She pauses when she sees Simran. Smiles a little too brightly. "Hey."

Simran glances at the suitcase. The tears in her throat recede enough that she can speak. "You're . . . leaving?"

"Well, yeah." Kiran shifts from foot to foot. "I've been here more than a week. Just booked my flights. I'll be back for Neetu's wedding."

That's in July. Simran stares. "You can't even stay for Mom's surgery?"

Kiran avoids her gaze. "Why would I? The doctors are handling everything."

"But—"

"I can't deal with you guys acting like it's the end of the world. Cancer isn't a death sentence anymore! And besides, I have a job. I have other responsibilities. I have a *life* in Toronto. You can't expect me to be here all the time."

She busies herself with her suitcase again. And something in Simran *snaps*.

"Fine. Then go." Simran grips the door handle hard. "Go back to your job and your friends and whatever else is so important to you. Go live your *great life* in Toronto. I'll stay here and live the one you were too good for."

She slams the door behind her, just in time to see Kiran look up in shock.

But Simran doesn't stop. She goes to her own room and closes the door, far more gently. Turns the lock. Only then does she let the tears fall.

It's hard to say when, exactly, Simran began resenting Kiran. Maybe when Kiran started her personal war with their parents during her teens. Sneaking out, partying, coming home drunk, arguing about *everything*. Didn't she see the toll that took on their parents? Could she not have ever compromised—on at least some of those things? Because by not doing so, she left Simran no margin for error.

Simran climbs onto her bed. It's a mess as usual, clothes and books strewn everywhere, along with crumpled napkins and pens. She shoves everything off the mattress on her way to the windowsill. Her dad's words echo in her mind.

Growing up, she always thought her family was a constant. But of course it's not. Families are fluid, constantly growing and shrinking. And hers . . . she can only foresee a subtraction. Her parents will be gone, her sister's running away, and who is Simran kidding—any long-distance friendship she has with her cousin will fade the longer Simran has to lie to her. Maybe in the end she'll be completely alone.

Simran forces herself to breathe deeply. There's no sense crying about it. Besides, she has exam material to study. Grades are important, even if school doesn't interest her anymore. But as she twists to pick up her textbook, something falls out of it. A Hillway brochure. The newest version, showcasing the revamped program she helped design.

It takes her back to yesterday—the volunteers were at an art festival, taking apart Legos for the next group of kids to use. Rajan was there. He greeted her as usual, but then kept his distance. She wondered if Nick had contacted him again, but she suspected he wouldn't tell her, so she watched from afar. He took apart Legos faster than anyone. He also built some during his break, and the spaceship he was idly making looked amazing. He was *creative*, she realized, not for the first time, and she went over to say she wanted to put it on display, but Paul got there first to tell him break was over. And Rajan dismantled it automatically, without even blinking. Like he was used to having the things he built fall apart.

Suddenly Simran has her phone out, her thumbs hovering over the screen.

The thing is, she can't solve her problems. Those are inevitable. But despite what Rajan thinks, his don't have to be.

She dials the number she memorized Saturday night.

Nick answers on the first ring. "What."

"It's Simran."

"Oh, right. Okay. Wow." Nick yawns. "We were taking bets on whether you'd call. So? What's the verdict?"

He sounds impatient, bored. But she's not fooled. This is her chance.

"I'll do it." Simran takes a deep breath. "I'll be your bookkeeper."

FIFTEEN

THE ADDRESS NICK gives is a nondescript café close to the industrial side of town. The online reviews are scathing: *All the pastries are stale*, one customer complained. *The "bakers" can't operate a microwave. How they stay in business is anyone's guess.*

Simran has a pretty good guess: money laundering.

The bell jangles as she enters. There are no patrons; just Nick, leaning over the front counter, with a few other men she's never seen. One of them—white, shaved head, leather jacket—scowls at her so hard she wonders if she's met and personally insulted him before.

Nick glances at the clock. "You're twenty minutes late."

"I had an exam." Which didn't go great. Her usual all-nighter to study didn't do the trick, possibly because she couldn't concentrate. Kiran had left the night before. She and Simran shared a very stiff departing hug. Their father shook his head, and remembering his earlier lecture, Simran had known she was disappointing him yet again.

The man in the leather jacket raises an eyebrow.

"You hiring schoolgirls to do our books, Nick?"

"Relax, Rory. We're just trialing her." Nick waves Simran to the back. She wonders if he's regretting this, or replaying their conversation from the ice-cream truck in his mind, as she is.

It had been before Rajan arrived. She'd glanced at the brown-papered bricks in the freezer. "You said your accountant got arrested? Your books must be a mess."

"You need to keep your trap shut, Nick," Zohra commented. Nick waved this away.

"Let her try and bargain. It's funny."

They weren't even taking her seriously. But, he didn't say they had a new accountant. This was good news.

Simran had recalled the time she went on a month-long trip to India a few years before—the Northridge student council books were a disaster when she returned. No one kept track of transactions, and several hundred dollars simply went missing. The Lions must be hemorrhaging money the same way. Which meant they had to be desperate. "I can keep your books for you."

Nick's answer was instant. "You're not an accountant."

"I'm good with numbers. If you know who I am, you at *least* know that. I've been bookkeeping for years—"

He barked a laugh. "This is a little different from your high school *clubs.*"

"How? You have profits. You have losses. You have expenses, and things that slip through the cracks if you're not keeping good records. I'm not asking for payment—I'll do it for as long as it takes to pay Rajan's debts. It'll buy you time to find a real accountant."

Nick's nasty smile had faded throughout her spiel. Zohra looked at him sharply. "Don't tell me you're considering this."

But here they are now. Although, no one looks happy about it.

The kitchen is an industrial setup of metallic counters, large fans, and grills. No baked goods are being prepared here, though. There are just a lot of . . . packages. Wrapped up in paper. Plastic wrap. Crystals. Thick black pucks—

"Don't mind the product." Nick sounds bored. "Your workstation's over there."

He points to an old-fashioned maple desk in the corner, starkly out of theme with the rest of the room. On it is a scale, a calculator, and a blue spiral-bound notebook.

Zohra pulls from her purse a few more items: a notepad, a calendar, and a piece of cardboard, all of which she sets on the table, too. "You want to prove you can do this work? Here's a few transactions we need recorded."

Simran stares at the items. "Those are . . . transactions?"

"You think we always have a nice ledger around when we're doing business?" Nick rolls his eyes. "Our people record on whatever they have on them."

He gives no further direction, so she opens the notebook. She's greeted with the debit and credit columns she's seen a million times. It's so normal it takes her by surprise, although it shouldn't. Any functional business needs to keep their finances straight. Even illegal ones.

But the more she examines it, the more she realizes it isn't so normal at all. For one, it's messy. The handwriting is nearly illegible at points, ignoring the ruled lines and going off in diagonal tangents, running into other calculations, sometimes smudged beyond recognition. Her math teachers would pop a vessel if they saw the egregious lack of BEDMAS adherence. Not only that, but the numbers aren't all written out fully, leaving plenty of room for error. It's only through context that Simran can understand them. And those numbers . . . are a lot. Far more zeroes than she's ever dealt with.

She flips a page and is greeted with a list of dates, next to numbers of pounds, next to four-digit codes. Some of the four-digit codes are repeated. Are they codes for certain clients, maybe? Buying whatever product here is measured in pounds? There's no legend to follow. How can she use this structure without understanding what it means? She glances up at Nick. He stares back. All of them do.

Rory says, "She doesn't know what she's doing."

"Looks that way, doesn't it?" Nick's voice is taunting.

They *knew* it wouldn't be straightforward. Of course it isn't; they don't want just anyone to be able to read it. "You're not going to at least tell me what these code words mean?"

"I don't have time to teach you how to do this job." Nick examines his fingernails. "I thought you said you were practically an accountant? If not, get the fuck out and stop wasting my time."

His voice is harsh. She swallows.

But. Nick wouldn't have gone to all this effort only to humiliate her. He may be mocking her, but he's also curious.

She holds her hand out. "Give me a pen."

Nick tilts his head, and a ballpoint is shoved in her hand. Instead of recording the new transactions as she was asked, she continues flipping through old pages, searching for patterns. From the looks of it, several people have worked on this ledger—with variable skill levels. Every time she thinks she has a grasp on their system, something changes and she has to go back again.

They talk about her while she's reading.

"Bitch doesn't know what she's doing."

"Where'd you even find her?"

"Nick, you on something? Why bring her in?" Something soft glances across her temple. She flinches, only to find a cigarette butt dropping onto her arm. She can't tell who threw it; they're all staring at her balefully. She looks down at the page and closes her eyes briefly.

These intimidation tactics are nothing. *Nothing*, she tells herself. In her last chemistry lab exam, she had to identify a compound in fifty minutes using only the equipment in front of her. The TAs stared them down, making Simran's hands shake as she attempted to use the mass spectrometer. How is this any different? Same game. Different substances.

She reopens her eyes to brush the cigarette off her cardigan. "Who's been keeping these books recently? They're a mess."

Rory makes a disbelieving sound and wheels on Nick again. "You should've asked me before you hired an outsider. How're we supposed to trust her? What if she's working with cops?"

"She's not. She hasn't had any contact since we met her."

A chill races down Simran's back. They've been . . . watching her?

"I was doing the books just fine," Rory snaps, and Simran's eyebrows rise. *He* was the accountant's replacement?

"Your notes are shit." Nick sniffs. "The schoolgirl isn't wrong about that."

"Fuck you," Rory retorts. "You're not even *from* here. You can't just come here and decide what *we* do in *Kelowna*."

Something in the air changes. A few of the men stir. Rory, apparently, took it too far with that comment.

Nick tilts his head, like a wolf hearing a rustle in the bushes. His voice becomes silky. "In case you've forgotten, Manny asked me personally to take over, because you've been doing a shit job. So you can either put up or shut up." He gives a nasty smile. "Or die."

The silence deepens. Simran doesn't doubt the sincerity of his threat. But somehow, she thought there'd be more loyalty within the Lions themselves. Or at least enough to avoid questioning each other in front of an outsider.

Zohra notices her staring. "What're *you* looking at? Get to work."

The hostility in her voice is so different from that day she walked Simran to her car. Simran refocuses on the series of subtractions she was reading.

$$13.13 - 5$$
$$20.01 - 8$$
$$17.45 - 6$$

Several columns of this, with the word *kilo* repeated a few times. They must be talking about one of their . . . products. But what are they subtracting? She glances at the paper-wrapped bricks. Those paper layers surely weigh something significant. They must take that into account when they sell. She flips a several pages back. There's a calculation here for 21.11 - 5.

She frowns and flips forward again. A few weeks ago, a new recorder had taken over. And their handwriting isn't the only thing that's changed.

She speaks before thinking, only realizing she's interrupted a conversation when they all stop. "There's something off about these calculations."

"Bullshit," Rory scoffs immediately.

"I can show you."

"Listen, you little bitch——" Rory surges toward her, and she jumps a little. But Nick grabs the back of his jacket.

"Rory, shut up." Nick hauls him back and glances at Simran. "Explain."

Trying not to let her hand shake, she taps the page. "I assume these calculations are all about the same product?" She takes the silence as a yes. "The proportion of wrapping paper to product weight is different between these two recorders. With the old recorder"—she flips to several weeks ago—"wrapping paper for the same amount of product weighed significantly less than it does now. Either you've started double-wrapping your product, or there are . . . roughly twenty kilos unaccounted for."

Dead silence meets her words. Simran finally looks up to find that the whole configuration of the room has changed.

Nearly everyone has a gun drawn. Nick isn't looking at her anymore. His focus, along with his gun, is directed at Rory.

"So, Rory," he says, "making a little money on the side, are we?"

Rory glares, but his hand has drifted to his waistband, too. "Are you seriously gonna believe this bitch over me?"

"I don't know." Nick nods to the Rolex on Rory's wrist. "But your expensive tastes are starting to speak for themselves."

He cocks the gun.

Simran stands without meaning to. "Wait!"

She hadn't meant to speak so loud, but everyone's heads swivel to her. A few guns, too. She holds her hands up, heart beating furiously. "I don't think he's—skimming. It could've been an honest mistake."

Zohra scoffs, and Simran can't blame her. She knows how naive she sounds. But she wasn't trying to cause whatever *this* is. She was just excited to find a mistake in the ledger.

Nick ignores her. He speaks over his shoulder, to the others. "Search his car."

Nick's men advance on Rory. For one wild moment, Simran thinks they're going to kill him right in front of her, and she squeezes her eyes shut. All she hears is flesh hitting flesh, grunts, the screech of shoes against tile, and a slam against the wall. Then silence. When she opens her eyes, a disheveled Rory is pushing off the wall, breathing hard and looking furious while the men retreat, one holding a ring of keys.

Zohra takes the keys and heads out the door. Nick remains, keeping his gun on Rory, whose nose is bleeding from the scuffle.

This is a nightmare. "Nick." Simran can't keep the desperation from her voice. "Please put the gun down."

Nick doesn't even look her way. "I knew there was something off about you, Rory."

Rory is beginning to pale. "It *was* an honest mistake," he says. "She's right."

"A minute ago she was a stupid, untrustworthy bitch. What changed?" Nick raises an eyebrow. "You were so reluctant to hand over the ledgers today. I wonder why."

Rory's jaw works.

"Please," Simran says. "I—I wasn't trying to—"

The store door opens again. Zohra, lips thin, tosses something at Nick. "Just this."

A bundle of cash.

Nick turns it over in his hand, expressionless.

"You can't prove where that's from!" Rory's eyes dart around. "And your shitty weighing scale wasn't calibrated. I had to correct the number at the end after figuring it out."

Nick's lip curls, like he's enjoying this a little. "Really, Rory? Why didn't you say that before?"

Rory makes a break for it. He gets two steps before the Lions close in on him again. There's another violent-sounding scuffle. Grunts. A flash of a knife, and Simran covers her face. She can't watch, yet she can't stop peeking from behind her fingers.

"Please, don't, *don't*—"

Zohra speaks. "Stop."

And they do. Just like that.

"Take it outside," she says, giving Simran a somewhat pitying look.

Someone gives Rory a shove, and he stumbles toward the door. Before he disappears, he turns to look at Simran.

The hatred in his eyes shakes her. She's still staring after him when Nick comes up to her.

"Get back to work."

Her hands are shaking. She strains her ears for a gunshot that will confirm her worst fears. "What will they do to him?"

Nick and Zohra exchange impatient looks, like Simran's a bratty kid having a tantrum. "He knew the consequences of what he was doing."

"Which are?"

Nick barks a laugh. He doesn't answer her, though. "I want you to look over the rest of his work. Find out exactly how much Rory stole from us."

The implications of that catch up to her. She's in.

But Nick seems to read her mind. He leans over the table, getting in her face with those cold dark eyes. He seemed young to her earlier, but right now he seems ancient, barely human at all.

"Don't get it twisted—you work for *me*. Don't think about getting smart like Rory did. Don't try being a hero, either. There's no legal evidence in any of the ledgers you have access to. Got it? I have no problem snuffing you out if you decide to become a problem."

She stares.

He slams his hand down on the table, making her jump. "I said, *got it?*"

A scream tries to work its way up her throat. She swallows it down. "As long as you leave Rajan alone."

Nick digs into his pocket and produces another notebook. He throws it at her feet. "Fine."

"And don't tell him about this," she adds, but he's already swept out of the room, leaving her with Zohra and one of the men. Still, it's a victory. She bends to pick up the new ledger. It takes her two tries because of her trembling.

When she straightens, Zohra sits on the countertop watching. "I used to be like you, you know. Soft."

Used to be? How did she end up here, anyway? She doesn't have the tattoo, but she clearly has power. Enough authority to get a bunch of grown men to take a murder outside. Enough experience to con Simran into trusting her, and enough audacity to act like it never happened.

Simran can't help the bite to her words. "You mean, human?"

"Whatever it is." Zohra's expression doesn't change. "It won't last."

SIXTEEN

AFTER OVER A week of radio silence from the Lions, Rajan starts to think Nick is playing some kind of sick game. The point of kidnapping Simran was to get Rajan back on the payroll. So why aren't they calling?

All he does at home is think about what the Lions' next move will be. All he does at work is guess which of his coworkers is on their payroll. All he does at Hillway is wonder if he's putting everyone he talks to in danger. At this point, if Nick reappeared, Rajan would *beg* for a job, just to end this torture.

Which, maybe, is the point.

Ahead of his next probation meeting, he stands in the kitchen, tuning out his brothers' latest hallway cage match while he finishes a mandatory gang violence module for the social worker Kat works with. It's full of stupid advice that would likely get him shot if he tried it with Nick, but he obligingly presses the correct answers. Then he pushes away the old laptop and sighs. The fight in the hallway still hasn't stopped.

"Dad said—"

"If you tell him, I'll—"

Sukha cuts himself off when Rajan steps into the hallway.

"Do you guys do this *every* morning? Just try to kill each other?"

"Go away," Sukha says. That's when Rajan notices Yash is holding something. A bag of what looks suspiciously like . . .

Yash quickly holds it out. "It's not mine."

Sukha snatches it out of Yash's hands with a glare. "Kind of like how my room isn't yours, but that doesn't stop you—"

"Yash," Rajan interrupts. "Go to your room for a sec. I wanna talk to Sukha."

Even Sukha seems a little surprised by that. Yash backs up, eyes wide. Rajan waits until his youngest brother has closed his door before rounding on Sukha.

"What the hell is this?"

"This?" Sukha holds up the baggie. "It's your whole personality before you went to jail."

Sukha always goes for the personal blow. "You want it to become *your* personality, too?"

"Not everyone is like you. Some of us do it for fun. Some of us aren't *addicts*."

That hit lands. Sukha seems to realize it, too, because his glare falters, as if he's afraid of what Rajan might do.

Rajan turns and walks over to Sukha's bedroom.

"What're you doing?" Sukha's voice changes, from anger to something else.

Rajan kicks open the door. Because now *he's* mad. Sukha doesn't get it. Rajan never thought he was an addict, either, but here he is, waking up every morning for the past week with actual, *physical* cravings thanks to the Lions. He may as well be that Oliver guy.

And he wouldn't wish that on anyone, but especially not on his own brother.

He flings open the closet; clothes fall out. "Just having a look around." He turns and rifles through a half-ajar sock drawer, then picks up the baseball on Sukha's desk. He examines it for open seams before tossing it over his shoulder. "What else do you have? Meth under your bed? Crack on your bookshelf?"

He's ready when Sukha takes a swing at him, catching his fist and shoving him back. Sukha staggers, his back hitting the doorframe, and Rajan expects another swing—expects a full-out *brawl*—but then Sukha laughs, the sound bitter.

"This is so rich. You came back from juvie on such a high horse. As if you're better than us now. You can't pretend to give a shit about this family when you're the one who ruined it."

Those words ring into the silence. The floor creaks in the hallway, and they both look out to find their father standing there.

Rajan stiffens. His father looms before them in shorts and a faded T-shirt, squinting and rubbing his five o'clock shadow. He must've just woken up. "What's going on." His voice is flat, eyes red-rimmed. Rajan might think he was hungover, but his father is rarely sober enough for that to happen anymore.

Sukha answers instantly. "Rajan barged into my room for no reason."

"*Sukha's* hiding weed." Rajan snaps. "And god knows what else—"

"Liar," Sukha shouts, but their father interrupts.

"Enough." He only looks at Sukha. "Come have breakfast. And apologize to Yash."

"That's all you're gonna say?" Rajan demands. "Tell him to turn out his pockets."

His father, as usual, acts like he didn't hear. Just heads to the kitchen. Sukha sends Rajan a triumphant look and follows, picking up the baseball as he goes.

Rajan kicks over Sukha's laundry basket and leaves for the bus stop. He and his father spend most of their time ignoring the other's existence, but this is extreme even for him. Rajan probably could've said Sukha set the neighbour's house on fire last night and their father would just ask someone to pass the milk. It's like he's just given up.

Rajan's still fuming when he arrives on the Correctional Services floor, just in time for Kat's last appointment to walk out. Snake Tattoo again. He slams into Rajan's shoulder as he passes.

"Fucking prick," Rajan stage-whispers. From the grapevine, he knows for a fact this guy breaches probation more often than he showers. That is to say, not that often, but often enough that he'd be totally screwed if it got out. Sometimes Rajan fantasizes about "letting it slip" to Kat.

But that would be the pot calling the kettle black. He checks his phone as he continues down the hall. Still nothing from Nick.

When he arrives, Kat's not there. Her chair is swiveled toward the door, as if she got up in a hurry. Rajan, still restless, wanders to the rickety cabinet near the wall. He flips through random books. Opens and closes the blinds. Doodles on the whiteboard. Tries locked drawers out of boredom.

Several minutes pass before he wonders if he got his appointment time wrong. He should've checked with the secretary, but there was a long line. Technically, he could also ask the office social worker, but then she's gonna ask him about that gang violence module and he'll have to pretend he remembers anything from it. Line it is.

He turns for the door, and his shoe crunches over something on the industrial carpet. A sparkle catches his eye—it's a fine sprinkling of glass. And next to it, near the wall . . . a photo frame, facedown.

Careful of the glass, he turns it over. It's the photo of Kat and the boy that's normally on her desk. The glass of the frame is shattered. He puts it back on the desk and leaves the room.

He's halfway down the hall when the washroom door swings open and he collides with someone. "Shit, are you—" He stops when he realizes it's Kat. Kat, wiping her face with a paper towel.

She jolts upon seeing him. He does, too, because her eyes are red. She's either found an interesting new hobby in the washroom or she's been . . . crying?

Kat recovers so fast he thinks he imagined it. "Hello, Rajan!" The paper towel disappears into her pocket. She bustles past him. "Let's talk in my office! I hope you weren't waiting long." She sits at her desk, gesturing to her reddened eyes and nose. "My allergies always act up in May. Have a seat."

Rajan sinks into his chair. Kat glances to the photo frame, back on the desk. She puts it in her drawer. When she catches him looking, she explains with a smile. "I don't want more glass to fall out. The photo fell during my last appointment, and the cleaners won't be in until evening."

"It broke on carpet?" This sounds like bullshit. "How'd it get to *your* side of the desk?"

Kat retrieves his file instead of answering. Rajan glances at the door. Wasn't her last appointment with Snake Tattoo?

He tries for a moment to imagine he's Snake Tattoo, sitting in this very chair. Getting irritated with Kat's never-ending questions, like Rajan. But unlike Rajan, acting on it. Grabbing whatever's in his reach and throwing it.

But not right *at* her. To intimidate her, he'd throw it—*there*. There's a dent in the drywall right beside Kat's head. And it's definitely new.

"How's Hillway been?" Kat jars him from his thoughts. "Last time, you said you didn't like your mentor. Is that still true?"

"I never said that." He feels like an asshole now, knowing what Simran was actually going through. God, he hopes she's okay. He would ask her, but he's trying to keep his distance. For her sake.

At the thought, he reaches into his pocket for a toothpick. And winces at the twinge in his shoulder.

Kat notices. "Your work takes too much advantage of you, Rajan."

She sounds a lot like she suspects he's working overtime. "*You* guys got me this job."

"We could consider other options." When he shakes his head, she shrugs. "Let me know if you change your mind. How're things at home?"

By this point, he's gotten used to her swerves. "Well, the tree in our yard fell down yesterday. Missed the roof by inches. So I guess it could be worse."

Kat smiles, clearly aware he misinterpreted her question on purpose.

But she plays along. "Goodness, that's lucky. Have you called anyone to remove it yet?"

"No. Nobody's going to care, anyway. Whole neighbourhood is a shithole."

She chuckles. "You and your family used to live in a very nice neighbourhood, if I read the reports right. Why'd you move? Too many memories of your mother?"

Rajan scowls. "It had nothing to do with Mom dying. My parents couldn't afford that house in the first place—they had to declare bankruptcy."

"That's unfortunate. Did they think they could afford the house before?"

"No."

Kat's smile grows confused. Rajan chews his toothpick another moment before putting her out of her misery. "Some Punjabi people like to flex to each other. Who's got the biggest house, the most expensive cars, the nicest TV. You do it so you can say your kids will have a good time growing up. You do it even if you don't have the money. That's why my parents worked so much. They had to."

"Your mom, too? I thought she was sick."

"She got sick after. And the house . . . was her idea." His mom was stretching herself too thin by the time he was in grade seven. Almost never home, and when she was, she was in bed. It took almost a year for the doctors to figure out that she wasn't just tired. Her own immune system was trying to off her. "But even then, she kept trying to work, because the mortgage was nuts. She got sicker and the stress of everything . . . I think it made it worse. And definitely, *I* made it worse." His throat closes and he stops abruptly.

Kat steeples her fingers. "So really, then, maybe your predicament was partly your mother's fault."

Wait, what? Rajan blinks. "Where'd you pull *that* from?"

"It makes sense, doesn't it?" Kat's smile doesn't reach her eyes anymore. "She, along with your father, knew what taking on all that debt would mean. How much they'd have to work, and what that'd do to you and your brothers. But they did it anyway."

"What it would *do to us*?" Rajan's blood heats. "Did you hear anything I said? She did it *for* us. She loved us."

"People can love you and hurt you at the same time," Kat notes. "Even if she did it so you could live well, she also did it partly to look to other people like she had money. Wouldn't you say that was maybe a little . . . selfish of her?"

Rajan's up from his seat in a flash, so fast his chair topples over and the candy jar falls on its side. "Don't talk about her like that," he snaps. "You don't know her—you don't *fucking know*—"

He cuts himself off, because Kat has flinched.

She recovers almost immediately, but he still notices. His anger falters. And his eyes are drawn back to that dent in the wall.

With effort, he reins himself back in. She's sitting very still, and when he reaches to right the candy jar, she watches it like it's a grenade.

He weighs it in his hand before setting it down. "You should be careful, provoking guys like me," he says lowly. "Some people aren't going to appreciate it."

She takes a long time to respond. "I'm sorry. I just want to do more good than sending people back to jail."

He gets the sense that Kat is somewhat new to this game. Still thinks she can change people.

He pulls his chair upright and sits again. "You're in the wrong profession."

Her smile returns, now wry. "Maybe so. Can I finish my thought, though?"

"If you're asking if I'll throw shit at your head, I won't." He glares at her. "But if you cross a line, I'm gonna say so."

"That's fair." She pauses. "I don't know your parents, you're right. But I know *you*. And I'm sure you would've preferred they were around, asking you about your day, helping with your homework, coming to your baseball games. Of course you started looking elsewhere for family. For people who would pay attention to you. You were lonely."

She's making him sound like the world's biggest loser. "That's *not* why—"

"How did you first start running with this crowd? You were a boy from a well-to-do family with no gang ties. How does that happen?"

"What does it matter?"

"Humour me." She hesitates. "If it's okay."

The fact that she's willing to back off is what makes him cooperate. He rocks his chair on its rear legs and thinks back to grade eight.

How great was it back then when guys from tenth grade started paying attention to him? Gassing him up? Of course he let them egg him on to do stupid shit—like shoplifting. But, he got caught. It was the first time he saw the inside of a police station. All his other friends stopped talking to him after that. Suddenly, he only had one crowd to run with.

"It doesn't matter," Rajan repeats. Loneliness is no excuse. Everybody's parents work a lot. And yet, *he* was the one who acted out, started fights, used drugs, and toed the line of expulsion. *He* did this; he drove his parents away. He saw how they tried at first, how their ability to forgive him wore down over time, until it was metal on metal.

"Sure, not everyone in a situation like yours ends up like you. But the point is," Kat says, "anyone *could*. Put someone in a vulnerable frame of mind, in the wrong time and place, and they could fall victim, too."

Rajan scoffs. "Right."

"Believe it." She gestures to her folder. "The difference between you and your Hillway mentor is actually very thin. Maybe remembering that will help you resent her less."

He opens his mouth to tell her yet again that he *likes her just fine* and also that he *somehow can't imagine Simran beating people up with a bat*, but then he pauses.

A few weeks ago, when he saw the news of the drug bust on the TV in Kat's waiting room . . . it wasn't just drug dealers who got arrested.

There were people you'd never expect. Like that dude who owned a car dealership, and an accountant.

Rajan's next thought is truly bizarre. So bizarre, he immediately tries to dismiss it. There's no way. The Lions haven't contacted him because they're playing with him. That's *it.*

Isn't it?

Kat doesn't seem to notice his sudden quiet. She closes his file, a faraway look on her face.

"Wait, we're done?"

"Yes." Her smile is perfectly in place again. "It's a nice afternoon, isn't it? Go enjoy it. We both have a lot to think about."

SEVENTEEN

THE ONCOLOGIST FOLDS her hands. "I have mixed news."

Simran tries not to tense. Her parents, sitting next to her in the appointment room, are already tense enough.

It's been weeks since her mother's disastrous birthday party—weeks of a cloud hanging over them all. Right up until now. But the doctor doesn't seem to notice, swiveling in her chair to face them. "The scans don't show any *obvious* spread. But there are some ambiguous findings on your imaging. We won't know for sure until the surgery, when they biopsy your lymph nodes. You should probably prepare for needing . . . more treatment, though."

A long silence. If what Simran read in her internet spirals about cancer treatment is true, there's a *lot* to prepare for. A headache builds behind her eyes. She can barely even get through *this*, how's she supposed to deal with all that?

Simran's mother speaks up. "About this surgery. I want to make sure this is done discreetly. I don't want—"

"Your sister, who's a physician, to know. Yes, I remember," the oncologist replies, somewhat drily, likely because Simran's mom says this at every appointment. She stands to open the door for them. "Your procedure is scheduled on a day that Dr. Powar isn't in the OR. Don't worry."

As they're walking out into the parking lot, Simran's dad nudges her. "Tell Kiran the news."

This is clearly an excuse to make her phone her sister. Simran sighs. She knows what Kiran will say, and it's already, preemptively, annoying her.

She half hopes it'll go to voicemail, but instead, Kiran picks up first ring. "How'd it go?"

"No obvious spread—"

"See!" Kiran sounds triumphant. "Told you—"

"—but it's *ambiguous*. We don't know for sure yet."

"Sure, but this is great news. I'm busy right now, but tell Mom and Dad hi, okay?" And she hangs up. That's clearly all she wanted to hear. Must be nice to get updates and go, and not have to deal with how suffocating the house has been leading up to this appointment. And it's only going to get worse with this surgery hanging over their heads.

The prospect of going home suddenly feels unbearable, and Simran's again guiltily glad she has plans today. "I have to go. I'll be home in a few hours."

Her father nods, squeezing her hand. Her mom barely appears to hear. They never ask where she's going anymore. Which is too bad, because today, unlike many days in the past few weeks, she would've been able to answer honestly.

She separates from her parents to drive to UBCO. She's running another errand for the undergraduate student society: clearing the event boards in preparation for the incoming year. All the posters, tutoring ads, and sign-up sheets from the last eight months have to go. Dull work, but Simran doesn't mind. Especially not these days.

Surprisingly, when she arrives, Chandani is also there to help.

"Why even *put* your ad this high up?" Chandani holds up a flyer. She's on the stepladder next to Simran's, pulling pins from the wall and offering commentary the whole way across. "Who's going to come to this event, giraffes?"

Simran shrugs as she takes down the SPRING EVENTS sign at the top of the board. When it comes to Chandani, Simran says very little in general. Usually Chandani finds a way to carry the conversation on her own.

But this time, Chandani leans against her ladder. "Okay, I'll be honest. The only reason I came today is because TJ told me to check on you. She thinks you're acting weird."

Simran pauses. She *knew* Chandani volunteering was suspicious. As for TJ . . . they've talked briefly since exams ended, but Simran finds it difficult to maintain conversation when TJ's so *nosy*. Which usually leads to Simran ending the call for fear that she'll expose her mom's secret.

Or maybe her own.

Thankfully, Simran's phone buzzes at that moment. She fishes it out of her back pocket. Private number. "Hello?"

"Don't 'hello' me, it's Nick," Nick says. "As you know. I need you tonight."

Next to Simran, Chandani mouths, *Nick?* with a gleeful grin on her face. Simran leans away slightly. The last thing she needs is Chandani overhearing a call with the *Lions*.

When Simran had left that initial meeting, Nick didn't offer any clarity on whether she'd hear back. But a week later, he called . . . and the week after, too. Now Simran's in the café every week, running the books under the supervision of Zohra and a rotating group of Lions. She hasn't seen Rory again and hasn't asked. Her job is the numbers only. There's a lot of work to do, tidying old calculations and recording new ones. She's starting to understand parts of it—four-digit codes, buying product from other four-digit codes—but she finds herself trying to go a step further each time. Trying to glean their patterns. She likes putting the stories together, even if the characters remain anonymous.

But . . . "I can't tonight," she tells Nick. "I'm busy." Usually he gives her more heads-up. Tonight she's helping Neetu pick out decorations for the engagement party.

"That wasn't a request," Nick says. "That's an order, from someone above my paygrade. We found something we need your skill set for."

Chandani leans in farther, and that's it, Simran can't risk her hearing more. She climbs down her ladder. "And what's that?"

"How many times do I have to say this? If you want to keep this arrangement up, you don't get to ask questions. Six. The usual place."

She was supposed to meet Neetu at six. "But—"

He hangs up, leaving Simran with a sinking stomach. Hopefully she can finish fast and make it to Neetu's just a little late.

Chandani descends her ladder with the last posters and jabs Simran's arm. "I can't believe this. I thought you were some kind of saint! Is this why you've been avoiding TJ? You don't want her to know?"

She sounds gleeful. Simran blinks, still disoriented from her call. "What?"

"Don't act all coy." They've finished here, so they line their ladders up against the wall and set off to the admin building, where the next set of boards await. "You and Jassa flirt after every council meeting *and* you have another man on the side? *'I need you tonight.'* Who's Nick, bitch?"

Of course she overheard. "Nick is a friend from a community org," Simran says as they walk outside into the May sun, passing a construction site. "They recently lost their bookkeeper, so I'm helping out. Also, me and Jassa don't—"

"So *this* is what I have to do to get you to talk to me," Chandani muses. "Ask about your love life. And here I was this whole time, trying to make our friendship pass the Bechdel test."

Their *friendship*? "Neither of them are my—"

Chandani stops in place. "Speaking of men with a capital *M*. Oh my god."

Simran follows her gaze, and stops, too. They've found themselves in front of the new dorm's construction zone. And there's a familiar figure on the unfinished landing above them.

Rajan's got his hands hooked on the beam above his head, watching them, but . . . oh. Gone is his usual shapeless hoodie. And in the light of day, there's a lot on display. *Arms*, is Simran's most intelligent thought. Gleaming-from-sweat, rich-brown-from-the-sun, sculpted-by-God kind of shoulders and arms. A black tattoo crawls up the side of his neck from under his white tank, the same as Nick's. She hastily drags her eyes away, but then she's staring at the shirt, or rather the way it's smudged with dirt and clinging to him, and those dark olive cargo pants, tucked into black work boots . . . She doesn't know where to look at him. Everywhere seems obscene.

So she refocuses on his face, and the small grin unfurling on his mouth, in his eyes too, like he knows exactly what she's thinking. He doesn't call her out on it, though. "What's up, Simran Sahiba?"

He takes off his hard hat, which has got to be against safety protocol. She has to think about safety protocol instead of the careless way he tucks his hat under his arm. She looks over his shoulder instead. "Hi, Rajan."

She feels his gaze heavily before he turns his attention elsewhere. "Chandani. What're you doing with my girl?"

Simran's eyes jump back to him. He winks. Chandani, meanwhile, examines her fingernails. "Who're you, again?"

"I can always remind you if you forgot," Rajan says.

Simran blinks. This goes slightly beyond his usual flirtation. And Chandani—Simran glances her way—Chandani's cheeks seem bright suddenly. Several clues slide into place. Didn't Nick say Rajan was with some girl at his construction site? Some girl they confused with Simran? It couldn't be—

"*No* thanks. You suck in bed," Chandani snaps. Then she whips around and tries to steer Simran away. Simran, dazed, lets her. At least until Rajan calls to her.

"Simran Auntie. Can I talk to you for a minute?"

She turns immediately. He's still standing there, and all she can think about is him with Chandani and—*things* they might've been doing. "M-me?"

"Yeah, you. Come here." He crooks his fingers at her.

"What the hell?" Chandani mutters, which spurs Simran to coherent speech.

"We volunteer together at Hallway House. That's probably what this is about. I'll meet you at the admin building." She shakes Chandani off and marches over.

Rajan sits on the landing and jumps the rest of the way to the ground. Then he straightens to full height. Simran's never felt more childish next to him than right now, knowing this new information about him and Chandani. It's so strange knowing people her age casually do that sort of thing, while *she* has only a concept of it—

Rajan asks, "What did Nick say to you before I showed up that night?"

Simran stares. It's been weeks since then. "Why?"

"Curious." The flirting tone is gone. Her heart jumps. Something tells her this isn't a random question. Somehow . . . he suspects.

She looks him in the eye. "He said they wanted you working for them again. That's it."

"And you haven't heard from them since. Right?"

"Of course not."

"Good. Just making sure. They better not be bothering you, because I've been doing everything they asked lately."

"*What?*"

Too late, she sees the trap, right after she's said it. Rajan immediately steps closer. "Why is that so surprising? Of course I'm with them again. That was the whole point of them taking you. Wasn't it?"

Her throat closes. "Yes, but . . ." *Come on, Simran, think!* "It's stupid, but I was hoping they wouldn't bother you again, anyway. I never wanted this for you." She doesn't have to fake her trembling voice. "What . . . What are you doing for them?"

He studies her. She keeps her chin lifted to maintain eye contact. His height isn't normally intimidating. The way he normally carries himself is so *un*intimidating that she forgets how tall he is. But now she's realizing he probably does that deliberately. Of course he knows how to unnerve people when he wants to.

He speaks, low. "You're good, dammit. You're so good."

Her heart thunders. "What are you talking about?"

"I dunno. What *am* I talking about?"

The ensuing silence is only broken when Chandani marches up and shoves Rajan away. "That's enough."

And just like that, his expression transforms. The dark veil over his eyes lifts, he's smiling harmlessly, and he backs up. "Chill out. I was only asking a question."

"Don't *chill out* me," Chandani retorts. "Look, you've scared her—"

That compels Simran to speak. "I'm fine. We were talking about the Hillway schedule. Let's go, okay?"

Chandani allows herself to get tugged away after one last glare at Rajan. Simran, however, doesn't dare look back. Did he figure it out? No. He couldn't have.

"Okay, what'd he say?" Chandani asks once they're out of earshot. "That was way too intense to be about *scheduling*."

"Scheduling can get quite intense."

"Bitch, be serious. Do you even know why he's stuck doing community service? It's disturbing."

Even *Chandani's* warning her off now? She can't help herself. "Didn't you sleep with him?"

"So?" Chandani raises her eyebrows. "He's not the type you bring home to your parents. He's the type you use to get over your bad-boy phase before he goes back to jail."

Heat rises up Simran's neck. "You don't know that he's going back to jail."

"You're right," Chandani muses. "He might actually go to prison. Or die first. Who's to say?" She sighs, seemingly not noticing Simran clutching the posters in a death grip. "Tragic, really. The boy really knows what he's doing."

EIGHTEEN

RAJAN REMEMBERS EXACTLY where the old LS bookkeeper used to pick up his work. That shitty café downtown, right next to a laundromat and a storefront that was perpetually for rent. Rajan's been there a few times, dropping records off. He never thought he'd be back.

Inside, Zohra's at the counter, elbows leaning on the table while she reads a book. She looks up when he enters.

"Where is she?" Rajan demands. Zohra laughs.

"Wow, Rajan. Maybe start with hello— Wait, stop!" She darts in front of him, because he's reached the door to the kitchen.

He's not in the mood for games. "Get out of my way."

She doesn't. "Just *listen*—"

Rajan pushes her aside—gently, because even now he's conscious of what she's been through. When she grabs his arm, he shakes her off and continues on. Nothing's stopping him now.

Ever since his last meeting with Kat, this absurd thought had been niggling at him. But he dismissed it every time—it was way too stupid-sounding. Simran? Running with the *Lions*? No way. And yet, when he saw her with Chandani, he *had* to ask. Just to reassure himself.

What he got was the exact opposite of reassurance. And if Simran slipping up wasn't enough evidence, calling Nick afterward sure was.

"I'm not getting involved in your drama," Nick said when Rajan demanded the truth. "Sort this out yourselves. Tonight, at six."

Rajan couldn't concentrate at work after that. He kept thinking about the old accountant who was arrested. The Lions' money issues lately. He started to piece it together, and it horrified him.

Now, he pushes into the café service hallway only to be caught around the middle by some LS dude, who pats him down for weapons. The second his hands are off, Rajan surges into the kitchen.

The industrial space is the same as he remembers. But now there's a desk in the corner, piled high with notebooks and paper. Nick's there, bending over the page Simran's scrawling on. She sits at a chair there like she owns the place, a pen in her hand, using a brick of brown-papered cocaine as a paperweight.

Rajan's done shrooms once or twice, and the experience has nothing on what he's seeing right now.

"What the fuck is wrong with you?" he says without preamble.

Both her and Nick look up, but Simran answers. "You should leave, Rajan. You can't be seen here."

Of course she's not even surprised. Simran knows everything—or at least she thinks she does.

Rajan braces his hands on the table. Simran continues writing like he's not there. "I get what you're trying to do," he says to the top of her head. "You're trying to stop me from getting caught and going to jail, right? And let's pretend for one second that I'm okay with it. Not that you even asked, but let's pretend. Have you thought about what'll happen if they catch *you*?"

Her pen pauses briefly.

"Do *you* want to go to prison? Screw up your future? Do you wanna die for them?" He gestures to the room. "Because that's where this ends. The Lions' last accountant is locked up. The guy before him got strung up in his own office. This isn't some fun little math problem for you to solve at school. This shit is *real*."

"I know that." Simran's voice is sharp. "I'm not doing it forever. It's temporary."

He laughs. "Temporary? Fucking *temporary*? Is that what they told you?" His voice rises. In his peripheral vision, someone casually reaches under their jacket.

"Okay." Nick grabs Rajan's arm. "Take a walk."

Rajan wrenches his arm away. "*You* take a fucking walk, you prick. I'll deal with you later—"

"Let me rephrase." Nick shoves him. Hard. "Let's take a walk, or this isn't going to be pretty."

Rajan's about to shove him back, but he pauses. The circle has tightened around him. Subtly. He ponders his odds, but Simran's eyes are huge, and he doesn't want her to see any of that.

So he lets Nick push him into the service hallway. As soon as they're alone, he wheels on him. He wants to pummel him, but Nick just casually has his gun out right now. Rajan settles for: "You're *sick* for taking advantage of her like this."

"She offered."

"And you accepted because you thought she *had* something to offer."

Nick doesn't reply for a moment. "I don't let opportunities pass me by. You know I have a talent for finding talent."

Rajan sees red. "You piece of—"

"It's like she said. Until the end of July only. That pays your debts, and we should have another accountant by then."

He's being way too casual about this. "Seriously? She's not an accountant. Why even trust her with these ledgers?" Rajan's only glimpsed them rarely, passed between the hands of people much more important than him. "You're handing her all the LS's info."

"Nobody has *all* our info," Nick scoffs. "Well, except Manny, maybe. But Simran isn't even allowed her phone while she works. And you know what? She's *good* at this." He nods to the kitchen. "We snagged ledgers from the Aces last night. The *Aces*. Manny wants one cracked tonight— he thinks the Aces' don has been sending messages from prison, ordering a hit on an LS member. And Simran was the first person I thought of to do it. I wasn't wrong. She's pulling it apart."

His glee turns Rajan's stomach. "If something happens to her . . ."

"She's doing the *books*, not coming to shoot-outs. Be grateful. She's giving you an out."

"I'd rather go to prison."

Nick looks at him with something like pity. "Go tell your PO you were here, then." He tucks his gun away. "But Simran's still in it for the summer, whether you like it or not."

Rajan breathes deeply through his nose. A shitty, shitty situation, and he's losing control of it. "I want to talk to her."

"Promise you're finished with your tantrum first."

Rajan rolls his eyes and shoves past him.

Simran stiffens slightly when he reenters, as does everyone else. He grabs a chair from the corner and drags it over to her. She watches warily as he turns it around, sits, and rests his chin on the back to stare at her. "If you're not gonna listen to me, don't expect me to listen to *you*. Every minute you're here, I'll be here, too."

"That's defeating the point."

"I'm glad it feels pointless."

Her lips thin. She looks down at her book. Hopefully, she's starting to see for herself how fucked up this is.

The room lapses into silence. For the next few minutes, he watches her write, cross things out, and occasionally stare into space with an expression he associates with her mental calculations. He's pretty sure she doesn't even register the brick of cocaine sitting in front of her. Which is unfathomable to him. God, how many highs could he get out of that much coke . . . ?

His fingers start to itch. He puts his hands in his pockets. He could never afford it. More importantly, he *isn't into this shit anymore*, right? He's here to watch Simran. Not daydream about scraping off just a *little*—

Simran bends forward suddenly and starts writing furiously. It snaps Rajan out of it. Even though he told himself he wouldn't care, he's curious. He can't help but bend with her over the book.

A faint popcorn smell wafts from the page, which contains complete gibberish—the letters don't form real words. But Simran scrawls a formula at the top, frowning. It's entrancing. He may be shit at math himself, but she makes numbers her bitch.

The minutes crawl by. Half an hour. An hour. Everyone drifts into more relaxed positions. Nick's off having a smoke break; Zohra's on the floor studying her LSAT prep book. Rajan continues watching Simran work despite himself. She's decoding, all right. From what he can gather, all the letters have been shifted three letters forward in the alphabet, and when she shifts them back, it starts making sense. *D* is actually *A*. *E* is *B*. *F* is *C*.

"How'd you figure that out?" he asks, quietly, unable to help himself.

Simran glances his way, as if surprised he's still there. She pushes her glasses up her nose. "It's called a Caesar cypher. We talked about it once in calculus. The most common letter in this code is *h*, but the most common letter in the English alphabet is *e*. Therefore, they're probably substituting *h* for *e*." She points to the formula she's scrawled. "If *i* is a letter from the alphabet, *i* plus three is the letter it turns into. If *C* equals Caesar cypher, and *i* is the letter, the Caesar cypher of *i* is *i* plus three—"

"Forget I asked," Rajan says. She grins.

"These pages are just inventory transactions, which is probably why they encrypted them so poorly. Nick must be looking for something else." She flips to another section. Here, there are symbols instead of letters: Stars. Pitchforks. Crowns. Rings.

Nick walks back in the room. "Simran, you keep getting calls from a Neetu."

It's only when Simran tenses up again that Rajan realizes how much she'd relaxed in the last few minutes. "Neetu?" he repeats. That name sounds familiar. "The one from the kitchen?"

"Yes. I was supposed to meet her tonight— Never mind." Simran rubs her eyes. "It doesn't matter."

But clearly it does. Rajan glances at the page. He shouldn't help. He really, *really* shouldn't encourage this. But . . . the thought of her being trapped here . . .

"Listen, I might know some of these." He picks up her pen, ignoring her blink of surprise. "This upside-down *L*. That's probably referring to us—I mean, them. The Lions." Talk about a Freudian slip.

"Why's it upside down?" Simran asks.

"Disrespect." He's seen it in their graffiti before.

Simran takes the pen and notes it in the margin. He points to another symbol.

"The ace of spades is Aces."

She writes quicker now. "Tell me everything you know about the Aces. I think this is the kind of code you have to understand your enemy for."

As it happens, Rajan knows a lot about the Aces. "They're older and more established than the Lions. They're exclusive about who they let become full members, but they've got tons of wannabes doing their dirty work." That asshole Zach Singer from school was one of them. "And they've got rules. No stealing each other's shit, no going after family members—don't be a coward. Don't use what you sell."

"Half those assholes smoke crack anyway," Nick mutters.

"They don't always follow their own rules," Rajan agrees. "But they pretend to."

Simran nods thoughtfully. "Any . . . symbols? The Lions have tattoos. Do they?"

Snake Tattoo immediately comes to mind. "Snakes. And they have this motto. 'Reign in hell.' They write it fucking everywhere." *Also* seen on graffiti. The lack of imagination is inexcusable.

Simran taps one of the symbols—a palm tree crossed out. "'Better to reign in hell than serve in heaven.' That's from *Paradise Lost*. Who decided on the motto?"

Nick speaks up. "Otis. He's the don Manny thinks wrote this message."

"Otis," Simran murmurs, then scrawls the letter *O* next to the symbol. "If they really write their motto everywhere, maybe they wrote it here, too. Let's look for a five-letter word, two-letter word, and four-letter word."

They scan the page. Rajan spots it first. "There, at the bottom."

"Good eye," Simran says appreciatively, and *god*, he'd completely forgotten the rush her praise gave him. "We can crack the alphabet way faster now."

And they do. They put letters together, some through context clues and others through meaningful symbols. Nick and Zohra drift closer, as if too curious to help themselves.

When it's done, they all stare at the message.

"Letter to Adrina," Nick reads. "That's his wife."

Dear Adrina,

Looks like the online order's delayed. The shipment could come soon though. Is everything going okay otherwise? Moving is hard. Once I'm out, I want to help. Soon we'll be together and hit up that donut place Manny loves. Just you wait. Before you know it!

Until then,

Otis

REIGN IN HELL

"Any guesses why he's acting like Manny's his son instead of his mortal enemy?" Zohra mutters.

Nick picks up the notebook. "Because it's coded." He squints for a minute, then tosses it back on the table. "Every fifth word. Read it."

And suddenly it becomes clear. THE SHIPMENT IS MOVING OUT SOON. HIT MANNY BEFORE THEN.

"Shit." Rajan breathes. A hit order on an LS godfather? This is *big*.

The last time a godfather got killed was before Rajan's time, but he's heard the stories. It was chaos.

Nick rips the message out of the book. He's trying to be casual, but Rajan can tell he's shaken, too. "You can go now."

There's a collective exhale; chairs scrape back. Zohra wanders off to pick up her textbook, and Nick's already making phone calls in the corner. But Simran stays put, staring at the inside back cover of the Aces ledger.

"What?" Rajan asks.

She tilts the book his way. A small slip of paper tucked into the inside cover falls out. Written on it:

June 18
Pack my bag with five raisin strudels today.
1, 86, 81, 82, 29, 56, 29, 58, 18, 59, 92, 19, 55, 69, 56, 81, 18, 98, 58, 85,
98, 68, 98, 52, 92, 81, 95, 89, 25, 89, 16, 85, 28, 21, 56, 56, 65, 65, 91, 18,
85, 89, 65, 89, 58, 92, 91, 85, 2

Yeah, not suspicious at all. *Raisin strudels* has to be code.

Simran taps the date. "Maybe it has to do with the shipment they're talking about moving?" she whispers.

Rajan has no clue, of course, but he doesn't like the way she's gazing at the numbers. Entranced. Nick hangs up his phone, and Rajan makes an executive decision. "Doesn't matter." He tucks the slip back into the cover, closing the book in her hands. "Don't let them see, or who knows how long they'll keep you here."

Simran glances Nick's way and hesitates before nodding. She looks exhausted. Rajan wonders how much of that is from her own life and how much of it is from his.

"Still think this was a good idea?" he asks her quietly, and she doesn't respond.

NINETEEN

TO BE CLEAR, Simran never thought this was a good idea. But it's the only one she had.

And even if Rajan's always present when she's working, at least he won't be out *there*, on the streets, doing whatever Nick would have him do. The chances of him being caught for this are much less. Although admittedly, his presence *is* rather inconvenient. She had to be careful yesterday, slipping the list of numbers into her sleeve.

She's just *curious*. There's no harm.

When she gets home, she inputs those forty-eight numbers into Excel. She orders them from low to high, then vice versa, examines their frequency, tries another alphabetical substitution algorithm. Nothing works.

So she examines the accompanying message instead. A Google search doesn't tell of any drugs that are referred to as *raisin strudel*. It must be Ace-specific. Or just another part of the cipher.

A little while turns into a long while, and the next thing she knows, the sun's first rays hit her laptop screen. She puts it away and kicks clothes off her bed to sleep. But ten minutes later she has a different idea and is up again.

She does the same thing the next night, only nodding off a few hours before her father wakes her for the gurdwara. Apparently, he's tried to wake her three times already, and they're going to be late.

It's a big day for her mom—she hasn't been to the gurdwara in weeks, and when Simran comes downstairs, she's wearing a dark gold suit rather than the grubby home clothes that have become her norm lately. But not even that can hide the deepened lines in her face. All this, in a month.

Several people at the gurdwara notice, too. As they enter, Simran's mother is greeted with questions like *Are you ill? My, you've lost so much weight, what's your secret?*

Her mother takes it all with a strained smile. Simran suspects the only reason she came today was for this purpose: to stop rumours from growing.

While her mother's smoothly explaining how a nasty virus kept her home for weeks, several kids run past clutching backpacks. One is crying. Simran automatically reaches out to touch her shoulder. "What's wrong?"

The little girl immediately turns to Simran, her face tear-streaked. "Preeti won't give my backpack back. We got them from the playplace field trip yesterday."

Simran turns her gaze on the other girl, who now looks guilty. "Preeti, come on. Give it back."

Preeti does so immediately. Simran smiles, pleased. While she doesn't exactly *enjoy* being seen as a paragon of virtue, it does have its benefits at times like this.

As the backpack passes hands, the pocket slides open a bit, and the lingering smell of yesterday's popcorn wafts over to Simran's nose. It immediately takes her back to the ledger.

Her smile slides away. She mentally shakes herself. First, two all-nighters, now this? *Why* can't she stop thinking about it? It wasn't like the message was especially outlined or highlighted. In fact, it was plain scrawl in a fine-tipped blue pen, like an afterthought.

But that makes her wonder if it was the most crucial thing of all.

"Will you be doing kirtan today?" a passing auntie asks, snapping Simran out of it. Simran hums her confirmation. She prepared one of her mom's favourite shabads for this day.

But her mom isn't the only one making her return, as Simran discovers when she gets onstage to sing. As she's puffing air into her harmonium, Jassa settles behind the tabla beside her like he never left. She looks at him, but he only covers his mic to ask *Which taal?* and she covers hers to reply *Dadra*, and then they get to it.

They are, as always, a good duo. Her mom clearly thinks so, too, because every time Simran looks up while singing, she spots her face in the crowd, those lines in her face smoothed away for the first time in weeks.

Simran doesn't speak to Jassa right afterward, but later, in the langar hall for lunch, she spots him approaching while she's sitting to eat. He's holding a steel water pitcher and cups, going down her row to pour water for people. When he kneels in front of her, Simran says, "I thought you wouldn't be back in Kelowna until fall."

He hands her a cup. "I'm taking summer classes."

Smart move, getting ahead of the next school year. She should've done that too. "I'm sorry about your dada. How's your family?"

"Adjusting. Somehow, I never imagined him dying. Kind of stupid, right? He was, like, eighty." He laughs a little, shaking his head. "I just wasn't ready."

"Can you ever be ready?"

"Exactly." He doesn't seem to realize her question wasn't rhetorical. "But listen, I really am sorry about before. There was a lot on my mind, but that's no excuse. I should've texted you before I left that I'd miss our—"

"It's okay," Simran says quickly, not wanting to hear whatever he was about to call their coffee date. "I understand."

He smiles apologetically and picks up his pitcher again. As he pours, she can't help but admire his ever-graceful posture, the way the fabric of his dress pants and shirt stretch over muscle. What on *earth* does he do to maintain that physique?

"How're you doing, anyway?" Jassa asks. Simran hastily tears her eyes away.

"Fine, why?" She shoves a piece of roti in her mouth to give herself something to do.

"You came in pretty late today. And . . . Neetu told me you've been acting off."

Simran pauses in chewing. She *has* been acting off. Missing Neetu's decoration night was just part of her new pattern of avoidance—of people *and* social functions. Half because of her mom, half because of the Lions.

Thankfully, Toor Uncle, who's sitting next to Simran, bangs his cup on the ground at that moment. "Are you socializing or doing seva, boy?"

"Coming, Uncle ji." Jassa grins at Simran and moves on. Simran exhales. Close call. Jassa's too smart for her excuses.

As he's leaving, another kid with a playplace backpack runs by, wafting that popcorn smell at her, and she sits up quickly. Wait. Jassa *is* smart. And he knows his way around a mathematical quandary as well as she does. If anyone could help with the Ace cipher . . .

"Jassa," she calls impulsively. He turns. "Come eat with me."

Jassa looks surprised at the request. She has a tiny amount of déjà vu—but this time, there's no room for embarrassment. "Sure," he says. "Just let me finish."

Once Jassa moves on, Toor Uncle nudges her. "I understand your game, Birdie. Very clever."

She blushes, and he cackles. Toor Uncle has no idea what game she's really playing.

Jassa eventually shows up with his tray, and Simran makes room for him by tucking her legs beneath her. It's a tight fit—their shoulders press together. They eat in silence as Simran tries to figure out how to approach her question.

Jassa speaks after a minute. "Another example of you acting off: You didn't get the academic award this semester."

It's true. Her GPA slipped. Her exams . . . well, some of them hadn't gone *great*. She knew it deep down, but it still stung when she didn't get the email. Now she knows who did. "Congratulations."

"I didn't think I could beat you."

His voice is curious. Time to segue. "Well, since you're my academic superior now, can I ask a favour?"

Jassa laughs. "Yeah, okay."

"This is going to sound strange." She puts her napkin between them. "My cousin sends me on scavenger hunts sometimes, but this time she's sent a code I can't crack."

He's still smiling, clearly thinking it's a joke. "*You?* Can't crack it?"

"Give me a pen."

He reaches into his front pocket to hand her one. She takes it, then writes the memorized list of numbers on her napkin.

Jassa looks much less amused now. "What the hell?"

"I know. But I need to crack it. I think it's a hint of where I'll find the next clue."

Jassa pulls the napkin toward himself for a better look. "Your cousin sounds intense."

"You've got no idea." That reminds her, she has to stop avoiding TJ one of these days. The fact that her cousin tasked *Chandani* with mining information shows how bad Simran's been at acting normal. "I've spent so long looking at these numbers. Why aren't three, four, seven, or zero used? And if I replace the most frequent number with the most frequent letter in the alphabet—"

"*E*," Jassa says softly. "You thought it was a Caesar cipher variation?"

Simran nods. Jassa speaks her language. "It didn't work, though."

He examines the napkin again. "Did your cousin use the Enigma machine to encrypt this or something?"

He's starting to sound suspicious. Simran adds another layer to the story. "She got help from a math prof. She knows I like figuring things out. Well? Want to help?"

Without hesitation, Jassa takes the pen. "I do like a challenge."

So, over the next few minutes, Simran watches as he repeats many of the strategies she's already tried: frequency analysis, writing out the unused numbers, ranking high to low. Finally, he sits back and frowns. "Maybe this isn't just numbers at all." He taps the list. "These commas. Were they part of the original code?"

Simran stares down at the list. He might be onto something here. The fact that only the first and last number is single-digit . . .

"Maybe these commas aren't separating numbers at all," Jassa says. "Maybe they're—"

"Coordinates," Simran finishes. "Ordered pairs of numbers, like on a—"

"Cartesian plane." Jassa flips his napkin and draws a graph. "Maybe all you need is an x and y axis." He marks each axis with the numbers one through nine. "Give me the coordinates."

Simran reads them out—*1,8; 6,8; 1,8;* and so on. He marks each point. There doesn't appear to be a clear shape between the dots. But she copies the graph anyway, and silently, they study their respective napkins.

A pair of feet stops in front of them. Jassa looks up first, Simran too busy trying to connect dots until he says, "Sat Sri Akaal. Auntie ji."

Simran finally tears her gaze away to see her mother, greeting Jassa with a warm smile. Then she looks down at their napkins, eyebrows raised. "What's this?"

"A puzzle," Simran says before Jassa can.

She tilts her head. "Odd puzzle."

"Mom, you have no idea." Simran grimaces. "It's a math thing."

Her mother's smile widens. "Well, I'll get a ride with Rupi, then. See you at home."

Simran blinks. No tearing her away to leave? No meaningful look? Her mother is going out of her way to get a ride with someone else—someone *nosy*, who might question her on her absence—just so Simran can . . . what, hang out with Jassa?

Simran's mother bids goodbye to Jassa before retreating. Simran watches her go, confused. Jassa says, "Your mom's really nice."

Simran wants to laugh. "To *you*."

"And you." At Simran's skeptical look, he adds, "A few months back, I overheard her telling some other aunties about you. Apparently when you were little, you used to space out a lot, and she could tell because you'd chew your lip and ignore people talking to you."

Embarrassing. "How is this an example of her niceness, again?"

"She said she always tried to make you stop, but looking back, you were probably just thinking about something. She said you were brilliant even then."

Simran stares. "She . . . said that?" She almost can't imagine.

"Typical *nice behind your back* parenting, isn't it? My mom's the same." He clicks his pen. "She's right, you know."

"About what?"

"You're brilliant." He says it casually, but Simran's face heats. She ducks her head back down at the napkins. If she's so *brilliant*, why can't she crack this cipher?

Jassa's not done. "Also, you still do it. Chew your lip, I mean." She stops chewing her lip immediately, and Jassa smiles. Now Simran's certain her face has burst into flames.

She can't look at him, so she bends over her napkin and adds, impulsively, "There's more to the message, by the way." She scribbles the date and message that were on the slip. It's a long shot, but maybe it *is* part of the code.

When she's done, Jassa says, "Are we sure your cousin's not messing with you?" He pauses. "Or that you're not messing with *me* as revenge for leaving you hanging?"

"I promise it's real." Now that she's transcribed the message—*PACK MY BAG WITH FIVE RAISIN STRUDELS TODAY*—something about it niggles her. Written in all caps, letters evenly spaced out . . . something. She can't figure it out.

"Maybe it's an anagram?" Jassa suggests. Now that's an idea.

But it doesn't come to anything. Simran barely notices as people drift away, their plates get picked up, and an auntie brings them refills of chah. The sunlight from the window has slid halfway across the room by the time Jassa drops his pen. "As much as I wish I could keep at this, I have to go."

"Sorry." Simran sits up and sighs. They're surrounded by crumpled napkins. "My cousin outdid herself this time."

"Don't be sorry. This was fun. But god, I have a headache." Jassa stands and stretches, and then, eyes landing back on her, grins. "You really know how to put a guy through the wringer, Simran."

And he's gone, strolling out of the langar hall, before Simran can figure out whether he's flirting with her.

TWENTY

CLANK.

Sweat drips into Rajan's eyes as he hammers a particularly stubborn nail into place. Today, the roofing crew is working on a house, and while the other guys are having a smoke break in the backyard below, he remains on the roof, only half listening to them complain about their allegedly bitchy wives and annoying kids. The other half is thinking about *her*.

Clank.

The image of Simran at the table, surrounded by Lions.

Clank.

It's amazing, really, how he somehow sucked her into this mess without trying. It just happened because he was *there*. He raises his hammer higher.

Clank. Clank. Cl—

Pain lances through his left shoulder. He drops the hammer, cursing, and it topples down the side of the roof before coming to a stop in the gutter. He lets his arm dangle until the pain ebbs to a dull throb.

Fantastic. The foreman yells from below to *watch it with the hammer*, while Trevor adds a cheery *You got this, brother!*

Rajan curses them both inwardly as he retrieves the hammer. This job seriously sucks. His coworkers are on the LS payroll, the foreman's a dick, and his shoulder's about had it with roofing. Too bad he doesn't have the qualifications or temperament for anything else.

Your shoulder wouldn't bother you if you had a line of coke, some voice in the back of his head singsongs. Nothing *would bother you*.

Rajan shakes his head vigorously. Not this again. The cravings have been getting steadily worse. What did the shrink in juvie always say? Make a plan to deal with your problems, not run away from them?

He settles back on his perch and calls Nick. It goes to voicemail. Rajan calls again, then again. On the fourth attempt Nick picks up. "I'm blocking you—"

"I have a proposal." That shuts Nick up. If there's one thing that prick loves, it's a good deal. Rajan just has to make it sound like one. "You have my Hillway mentor tied up in illegal shit. I can't have that on my conscience, okay? So listen. You're only taking her help because you can't find a real accountant. If I find you one, you won't need her anymore. Right?"

"Is *that* what you took away from that conversation?"

Rajan takes that as a yes. "That dude Oliver was an insurance broker. There's got to be other people like him who buy from the Lions. People who have the skills to run the books."

"Of course there are." Nick sounds irritated. "But finding the right person takes time, and I'm starting from scratch. Rory wasn't exactly looking for an accountant before I got here."

"Then let me help."

He can practically hear Nick's raised eyebrows. "*Now* you wanna come back to the Lions? Simran's only with us because you were too chicken to do that in the first place—"

"This isn't me *coming back*," Rajan snaps. "This is me getting you a bookkeeper to clear my debt. That's the exchange she made, right?

You're losing nothing. You're actually gaining someone better qualified."

A pause, where Rajan can practically feel Nick pondering that. Then: "We'll see." Nick hangs up. Rajan, unfazed, lowers the phone and picks up his hammer again. The fact that Nick's even considering it means the Lions' financial situation is serious. They really *are* desperate. And that, he can work with.

Hours later, Rajan heads home with the intention of icing his shoulder and taking as much Tylenol as possible without overdosing. Hopefully it'll stop hurting by the time he wakes. That damn fallen tree's still in the yard, after all, and nobody else is gonna move it. But when he rounds the corner from the bus stop, he stops short.

In front of the house is a police cruiser.

No. This can't be happening. He can't be caught *already*. Technically, yes, he's been breaching probation, but *barely*. How is Snake Tattoo getting away with it and he isn't?

He debates turning around, but he knows from experience they'll wait until he shows. And they'll spook Yash—Yash always hated when they came, before. Rajan takes a deep breath. He'll just suck it up, then. And stay calm. They can't pin him for shit yet.

As he enters the house, a stranger's low murmur floats from the living room. Slowly, he removes his shoes and rounds the corner. His dad's there, arms folded. And two white cops stand in the middle of the room, boots sinking into the carpet. One glances at Rajan, and Rajan's breath catches. He recognizes him. This guy arrested him in high school . . . more than once.

There's a flash of recognition in the officer's expression, too. His eyes flick down a little, and Rajan realizes his hood has gone lopsided, exposing his tattoo.

From the smirk curling the officer's lip, Rajan knows he's recognized it. And when he meets his eyes again, it's like he's analyzing prey.

Rajan's skin crawls. Back in the day, cops always treated him like an animal. The majority of Vancouver's Most Wanted list were brown, and therefore Rajan was automatically suspicious. It didn't matter that by sheer numbers, white people in the gangs far outstripped them. People only saw what was different.

The cop turns back to the couch where—Rajan realizes with a start—Sukha is sitting sullenly. "Following in your brother's footsteps, are we? Thought you looked familiar."

It takes Rajan a second to understand: The officer's there for *Sukha*, not him.

He strides forward. "Wait—what happened?"

"Your brother was vandalizing public property," the cop says. "He and his friends thought it'd be funny."

What. The. Hell? Rajan glances at Sukha, who's avoiding his eyes.

The cop goes on. "We're choosing not to pursue an investigation or charges, considering it's your first offense." His tone makes it clear he thinks it won't be the last.

"Thank you, Officers. I'll talk to him," their father says. "I'm sorry you have to deal with this."

The cops file out. One has the audacity to pause next to Rajan and say, "See you later."

Rajan doesn't trust himself to speak. There's silence as the door shuts behind them. Silence as their boots crunch over gravel to their cruiser, car doors close behind them, and they pull out.

It's only once the engine noise fades that Rajan wheels on Sukha. "Are you fucking serious?"

"Those cops should be thanking me." Sukha lounges on the couch with an insolent smile. "That statue has a lot more personality now."

"They could've *charged* you. You're lucky Officer Dipshit let you off."

"Never seemed to occur to you," Sukha fires back. "Then *or* now. Aren't you still running with the Lions?"

His words hang in the air. No one's ever spoken the name in their house before. Also, they're called the *Lion's Share*. The only people who shorten the name are people who are *in* the Lions.

Rajan steps closer. "What do *you* know about the Lions?"

"Just that you're clearly still with them."

"Yeah? How would you know?" Rajan stares him down. "Don't tell me you've been running with them, too."

His voice is deadly quiet, and for a second, Sukha pales. Then he raises his chin. "None of your business—"

Rajan explodes. *"Don't fucking tell me* you've been running with them too!"

Sukha's eyes widen. Rajan knows he's lost it, but he can't get himself together right now. First the weed, now this? The thought of his brother getting into the same mess he's in has him completely scattered—

"Enough," thunders their father. He wrenches Rajan away by his hoodie, but it's more out of shock that Rajan stumbles back. His father so rarely talks to him directly.

But now he even looks at him. "Leave. You're not helping."

"Oh, because you are?" Rajan shakes him off. "You can't even stay sober for them for one day."

He kicks the crate of empty bottles for emphasis. No one speaks. Sukha's eyes dart between Rajan and their father. From the end of the hall, Yash's door opens a hair as if to listen better. Rajan knows he took it too far, mentioning the drinking. But it pisses him off that his dad acts like he's better than him. As if Rajan's the only one with a problem—at least Rajan *quit.*

His father finally speaks, voice gravelly. "I was completely sober when you were younger, Rajan, and that didn't do shit, as we all know."

It takes everything in Rajan not to flinch. But his dad's not done.

"You want to play the blame game? Fine. If Sukha *is* involved in a gang, it's because he learned it from somewhere. The *same* place he got his little drug habit and his habit of disobeying everything I ask him to do for his own good." He turns away. "Your mother would be heartbroken if she saw you now."

This time Rajan does flinch. "She—"

"I'm talking to Sukha. *You* already broke her heart, before she died."

His father looks back, eyes suspiciously bright. "Remember how she got clots in her lungs at the end? It happened because she laid in bed all day. She was tired, sure. She was sick, sure. But I bet she could've gotten up. If you ever just gave her a *reason to*."

His voice has lost its usual apathetic undertone by the end. Now it's downright vicious.

And effective.

"Dad," Sukha says quietly. "Dad, that's not—"

But Rajan doesn't hear the rest. He can't look at his father or brother any longer. Instead, he strides out without another word. Out of the room and then out of the house, slamming the door behind him.

The night air is chilly, but he barely notices. He just has to get away. He walks and walks until he's met with the chain-link fence of a ballpark several blocks from home. He grabs onto it, bending over, trying to breathe. It feels like there's a band wrapped around his rib cage, squeezing the air out of his lungs. He sinks to his knees, still clutching the fence. Gasping for air. Black spots appear in his vision. What's wrong with him? What is *wrong* with him?

He slams his fist into the fence. Pain lances immediately through his shoulder, and with a cry, he drops it. But at least the pain has jarred him out of that suffocating feeling.

He sits in the grass, holding his shoulder. Tonight the ache is relentless. So bad, he might actually cry. He's tired of hurting. He wants it gone, *god*, he wants to stop feeling this way for one fucking *second*.

And so, on impulse, Rajan tugs his phone out of his pocket and dials.

Zohra picks up. "Hello?"

"Come get me," he says.

Rajan remembers his psych eval from juvie very well. *Drug-seeking behaviours* was noted in his chart early on. *Probable substance use disorder.*

In a way, juvie *was* like kindergarten, like he told Nick. There *was* finger painting. He *did* play a lot of basketball. Hell, he played the cymbals in the Christmas concert they put on. But they also did some serious shit while there. Therapy. Drug rehab. He got the "kicked the habit" sticker.

But the thing is, he's not wired normal anymore. Whenever something goes even slightly wrong in his life, he starts thinking about it again. He knows it's bad. He feels like a bad person right now, asking Zohra to take him to Nick, but that doesn't stop him. He's so tired of fighting it. And for what? Trying to set a good example for Sukha? That's already failed. So who the hell is he suffering for?

Zohra picks him up in the ice-cream truck. She's driving tonight, in a little black dress. She gives him a once-over when he clambers into the passenger's seat. And clearly, she picks up on his mood. "Nick's not at the café. He's at Manny's for a party."

Nick has the good stuff. "Then take me to Manny's."

Zohra hits the gas without asking more questions. Rajan's used to her reckless driving and therefore knows to brace his shoulder against her sharp turns. His father's words, meanwhile, continue to echo in his mind. They were too calculated to be spur-of-the-moment. No, his father's held his tongue for a *long* time.

Rajan's reminded of the end of grade twelve, when he accompanied his mother to Surrey. She was going to see new specialists for her transplant issues. His father had work and his brothers had school; Rajan was the only one available. His father begged him to stay out of trouble for once. Rajan had scoffed. He wasn't *that* much of an asshole. He could keep it together for his mom.

But, the move was hard. The appointments were painful. Watching his mom waste away was excruciating. It didn't help that his aunt's family, who they stayed with, knew his reputation and treated him like shit. It helped even less that his mother never tried to defend him when they criticized him. She was probably too exhausted, but it still hurt.

He took it for her sake. Sometimes he needed help staying mellow enough to do so. It was easy to get connected—and then, of course, he met Nick and Zohra. With them, he drowned his frustration in stronger ways. It was the exact opposite of the bare minimum his father asked of him.

Knowing that, Rajan supposes he should be grateful his father didn't scream at him at the funeral. At that time, his father hardly showed any emotion at all, not even when Rajan said he was sorry. He just looked at the casket and told him the bank was taking the house. And it would be best for everyone—particularly his brothers—if Rajan didn't come back to Kelowna. At least until things "settled down."

He did not elaborate on what "settled down" meant. He also did not look at Rajan as he said it. But, for once in his life, Rajan did as he was told.

He dropped out of the community college his mom had convinced him to enroll in. He spent his days sleeping off the night before. He regularly came home with blood on his shoes, wasted at all hours, and when he stumbled in one morning with an LS tattoo he didn't remember getting, his aunt finally kicked him out.

Life accelerated; time loosened and flew. His nights became a blur of jobs with Nick and Zohra, with his baseball bat and gun and the lines of coke Nick provided to keep him happy. The only thing he remembers clearly is that he was *good* at what he did—at being a Lion. It was the only thing he was ever truly good at.

Rajan's pulled out of memories when Zohra says, "We're here."

They've driven up a long winding hill in a rich neighbourhood, the houses bigger and more sprawling the farther they've gone. And now they're at the gates of one of the grandest. Real fancy gates, too, with black statues of lions perched on stylized khandas. Rajan stares at them as they pass. The irony of the Sikh symbolism in the LS isn't lost on him. Just like the Sikh warriors of old, they want you to feel like you're part of something bigger. Like a soldier fighting for a cause you would die for. Except in the Lions' case, it's not a very good one.

He jumps out of the truck before Zohra has fully parked next to a bunch of BMWs. She catches up and grabs his hand. "Put your arm around me. We have to look like we're together."

He pulls away. "You and me are done, remember?"

"This is for *you*. There's a lot of people here." She leans into him. "You haven't seen what it's been like. After . . . you got arrested. What people think of you."

"That what? I'm not loyal?" He rolls his eyes and presses forward. "Well, nobody's killed me yet."

Zohra doesn't answer, just hooks her hand around his elbow.

They cross the manicured lawn. From what Rajan can see through the glass, this is a rich-people-only event. Diamonds glint from ears, pale champagne is passed hand to hand, and he catches a flash of white powder on a glass table. He turns to Zohra abruptly. "Where's Nick?"

"This way." She steers him away from the grand front doors, away from the curious eyes, and they circle around back until they reach a service entrance. The music is quieter here. Once inside, she leads him up a staircase. In different circumstances, Rajan might be intrigued by the bird's-eye view he now has of the party scene below, but today, he's more interested in where they finally come to a halt: a door with a lion's crest.

Nick opens it at Zohra's knock, lit joint in hand. His eyebrows rise at the sight of Rajan behind her. "I don't have a job for you yet, it's only been a few hours."

Rajan steps forward. Now that they're face-to-face, a different question has sprung to mind. "Is my brother in the Lions?"

The only indicator of Nick's surprise is a slow blink. After a moment he says, "Rajan, you know I don't keep track of every low-level shithead in the Lions. Especially not in Kelowna. Or have you forgotten I'm only here temporarily?"

Rajan honestly cannot tell if he's lying. But then again, he's got a point. When Rajan was younger, he, too, was on the fringes. Running drugs, doing dirty work. People didn't know him. He was expendable. That was part of why he worked so hard to *get* known. And it didn't really happen until he met Nick.

Rajan narrows his eyes at the thought. "If you ever come near him, I'll kill you."

Nick yawns theatrically. "I'll keep that in mind. Now go away."

He starts closing the door, but Rajan sticks his foot in the way. "Wait. That's not . . . what I'm here for."

Nick scans his expression. Rajan doesn't know what he sees, but whatever it is makes him turn to Zohra. "You brought him here *why*?"

"You know he doesn't stop when he gets like this." She sounds slightly defensive. "Better he uses with us than somewhere else."

"Well, too bad. I don't have anything."

Rajan scoffs. "You have a joint in your hand, asshole."

Nick takes a drag from it. "Haven't you been sober for months?"

Rajan doesn't like his insinuation. "It's not *heroin*."

"For you, it might as well be."

He's right, some part of Rajan knows this. At the start of juvie, going cold turkey on everything was a shock to his system. He was keyed up all the time. When they finally dragged him to the addictions counselor, he denied it at first. He wasn't some clichéd *drug addict*. It was all just for fun. Yes, his use had ramped up over the last year, yes, he was trying new stuff, but nobody else was having issues—

It's not really about the drug, Rajan. It's about you. You can't have one thing giving you all your happiness, whether that's a drug or something else. It'll suck the life out of everything else. Until that's all you have. The opposite of addiction is balance.

Currently, he couldn't give less of a shit about balance. "Is this because you think I don't have money? I have a job I can pay cash. Tomorrow." He's desperate. The pain is so bad he wants to rip his arm off. "Give me *something*."

"Do you even hear yourself right now?" Nick asks. "I thought you didn't want to breach probation. What if they find out?"

"Who's going to tell them? You?"

Nick blows out smoke, considering him. Then: "Zohra, take him home." He closes the door without warning. It pisses Rajan off. He slams at the door, but it's now locked.

"Isn't this what you wanted?" he shouts at the lion's crest. "Me, relying on you for everything I need? Here I am, and you don't want me anymore?"

No answer. It feels like he's been shut out of the only place that has consistently been home. A twisted thought, but it's true. Simran did that—shut him out. For his own good, maybe—but right now, it feels like he's lost everything. It feels fucking cruel.

"Rajan," Zohra says quietly, and he looks up, vision blurred, to find her reaching for him.

He lets her wrap her arms around him, his fight gone. She smells like her usual perfume, the one that stuck to him for hours when they were together. A confusing mix of emotions rise in him. Desire. Disgust. She, and Nick, and the Lions reduced him to this. Having a breakdown because he can't get high. He used to be a good person, damn it.

Self-loathing crawls under his skin. "Zohra, you know you owe me. Get me something. Please." His voice cracks.

Her resolve seems to break at that. "Okay, okay." Her voice is gentle and soothing. So are her lips, when they press against his. "Come with me."

TWENTY-ONE

ABSURDLY, SIMRAN'S MOTHER looks almost childlike in a hospital gown.

It's the morning of her surgery. Simran waits with her in the OR lounge, unable to stop herself noticing how odd her mom looks without her kara and kirpan, her grey hair covered with a surgical cap instead of a turban. She looks like a nobody.

Her mother speaks first. "Stop biting your hangnail. It'll bleed."

Simran sighs. Of course *that's* what her mom is thinking while they're holding hands.

"And those jeans need washing. Look at the scuff marks. Did you even eat breakfast?"

"*Mom.*"

"I'm serious. You need to take better care of yourself. And stop slouching—"

Simran starts to pull her hand out of her mother's grip, but the grip tightens. Simran looks up at her. And although her mother doesn't say a word, her stony expression giving nothing away, Simran understands everything in that moment.

"Mom, the surgery will be okay," she says gently, and that mask cracks. A bit.

"I'm afraid of what they'll find." Her mother's voice wavers, suddenly as stripped down and vulnerable as her appearance. "I shouldn't have waited so long to see the doctor."

"You—you waited?" Simran stammers despite herself. Her mother's never gone into detail about how the diagnosis was made.

"I was embarrassed, you know. That I was having bleeding again at my old age. I hoped it would go away, and now I learn that when this cancer is caught early, surgery usually cures it." Her mother's lips tremble. "Shame. *That* is the reason I might die."

Simran's throat clogs. It's a horrible thought, that all this could've been prevented, but she tries not to show it. Her mother is scared enough already. "It can still be cured. Remember the pamphlets? There's radiation, chemotherapy—"

"They say you lose your *hair* with chemotherapy, Simran." Her mom's voice comes out in a rush. Clearly she's thought about it. "I don't want that. You . . . *You* know what it means to me."

There's nothing Simran can say to that. She does not offer to get rid of hers in solidarity. It's the last thing her mother would want. The image of her mother's long hair, cultivated over a lifetime practicing Sikhism, falling out in chunks, in the drain, on the floor, is gutting. It would be a destruction of her spirit more than her body.

Her mother smiles wanly in the silence. "Your father would cry if I said such things to him. I knew you wouldn't. You would just . . . understand." She sighs. "Your father's right. You are so brave."

Simran blinks. But her mother's gaze is steady, as if delivering compliments to Simran comes easy. And—she remembers Jassa's words—maybe it does.

A cough comes from behind them. "We're ready for you now, Mrs. Aujla."

Simran finds she doesn't have any words left. Their gazes connect, large brown eyes that Simran inherited. They hug. She manages to keep it together. At least until her mom is being led away by one of the nurses, and the other pats Simran's shoulder. "Don't worry, hon. We'll take good care of your grandma."

Simran flinches. The nurse doesn't notice. No one seems to notice how fast Simran flees as soon as her mom is gone.

Simran's father rises off the couch as soon as she returns home. "How'd it go?"

"Fine. She's in surgery now." Simran clears her throat. "I'm—I'm going upstairs. I'm tired."

He doesn't stop her, although she feels his worried eyes on her back.

She's nearly at her bedroom door when her phone vibrates. She's so numb, so keen on a distraction, that she picks up instantly. "Hel—?"

"Finally!" TJ says. Simran closes her eyes momentarily. Of *course* it's TJ. "If it weren't for Chandani confirming you were alive, I'd be putting out Missing Person ads by now. What is going on with you?"

Simran clamps down on the hysterical laugh that wants to rise. "Nothing."

"Nothing?"

"Nothing. Now please stop siccing Chandani on me."

"No," TJ says pleasantly. "She gives me more deets than you ever will. For example, what's this about some crush you have?" Simran's heart leaps in panic, at least until TJ says, "Jesse, or something?"

Simran exhales. She's not sure why she thought TJ was about to name someone else. "Jassa," she corrects, and when TJ snickers, corrects her again. "And it's not like that."

"Okay." TJ sounds amused. "What's it like, then?"

Simran turns her eyes to the ceiling. For a second, she imagines trying to explain. *Well, it's like this, TJ: I didn't think of him that way until I found out my mom has cancer, and she approves of me dating him. And now I can't tell if my feelings are real or if I'm trying to* make *myself feel them. Want to unpack that for me?*

After a long silence, TJ sighs. "You know you can't avoid me forever, right? I'm coming home after my June exams."

"I know. I'll be at your dinner, like I said." That gives her two more weeks to prepare some convincing lies. "Look, I have to go."

"But—"

Simran hangs up and resumes biting her hangnail. Despite what she just told TJ, she's spent a lot of time thinking about Jassa lately. Particularly since that afternoon in the gurdwara, working on the cipher with him. Things felt . . . real, during that.

She throws herself on her bed and flips open a notebook. Now's as good a time as any to continue working on it. It felt like they were getting close that day.

She writes the numbers out as coordinates again; this time, she notes some of them are repeated. What if it *is* like frequency analysis? What if each coordinate represents a *letter*?

Excited now, she draws a table. The only numbers in the list are 1, 2, 5, 6, 8, and 9, so she makes the table six-by-six and uses those numbers as the headings for the rows and columns. Which leaves her with . . . thirty-six cells to fill. But the alphabet only has twenty-six letters. What would be in the other ten cells? Numbers? Punctuation?

She realizes she's chewing on her lip and forces herself to stop. Jassa is really getting to her.

Her gaze drifts back to the message accompanying the code.

Pack my bag with five raisin strudels today.

Slowly, she counts the number of characters in it.

Excluding spaces, thirty-six.

Ignoring the way her back aches from her hunched-over posture, she inputs the characters into the table, one letter per cell.

	1	2	5	6	8	9
1	P	A	C	K	M	Y
2	B	A	G	W	I	T
5	H	F	I	V	E	R
6	A	I	S	I	N	S
8	T	R	U	D	E	L
9	S	T	O	D	A	Y

It fits. That can't be coincidence, right? She glances at her list of coordinates. Only one way to find out.

But, to her dismay, her translation makes no sense.

mnmaoiotuybovonpluerdluti yeaesnfrcsivrpeedeoltme

She must've filled out the table the wrong way. There's some angle she's missing.

She doesn't know when she falls asleep, but it's dark when she wakes. There's a note on her bedside table, pinned down by a plate of digestible biscuits.

Gone to see your mom, reads her father's elegant script. *She's in recovery. We can visit her together tomorrow. Sleep, sher putt.*

He signs it off with love. Simran pops a biscuit in her mouth. If her mom were here, she'd admonish her for eating in bed, getting crumbs everywhere. She'd look at the state of Simran's room and tell her to clean or she'll never be able to find anything. Simran would sigh and wish her mother would stop coming into her room.

Well, she doesn't anymore, a voice in her head says. *You got your wish.*

She doesn't realize she's crying until her tears hit the pillow. Instantly, she tries to wipe them away. This is ridiculous; the surgery went *fine.*

But it's the future she's scared of.

Despair she suppressed earlier, accompanying her mom, crashes down on her. She wants to hit pause on time. She doesn't want to witness her mother postsurgery, she doesn't want to watch her beautiful hair fall out. She doesn't want to watch her father's beard turn more white than grey. She doesn't want to endure the kind of inevitable suffering their family has yet to go through. If only she could be like Kiran, and fly so far away she wouldn't have to partake at all.

Impulsively, Simran reaches for her phone.

Nick picks up first ring, sounding irritable. "What?"

"Can I come in tonight?"

A pause, filled with background noise of loud music. "You were in two days ago."

"Yes, but . . ." She racks her brain. "I should get ahead of things. Aren't there still some Ace ledgers to decode?"

"Well, I don't know how important—"

"They might be useful." He remains silent, and she breaks. She can't take more of her own dark thoughts tonight. "Nick. *Please.*"

Another pause. "Did something happen between you and Rajan?"

Where did that come from? Simran frowns. "No. I haven't seen him in days. Why?"

"Because you're both testing my nerves tonight." Nick sighs. "Fine, you can come. But I'm warning you, your boy's here, too. And you're not gonna like it."

"He's—with you?" Simran grips her phone harder. "But you said you'd leave him alone!"

"Yeah," Nick replies darkly. "But I can't help what *he* does."

Those words give her a very bad feeling. "Nick," she says slowly, "what exactly is Rajan doing?"

Simran's never been to this neighbourhood before, packed with multi-million-dollar homes, but she doesn't need Nick's directions to know which house she's looking for. The black gates have lion statues on them.

When she stops at them, a man walks to her side of the truck and flashes his phone light at her. "Who're you?"

"Friend of Nick."

He snaps a photo of her without warning and wanders off to text someone. A minute later, the gate opens. There are plenty of luxury vehicles already parked in the lot, but she spots Nick's ice-cream truck at the end of the line and parks beside it.

Someone with expensive taste is hosting this party. She feels out of place immediately in her old sweatshirt and jeans. No wonder Nick told her to avoid the main entrance; as she enters through the side door he specified, she keeps her head down, catching only flashes of scenes through doorways—chandeliers, glass tables, tiled floors, strappy shoes. The indistinct noise of chatter and music.

Nick's waiting at the bottom of the stairwell, looking impatient. As soon as he sees her, he strides forward and grabs her arm. "Let's go."

He more or less drags her up the stairs, and she stumbles trying to keep pace. "Where are we going?"

He doesn't answer. Up the first flight, things are quieter. The air is hazy. A pair in formal wear sit on the carpet, heads leaned together, staring off into space and giggling at nothing.

Oh. It's *this* kind of party up here.

Nick releases Simran when they round a corner and come across a smoke-filled living room. And on the couch . . . Rajan and Zohra.

Simran stops short. Rajan's sprawled on the cushion, although she can't see his face because Zohra's in his lap. They're kissing. In such a clearly *involved* way that Simran's face heats. But she can't look away. His hand is on Zohra's mid-back, the other tangled up in her straw-coloured hair. Zohra's practically glued to him.

Nick makes a gagging sound. "I thought we left this behind in Surrey?"

They wrench apart immediately. Simran blinks out of her trance. Now she notices what's on the table in front of them: a fine dusting of powder, a crumpled up five-dollar bill, rolled-up paper. More important, the euphoric haze clouding Rajan's expression. Chemically carefree.

His eyes land on her, and immediately sharpen.

"The fuck?" His voice is hoarse, head swinging toward Nick. "You brought *her* here?"

Nick shrugs. "She came here herself."

Rajan pushes Zohra off. She settles beside him instead and picks up a joint from the tray. Simran can't help but notice how rumpled the front of her dress is. Rajan, meanwhile, glares at Nick. "I know what you're doing, asshole."

"What, showing Simran the ledgers?" Nick raises his eyebrows. "Yeah. Come on, Simran, they're this way."

He continues down the hall, and Simran mechanically turns to follow, still reeling—

A hand lands on her shoulder. "Wait."

She doesn't want to. She doesn't want to look at Rajan and feel disappointed again. She stares down the hall, at the doorway Nick's disappeared into, until Rajan speaks.

"I'm sorry."

"It's none of my business."

His hand falls away. "Right." His laugh sounds bitter. "Of course not."

Simran suddenly isn't sure what they're talking about. The drugs? Or Zohra? She has to draw the line. Fast. "What if they find out?" She turns to face him. Up close, his pupils are dilated. "They could send you to jail for this."

"Then I guess you're finally rid of me."

"Don't joke about that!" she shouts. He balks. The pair who were giggling near the wall fall silent to watch, as if this argument is now more entertaining than their hallucinations. "I can't watch you throw it all away. What were you *thinking*?"

Rajan's eyes flash, and she knows she's hit a sore spot, because he draws closer, into her space. "What was *I* thinking?" he repeats. "Why're *you* here off duty? You working for free now?"

She's suddenly on defense. "I'm getting ahead on work."

"Oh, really?" He laughs again. "What about the rest of your life, you on top of all that?"

Now *he's* hit a sore spot. Without answering, she wheels around and into the room Nick went into. Rajan doesn't follow.

It's a home office, the ledgers stacked neatly on the wide desk. Nick raises his eyebrows—he clearly heard everything—but she ignores him to sit behind the desk.

"Need help?" Nick asks.

She opens a ledger. "No."

Nick seems to take the hint. He leaves, but Zohra drifts in. To babysit as usual, probably.

Simran glares down at the new Aces ledger. The coded math in it would normally intrigue her, but she can't focus. She's angry at Rajan. But more so, she's . . . *sad* for him.

Neetu and the others at the breakfast kitchen would call her naive for that. They'd question whether Rajan was *ever* sober, or if he's been hiding it this whole time. She doesn't want to believe that, but she forces herself to turn that possibility over in her mind now. Has she been seeing what she wants to see?

There's a sudden pain in her thumb, and she looks down to realize the hangnail she's been biting is now bleeding. While she's wrapping it with a tissue, Zohra hops up on the desk beside her. "Back there, with Rajan, it wasn't what it looked like. I swear I'm not playing jealous ex."

"We're not together."

Zohra continues like she hadn't spoken. "I was trying to distract him. He was losing control. Dangerous place to be in, when you don't have the tolerance anymore. He hasn't done any of this stuff in months."

So it's his *first* relapse. Relief floods her, mixed with another emotion that urges her to ask if Zohra kisses everyone in danger of overdosing. She wrestles it down. "You sound like you know from experience."

"I've seen my fair share of bad things happen."

Her voice is dark. Simran's curiosity finally overpowers her. "How did you even end up here?"

Zohra lifts a dark brow. "As in, with the Lions?"

"It's just . . ."

"I'm a girl? And you don't see girls on the news being arrested at shootouts?" She shrugs. "That's exactly why I'm useful. People don't expect me." A flash of teeth. "You definitely didn't."

Simran would rather not reminisce about that. "You didn't answer my question."

"It's not that interesting. I dated someone in the LS." Zohra pauses. Hesitation, Simran might almost call it, but Zohra doesn't seem the type. "He was older, and gave me all the attention I wanted. Plus, he was loaded. I was shopping seven days a week, driving luxury cars . . . first time in my life I had money."

"You didn't question where that money came from?"

"Of course I did. I knew Jai was involved in the LS. But honestly, I liked it. Hard to resist the sexy bad-boy thing." She shoots Simran a knowing look. Simran pretends not to notice. "So when he started asking me to do things for *them*, I didn't mind. Like, I'd put his gun in my purse when we went out. I'd drive him and his friends around because cops wouldn't suspect a seventeen-year-old girl. Things like that. I didn't care. Especially because on top of everything else, Jai's friends were offering to pay my university tuition. Before that, I never thought I'd get to go."

Simran has to admire the Lions' resourcefulness. Of course they'd invest in a future lawyer on their payroll. Of course an organization of their magnitude has people in high places. She waits for more, but Zohra doesn't offer. "You're using a lot of past tense."

Zohra glances at the door, still slightly ajar. "Don't you have work to do?"

Simran hears the signal loud and clear. She finally turns her attention to the transactions in the book, fixating on one in particular.

$$
\begin{array}{r}
AYUBB \\
PTUB \\
+\ PUB \\
\hline
NPYBB
\end{array}
$$

"Give me a pen," she says after a moment. Her focus has returned.

Zohra does. "How're you going to figure it out?"

"By context." She taps the page. "Add up all the digits in the ones place. If B plus B plus B *equals* B, B has to be either zero, because zero times three is zero, or five, because five times three is fifteen. Right?"

Zohra frowns, seemingly doing the math. "I . . . guess so."

Simran points at the tens place. "And here, B plus U plus U *equals* B. For that to work, B *has* to be zero. And U has to be five."

Zohra nods slowly. "Because . . . if *B* were five, you'd have to carry a one to the tens place, and it would've fallen apart."

"Exactly." Simran smiles. "Now we have a foothold to figure out the rest."

And so she does. Zohra's silent at her side while she works, and several minutes later, she has the code: the numbers zero through nine are encrypted with the letters of the word BANKRUPTCY.

Zohra laughs softly when she writes it down. Then pulls up a chair to sit. "I wanna help." Whatever she's been using tonight has made her a gentler, warmer version of herself. Simran doesn't object, just places the ledger between them.

"Holy shit," Zohra says once they've decoded all the transactions. "That's . . . a lot of money, right?"

Simran nods. "And a lot of drugs they're keeping somewhere."

Somewhere. She can't help but think about the cipher in her notebook at home. Can't help but wonder if it holds the key.

Zohra pushes the ledger away and stretches. "Well, this was fun. I can see why you're a good math tutor." At Simran's expression, she shrugs. "What? We read up on you. Mathlete. A-plus student. Golden girl of your school, awards from the city, involved in apparently every nonprofit in town. Pretty impressive."

"I like to keep busy."

"Or you're a people pleaser."

Simran frowns. Zohra, meanwhile, glances again at the door. She appears to be warring with herself, but finally, she rises to close it. The sounds of the party fade.

Zohra turns to face her. "I didn't tell you the full story with Jai."

A chill runs down Simran's spine. Where this is coming from, she doesn't know, but when Zohra sits again, her voice is hushed.

"The older I got, the more Jai asked me to do. He'd rent properties and insure cars in my name. He had me get my firearms license and buy guns, so his friends could break into my car and steal them. It made me nervous. But when I started pushing back, Jai said I owed him. That's when I saw a new side of him." She wraps her arms around herself. "The only control I had was when I cheated on him. But he didn't even seem to care. In fact . . ." She takes a deep breath. "He was more than okay with me having sex with other people. Last fall, he tried to talk me into doing it with his friend."

Simran stares. "Why?"

"For money. We'd split the profits, right? Except I knew it didn't work like that. I'd seen some of those girls . . . they weren't exactly on equal footing with their pimps." Zohra smiles grimly. "I finally said no to him."

"And?"

"He got mad." A shadow crosses her face. "I ran out of the house. Rajan was there. I got in the car, Jai was waving his gun around, screaming that he was going to kill me, and . . . I didn't think."

Simran realizes, suddenly, where the story is going. "It was you," she breathes. "*You* ran him over."

Zohra's eyes dart around, like someone might hear. "Listen, I was *nineteen*. I was freaking out. Murder? I could go to prison. And even if not, all my law school dreams would be over. But . . . Rajan was seventeen."

Simran's still processing this. "He took the fall."

"I didn't ask him to," Zohra says defensively. "He jus⌐ . . . did. The cops bought it. So did the courts—Rajan pled guilty, it was an open-and-shut case. Jealous boyfriend, they see it all the time with the gangs. They'd kill each other over a parking space, you know? Even the *Lions* thought Rajan did it. Everyone knew we were sleeping together. Only Nick knows the truth." Her eyes take on a faraway look. "I guess I owe him for that. I always will."

Simran is quiet. Rajan went to juvie, got all sorts of labels that will stick to him for life, for something he didn't do. What if they'd tried him as an adult? Does his own life mean so little to him? Or does Zohra mean that much?

Zohra's voice brings her back. "Being a people pleaser got me to the worst place of my life. I have a feeling you're like me that way, so I have a question for you that would've saved me a lot of trouble: How far are you gonna take it?"

Simran raises her eyes to Zohra's.

"Have you ever asked yourself that? Because you should. You need to find the point where doing what other people want makes you more sad for yourself than happy for them." Zohra rises from her seat. "And you need to figure it out *before* it happens."

TWENTY-TWO

RAJAN AWAKENS TO his head pounding.

For a second, he doesn't know where he is. The leather couch is unfamiliar. As is the crystal table in front of him, the fireplace, and the floor-to-ceiling window allowing sunlight to assault his eyes—

Shit.

Memories of last night flood back. The cops. Sukha. His father. Nick and Zohra. And . . . his eyes fall on the table. The remnants of what he's done, still there.

Unexpected disappointment crushes him. He drops his head back to the cushion. *Why?* Why couldn't he just hold on? He got *so far*, and now it's for nothing.

But god help him . . . it felt *good*. And if that isn't the part that makes him feel the shittiest—how, in the moment, it was a *relief* to relapse. Like finally coming home after months. As if no time had passed; as if all the cravings he fought, and the drug rehab he went through, didn't matter. As if it never will. Because whether he's one week, one year, or one lifetime away from his last cocaine binge, it will only ever really be one bad day away.

Nick chooses that moment to walk into the room. "Oh, you're alive?" He plops onto the opposite couch, voice gratingly loud. "In case you were wondering, Simran got home safe. Don't worry. I doubt she'll report you."

Rajan glares. He did *not* need the reminder that Simran saw him like that, too. "I get it, okay? I fucked up."

"That's not why I'm here." Nick tosses a bunch of books on the table between them.

Rajan struggles to his elbows to squint at them. Patterned hardcover notebooks, the nice-stationery types. "What—"

"Have you already forgotten you were begging to help find a book-keeper?" Nick taps one of the notebooks. "Here's the accounts. I've been researching these people. If you were serious about wanting to help, this is your chance."

Slowly, Rajan takes one. It takes his sluggish brain several seconds to make sense of what he's seeing. Pages and pages of *names*, each corresponding to a different code. Four-digit codes . . . just like those used in the ledgers. This is the key to it all.

Simran would probably drool over this information. Rajan, however, just rubs his eyes. "It's six in the fucking morning. Can't we do this later?"

"No." Nick picks up a ledger, too. "These records don't leave this house."

Sighing, Rajan sits upright. Instant vertigo forces his eyes closed. He kind of, sort of, very much wishes he could do a line right now to wake himself up. He already broke his sobriety streak. What's the point of trying again?

"I know that look on your face," Nick says. Rajan opens his eyes to find him staring. "And the answer is no. You're brainless when you're using."

Rajan scowls and returns to reading. Potential candidates have already been highlighted, with notes stuck in the pages. Nick's clearly

been doing some light stalking on clients. There's an economics professor. An accountant. A financial consultant . . . Rajan lowers the book.
"Couldn't you pay off any of these people?"

"I'm looking for something specific."

"Which is?"

"Vulnerability," Nick says simply. "For example, take Brenckmann's
file over there. Highly regarded accountant. And careful. His assistant
picks up product for him. The guy practically never leaves his office. No
one has anything on him. Therefore, he's not a good mark."

Rajan, undeterred, flips to Brenckmann and opens his envelope.
Lots of info on Brenckmann, but Rajan focuses on the assistant. She's
an international student, runs all his errands, prepares his presentations.
Probably wipes his ass, too. Rajan studies the blurry photo. It's a candid
of a woman with a black ponytail and work uniform crossing a street. A
gas station sign looms overhead, one he recognizes from downtown.

"You've gotta really trust your assistant if they're picking up your
drugs," Rajan murmurs. "But she's got a second job, too."

"So?"

"So the first doesn't pay enough. Your accountant's stingy with his
employees. He may not be vulnerable, but *she* is."

Nick leans over and snatches the book from his hands for another look.
Rajan picks up another in the meantime. Opening it makes him pause—
it's got Simran's handwriting in it. She must've been using it last night. Her
calculations cascade down the page, much harder to follow after the fact.
If he was there, she would've explained as she was doing them. But he
wasn't there. So instead all he can do is stare at her writing and add it to the
list of things he's missed out on because he was getting high.

As if on cue, his phone chimes—a reminder for Hillway this afternoon. Fantastic. He has no desire to face Simran today. That's the worst
part of a comedown—the consequences. Of course, if he keeps using, he
won't have to face any . . .

Cut it out, he tells himself firmly. Out loud, he says, "So what do you
think?"

"Not viable." Nick throws down the book. "She may be desperate for money, but she's not gonna sell out her boss. He's her best source of income. You need an angle to make people *want* to cooperate."

Rajan takes another book from the pile. They read in silence until the sounds of voices from downstairs float through the vent. Nick looks out the window. "You should go."

It's not even eight. "But—"

"If I were you," Nick interrupts, "I'd leave before people start waking up. You don't have many fans around here."

It's a little too similar to what Zohra said yesterday. "So? That's never been a problem before."

Nick shrugs. "Stay, then." He props his feet on the table. "I like you being here anyway. It's like old times."

That gets Rajan to his feet. "That's not what this was." He throws the ledger at Nick's chest.

Nick catches it, looking amused. He doesn't argue. He just taps the tattoo on his neck, and Rajan can almost feel his burn in response. "Sure it wasn't."

By the time Rajan sulks home, it's midmorning and everyone's gone. Good. He doesn't want to face his family. It's obvious what he did all night, proof his dad was right. And the idea that Sukha might follow in his footsteps with *this*, too, makes him want to get fucked up again. Which he knows doesn't make much sense, but in his brain it does.

He compromises by crashing until it's time for Hillway. Today's volunteering session is at the public library, and when he arrives, most of the other volunteers are already dispersed. Simran's the only mentor still standing at the door with—Neetu, he recognizes. Her friend.

Simran spots him first. God, kill him now. But when he reaches them, she smiles.

"Neetu's a librarian here," she tells him. "She's managing the group today."

There's a fakeness to that smile. They're putting on a performance, then. He turns to Neetu, and Neetu explains their task for the day. They're cleaning up after a Nerf war organized by the teen book club yesterday; many rubber Nerf darts are still missing after the initial collection.

"This feels like a made-up job," Rajan comments once she's handed them a basket.

Neetu laughs. "It's not. Last time we had a Nerf war, I was finding darts in bookshelves for months. I'd rather not have to keep buying more. Do you know how much those things cost?"

And with that, she directs them upstairs to begin their search.

But even when they're left alone on the top floor, Simran still says nothing to him. Minutes pass. Eventually, Rajan can't take it anymore. "Should we talk about yesterday?"

Simran's scouring the place with her eyes. "We should look for darts."

So that's how she's gonna play it. She'll ignore his vices if he ignores hers.

But he *can't* ignore hers. He grits his teeth, knowing he's about to open himself up to this. "You have to keep boundaries around this bookkeeping thing. If they think you're open to getting called whenever . . ."

"I know. I just needed to take my mind off things." Her fingers twitch. "My mom had surgery yesterday."

Oh. He watches her carefully. "And?"

"It went fine." She strides off in the direction of the computers. After a moment, he follows. She can't possibly think he bought that.

He backs off, though, and they comb through the top floor in silence—first around the computers, then between rows of books. It's easy. All he has to do is picture a shootout, where the last stand might've taken place, and the bullets are right where he imagines.

"You're good at this," Simran comments after they've filled half their basket.

He bends to pluck a dart from where it's suctioned to the bottom of a bookshelf. "Yeah, I'm your guy if you want to strategize a gunfight or finesse all the coke off its paper. Not much else."

"That's not true."

He drops the dart into the basket. "You saw me last night. You know it is." He can't help how bitter he sounds.

"What I saw last night was my friend making a mistake. Like we all do. It doesn't mean he can't come back from it."

He pauses to peek at her. She sounded so angry last night, yet now her expression is soft. Damn it. Why can't she just be disgusted like everyone else? Then he could lean into his little relapse knowing he'd already disappointed her, and there was nothing to lose.

After a moment, he heads into the next aisle. "Your friend sounds like a fucking loser. Who is this dude?"

He hears her amused little huff and grins to himself, feeling lighter.

They search several more aisles without luck. At some point, Simran stops searching to pull a book off the shelf. Rajan throws a dart at her back. "Focus on the task, Simran Auntie."

She brushes the dart off. "*I'm* not the one doing mandatory community service hours."

"Smartass," he says, delighted she's joking with him again. "Can't believe you're abandoning me for some book about"—he ducks to read the cover, but she returns it to the shelf— "nerdy shit."

She picks up another. "Maybe reading some 'nerdy shit' now and then would do you some good."

Swear words are so funny coming from her mouth. "Why don't you read it *to* me, Sahiba," he suggests, leaning his good shoulder against the bookcase. "In your sexy, monotone voice."

Simran rolls her eyes and throws the book at his chest. He catches it with a grin, then reshelves it. As Simran moves on, he pauses at the other book she had so quickly shelved when he came by. "Why are you interested in—*Mathematics in Cryptography?*"

"School."

Rajan might've accepted this normally, but there's something about her perfectly neutral tone that has him opening the book up. Hell *no*.

"Code breaking?" Suddenly, he knows *exactly* what this is about.

"Don't tell me you're stuck on that note in the Aces' ledger. That was weeks ago."

Her eyes dart away. "I still haven't figured it out."

"And *nobody* is asking you to." He almost face-palms. This is so typical of her. "Leave it alone or they'll—"

He stops because of footsteps behind him. Simran's eyes flick over his shoulder and widen. When Rajan turns, there's a brown guy their age approaching. Bright eyes, scruffy jaw, one of those modern-style turbans, a gym bag slung over his shoulder. Rajan dismissively turns back to Simran, but then she says, "Hi, Jassa," in the most fake peppy voice he's ever heard.

And the guy responds, "Hey, Simran."

Wait. *Wait.* Rajan unwillingly glances back. Jassa is looking only at Simran.

Rajan doesn't need math skills to add it up. *This* is the guy who stood her up. The one she's *into*. Rajan side-eyes him as he comes closer, his dismay growing. Not only is this guy jacked, but he looks like a *Vogue India* model.

"I was on my way out and saw you," the guy says. "What's up?"

Simran twirls her kara around her wrist. "I'm actually volunteering right now. This is my mentee at Hillway House." She nods to Rajan. "Rajan, this is Jassa Singh. A friend . . . from school." Her smile is big and wavering and . . . dammit, she so desperately wants this to go well.

Rajan pastes a bullshit smile on his mouth. Simran owes him bigtime for this. "Hey."

Jassa nods at him. "Nice to meet you."

The dude has said his hello. It's time for him to get lost, but he doesn't. Instead, Simran strikes up a conversation with him about some school thing. Feigning boredom, Rajan flips through the book in his hands without reading a word. From the conversation, he gathers several things: Jassa's involved in all kinds of committees, like her, and goes to the gurdwara, like her, and apparently plays a mean tabla, and is also really smart. They start talking biochemistry at one point and his brain melts— Is this the kind of talk Simran actually *enjoys*? Does she consider her conversations with Rajan mind-numbing in comparison?

Finally, Jassa says, "I should probably get going."

"Where to?" Why does she *care*?

"My martial arts club."

"Martial arts?" Pause. "That explains a lot."

Jassa laughs lowly. "Does it?"

Rajan's *this* close to banging his head against the bookshelf. Simran mutters, "I've only ever seen that stuff on TV."

"You could come watch, if you want. Fridays are fight nights. We could have another crack at your cousin's code, too."

What code? *Another* crack at it? Rajan turns just in time to see Simran stiffen. She never told him she met up with Jassa again. And . . . Jassa couldn't be talking about the Ace code. Surely Simran's not going around giving randos information out of a gang ledger. *Surely.*

Simran doesn't return Rajan's pointed stare, which confirms she is. "Maybe. I'll text you later." She speaks to Rajan without looking at him. "We should go wrap up."

Rajan snaps the book shut. "Yeah, you really *should* wrap this shit up."

Jassa glances at him again, this time somewhat warily, but doesn't comment.

He accompanies them down the stairs, even hanging around while Simran hands in the darts basket to Neetu and signs them out. It's only at the exit doors that he nods at Rajan again. "Nice to meet you. Maybe I'll see you around."

Preferably when Rajan's bludgeoning him with a baseball bat. "Maybe."

He disappears, and Simran looks ready to escape to the parking lot. Rajan catches up. "He knows about the Ace code."

She doesn't deny it. "I thought he'd be able to help."

"What if he figured it out? What if the message was creepy and illegal?"

"I would've come up with an explanation."

He stares at her as they enter the parking garage. Coming from a person whose logic he once implicitly trusted, this is really something. "Dude, you're obsessed. You have to stop before you get hurt." He definitely needs to get the Lions their new accountant. Fast.

Simran's lips flatten, a telltale sign of her annoyance. "Are you upset I told him or upset I met with him?"

Oh, she went there. "Both. Didn't he stand you up?"

"He had a family emergency."

"So? He could've at least answered his fucking phone."

She unlocks her truck as they approach it. "Rajan, it's fine. You don't need to act like some kind of overprotective relative. I have enough of those already."

A relative? *Relative?* Rajan actually stops walking for a second. Is *that* how she sees him now? Evidently even Simran thinks she went too far, because she stops, too. "That's not what I meant."

Rajan wrenches her truck door open for her. At this rate he wouldn't be surprised if she tried to tie a rakhri on him. "Never mind. If you wanna see him again, fine, he's clearly into you. Just . . . don't bring the Lions into it, all right?"

"Okay," she whispers. God, she really *is* going to see him again. Probably when he's in a boxing ring because she's *oh so interested* in martial arts..

While he's wrestling these incredibly stupid thoughts back, he almost—*almost*—misses the shadow crossing her face.

"What? What's wrong? You don't like him anymore?"

Simran slowly buckles herself into her seat. Her truck is high enough off the ground that they're at eye level. "How do you know he's into me?"

"I know what people look like when they're into someone." And thank god Simran doesn't.

She bites her lip. "I don't know how to do any of this."

Rajan's every sense is suddenly on high alert. "Any of what?"

"Well, everything." She swallows. "Like . . . what if he kisses me?"

Jesus. Christ. Rajan takes his cap off to run a hand through his hair. "What about it?" he says moodily. Imagining Simran kissing that dickhead has him wanting to go back upstairs to the library just so he can throw himself down. "If you like him, go for it."

"I don't know how to kiss. I've never done it." Her words are whispered. He can't be sure, but she seems embarrassed.

Slowly, Rajan puts his cap back on. This conversation is literal torture, but it isn't about him. It's about *her*. The fact that she's asking him for advice shows she really has no one else.

So he says, as evenly as possible, "That's okay. It's usually a little awkward at first."

"I don't want it to be awkward. I want to do this right Can you even kiss with glasses on?"

He barks out a laugh. Yet another mental image he didn't need. Simran, taking off her glasses to kiss someone. Someone else kissing her back. Someone else touching her.

Simran fiddles with her braid. "Never mind, I—"

Rajan takes a long, slow, deep breath. "You can kiss with glasses. But if you're having a full make-out session, you should probably take them off."

"I don't know how to do that either."

She sounds troubled by the fact. It's kind of funny "You can't be perfect at everything from the start, dude. I'm sure you had to work on your singing skills, too."

"Well, yes," she bursts, "but with singing I *practice* before I perform."

Their eyes meet. In that moment, Rajan swears everything else fades into the background. She's in the driver's seat half facing him, one hand dangling from the wheel, the breeze coming into the parking garage stirring her hair loose from its braid. Those long-lashed eyes, huge behind her glasses. Her half-parted, half-parched lips.

Rajan is sure the same thought passes through her head as through his.

He never, ever allows his brain to go there. Never. If it starts sliding that way, he thinks about the least sexy things he can think of. Gunshot wounds. Socks with Crocs. Nick's goatee. But she's sitting there now, and it's too late, because the thought has seeded in his mind, a possibility of kissing her with no consequences, only to *help*—and it's all his brain needs to slide there all at once.

He'd put his hand under the base of her braid and gently tug her in. He'd press his lips to hers—chastely at first, to get a feel of her, to let her get used to him. Once her body relaxed, he'd go for it. He has a feeling she'd like that. That she would sigh and reach for him, too. He'd unbuckle the seat belt at her hip to pull her right to the edge of her seat and into his arms. She would say his name. He'd kiss her until that was the only thing she could remember—

His phone buzzes in his pocket. He blinks back to reality. Simran is still gazing at him with an indecipherable expression. With Herculean effort, he steps back. "Stop worrying. You'll figure it out."

He didn't realize she was holding her breath until she exhales, sticking her key in the ignition. Her hand is shaking. "Right. See you later, then."

"Later, Sahiba," he whispers. Closes her door gently. He remains standing there as she drives off.

Rajan knows Simran wanted him to kiss her. It *killed* him not to. Problem is, it might just be practice for her, but for him, it'd be like someone put a line of coke in front of him. He can't have only one. He'd keep going; he would tell himself he could stop, but he wouldn't. The consequences wouldn't matter. He would devour her until there was nothing left, and even then, he would be craving her for the rest of his life.

And she never asked for that—she just asked for one kiss.

He shakes his head and checks his phone for the text he got. Probably Yash, pestering him for Oreos again—

It's not Yash. Rajan stares. This has to be some kind of cosmic joke.

The message is from that hard-ass social worker at Kat's office. It has an attachment, and it reads: I will have to send this to your PO. I am giving you a heads-up as a courtesy. I recommend that you attend that appointment, as another breach will not do you any favours.

Rajan clicks on the attachment. It's a photo—of himself. Blurry, but unmistakably his black hoodie, unmistakably him at Manny Khullar's mansion last night, unmistakably with a white line in front of him that even now, he has trouble tearing his eyes away from. The angle is from a corner of the room. Rajan doesn't even remember this moment or who would've been there to witness it.

But he knows that it happened. And now Kat will, too.

TWENTY-THREE

WHEN RAJAN'S NAME gets called by Kat's secretary at his next appointment, he considers walking out.

He's been in the waiting room debating the merits of doing so for the past five minutes. But as the social worker said, if he misses a check-in, that's yet another breach. They could put out an arrest warrant. And wouldn't Officer Dipshit love the excuse to track him down?

Was it worth it? some voice in his head taunts as he heads to Kat's office. *Did it solve your problems? No. Your shoulder still hurts, your mom's still dead, Simran's still with the Lions, and Sukha's still headed the same way. You actually made your life worse. Congrats! We all know it won't stop you from doing it again.*

Man, his subconscious is a real asshole.

The real question, of course, is who ratted him out. Nick? But that doesn't make sense anymore. Nick got what he wanted through Simran. So, maybe someone else at the party. If what Zohra said was true, and the Lions have stopped trusting him, it could've been anyone.

When Rajan enters Kat's office, she's busy at her filing cabinet, wearing yet another Ms. Frizzle–like dress. A familiar sight now. He's been here several times since that day with the broken frame, and she goes off-script often to ask him about his life. His past. His family. Sometimes he answers; sometimes he tells her to back off. He suspects he's become her test case for counseling strategies, because she knows he's safe.

He hadn't realized until right now, listening to her hum, that he took pride in that. In being *trustworthy*.

She turns and beams. "Rajan. Come in."

He sinks into his chair. That doesn't sound like the voice of someone who's sending him back to court. Right?

Kat sits down with his file. Immediately, he notices a red sticky note poking out.

She flips through the first few documents, occasionally commenting ("Glad you enjoyed the library," "Simran speaks highly of you in her reviews," "Have you thought about continuing volunteering after probation's finished? I think it'd be good for you."). He only half pays attention. She'll get to the (literal) red flag soon enough.

He puts his feet up on her table, since this'll probably be his last opportunity. The photo frame is still noticeably absent. "What happened to your photo?" The more he talks, the longer he can delay the inevitable.

Kat glances at the empty stretch of desk. "I haven't gotten a new frame yet." She flips through his file some more. She's about to reach it. His sense of dread climbs. "Who is it in the photo, anyway?" he asks, and *that* makes her fingers pause, a few pages away from the red sticky.

"My son."

She starts flipping again. Shit, shit, shit— "Is he batshit like you?"

Luckily, his blatant attempts at distraction make her pause again. "I wouldn't know." She glances at the wall calendar. "He died nearly eight years ago."

Oh. He starts feeling actual curiosity. Screw it, no one's ever accused Rajan of being tactful. "How?"

"Shot dead." When he stares, her smile becomes a little sad. "That's why I do what I do."

And before he can ask more, she flips to the last page.

The red flag is taped to it, and Kat's smile falters. This is it. Rajan's lack of control is coolly laid out on that page for anyone to see. Humiliated, he stares at the desk, gritting his teeth, waiting, waiting—

Kat flips the page. "Have you thought about going back to school?"

Wait, what? Hesitantly, he looks up. Her expression remains neutral. Was he imagining things?

Maybe that red sticky was always there. Some older page he didn't notice until now. Maybe the social worker hasn't had a chance to send the photo yet, or Kat didn't see the email.

Rajan relaxes slightly. Topic changes are good, even if they're fucking annoying topics. "I don't like textbooks."

"Education doesn't have to mean classrooms or textbooks. You should give yourself a chance to explore something you might enjoy doing."

"What if I enjoy roofing?" When she gives him a pointed look, he shrugs. "Who cares if I like my job? It's just a job." Kat smiles a bit. "What?"

"Sometimes you don't talk much like an eighteen-year-old boy."

"Dude, are you saying I sound old?"

"And other times you sound very much your age." Her smile turns wry. "Most teenagers care a lot about their futures. You haven't had that luxury—you grew up too fast. That means some people will mistake you for an adult, and will want to treat you that way . . . and punish you that way, too."

Her fingers toy with the red sticky. Rajan's breath stalls. This is the moment, isn't it, where she—

Kat closes his file completely. "What do you think your strengths are?"

"My— What?" He's still staring at the sticky.

"Your strengths. Might help you decide where to go from here." At his expression, she adds, "You were successful in criminal activities because you have valuable skills. Creativity. Resourcefulness. An ability to make decisions in high-pressure situations. The Lion's Share recognized them. You should, too."

"Right."

"I'm serious. Have you gotten rid of that tree in your yard yet, by the way?"

Rajan gives her a wary look. She's asked him this before, and each time he's had the same answer. "No. Why do you keep asking?"

"Just wondering why you haven't."

He picks a toothpick from his pocket. "It's maple, you know. People pay for that shit. I was gonna get a chain saw from work and see if I could cut it up, but I dunno. It's probably rotten anyway." He stops because he doesn't like the change in Kat's expression. Like she thinks the fact that he hasn't gotten rid of a fucking tree means something. It doesn't.

But Kat's right about at least one thing: The LS knows how to recruit talent. Simran's a prime example. Sometimes, the best targets are the ones who aren't immediately obvious. He thinks back to Nick's files of potential bookkeepers. *Those* were all fairly obvious picks, but only one stayed on his mind—that accountant, Brenckmann. Yet, it wasn't Brenckmann himself that intrigued him.

Rajan sits up. "Actually, there *is* a different job I wanna try."

She brightens. "Really? What is it?"

She looks so hopeful, he almost feels bad as he says, "The Chevron on the highway."

Kat blinks. "The . . . gas station?"

Ick. "Yeah. Could I get in there? Just see how it goes?"

Kat's eyebrows have reached her hairline by this point. "I'll admit, I didn't think you would enjoy customer service—"

"Can you get me the job or not?"

She studies him. He holds her gaze. Finally, she exhales. "I'll see what I can do. We might have to reduce your hours at the roofing company to follow your probation conditions, that's all." She pushes his file away. "We're done for today."

He rises, feeling invigorated. *Finally*, a lead to follow, even if Nick doesn't agree. Something tells him there's more to that accountant's assistant than meets the eye. After all, how does a new international student get a job like that, working for a prestigious accounting firm? If he can figure her out, he's one step closer to freeing Simran.

He's almost at the door when he remembers the red sticky. He turns to find Kat watching him. "Was there . . . anything else we were supposed to talk about today?"

Kat tilts her head. "Did we miss something?"

Her question hangs in the air. Has she been waiting for him to confess? Is this some kind of fucked-up test?

Rajan's never been good at tests.

"Nope," he says. "Nothing."

TWENTY-FOUR

IT'S JUNE 18. The date in the ledger.

Simran sits hunched over her desk, half dressed in jeans and a pajama top, crumpling up another idea that's gotten her nowhere. She tosses it in her overflowing wastebasket.

Every night for the past week, she's stayed up until sunrise with the Aces' code. Her father thinks all her time at her desk is spent getting ahead of coursework. Her mother, however, has barely noticed. She's been in a lot of pain since returning home from her surgery a few days ago. Speaking of . . . Simran should probably check on her before she leaves.

Sighing, she selects a random T-shirt from her closet. TJ's dinner is tonight, and although a large part of her wants to ignore it, she already slept through kirtan practice with Neetu today. Besides, she *promised* TJ. So the cipher will have to wait.

After rebraiding her hair, she knocks on her parents' bedroom door. "Mom? I'm going out for a bit." No answer. Simran pushes inside. "Mom?" The bed is unmade; the adjoining bathroom door is open. Simran peeks through, and her heart stops.

Her mom is hunched over the side of the toilet.

Simran skids to her side, trying not to panic. "What's going on?" There's vomit in the bowl. "When did this start?"

Her mother only gags, lurching for the toilet again. Simran instinctively holds her hair back, the once-shiny waves a mass of greasy tendrils. Is this supposed to be normal? "I'll get the pain meds."

"I don't need them."

"Mom—"

"I used to hate my womb, you know." Her mom lifts her head from the bowl, her face flushed and sweaty. "It wouldn't help me. I'd almost given up on it when you came along." She hiccups. "I *made* you in there. And now it's gone."

Simran doesn't know what to say. She'd never considered her mother might be attached to the organ that was trying to kill her. And when she hiccups again, this time sounding suspiciously like a sob, Simran makes a decision. Forget her plans, forget the cipher. "Let's go to the ER."

At the mention of the ER, her mother's entire demeanour changes. She sits up. "No. I'm fine."

"Mom, you're throwing up."

"So?" She sniffs, somehow regal despite grasping a toilet for support. "It's good. I'm getting rid of toxins."

Simran would laugh if she weren't scared. "I'm not sure that's how it works."

"I thought you had plans today."

So she *did* hear. "It—doesn't matter. I'm not leaving you like this."

"Yes, you are." Her mother wipes her mouth, sounding more lucid. "Your father will be home soon. Go. Or are you just looking for a reason to be late? Is it so painful to be on time for once?"

Despite herself, Simran smiles. "Maybe a little."

Her mother smiles too and pinches her cheek. Maybe it's like Kiran said—she just likes being dramatic. And it's with that reassuring thought, and the knowledge that her dad will be home in a few minutes, that Simran finally departs with a kiss to her mother's forehead.

———

When Simran rings the doorbell of TJ's house, TJ's mom opens it, wearing a button-down cardigan and slacks, her black hair curling loosely around her shoulders. She's much younger than Simran's mom, and she looks it. When she sees Simran, she blinks in surprise.

"Sat Sri Akaal, Masi ji," Simran says.

"Simran!" TJ's mom recovers quickly. "It's been too long. Come in, have chah?"

Her question hangs in the air. Despite the warm welcome, Simran senses the tense undercurrent. She doesn't want Simran around, tonight of all nights, when TJ's bringing her boyfriend home. She's hoping Simran's only here to run a quick errand.

No such luck. "Sure, Masi ji. I thought I'd come see TJ. She just arrived, right?" She holds out the container of ras malai she bought on her way. No one can say Simran doesn't fully invest in her scams. "But if now's not a good time . . ."

Simran can practically see her aunt's ingrained manners battling her panic. "No, no, of course! It's just—we're expecting a guest very soon."

Simran widens her eyes. "I'm sorry. I should've asked before coming. I'll come tomorrow." She turns to leave. Three, two, one—

"No!" her masi practically shouts. "No, of course you should come in."

Simran turns, the picture of contrition. "Are you sure? It isn't a big deal—"

"You *must* come in."

With a helpless shrug that suggests this was all her aunt's idea, Simran strolls inside. Her masi sighs behind her. Simran bites back a smile. If nothing else, playing this role is at least an amusing diversion.

Her amusement ends when her masi says, "How's your mom?"

Simran takes her shoes off. "Fine, why?"

"I heard she hasn't been attending events lately." When Simran gives her a surprised look, she shrugs. "We have some mutual friends. I just wondered . . . She's okay, right?"

Something in her voice is less than casual. It reminds Simran that she and her aunt were both raised by the same woman.

Simran faces her. "Yes, she's okay."

Her masi's face breaks into relief. "Good. Good."

That relief twists Simran's gut with jealousy. She wishes she could tell the truth. She wishes she could drag her masi out of her peace. Then, at least, Simran wouldn't have to endure this alone.

TJ's dad appears in the doorway. There are bags under his eyes from his night-shift work, but he smiles at her. Simran automatically slides back into socializing mode, going to hug him. "Are you on your way to work, Massar ji?"

"Uh, no." He exchanges a glance with his wife. "We're having a guest."

Simran looks between them, smiling guilelessly. "Really? Who?"

Her masi seems to panic and glances at the staircase. "TJ!" she yells. There's a note of strain in it.

A moment later, footsteps run down the stairs. Simran would recognize those bounding footfalls anywhere. And despite herself, a real smile pulls at her mouth as she turns to face her.

Her cousin TJ always brims with energy, and today is no different. She barely comes to a halt on the last stair, her brown eyes sparkling. Her dark hair is tossed up into a messy bun. She's dressed in a form-fitting black sweater, jeans, and simple makeup. She and Simran don't look much alike—aside from how hairy they both are. Those genes are *very* strong.

"Simran!" TJ hops off the last stair. Simran steps right into her perfumed embrace. "I missed you," her cousin murmurs, leaning her fuzzy cheek against Simran's equally fuzzy one, and Simran finds herself relaxing into it. They rock from foot to foot, and for some reason, tears prick at Simran's eyes. She missed being hugged like this. Tightly, carefree, as much a comfort to her as it is to the other.

By the time TJ steps away, Simran has pulled herself together. She clears her throat. "I heard you're having guests. I can come back later."

TJ jumps up and down as if they haven't rehearsed this. "No! This is perfect. It's Charlie. He'd love to see you. I think he misses having you in all his student council stuff. How long has it been?"

"At least since graduation."

TJ's dad parts the window curtains and squints; headlights hit his face. "Does he drive a sedan?"

"*Dad,*" TJ groans. "Get away from the window." She looks at Simran, pitching her voice low. "See what I'm dealing with?"

"Want me to say a prayer?"

TJ smacks her arm. There's a knock on the door, and TJ freezes. She and her parents stare at it like they're in a horror movie and the killer has found them. After a moment, Simran goes to open the door herself. "Hi, Charlie."

Charlie stands in the doorway bearing a bouquet of flowers. He blinks; clearly, he wasn't told to expect her. But then he gives her a warm, wide smile. It strikes her that he looks older now. High school really is behind them. But his brown hair is parted in his familiar neat style, and he's dressed in a navy button-down and white chinos—always erring on the side of formal. "Simran. Haven't heard from you in a while."

"Sorry. I got busy." It's true she doesn't text anymore. Charlie's too close to TJ—and apparently gets his phone stolen by her a lot—for Simran to risk it. "I hear you're here for dinner."

"Yes. You should stay, if you can. We need to catch up."

He might just be acting polite, but Simran doesn't think so. Their countless caucuses between council meetings in high school led to an inevitable friendship. It'd sure be nice to have a friend on council these days. She's missed him, she realizes right then. She's missed a *lot* while she was shutting everyone out.

"Of course." Simran opens the door wider, revealing TJ and her parents behind her. "This is a family event."

Simran has to hand it to Charlie. He does everything right.

He never once implies his relationship with TJ is anything but platonic. He sits on the opposite end of the table, next to Simran and TJ's dad. He barely even speaks to TJ directly. If you didn't know better, you might think she and Charlie were just acquaintances, although Simran does catch them having prolonged staring contests when the parents are otherwise distracted.

Simran suspects he and TJ had a lengthy strategic meeting prior to this dinner. Particularly to prep for the seemingly innocuous questions about his *career goals* and *family background*. He handles them all well. Charlie's always been good at making people feel comfortable.

As the conversation continues to flow easily, she grows restless. What was TJ worrying about, anyway? Simran isn't needed here. She could be working on the cipher right now—there's only hours left to solve it.

At the thought, she glances down at the checkered tablecloth. She's got no pen, but she has her imagination. She mentally lays the letters out. One letter per square. The long string of letters runs off the tablecloth. She rearranges them, breaking the string into several lines so it can stay contained in a grid next to her plate for easy viewing. Pleased, she picks up where she last left off.

Eons later, TJ's mom says, "Well, let's eat some of that ras malai Simran brought."

Simran, who has gotten nowhere with the cipher, immediately rises. "I'll get it."

She doesn't realize she's been followed to the kitchen until TJ grabs her arm.

"TJ, I've got it—"

"Stop for a second." TJ searches her eyes. "Is everything okay?"

Simran stills. "Why wouldn't it be?"

"Because you're somewhere else. This whole time." TJ gestures to the dining room. "You're nodding, you're smiling, but you're not really here. I *knew* I wasn't just imagining it on the phone."

Simran's silent. She thought she was doing an excellent job acting okay. What about her performance was lacking?

TJ goes on. "Did anything happen while I've been gone?"

Everything. Everything.

"My grades weren't as good this semester as usual," Simran says. "I didn't get the academic award." She spins another believable lie. "My parents weren't happy."

TJ winces. She gets what a big deal grades are to Simran. Well, *were*. "What did they say?"

"I'm grounded. I barely got out for this." It's not the first time she's used the strict-parents excuse. Although she feels guilty painting them that way, especially when her father's currently home caring for her sick mother, it's the perfect way to get TJ off her back. "Don't expect to see me much for a while."

"What the *hell*?" TJ looks outraged. "Your parents need to chill out. No one tries harder in school than you. How long are you grounded?"

Simran shrugs. TJ looks even more indignant, but luckily, at that moment, her father pokes his head in. "Everything okay?"

TJ snatches the ras malai before Simran can. "Yep."

They return to the dining room, but as TJ sets the bowl of ras malai down, she looks sharply at Simran again. "Oh my god. I totally forgot. Chandani told me you and her ran into—" she glances at her parents— "you'll never guess—*Rajan Randhawa* a few weeks ago?"

Simran sits slowly. Honestly, she's surprised this didn't come up before. Of course Chandani told her. "Yes."

"Randhawa?" her masi asks curiously. "I remember his mother. Shame, what happened to Arshdeep. No wonder her boys are so lost."

Finally, someone granting Rajan leeway. But TJ waves it off. "Okay, but did you hear what he did? Chandani told me."

"Well, yes," her mother says. "*That* part is horrible."

Simran's heart sinks. Charlie, meanwhile, sets down his spoon. "Why? What did he do?"

TJ turns to him with glee. "Apparently he *killed* somebody."

Her mother tuts. Her father, who's been helping himself to ras malai, pauses to shake his head.

TJ continues. "Plus he got charged with weapons possession and stuff. I heard he's in a gang. He's got the tattoo and everything." She jabs her finger at Simran triumphantly. "I *knew* there was always something deeply wrong with that guy."

"Yes, because you're the most well-adjusted of all of us," Charlie says. TJ rolls her eyes.

"Well, I haven't *killed anyone* yet, Charlie—"

"He didn't," Simran says.

All eyes turn to her. Simran seals her lips, but it's too late. Even Charlie looks somewhat bemused. *Why* did she say that? How can she explain knowing the true story behind Rajan's arrest? To give herself time, she takes off her glasses to polish them with her shirt. "I mean," she mutters, "I'm pretty sure it was an accident, what happened."

When she puts her glasses back on, everyone is giving her strange looks.

"An *accident?*" TJ scoffs. "Simran, I know you're a softy, but puh-*lease*. You don't get that involved in a gang without doing horrible things."

Simran says nothing. As usual, she can't deny the facts. Rajan is *not* innocent. Even if he didn't kill Jai, she knows what he used to do for the Lions. Her stance is objectively naive. And yet.

Surprisingly, it's Charlie who speaks up. "Why can't it have been an accident?"

TJ rounds on him, thankfully taking her intensity off Simran. "What's *that* supposed to mean?"

"Just that no matter their background, people deserve to be innocent until proven guilty."

"He *was* proven guilty," TJ scoffs. "In court. That's literally why he went to juvie."

Simran suppresses the urge to correct TJ about the plea deal. Knowing that level of detail would only make her look more pathetic. Luckily, Charlie again comes to her aid.

"Were *you* in that courtroom?" He tilts his head at TJ. "We don't know what discussions were had there. What if it was full of people as quick as you to judge based on heuristics?"

"Are you seriously building a case off of Simran thinking it was an accident?" TJ's nostrils flare. "You literally found out about this thirty seconds ago and you're already playing devil's advocate, this has to be a record. You don't even know what happened. There. Are. *Facts.*"

"And you're choosing to read the facts a certain way," Charlie retorts. "A familiar way—"

As their voices rise, TJ's dad shoots Simran an alarmed look. Simran shakes her head. She knows TJ and Charlie well enough to recognize the difference between their serious disputes and flirting. And they're both definitely hot under the collar right now.

But Charlie . . . she hadn't expected that. She's never heard *anyone* defend Rajan. Ever. Her respect for him grows. Even if it was a theoretical exercise for him, he made a good point.

Her eyes fall back to the cipher she's mentally drawn on the tablecloth. The letters continue to rearrange themselves as Charlie's words from a second ago echo. *You're choosing to read the facts a certain way. A familiar way.*

She pauses. Wait.

She runs her eyes over her letters—the way she always automatically does. Left to right. But with the letters stacked on top of each other, in grid format, she realizes something very important: There's more than one direction to read them.

Meanwhile, TJ is saying, "Simran can *handle* him? Do you hear yourself? He ran somebody over! On purpose!"

Simran stands abruptly. "I'm going to the washroom."

No one seems to hear; TJ's parents are clearly engrossed in the argument before them. So Simran excuses herself down the hall to the bathroom.

Once she locks the door behind her, she takes a long strip of toilet paper and lays it on the edge of the bathtub, then digs through the drawers. In her haste, a few items clatter to the ground. She ignores them, pausing to select a dusty eyeliner pencil. Then she kneels next to her makeshift paper to write.

mnmaoiotuybovonpluerdlutiyeaesnfrcsivrpeedeoltme

There are forty-eight letters. She needs a grid with forty-eight cells. But what dimensions for the grid? Forty-eight has so many divisors.

One and forty-eight are automatically disqualified. She decides to skip two-by-twelve, and starts at a three-by-sixteen grid.

m	n	m	a	o	i	o	t	u	y	b	o	v	o	n	p
l	u	e	r	d	l	u	t	i	y	e	a	e	s	n	f
r	c	s	i	v	r	p	e	e	d	e	o	l	t	m	e

No sensical message when she looks top to bottom, vice versa, or diagonally. Undeterred, she next draws a sixteen-by-three grid. Then four-by-twelve.

Someone knocks on the door.

"Just a minute!" Her feet are starting to cramp from her squatting position.

"Simran, are you all right?" It's TJ's mom.

"Yes."

"Okay." A pause. "There's pads under the sink if you need them."

"Thanks."

"Also a plunger behind the toilet."

Now this is getting humiliating. "I'm just washing a stain off my shirt."

"Oh, is that all?" She sounds surprised. "Don't worry. You can take one of TJ's."

"Thanks," Simran says without taking her eyes off the grid. "I'm going to give it one more try."

Her masi's footsteps fade, and Simran takes a deep breath. She's *so close*. She can feel it, the frantic energy of an approaching epiphany, gripping every cell in her body.

With trembling fingers, she draws a six-by-eight grid. Runs her eyes over it, column by column.

Her breath catches.

TJ knocks on the door. "Simran, I've got—"

Simran stuffs the wad of toilet paper into her pocket and opens the door. "I have to go."

TJ stares. She's holding a blouse in her hand. "What?"

"I just remembered something I have to do." Simran brushes past her, to the door.

TJ follows. "Where're you going?"

Simran's so frazzled by her own discovery, she can't even think of a lie. "I'll tell you later." She shoves her shoes on. Distantly, the conversation between TJ's parents pauses in the kitchen. Soon they'll come too, and Simran can't handle more questions.

"But—you said you'd stay." TJ sounds bewildered.

Simran pauses. Right. She promised she'd stay overnight. And yet . . .

"I can't." She finds herself rationalizing it as she goes. The dinner's going *well*. Simran staying would only delay the inevitable, big questions TJ's parents want to ask her. Well, TJ can't avoid the big questions about life all the time. Simran's never had that luxury.

"You forgot your jacket!" TJ shouts as Simran flees out the door, but Simran doesn't turn back. She half jogs to her truck, ignoring her masi calling her name. She starts the vehicle.

While turning out of the cul-de-sac, she calls Nick.

He answers after a few rings. "I don't have time to babysit right now. This better be good."

"It's better than good." Simran swerves onto the main road, causing a passing truck to honk. "How do you feel about intercepting that huge shipment the Aces were talking about tonight?"

TWENTY-FIVE

PREDICTABLY, RAJAN HATES his new job.

It's only been three days and he's almost looking forward to returning to jail. At least behind bars, he can cuss people out who irritate him. Here? He has to keep his mouth shut with customers or risk this all being a waste.

He's in the back of the convenience store mopping the floor when his coworker walks by, black ponytail swinging. There she is. The reason he's enduring this hellhole.

Unfortunately, he hasn't learned much about Maya other than her name. She works in the back. She's in her mid-twenties, newly emigrated from India, although he can't tell where specifically. Hard to pin down accents when someone barely talks.

"How's it going?" he asks. She side-eyes him before heading to the front to watch the TV. She probably thinks he's hitting on her, given the number of times he's attempted conversation. With a frustrated sigh, he takes his mop to the back. Nick would laugh his ass off if he knew what Rajan was up to. Three days in, and he's already out of patience.

It's incredible, really. If only there were some way to cope with his failure, to take the edge off his anxiety . . .

No. He drops the bucket and, in the dark of the closet, squeezes his eyes shut. He won't, he can't let himself think about—

Too late. *Would it really be so bad?* some part of him (sounding pretty reasonable, really) questions. *Just for now. You're not like that Oliver guy—once Simran is out of the LS, of course you'll stop, but for now, it'll help you focus. You know where to get it. Take your break and go to the café. You can use some savings on it, it doesn't have to be on Simran's tab.*

Rajan clutches his head. *Distract, distract,* he thinks wildly. But he hasn't used those techniques since juvie, and the impulses are a helluva lot stronger suddenly. What did the shrinks used to say? Something about how cravings shouldn't be seen as something bad, but a natural part of getting clean? It's normal, it's fine. It'll pass. He just has to wait it out.

With fumbling fingers, he reaches into his pocket only to find his toothpick case empty. Jesus. All the stress lately is turning him into a fucking beaver. Well, he's always known that's a shit habit, too. Maybe today music will work.

He jams his earbuds into his ears, but totally blanks on what to play. He needs something new to distract himself—something totally different than his usual.

His mind reaches back for any ideas. And, as often is the case, it lands on a high school memory.

Grade ten, the first time Simran asked what he was listening to during tutoring. Rajan told her to take an earbud and find out. Then he put on a song with extremely offensive lyrics. But she nodded along wisely, the slight uptick of her mouth the only indication she knew she was being messed with.

When it finished, Rajan handed her his phone. She didn't have her own back then.

"Now you choose," he said.

"Me?" She seemed shocked. "I . . . don't think you'll like what I like."

"Simran Auntie, if you can make me *not hate* math sometimes, you can make me like anything."

She blushed. Then she took his phone and carefully typed. Rajan recognized the music immediately—kirtan, basically Sikh hymns. He could see how it relaxed her. She stopped slouching, a light came into her eyes, and as she waited for him to work through a word problem, she *hummed*. He pulled out his own earbud halfway through and confirmed his suspicion that even without the instrumentals, Simran's voice was goddamn angelic.

"What do you think?" she said at the end.

He could tell she was nervous by the way she twirled her kara. "It's a banger," he told her.

The store bell jingles from the door, jarring Rajan back into reality. Whatever, Maya can deal with the customers for once. Strangely, though, he's feeling more in control now. It really *does* pass.

A distant voice from the storefront asks if they have any key chains with bears on them. Rajan rolls his eyes. People come in here asking the stupidest shit.

Maya's voice comes, quiet. "I—um—"

Rajan peers around the doorway. Maya's back is turned, but her body language tells all. She's nervous.

"Key chain?" she says. She points at the rack of key chains beside the counter.

The guy blinks. "Well, yeah, but I'm wondering if you have any key chains with bears on them?"

"Um," Maya says again, faintly. "No—no bear. No."

It dawns on Rajan the real reason Maya doesn't talk much.

"Can't you check?" the customer asks.

Rajan comes around the doorway and back to the counter. "Look." He spins the key chain rack three-sixty degrees. "No bears. Are we done?"

The guy now looks irritated. "Can't you check in the back?"

"No."

With a huff, the guy pushes off the counter and leaves. As soon as the bell jangles, Rajan glances at Maya. She's already trying to skirt around him, most likely to escape to the break room. This time, he doesn't address her in English. "Are you okay?"

It's funny how he never noticed the tension in her shoulders until it melts away. She whips around. There's clear relief in her eyes. And although he spoke Punjabi to her, she speaks Hindi back. "You speak—?"

"Punjabi. I've been *trying* to talk to you, if you didn't notice."

"My English is very poor." She looks down, fiddling with her shirt.

Of course. He shouldn't have assumed. "You could've just said so."

"It's embarrassing." She blushes. "I haven't been able to pass my exams because of it, in order to work here."

"But you *do* work," he says, confused.

"I work jobs like this one. But I'm not yet qualified here for the job I did before."

He stares at her, starting to get a feeling. "Which was . . . ?"

"I was an accountant." In his silence, she adds, "They don't recognize my training here. I have to keep trying, and my English is, well, what it is."

God, he *knew* it. Of course Brenckmann picked her up. Brenckmann, unlike the government, recognized her skills. And Rajan would bet he has her doing way more than whatever's listed in her job description.

"See?" Maya says softly. "I told you. Embarrassing."

"That's not what I'm thinking." He pauses, choosing his next words carefully. "What if I said I knew a place that needs an accountant, and they don't care whether you pass your English exams?"

She blinks. "They don't?"

"Nope. The only language you have to speak is numbers. Interested?"

"I didn't realize there were jobs here like that."

"You just have to know the right people." The bell jangles again; another customer. Maya starts, clearly still skittish, and immediately slinks away to the back. But not before Rajan catches the thoughtful look on her face.

He leans against the cash register and stares through the TV, nearly in disbelief at his luck. Maya's vulnerable, eager, and, should things go sideways, they have blackmail material—the photos of her buying product. She's perfect. Not even Nick could deny that now. Rajan should call with this news, right? He should feel *happy*.

But he doesn't. He feels disgusted. With himself.

Maya doesn't understand the system here. She just accepted there was a job that would look past her lack of credentialing. And Rajan took advantage of it.

He grits his teeth. Fine, then. He's as bad as the rest of them. But he'll gladly be a Lion a little longer for Simran's sake.

Nick doesn't pick up when he dials. Rajan's on his fourth try when a customer comes up to the counter with a Gatorade. He whistles at the TV. "Look at that."

Rajan's been ignoring the news channel all day. But now he looks at the screen and sees the yellow tape, the headline jumping out.

POLICE WARN GANG WAR ON THE HORIZON

". . . children's playplace broken into just before midnight. There were numerous casualties in the gunfire that followed. But as the story develops, we've learned new details—traces of illicit drugs have been discovered hidden under the playplace's floor. The owners of the business allegedly have connections to the Silver Aces. Police suspect a rival gang stole what appear to be massive quantities of illicit substances . . ."

Damn. That had to be LS. Rajan knew things were escalating between them and the Aces lately, but this sort of offensive strike seems risky. Did Nick sanction it? There wasn't any talk of a raid, last time he heard. It must've been a quick decision.

He pauses mid-yawn. Then turns back to the TV, and the date in the corner: June 19. It happened yesterday, June 18. That *date*. What is it about that d—

Simran's cryptography textbook pops into his head at the same time the customer says, "Pretty wild, huh?"

He's still waiting at the counter with his Gatorade. Rajan finally turns to ring him up. "Yeah," he says lowly. *"Wild."*

TWENTY-SIX

THE KITCHEN OF the Lions' café has become as familiar to Simran as her own bedroom, her constant presence marked by the mess. Papers strewn over the desk, scattered pens, a tea mug perched on the cryptography textbook she brought from the library. A calculator discarded in the middle of her work—working with her pen is infinitely more satisfying than pressing buttons. Nothing made that clearer than yesterday.

The Aces' message was so simple. *Move inventory from under playplace to blue semi outside.* The euphoria she got cracking it was incredible. She already wants to re-create it.

Which is why she suggested to Nick earlier today that she could help the Lions in other ways.

For example, she'd noticed the dealers that frequented the café for product didn't really plan their routes. This seemed terribly inefficient. Google Maps, after all, didn't factor in roads highly frequented by police cruisers, or Silver Ace territory that had to be avoided. How much gasoline was wasted overcorrecting each time? How long did their customers wait? After Simran explained how linear algebra could help map the travel routes that would allow them to meet their product demand, given limitations on labour, vehicle storage space, and time, while minimizing fueling costs, Nick held up a hand, said "Shut up," and—surprisingly—entrusted her with several more of the books. Zohra came to help upon Simran's request, too. The Lions' operations would require insider knowledge to streamline. And that was what they did. For hours.

Now it's late afternoon. Simran opens her laptop—which apparently she's allowed to have suddenly, because nobody's stopping her. No one took her phone either. Not that she's planning anything sneaky. She just wants to run some calculations through her math program. Zohra left an hour ago, but Simran can't quit yet.

Her phone buzzes. Simran tears her gaze from her computer to look. It's TJ. Where are you? I came by your house, but no one answered. Are your parents around?

Her *parents*. That's one thing that happened today she doesn't want to dwell on. She flips her phone over. She'll talk to TJ later. She's too tired—and wired—for it right now. The adrenaline from last night kept her up, eagerly awaiting updates from Nick. And then early in the morning, it hit the news.

It was surreal, watching a plan *she* had masterminded unfolding on TV. There were sirens. Yellow tape. White sheets, but that part didn't really register. She was so entranced she almost didn't hear the sound from upstairs . . .

With effort, Simran focuses back on the numbers. People mill in and out, some even greeting her. She has become a permanent fixture. Trusted. Especially after last night.

But then, there's a scuffle outside the kitchen doors.

"You're not allowed in here," a voice says just beyond them.

"And you think that'll stop me *why*?"

Simran drops her pen. Rajan.

"She's working."

"So what? She royalty or something? Let me in."

Simran sighs. It was only a matter of time before he saw the news and figured it out. "Let him in," she calls, and after a pause, the kitchen door swings open and Rajan stalks in, scowling. He's in a navy hoodie, his cap on backward. Simran's eyes fixate on that detail. Somehow it seems a sign of his mood.

"Bad day?" she asks, but he interrupts.

"You've *officially* lost it."

His voice is heated. Simran closes her laptop. She needs all her focus for this conversation. But, Rajan's next words are unexpected.

"Did you forget Hillway today?"

Her heart drops. She flips her phone back over to see the notifications she ignored the first time. Two calls from Paul. Of *course*; there was a booth at a community fair they were helping with. She herself organized the opportunity for the volunteers months ago. How could she have forgotten?

She mentally adds Paul to the list of people she has to beg forgiveness from. "I—I'm sorry. Did they assign you someone different?"

"Yeah, and he was a dickhead. Never mind that." Rajan turns to close the kitchen door, but one of the Lions holds it open pointedly. Rajan glares. "I'm gonna have a little chat with your bookkeeper. Stay out of it."

"It's okay," Simran adds.

The door finally shuts. Rajan turns to her. "They your personal bodyguards now?" He prowls right up to her desk, shoving aside papers and ledgers; several fall to the floor.

Not this again. "Rajan, I need those—"

He plants his hands on the now-clear desk. "You could've kept your mouth shut, just kept doing the fucking bookkeeping, which was all they asked of you. But you had to go and give them the keys to paradise. Why?"

With the tenor of his voice, the sound of something barely restrained, her heart rate quickens. She leans back to put more space between their faces. "To work off your debt. As you know."

"Yeah? Is that right, *Simran Sahiba*?" It's the first time in a long while that the nickname sounds mocking. "Then tell me something. Did you ask Nick about it after you pulled this stunt? Because with all the drugs they took from the Aces, you must've paid off my debts times a million. Did he say we were home free? Did he?"

Simran blinks. Because she hadn't asked Nick. It hadn't even occurred to her at the time, for some reason. She reaches for her phone. "I'll talk to him now."

"Don't bother." Rajan almost sounds regretful. "What you did, higher-ups are gonna notice. You made yourself too valuable. Doing our books, cracking Aces' books, now whatever the fuck *this* is." He sweeps his hand over the mess of ledgers and paper on the floor. "I was so close, you know. *So close* to getting us both out."

Simran stares. "What?"

"I found someone to replace you. An accountant."

"*Replace* me?"

She regrets how her voice sounds, because Rajan gives her a sharp look. Then he laughs. "You know what I think? This is fucked up, but I think it's true. You ready?"

"Rajan—"

"I think you *liked* doing it. Telling Nick you had a big prize for him. Got a little thrill, did you?"

Heat rises to her face. She busies herself picking up the books Rajan knocked off the table. "Don't be ridiculous."

He keeps going. "This isn't about me and my debt anymore. Nah, this is about you now."

"It's not—"

"I think you *knew* what the consequences would be. You knew you were painting a target on your back from both Lions *and* Aces. But all you cared about was cracking that code. Because whenever there's a problem in front of you, you need to solve it. If you can't, it drives you nuts. Just like—"

She straightens to look him in the eye. "Don't."

"—your mom's cancer," he goes on, and her hand tightens around the ledger she's holding, because *okay*, he went there. "So you go looking for something else you *can* solve. And if you can solve it, you can't leave it alone. You need everyone to know you can do it." He laughs again, softly. "It's about your *pride*. Maybe you really are one of us, after all."

Her grip on the ledger becomes painful. "What's the point of this conversation, Rajan?"

"To confirm how batshit you are, but also, to come up with a plan." He runs a hand over his jaw. "We have to convince Nick this was a fluke. Or that someone else figured it out, not you."

"Nick wouldn't buy that. And besides, the deal hasn't changed. I'm here until July's end—he knows that. It'll be fine." Her phone rings. She fumbles for it.

Rajan rolls his eyes and pushes off the desk to the other side of the kitchen. "If it's Nick, I want to talk to him."

It's not Nick, of course. Simran's hand trembles slightly as she brings it to her ear. "Hello?"

"Nikka putt." Her father's worried voice makes her tense. "I was looking for you. Where'd you go?"

She clutches the phone. "I'm at TJ's. Is everything okay with—" She cuts herself off because Rajan has whipped around, his eyebrows raised at her blatant lie.

Simran ducks her head as her father says, "The doctors said she has a blood infection. It's probably from the surgery, and probably the reason she . . ." He trails off, but he doesn't have to say more. After all, Simran was there.

This morning. She'd pulled herself away from the TV when she heard the thump. Took the stairs two at a time. And there her mother was: lying on the floor next to her bed.

For a moment, Simran's world fell apart.

Then she stirred awake, and the ambulance came. The doctors took over. Once Simran had answered all their questions, she left without telling her father. She couldn't handle it anymore. She came *here*, where she wouldn't have to think any longer about what her first thought was upon seeing her mother's body on the floor.

Her father goes on. "They say she needs antibiotics. And she's very dehydrated." Simran closes her eyes. She should've *known* that. She was throwing up. Acting strangely. Of *course* it wasn't normal. Why'd she let her mother convince her otherwise?

Because you didn't want to deal with it that day.

"Are you coming back?" her father asks hesitantly. "I was going to head home, but if you want to visit . . ."

The idea of sitting at her mom's bedside while she gets pumped with drugs, a scenario Simran could've prevented the day before, is too much. "Maybe tomorrow. Bye." She ends the call before her voice can waver. Robotically, she sinks back into her chair.

Rajan's voice breaks through her mental haze. "What happened? Is it your mom?"

Simran can't answer. She just wants this all to be over. She wants her parents back, not these needy echoes of them. It's a selfish thought, but she can't take it back or stop herself thinking it, and the frustration inside her builds and *builds* with nowhere to go—

Rajan takes her hand.

Her head jerks up, bewildered, as his fingers wrap around her wrist. She hadn't noticed him approaching, or kneeling next to her chair. His expression is strangely intent. When she doesn't pull away, he captures her hand entirely, their palms sliding together as if they've done it a million times before. But they haven't; the feel of his skin against hers is new. Dizzying. Dangerous.

"Sahiba," he says simply, and the dam in her breaks.

"She's in the hospital again with an infection," Simran says. "I can't . . . I can't. I can't visit her. I can't."

She's aware she's nearly hyperventilating, not making any sense, but he nods anyway. "The last time my mom got admitted to the hospital, I left, too."

His words are overly casual, despite the fact that he rarely talks about his mom. Right then, Simran understands why. "You don't have to—"

"She wasn't doing so hot. Hadn't been for a while. My dad was making plans to come down and be with us, but he never got a chance. She just . . . tanked so suddenly. I don't know exactly what happened that day, though, because I wasn't sober. And I must've been a real asshole, because security kicked me out."

"Rajan," she exhales, but he holds up a hand.

"That's not the worst part. I was *glad* they kicked me out. I didn't want to see her like that. She wasn't my mom anymore, she was just tubes and lines and monitors. I went out looking for a distraction—you know, *my* type of distraction. Not yours." He chuckles without humour. "I didn't find out she died until the next morning."

Horror clogs her throat. There aren't words to respond adequately. Rajan doesn't seem to mind.

"I haven't even told you the worst part yet. Part of me, a real fucked-up part of me, is still glad I wasn't there."

And in that moment, she realizes he understands her perfectly.

While she's reeling, he smiles bitterly. "Huh," he says. "I've never told anyone that before. Not even the shrinks at juvie."

Of course he didn't. This is what it feels like to be pushed to your limit, desperate for an escape. You think things you're not proud of. That you can hardly even admit to yourself in the dark.

She finds her voice. "I don't think it's bad to not want to watch someone you love die. But my mom isn't . . ." *Not yet, anyway.*

"She's suffering, though. And it's hard to watch people you love suffer. You gotta pick. Either you and me are *both* assholes, or we're not."

She doesn't know how to respond, and thankfully, she doesn't have to—the sound of conversation on the other side of the wall reminds her they're not alone. She jerks away, and so does he.

Rajan slides his hand back into his hoodie pocket. "Let's go home. You've done enough for them for one night."

And Simran finds, for once, she can't argue.

Surprisingly, Rajan agrees to let her give him a ride. It seems they've made a silent pact not to discuss their earlier argument, because the drive to Rajan's place is largely spent in the type of conversation that reminds her of simpler times:

"Nice monster truck."

"It's not a monster truck."

"Have you seen how high off the ground this thing is? You're a glasses-wearing math nerd, you should drive a little sedan or something. Where'd you even get this?"

After she explains an auntie gifted it to her as a hand-me-down, Rajan flicks her pine-tree air freshener, sorts through the CDs in the glove box ("What decade is this again?"), and comments on the random junk and snacks accumulating in the back seat ("You planning a cross-country road trip?"). Although he's making fun of her truck, she has a feeling he's delighting in exploring it.

At least, until he holds something up. "What's this?"

She glances over and her heart somersaults—Rajan's got the printout of Dr. Maxfield's email in his hand. She'd printed it ages ago, planning to show her parents. At least before everything went sideways.

She takes it from him and stuffs it in her driver's-side door. "Nothing."

But clearly, he's read enough. "You were thinking of going to UBC Vancouver for this hotshot prof? And you didn't?"

"I had to be here, Rajan. For my family." He says nothing, looking troubled. She attempts a smile. "I don't mind. I like it here. Either way, I get my degree. There was no need to go to Vancouver to pursue a few niche interests."

"But you wanted to."

Her gut twists. "Just tell me how to get to your house, please."

Rajan takes the hint and doesn't push her further, but he also doesn't crack any jokes for the rest of the ride. She follows his directions to his neighbourhood. She's never been here before; the houses seem to progressively shrink until they squat, almost indistinguishable from trailers at first glance. Rajan points at one.

"That's it."

It looks like it broke its hip and is leaning on its side. The white paint peels; the stairs to the front door have splintered edges. The lawn is more gravel than green. There's a bike tossed to the side with slit tires, a rusted swing set in the overgrown grass beside the house. A tree fallen next to it.

"Shithole, isn't it." Rajan chuckles. "Well, thanks for the ride. I gotta make dinner before my brothers order takeout again."

Simran watches him get out and thinks about her next move. Her father might be home from the hospital now, and if so, she'll have to pull herself together and endure talking about her mom. Then she'll have to face her growing apology tour and answer her messages.

She's not ready.

"Rajan," she blurts. "I could help."

He turns. "With what?"

"Dinner. If you want." She's flustered. "I . . ."

He looks at her—*really* looks at her—and his expression softens. "Yeah, why not. I'm a shit cook anyway."

So she hops out and follows him in.

The inside is nicer, with a lived-in charm. Worn carpet, walls yellowed with age, a wooden coatrack overflowing with jackets and hats. Various shoes are haphazardly scattered across the welcome mat. She toes out of hers and follows Rajan around the corner. The first thing she sees is a multiplayer shooter game on the TV. Two boys sit on the squashy salmon-coloured couch facing it; the taller one turns his head and stills upon seeing them. Simran pauses, too. This boy is almost the spitting image of scowling, fourteen-year-old Rajan.

The younger boy shoots the other's character. Rajan's lookalike whips back around.

"That's not fair."

"I won," the younger one gloats, but then he sees them, too.

"Sukha, Yash," Rajan introduces them, pointing first at his lookalike, then the younger one. "This is Simran Bhenji. Friend from school. Be nice or I'll drop you into the lake and let the Ogopogo eat you."

Sukha rolls his eyes and tosses his controller on the table. "I'm done."

"We *just* started," Yash protests, but Sukha's already brushed past them. A door slams somewhere down the hall. Yash says, to the air, "The Ogopogo's not real."

Rajan glares at the hallway Sukha disappeared down. "Guess we'll find out. What do you want for dinner?"

"Not hungry," Yash mumbles.

"Because what, you're filling up on Oreos again?" Rajan leans over the couch back and holds up the open box. "This is junk, dude." He stuffs one in his mouth, then offers the box to Simran.

Simran accepts one before heading to the fridge. There's not a whole lot inside. A bag of bell peppers; two have already gone significantly moldy. A block of paneer, with one corner also moldy.

She looks at Rajan. He nods. She nods. "Cut the mold off?"

"Obviously," Rajan says. "What kind of operation do you think we're running here?"

Rajan, despite his comments, isn't a bad cook; of course his creativity translates here, too. He expertly shaves the moldy parts off the peppers over the trash can. Dusts salt over the cubed paneer. Starts the tardka while Simran's peeling potatoes. They debate the ratios of each ingredient, since they've grown up using different proportions. He says they need more mirch. She says more haldi. Once they've agreed on a compromise, he puts the lid on. Then they're just standing there, watching it cook.

She doesn't want it to be over. "Do you have flour? For roti?"

"Haven't made roti in years, but all right, all right." He opens a cabinet and hauls out a bag of flour. "Let's make it a fuckin' occasion."

So Simran watches the pot, adding the last few spices and cilantro, while he kneads the dough. He's gotten rid of his hat and rolled up the sleeves of his hoodie, his muscular forearms getting dusted with flour. However, it appears he finally hits his Achilles' heel when rolling out rotis.

"Creative shapes you've got there," she comments.

"You find this funny?" He's grinning, though. She takes the rolling pin from him and rolls out a perfectly circular roti.

"Well, *I* don't make circle rotis," Rajan says, playfully shoving her aside. "Cuz I'm not a fucking cop. You flip them, I'll roll them out."

Simran obliges, hopping on the counter next to the stovetop and flipping, taking care to inflate the rotis completely. She doesn't normally enjoy the tedious task, but with him, it's fun.

Rajan throws the last one on the tawa with a great flourish. It looks suspiciously heart shaped. She looks up, and he winks.

"I thought you were supposed to be smooth, not corny," she tells him. "Is this what works for people?"

Rajan abandons the rolling pin and comes close, nearly slotting between her knees. "Seems to be working for *you*, dude. You're looking pretty hot and bothered."

She *is* overheating. "That's the stove."

"Yeah, yeah, that's what they all say."

She can feel her lips pulling into a smile as well. Some part of her notes how this is skirting into dangerous territory, him saying things like this, his hands braced on the counter on either side of her hips. They're not at school, or volunteering, or with the Lions. They're in a kitchen with the blinds drawn on every window, and they have been alone for the past hour.

His smile fades slightly, and he glances down, as if realizing where he is for the first time. Then—he looks back up, and their eyes meet. She has an electric, funny feeling in her stomach that they're both thinking the same thing.

They could do anything right now. And no one would ever have to know.

Rajan pushes away, back to the stove. "You're right. It's hot in here."

The rest of the world surges back. The dim lighting, the sound of water running distantly from down the hall. The burning smell . . . of roti on the stove.

Flustered, frustrated, Simran flips it quickly. "Maybe you should take off your hoodie."

"Trying to get me naked already?" He grins, but then immediately disappears into the hall to shout for his brothers to come eat.

Simran, meanwhile, tries to collect herself. It's one of those times she could swear she's not the only one who feels the pull. But that's ridiculous. Rajan gave her tips on how to kiss Jassa. A jealous boy doesn't do that. Besides, Rajan's type is people like Zohra and Chandani. Whatever category that is, Simran knows she's not in it.

She heads to the dining table with the food, where Rajan and Yash are already setting up. "Sukha's not coming?" she asks.

Rajan pours them all water. "Telling me to go to hell would be a weird way of saying he was."

Yash explains, "Sukha's turning into Rajan. I think it's a phase."

"Turning into Rajan?" Simran sends Rajan an amused look. "What does that mean?"

"I dunno, but I don't wanna go through it," Yash says. "I think it's like puberty, but worse."

Simran laughs, while Rajan goes behind his chair and puts him in a headlock. "Stop talking shit about me in front of her, you little dick." Yash pretends to get choked out. Rajan releases him and pushes his head forward, affectionate, before sitting next to Simran.

And then they eat. The sabji is delicious. The company is even better. Simran tells Rajan about her cousin's boyfriend drama, which Rajan is delighted by, and in turn he tells her what he's learned about the other youth on probation simply by eavesdropping on Kat's secretary's phone calls. Gossiping still comes easy to them, it seems.

Yash warms up the more Simran and Rajan talk. Eventually, he pitches in too, and Simran learns he's a chatterbox. When he brings up his math woes at school, Simran tells him to bring his homework over, and she helps with the word problem he was struggling with. They exchange numbers in case he gets stuck again. She loves it all—the low-stakes conversation, warm home-cooked food, sitting next to Rajan, who occasionally stretches and drapes his arm over the back of her chair . . . it's so normal. She's forgotten what that feels like.

When their plates are scraped clean, Yash excuses himself, taking the dishes to the kitchen. Rajan says, "He hasn't talked that much in a while. He likes you."

"Probably because I just promised to help him with all his future math homework."

"Nah, it's more than that. But since you brought it up." His hand on the back of her chair tugs her braid gently. "That was real nice of you, Auntie."

She blushes. Rajan drums his fingers on the back of her chair. She feels every vibration like it's on her skin.

"So how'd you do it?" he asks out of nowhere.

"How'd I what?"

"How'd you crack the cipher?"

She glances his way. His gaze isn't accusing anymore. He looks . . . curious. Begrudgingly so. Like he's been wondering this whole time and couldn't stop himself from asking any longer.

"Give me a pen," she says at last, and he gets up to find one.

She shows every step to him on a paper towel: how she went from a list of numbers to coordinates. From coordinates to a string of letters. And finally, from letters to a grid.

m	n	m	a	o	i
o	t	u	y	b	o
v	o	n	p	l	u
e	r	d	l	u	t
i	y	e	a	e	s
n	f	r	c	s	i
v	r	p	e	e	d
e	o	l	t	m	e

As she circles the words transposed in the columns, he says, fondly, "You are such a fucking nerd."

She grins widely. Even re-creating the process gives her an echo of the rush. "Could the accountant you found to replace me do *that*?"

"Sahiba, there is nobody on earth who could replace you." He takes the pen from her. "I was just hoping the Lions would never realize that."

She wants to ask how he found this accountant when the Lions were having so much trouble, but she doesn't want to argue again when tonight has been so wonderful. So she says nothing.

Her phone buzzes. Her dad, asking when she'll be home.

"Everything okay?" Rajan asks. "You need an alibi?"

She answers *soon* and tucks the phone away. "No. I don't need excuses anymore."

"And it makes you feel like shit," he surmises quietly.

She can't answer. So often growing up she wished she could go to a friend's house without it being a big deal. But now that she has that luxury—now that she's at a *boy's* house and no one notices—she just feels guilty. Of course her parents don't notice. Her mom's in the *hospital*.

She pushes her chair back. "I should go."

Rajan gets to his feet, too. "I better go lock myself in my room so Sukha can eat without damaging his pride."

Despite herself, she smiles. "He sounds like you."

"I sure hope not," Rajan mutters darkly. "Did you know he got arrested the other day? I think he might be running with the Lions."

So *that's* what's happening. "You know that for certain?"

"No. But he won't tell me anything." He shakes his head as he walks her to the door. "I don't know how to stop him from making my mistakes."

He sounds bitter. Simran chews her lip in thought. "Hillway has a program for at-risk kids," she offers. "The next workshop is in a few weeks. I'll send you the link."

"He won't go to that."

"Just suggest it. He might not listen now, but he'll come around."

Rajan glances at her sideways. "That approach hasn't been working on you."

Simran flushes. "We're not the same."

"Why? Because you're better than him?" His voice goes flat. "Because he's a fucked-up kid from a fucked-up family and his brother set a shitty example by joining a gang and going to jail?"

She flushes harder. "That's not what I meant."

"Then what *did* you mean?" He pins her with his gaze. She can actually feel the carefree evening dissolving, the lights flicking back on to reveal the mess between them.

Car headlights stream through the blinds. A vehicle is rolling into the driveway. Rajan glances out at it. "Never mind. You should go."

She sighs. Right when she's putting her shoes on, the door opens from the outside, and there stands a man as tall as Rajan, with a five o'clock shadow, wearing a wrinkled collared shirt. He's handsome; she can see Rajan's full mouth and high cheekbones on him, but his eyes are dull.

It must be his father. "Sat Sri Akaal—"

Rajan interrupts her. "This is Simran, my Hillway mentor. She just dropped me off. She's leaving."

Simran drops her hands. Does he really need to protect her reputation to his own father?

Rajan's father smiles at Simran, speaking in Punjabi. "Now, where are our manners? Please stay for dinner, or chah?"

"We already ate, but thank you. I should go. It's getting late."

"Yes. I'm sorry Rajan made you drive all the way out here."

She winces. That wasn't what she meant. "No, it's okay. I offered."

And then, because the silence becomes awkward, she bids her goodbyes and leaves.

Rajan and his father watch her get in her truck from the front door. His father's still smiling when he says, in low, sharp Punjabi, "Are you out of your mind? What are you doing with that girl?"

Simran waves at Rajan. He waves back, then watches her truck roll down the street. "Nothing."

"Don't give me that. Everyone knows the Aujla girl. She's got a bright future. Do you have no shame?"

"Like she *said*, she offered me a ride home."

"And had dinner." He nods to the kitchen. "If you get her off her studies or god forbid, *pregnant*—"

Rajan contemplates flinging himself in front of a bus. "I just said we're not—"

"I would say you'll feel remorse once you destroy her life," his father says. "But I already know from experience that isn't true."

He leaves Rajan at the door, staring at the footprints Simran left in the dirt on her way out.

TWENTY-SEVEN

SIMRAN'S NIGHT AT Rajan's is strangely revitalizing. When she gets home, she sends an apology text to Neetu *and* an email to Paul promising to make up for her absenteeism. And the next day, she visits her mother—who's thankfully doing much better. So much better, in fact, that a few days later Simran and her father come to take her home from the hospital.

Simran can't help but notice, as they're being given discharge instructions, that her mom has lost weight. Her head lolls as if keeping her neck upright is too much effort. She's in a wheelchair, out of precaution, they explain, just to get her to the car. Because she's weak.

The doctor adds, "And as for the cancer, your oncologist will call with the . . . staging results." He sounds a little apologetic at the end.

Once, these words would have sent Simran into a spiral. Now, she hardly feels anything. She may as well assume this nightmare will continue forever.

"When?" her mom asks quietly.

"Soon," the doctor says gently. "In the meantime, maybe focus on some hobbies. It might be a good distraction from all this."

Simran's mother stares. At first, Simran doesn't think she's going to respond, but then she says, "Hobbies?"

She sounds rather lost.

"Yes, hobbies," the doctor replies, oblivious. "Things you enjoy doing. What are yours?"

"I don't have any."

He pats her shoulder. "Well, the local cancer center has lots of activity groups. Maybe find one you like?"

Once he leaves, Simran steps in. "You *have* hobbies, Mom. You like reading cooking magazines. And biking in the summers."

Her mother gives her a blank look as they enter the elevator. "I bike for exercise. I cook to make good food for you."

She turns back to the front, and Simran sighs, punching the down button. Her uber-practical mother cannot fathom doing things simply for her own enjoyment. Even if Simran suspects she *does* enjoy them.

When the elevator doors ding open on the main floor, Simran pushes off the wall. But just then, *Rupi Auntie* walks by.

Simran flings her hand out in front of the wheelchair.

Her father gives her an odd look, but it's enough for Rupi Auntie to move on without seeing them. Close call. Simran peeks into the hallway, watching Rupi Auntie's back retreat. She must be visiting someone here, but, god, what a reminder that they've been lucky so far. And they only have to be lucky a little longer: through a long, winding hall to the atrium and exit.

Simran glances at her mom, who meets her eyes, even paler now. She clearly saw Rupi Auntie, too.

In unspoken agreement, Simran walks out of the elevator first, leading them cautiously. Her father pushes the wheelchair. She peeks around corners before they turn them, scoping out each room they walk by. As they near the exit doors, Simran picks up the pace. She can see the outdoors from this hallway. She steps into the atrium.

And runs directly into someone coming from the coffee shop.

"Simran!" TJ exclaims. "What are you doing here?"

Simran doesn't dare look back. Her mom will be wheeled out from behind her in a few seconds. She darts around TJ, circling her, forcing TJ to turn, too.

She does, laughing. "What're you doing?"

With TJ safely facing the opposite direction, Simran keeps one eye on the atrium entrance. "Volunteering. Let's talk somewhere quieter." She gestures to the chairs safely across the atrium.

TJ doesn't move. "Is there anywhere you don't volunteer? *I'm* only here because my mom got called to the hospital while we were shopping. She said it'd be *quick*." She rolls her eyes. "Thank god you're here. You've been avoiding me as usual, and I seriously need a ride."

Above TJ's shoulder, Simran's father finally wheels her mom into the atrium. They look at her. Simran jerks her head in a *just go* motion. It's as subtle as she can make it, but TJ starts turning. "What're you—"

Simran grabs her arm and wrenches her back. "You'll *never* guess what happened."

It works. TJ turns back, eyes bright with interest. "What? What happened?"

Yeah, Simran, what happened? She blurts the first thing that comes to mind: "Rajan's my new Hillway mentee."

"*What?*" TJ shrieks, loud enough to draw stares. Simran's mom is almost out the door. "Why didn't you say anything at dinner?"

"Just happened," she lies. Clearly Chandani hasn't told her *that* part. "Funny, isn't it?"

"Funny? No!" TJ looks upset. "This is worse than that girl who punched you. You have to be careful with him! Chandani told me how creepy he was with you—"

Simran already regrets this. "He wasn't. He was his normal self."

"Which is creepy."

By now, Simran's parents have left the building. Time to make her exit. "Well, see you later . . ."

She tries to turn, but TJ catches up. "You can't drop *bombs* and just leave! Besides, I still need a ride."

"Can't you wait for your mom?"

It comes out more callous than intended. A flash of hurt goes over TJ's face. "Did I . . . do something wrong? The way you left dinner the other day . . ."

Simran's heart splinters even as she tries to plot her way out of this. "I'm sorry about that. I'm a marker for a professor's summer classes, and I remembered I had exams to mark due that night. I panicked."

TJ's eyebrows rise skeptically. Simran doesn't have time to reinforce her lie because just then, the doctor who discharged them gets off an elevator at the other end of the atrium. He spots her and begins heading her way, waving a paper. Did they forget something?

Simran focuses back on TJ. Thirty seconds before she's exposed. "I'll come back and pick you up. I just have to go right now."

She's sidestepping her when TJ's voice sounds again, very small. "Why does it feel like you won't come back?"

"I will, okay?" Some part of Simran recognizes TJ absolutely has the right to feel this way, but she's so *tired* of tiptoeing around everyone's feelings. The doctor has almost reached them.

"But—"

Simran whips around. "Leave me *alone*! Can you do that for one second?"

Her voice echoes. The doctor pauses in his steps, and TJ's eyes widen. Simran braces for the blow-up, the *Fine! See if I ever talk to you again!* Her fiery cousin has snapped over less.

But instead, TJ backs away. "Okay." Her voice is soft, and that's worse. Simran closes her eyes momentarily, trying to scrape together an ounce of compassion. But there's nothing left.

So she leaves TJ standing there.

The doctor catches up to her. "Glad I found you. We forgot your mother's prescriptions—"

"Great." Simran takes the paper without looking. She doesn't slow, and the doctor falls back. Simran ignores the greeter bidding her good-bye and heads outside.

Her parents are waiting in Simran's truck. As Simran climbs into the driver's seat, her dad asks gently, "Everything okay? We saw you talking to TJ."

"She wasn't asking about me, was she?" her mom says.

Simran savagely turns the ignition. The engine sputters to life. "*No*, Mom. I didn't give up your precious little secret, okay?"

A shocked silence settles over the vehicle. Simran never talks to them like that. But, she doesn't care. She keeps seeing TJ's hurt expression.

Last year, in high school, they'd made a pact to stay in each other's lives, even if their moms refused to. Yet another promise Simran has been unable to keep. It's so frustrating. What's even the *point* of having friends who don't know her secrets? All she's doing is hurting them. It would be kinder to leave them alone.

It occurs to her, backing out of her parking space, that maybe she should do exactly that—cut them all off. TJ, Neetu, Jassa, all her other friends. Just until she's done with the Lions. Yes. That will make her life simpler. Simran doesn't have the strength to lead a double life anymore.

If only she were more like her mom. Her mom handled so much more at Simran's age. If Simran had her strength, maybe she wouldn't be falling apart at the seams, losing pieces of herself she took pride in, becoming bitter, pushing away people she loves just to function . . .

Oh.

A realization that has taken her entire life slides quietly into place.

"Sher putt," her dad says timidly as Simran pulls out of the lot, "are you okay?"

A hysterical laugh escapes her. "I'm great," she says. "I'm great."

TWENTY-EIGHT

WHEN RAJAN KNOCKS on Sukha's bedroom door, several days after Simran's visit, Sukha yells at him to fuck off.

So naturally, Rajan kicks it open. Sukha has barricaded it with his hamper, so it takes two kicks.

When he pushes inside, he notes Sukha's baseball rolling off the desk. Why does Sukha keep it there, anyway? It's not like they've played in years. Rajan never even sees Sukha touch it except to put it back in its place.

Which he does now, before turning back to his computer. "Get out."

"Smells like weed in here," Rajan says.

"Must be coming from your room."

Rajan forcibly wrestles down a comeback. He's not here to fight. Hoping to channel Simran instead, he comes closer. "I've got an offer for you."

Sukha turns up the volume on his headphones. Forget channeling Simran, then. Rajan rips them off. Sukha leaps up, eyes screaming bloody murder. But he pauses when Rajan holds up a hundred-dollar bill.

"I'm going to give you this, but only if"—Rajan tosses the Hillway pamphlet on his keyboard—"you go to this with me."

Sukha takes one look and scoffs. "I don't need your reform school." He makes a grab for his headphones.

Rajan holds them away. "Two hundred."

"I've got my own money."

"How? Got a job?" Rajan shoots back, and Sukha's jaw ticks. That was a slipup, right there. And Rajan definitely knows what *that* means. But he reins himself in with conscious effort. "What do I have to do to make you go?" Sukha stares ahead, bored. Desperation breaks Rajan's pride. "Please."

Sukha blinks. Clearly he didn't expect begging. Rajan waits with bated breath. At last, Sukha says, "Give me your bunny."

It takes Rajan a second to understand.

When they were little, their mother made all three of them these stuffed animals. Sukha and Yash have a bear and a tiger, Rajan has a bunny, and he's never cared what anyone said, he *loves* that fucking bunny. She bought all the fabric with his input and sewed it and stuffed it herself, then gifted it to him on his fifth birthday.

"Screw you, man," Rajan says finally. His heart is somewhere in his throat.

Sukha shrugs. "I'll go to your stupid seminar if you give me that."

"It got lost in the move."

"Too bad." Sukha snatches back his headphones. The movement again jostles the baseball, which he quickly steadies.

Rajan finds himself fixated on that action despite himself. Years ago, Rajan taught Sukha how to catch that ball. He always threw it gently underhand, and when Sukha caught it, he was always *so* excited. He'd talk Rajan's ear off about how he wanted to join the T-ball league, too. Their parents didn't let him because they thought, Sukha being a clumsy toddler, that he'd get hurt. *Wait until you're older,* their father had said. So

Sukha spent his time on the sidelines of Rajan's games. And he never did get the chance to step up to the plate—their family situation went downhill real quick after that.

Sukha's reabsorbed in his computer. Rajan studies him. He's never thought of himself as the lucky one, not until right now. But maybe in some ways he was. He, unlike his brothers, got a taste of normal childhood.

Rajan pushes off the wall and leaves.

Back in his own bedroom, he flings open his suitcase, the one that's remained unpacked since Surrey. He digs out a bundle of T-shirts and unwraps it.

The bunny falls into his hands. The fabric is yellowing, but it's still in decent condition. Except for one of the button eyes—it's hanging by a thread. He's been telling himself he'll fix that button for years.

He brings it to his face. Somehow, maybe because he barely ever touches it, it still smells like her.

Sukha actually pauses the game when he returns. Clearly, Rajan's got his full attention now. "You'll go to the seminar?"

Sukha nods.

Rajan hesitates before holding out the bunny. Sukha takes it, and Rajan braces himself. Sukha can do whatever he likes with it now. He could rip it apart to punish him. And Rajan would just have to take it.

But Sukha merely places it next to the baseball and adjusts his headphones. "You can get out now."

TWENTY-NINE

TRUE TO HIS word, Sukha attends the Hillway seminar with Rajan. He rolls his eyes throughout it, but most of the attendees do. Rajan's probably the only one listening as they explain *gang exit strategies, fostering connections in the community, healthy friendships, navigating drug use,* blah blah.

Admittedly, his mind starts wandering too while sitting in the back, doodling in the margin of a counseling brochure. At least until someone sits beside him.

Kat. He stiffens, as always now with his relapse hanging over him. She speaks in a whisper so as to not disrupt the presentation. "I didn't expect to see you here."

Their little game continues, then. Rajan exhales. He's counting down the days till end of probation, because this is *torture*. "I'm here for my brother. You?"

"Volunteering. I helped organize this seminar, actually. What do you think?"

"It's kind of bullshit."

She frowns. "Why?"

"It would hit more if it weren't just some do-gooder standing up there." He nods to the front of the room. "If it were someone who actually went through this and made it out the other side." As it stands, it's entirely theoretical.

Kat nods sagely. "Hmmm."

He eyes her. She looks like she wants to say something. "Spit it out, dude."

She doesn't. She just says, "So the gas station job didn't suit you, I take it?"

"Kat, not even you would be able to smile if you worked there." He quit the same day he discovered Maya. Now he's fully returned to roofing. And Simran's returned to bookkeeping with a vengeance. Nick hasn't acted on Rajan's Maya intel, and although he makes excuses, Rajan knows it's because Simran made it obsolete. They're back to square one—Rajan keeping an eye on her while she works.

Except some days, even that feels useless. That night at his house she seemed happy, but the next time he saw her with the Lions, she was listless, the shadows under her eyes deeper than ever. Her phone buzzed occasionally, and she didn't even look. But he did. He saw how many unread messages she had. And he mentioned it, too, only to receive glares from everyone else in the room. Nick even told him to shut up. None of them like it when Rajan reminds their bookkeeper she has a life outside these damn ledgers.

"Does that mean you're willing to explore other options now?" Kat asks.

A commotion distracts them from conversation. Rajan looks up to see Sukha has stood in the middle of Narcan kits being distributed. "I'm not doing fucking *IV drugs*," he snaps. "Fuck this." He stalks toward the exit. Rajan doesn't move to stop him. Sukha staying this long is already a win.

"Thanks for coming!" Kat trills as Sukha storms past. She turns back to Rajan. "As I was saying, I gathered some applications for the community college I think might interest you. There's funding we can apply for. Mechanics, woodworking, graphic design."

He pauses his doodling. Kat's psychoanalyzing is getting old. "Fine."

"Really?"

"Yeah." Only to get her off his back. Even *if* Kat got him into some program, starting something like that feels like asking the universe to screw it up again. He's not sure how much more of that he can take.

He crumples the brochure. "I've got to go. Work soon."

Kat's hand lands on his shoulder. "Wait."

He stills immediately. This is it. This is where she mentions—

"Be careful out there. You've seen the news, right? There's a gang war. People might not be thinking clearly, and you're very visible with your tattoo."

Rajan relaxes again. "Don't worry, dude. Everyone knows I'm a *reformed* Lion."

He punctuates that with a wink, but she doesn't seem reassured. She keeps smoothing out her dress. Weeks have passed since the playplace attack; why so nervous today?

He shakes his head and follows Sukha out.

Work today is at a three-storey house they're re-shingling. The cloudy July sky forecasts rain. Bad news for a roofing company, and the foreman is in a shit mood when Rajan shows up, barking at him to get to work already.

Rajan and Trevor are assigned on a section together. As usual, Trevor talks too much. As usual, Rajan tries to tune him out.

Trevor notices, though. "You're in a mood."

"Just noticed today, huh?"

Trevor doesn't seem to get it. Raindrops splatter the shingles they're laying down. "Trouble with your girlfriend?"

Rajan pauses. Was it Trevor that gave Nick the intel about Chandani? "One-time thing."

"That's not the one I'm talking about."

His voice is sly. As the rain comes down in earnest, Rajan processes what he means. There was that day—at UBCO—when Rajan talked to Simran on the worksite. Interrogated her, really, about her dealings with the Lions. It hadn't occurred to him that people were watching.

A foreboding feeling crawls up his neck. Today, Kat was warning him off from rival gangs. What she didn't realize was that he might have more to fear from his own people. They're watching, they're reporting on him to their higher-ups, they're narcing to his PO, and—he suddenly remembers Nick's and Zohra's warnings about him not being welcome— maybe they're waiting for the right moment to off him.

The thought feels ridiculous. At first. Because then he thinks about the stink eye everyone gives him when he talks to Simran at the café. Not only has Rajan become useless to the Lions, but he might now be actively getting in their way.

He's spared from answering Trevor because the foreman shouts to cover the roof. The rain's too heavy.

Trevor runs to grab the tarp, and they lay it down on the unfinished parts. Rajan reaches for the zip ties to secure it in his vest pocket, but it's empty. He could've sworn he had some earlier.

Trevor stands. "I'll get more."

Rajan sits back while Trevor darts over to the edge of the roof to his ladder. Something about the whole group—Trevor, the foreman, everybody—seems off today. He can't put his finger on it. God, Kat really got into his head, didn't she—

Thump.

Rajan looks up. "Trevor?"

No answer. Trevor's not on the roof anymore.

Rajan stands. He may not like the guy, but that doesn't mean he wants him to break his neck. "Trevor!"

He walks quickly to the edge of the roof. But right before he can look over the side, his boot connects with something heavy.

He barely has a second to look down and note the heavy hammer that's just *lying* there before he loses balance. Reflexively, he shifts his weight, but the tarp under his feet slips. He doesn't even have time to curse before he tips backward off the roof.

And falls. Headfirst.

Some instinct makes him stretch out his arms, looking for something, anything to grab onto. Miraculously, his hand hooks around something—a beam?—and his fall stops all at once, violently wrenching his shoulder.

Pain explodes through it.

It's so intense, he loses his breath. Along with his grip. He falls the rest of the way down.

His back hits the earth first. Then his shoulder—god, *his shoulder*. He blinks up at the cloudy sky, raindrops falling on his face. The pain makes him woozy. When he tries to roll onto all fours, his shoulder won't take any weight. It feels odd. With his other hand, he gropes at it. Something's . . . not right.

In his peripheral vision, boots splash through the puddles toward him. He struggles to his knees, fighting back nausea. Fingers pry at his shoulder, making him gasp. "Dislocated," someone says.

Rajan staggers to his feet, shoving them away with his good arm. The shock is starting to wear off, enough that he's aware of his frantic heartbeat, more frantic still as his coworkers crowd him. "Get the fuck away from me."

"Relax, Rajan."

"We can fix it."

"Don't touch me." Rajan clutches his injured arm. The nausea lets up a little. He rounds on Trevor. "Why was that hammer on the roof?"

Silence. Trevor pales. "It was an—"

"Why the fuck was it on the roof?" he screams. He's lost it and he doesn't care, all he can see is a hammer that never should've been there, a tarp that was loose, zip ties that were gone, and a blur of people he can't trust.

He backs away. They let him, watching warily.

Trevor sighs. "Kid, at least go to the hospital. You can't sleep that off."

Rajan doesn't answer, because he can't think straight. He doesn't like hospitals. Jesus Christ. This *hurts*.

"They'll at least dope you up," someone else adds quietly. And, pathetically, *that* gets him thinking as he trudges off the worksite. No one stops him. But he hears that *thump* again behind him—when he looks, it's just the wind knocking heavy tarps against the wall. That's all it was . . . right?

He takes the bus to the hospital, wincing with the jolt of every pothole. He's suddenly learning all the other hits he took on the way down. He closes his eyes to the pain and again sees that hammer on the roof. Is he losing it or was that *definitely* not there before?

At the hospital, the triage nurse directs him to the waiting room. It's crammed. His eyes snag on the woman holding a bucket for a little girl to barf into. God, he wishes he had one of those right now. A few rows away, a guy rocks back and forth, clearly tweaking. The security guards nearby are eyeing him. Too much déjà vu. Rajan hasn't been in a hospital since . . .

Anyway.

He scans for a patch of floor to sit. There. By a lady with a ponytail. It's only when he makes his way over that he realizes he knows her.

"*Kat?*" he blurts.

She's not in her preppy dress from earlier; she sits cross-legged on the floor in a black full-sleeve shirt and loose-fitting jeans. When she sees him, she smiles wanly.

"Hello, Rajan," she says, like it's normal for them to rendezvous in ER waiting rooms. Her eyes flit to how he's holding his arm. "Did you . . . dislocate your shoulder somehow?"

"How would *you* know?" He's wearing a big hoodie, it's not obvious. He squints at her, that paranoid edge returning as he recalls her parting words from earlier. "How the *fuck* did you know I was gonna get hurt today?"

His voice carries; out of the corner of his eye, the security guards straighten.

"Rajan," Kat says calmly. "Please sit."

"Answer me first." Some part of him knows he's being irrational, but his longstanding paranoia, combined with the mind-numbing pain, makes it hard to see it that way. "You had weeks to tell me to be careful and you chose today. What kind of fucking coincidence is that?"

One of the security guards comes up to him. "All right, buddy. Leave the lady alone."

Rajan opens his mouth to tell him off, not caring that he'll get kicked out, but then Kat's on her feet, holding a hand up. "It's fine. He's my—" She stops, and turns to Rajan. "Today's the day my son died."

He blinks. That was the last thing he was expecting her to say.

"Eighth anniversary. He was nineteen." Her throat bobs. "I always worry more about people on this day. Please, sit."

She's struggling to meet his eyes, and that's what sells him. His anger fades. This is the least fake she's ever been.

He sinks onto the floor next to her. Kat sits again, too, her expression composed once again. They're silent until the guards retreat to their corner. Rajan wants to ask her more, but another question distracts him first. "Why're *you* here?"

Kat merely says, "Did you get anything for pain? You're sweating."

Rajan raises his good hand to his forehead. She's right. Huh.

Kat presses her fingers to his wrist, making him jump. "Your pulse is high. It must really hurt."

He jerks away. "The fuck, Kat? You want to read my mind next?"

"Sorry." She looks anything but. "You know, I have military training. I could put your shoulder back."

"I'm sorry, *military training*? Who even are you?"

Kat's smile widens, genuine amusement entering her eyes. "Will you let me try?"

He mulls this over for exactly one second. "Yeah, fine." If he doesn't have to hang around the hospital, he won't. "You gonna shove it in place on the count of three?"

"Turn toward me." She shifts to face him, and he does the same. "Sit up straight and relax."

"Those are two different things," Rajan mutters, but he tries anyway. Kat takes his hand and puts it on her shoulder. She grips his arm with a gentle pull and, with the other, starts *massaging* his shoulder. "I don't need a warm-up, just do it. And warn me first."

"I said sit up straight. You're slouching. And relax."

He tries again. This is *so* weird. "Jesus, Kat. You sound like my mother."

The words are out thoughtlessly, and he freezes, but her expression doesn't change. "Well, once upon a time I *was* a mother. Just not a very good one."

Rajan remembers, not for the first time, what she told him about her son. *Shot dead.* "Why not?" he asks slowly.

She takes a long time answering. "I was young, and had my own problems . . . I wasn't ready to be a parent. If I were, maybe he wouldn't have gone the way he did."

She says nothing more. Rajan thinks again about the photo frame she hasn't replaced. Maybe she can't stand to look at it, the same way he could never take his bunny out of his suitcase. "You know," he says carefully, "I don't blame my mom for the stuff that happened to me. Maybe you're right, maybe she wasn't completely faultless. But I still don't blame her. She was trying her best."

Kat, still smiling, breaks eye contact to survey the waiting room for a long time. Then: "Well, I hope you also realize you didn't make her illness worse. She was sick long before you lost your way."

"Okay, but did you believe the bit *I* said?" Rajan arches a brow. "Because if you didn't, I'm not going to try to convince myself of *your* bullshit."

Kat laughs before dropping his arm. "All done."

"What?" He lifts his arm and crosses it over his chest. Holy shit. His shoulder is back in place. And he barely noticed. Now, it's more an ache rather than a red-hot knife. "But—I thought it was supposed to hurt."

"Not all healing has to hurt, Rajan." She pats his hand. "Go home now. And put it in a sling for a few days."

Rajan gets up, and it's only once he's out the ER door that he realizes he still doesn't know why Kat was there. He turns back. but his view is already obscured by the lineup.

He wanders down the street. It's getting dark. The buses run less frequently now. On a whim, he calls Nick instead. His paranoia needs to be fully satisfied.

But when Nick arrives in a slick-looking Benz, he seems surprised.

"What happened?" he asks as Rajan gets in, awkwardly holding his arm.

"Well, funny thing, Nick." Rajan slams the passenger door harder than necessary. "I fell off a roof at work."

"Sucks."

"Yeah. Someone *happened* to leave a hammer on the roof for me to trip on."

Nick doesn't say anything for at least a minute as he drives. Then: "Rajan, if I wanted you dead, I would just put a bullet in your brain."

Well, that's nice. But Rajan isn't done. "Someone also narced to my PO that night I got high."

"Remember how I said nobody in the LS likes you? Any petty little shit at the party could've done that. We all know you're on probation." Nick shoots him an amused look. "Christ, you're paranoid. A hammer? Come on."

Rajan scoffs. "Fuck you, dude." But now he's starting to feel stupid. Nick's right. That's not his style, and besides, would the Lions really want to kill him? Sure, Rajan is always in Simran's ear—but it's not like she listens.

Speaking of . . . "You have to promise me if anyone gives Simran a hard time about leaving at the end of July, you'll handle it. I found you a new bookkeeper. Hell, *I'll* come back if it helps sweeten the deal." Nick actually tears his eyes off the road to look at him in surprise. "What? I'll be done with probation soon."

"Don't be stupid."

"Yeah, yeah, I know, I can't replace her, but—"

"You don't want that. You don't want to come back."

That pisses Rajan off. "You're the one who tried to *make* me come back."

Nick's grip on the wheel tightens. "The godfathers wanted recruits," he says eventually. "But now they're focused on other things. Take advantage of it. Skip town. You found us an accountant we can maybe use, good. But you're not helping Simran anymore, being here."

Rajan latches onto only one part of his answer. "You mean the godfathers are focused on *Simran*." No answer. "They know about her, down south?"

"Not her name. Just that we've got one helluva bookkeeper." Jesus. Rajan rubs his face. Nick's phone buzzes, and he pulls it out of his pocket. "Yeah."

Moodily, Rajan tries the glove box while Nick listens to his caller. It's locked, of course. He's about to dig through the center console when the car swerves slightly.

Rajan glances at Nick. He's gone pale.

"Okay," he says. "On my way." He ends the call. "Shit. Shit, shit, shit."

"What?"

"The Aces are retaliating."

Big surprise. Rajan yawns. "Drop me off at home first. I don't give a shit about the mess you got yourself into."

Nick casts him a glance as he accelerates, seeming to consider his words before speaking.

"You should," he says slowly. "Because Simran is there."

THIRTY

THE CLOCK TICKS loudly in the café kitchen. Zohra and several of the Lions stare right at Simran. Keeping her face expressionless, she tosses her final card on the table.

Everyone sighs. Shane, one of the Lions, throws his hand down, too. "Are we all gonna pretend she's not counting cards?"

Zohra reclines in her chair. "That's the fun. Trying to beat a card counter." She pushes her chips toward her. "Damn it, Simran. I lost two hundred bucks to you."

"I don't want the money," Simran replies. But they always want to play with real stakes. "Take it back."

"See, that's plain insulting." Shane gets up to stretch. He's in his twenties, heavily tattooed, and had intimidated Simran until recently. "I'm starving. I'm gonna get one of those bagels in the display case."

"Ew," Zohra says. "Those things have been there forever. Wait five minutes and I'll go buy you something fresh."

"Too hungry. I'll risk it." The kitchen door swings shut behind him.

As Zohra puts the deck away, Simran pulls the ledgers toward herself. She's finished her bookkeeping for the day, but the Ace ledgers are her side project. There's only one she hasn't fully decoded yet. It's mostly simple transactions, which she deduced were encrypted with a Vigenere cipher ten minutes in, but she wants to finish anyway. It's like Rajan said: She just likes solving problems. There's no other excuse for being here. Things at home have actually improved. In fact, just this morning, her mom's oncologist had called.

"I have excellent news," she'd said as Simran and her parents crowded around the phone. "The lymph nodes came back negative."

It was like a spring released in the room. The oncologist kept going. "You'll get a follow-up about further treatment. If any."

If any. Her father silently cried right there, tears trickling into his beard. Once the call was over, he called Kiran. Her mother just opened the window and stared out for a long, long time. And Simran . . . didn't know what to do with herself.

She's spent months bracing for a train wreck. And now that it's not happening, she feels off balance. Like someone's playing a prank, and any moment now, the other shoe might drop.

Zohra reaches for the ledgers, but Simran's grip tightens. "I'm not done yet."

Zohra gives her a knowing look before straightening. "You remind me of Manny sometimes." She swings her purse over her shoulder. "His favourite thing to do is get high and then count his money. Except, for you, I think counting money is what *gets* you high."

Simran ignores her teasing tone in favour of a question she's been dying to ask. "Who *is* Manny?" All she knows is everyone seems to answer to him.

"He's part of the family from Van that founded the LS. They got rich in the nineties funneling drugs from Pakistan to India to North America. Biggest open secret ever, the Khullar family. Cops have never been able to pin any of them."

"Why not?"

"They don't do any actual dirty work. That's reserved for plebes like me and you." Zohra winks and pushes out the door.

Now alone, Simran resumes working. It's silent for a long while, the only sounds the ticking clock and cars occasionally driving by. The Aces have used "reigninhell" as their keyword in this book. Disappointing. It's too easy. She wanted a *challenge*. She wants the same rush she got on June 18.

She can practically see Rajan shaking his head at that. Which is why it's best he doesn't know about these extra sessions.

A gunshot rings out.

At first, she doesn't quite process it for what it is. It sounds like a firework. And then . . . glass breaking. Shouts from outside.

Simran scrambles up, a delayed reaction, and backs away from the door. It's probably nothing, right? Some Lions getting into a little tussle with each other. A gun firing accidentally.

But then there's another gunshot. And another.

Terror grips her. *It's happening*, a voice in her head whispers. *This is how the universe is balancing the end of one nightmare.*

With another.

As if to punctuate this, she suddenly hears *voices*. Horrifyingly close, and coming closer.

There are only two possibilities here: police or rival gang. Either way . . . she can't be here. She runs for the back door. It leads to a service hallway that has an exit. But as she reaches for the handle, it swings open on its own.

And there stands a tall man in a balaclava and hoodie, eyes glaringly blue and vicious. His gun is pointed right at her head.

A sound escapes Simran's throat. "*Please* don't." She puts her hands up. He descends upon her, and she backs up. Keeps going until she hits the wall.

He pins her against it. "Who the fuck are you?" His voice is gravelly.

Simran's frozen. It's like she's outside her body, watching this happen. *Think*, she begs herself. What answer does he want? *Think*.

The cold metal of the gun presses under her chin, making that impossible. "I'll ask one more time, bitch. Who are you?"

Her vocal cords feel like molasses. She cannot get her lips to form around any words.

Without warning, he raises his gun and hits her across the face. The metal is sharp and unforgiving, connecting against her glasses with a *crack*. They twist out of shape, digging into her nose, the lenses going lopsided.

She automatically reaches up to adjust them, but he grabs her wrist, then hits her across the face again. Her glasses skitter clean off. Her vision becomes a smear, the world losing definition, losing sense. "No—" she gasps, but he slams her against the wall again. A low chuckle.

"What, these?"

It's like watching through a windshield drenched in water, but she can see the blurry outline of his boot, stepping deliberately onto something on the floor. *Crunch.*

The sound snaps her out of her fear. He's had to shift his weight in order to destroy her glasses, so she shoves him as hard as she can. He stumbles—slightly. It's all she needs.

She barely makes it three steps before he yanks her back by the braid. Pain shoots through her skull, and she crashes down behind the table. Her chin collides with the chair back on her way down. Blood fills her mouth.

She hasn't even fully hit the floor before he's hauling her up by the back of her shirt. Then slamming her onto the desk. Papers scatter off. Her already bruised cheek smarts against the wood. All she can see is the blurry outline of a book and her pen beside it.

Disbelief steals over her. This cannot be the end. As her attacker wrenches her arms behind her back, absurdly, Simran thinks of her parents. She thinks of the police showing up at their door to say, *I'm sorry to have to tell you* . . .

Her mother would collapse. Her father . . . he would collapse in his own way. Inwardly. There would be nothing left for them. Nothing left *of* them.

An inhuman sound tears from Simran's throat. Some strength she didn't know she had possesses her, enough that she can wrench one arm free. She snatches the pen from the desk and twists, swinging it with all her might.

It sinks into something soft. Her attacker screams and releases her.

Simran rolls off the table, catching a glimpse of him clutching his throat before she takes off through the kitchen door. She collides with a wall on her way. Clumsily, she skids into the dining area.

It's dark. And quiet, other than someone gasping loudly. It takes her a second to realize it's her.

She attempts to gulp it back. Her feet crunch on glass unsteadily as she heads for the door. She's nearly there when headlights flash through the windows. Automatically, she ducks behind the front counter instead.

Somehow, the only light bulb still working is in the pastry display case, flickering from within. She ducks farther, not wanting it to illuminate her face, and nearly trips over something on the ground. Not something—some*one*. She drops to her knees, shaking, bringing her face closer to see who—

Shane. His eyes are open. His black shirt glistens as if drenched with water, but Simran knows better.

A silent scream builds in her chest, just as the kitchen door swings open.

"Crazy bitch," her attacker wheezes. He cocks his gun. Simran backs away from Shane's body and holds her breath.

Her attacker fires into the pastry display cases on either side of her. Glass explodes. She shields her face, so her forearms sting instead, but doesn't make a sound. His footsteps echo closer. This is it.

Her hand falls to her hip, where her kirpan is strapped. A curved blade, small as a pocketknife, and as familiar as her own face. She's had it since she was ten: a symbolic, smaller version of the weapon once used in war. She doesn't want to use it. Doesn't even know how. But it's all she has.

Her attacker is almost around the display case. Simran's hands tighten around her kirpan. Just two more steps . . . one . . .

Thunk.

Everything is quiet except for that calm, violent sound. She can't see what's happening, but the boots stop in their tracks.

And then her attacker pitches forward. He lands on his cheek, staring blankly at her. Out cold. She stares at his face as a different set of shoes crunch into the glass beside his head. Simran looks up. Although she cannot discern his features, she would recognize that silhouette anywhere.

Yet, she doesn't really recognize Rajan in what he does next.

THIRTY-ONE

RAJAN GLANCES DOWN at Simran, crouching on the floor, only momentarily. Only to reassure himself she's alive.

He'd thought the worst, when he leapt out of Nick's vehicle behind the café. He'd ignored Nick telling him to wait for the reinforcements.

He nearly got shot in the service hallway—bullet went clean through his hoodie. Rajan's fist, on the other hand, didn't miss. After the Ace was out cold, Rajan broke into the kitchen and saw Simran's ledgers scattered on the table, a pen rolling off, and . . . and . . .

Simran's glasses. Wire frame, completely dated, but always so straight on her nose. Now, twisted on the floor. One arm snapped off. The lenses crushed to dust.

Rajan felt like someone had punched him in the stomach. A cool rage swept over him, pushing out all other thought. Although he had a gun courtesy of Nick, he paused to select a heavy marble rolling pin from the rack. Weighed it in his hands. And set out to make whoever was responsible pay.

Well, he found him. Now that he's determined Simran's alive, he hauls her attacker up by the jacket and leans him against one of the busted pastry display cases. His head lolls into it, resting against the metal trays. The flickering light from the display illuminates a small wound oozing in his throat. Clearly it hadn't hit anything vital. Rajan can fix that.

He drops the rolling pin and takes out his gun. He raises it, and points it between the Ace's eyes.

His finger is curling around the trigger when Simran's voice cuts through the roaring in his head.

"Don't."

She sounds calm somehow. Rajan doesn't fire, but he doesn't lower the gun either. "He came for *you*."

She stands slowly. "That's not a reason to kill somebody."

"He saw your face."

"You just knocked him into next week. He's not going to remember his own face, let alone mine." Her voice softens. "Rajan. You don't want to kill somebody right in front of me, do you? Don't kill him."

He wishes she'd shut up. She doesn't.

"Let's go, Rajan. My truck isn't far." He doesn't move. Until her hand touches his wrist.

Then he looks at her. Her braid's coming undone. His own cold expression reflects back in her luminous eyes. Good. *Look at me*, he thinks. *See what you've been ignoring.*

But Simran doesn't look afraid. "Don't you hear the sirens?"

And then he does. Faintly, but getting louder by the second. Damn it.

He flicks the safety on and tucks the gun away, ignoring her relieved sigh. "Fine. Stay close."

He leads them through the dark back to the kitchen, avoiding the glass. She shadows every step, only pausing to pick up her purse. They peer into the service hallway. It's dark. Empty.

He beckons her to follow, stepping over the Ace he knocked out earlier. They've almost reached the exit when gunshots erupt outside again.

Automatically, he shoves Simran down, covering her body with his. But a moment later he realizes nobody's shooting into the café—they're shooting at someone *outside*. Nick and the others must've run across some Aces.

Rajan presses his face against the top of Simran's head. A minute passes; sometime during it, her body begins trembling beneath him. Eventually, the gunshots slow and stop. Tires squeal from the front of the store. Sirens blare.

He pulls away from Simran, then peers through a crack at the edge of the door. Coast is clear—Nick finally did something useful. "Okay, let's go."

He reaches for the door handle. Glances back.

Simran's still on all fours, her wide eyes staring at nothing.

"Let's go," he repeats, more urgently. Simran covers her face.

"I can't," she whispers.

"Why *not*?"

"I—I can't see."

The hitch in her voice hits him right in the chest. Of course. It's so easy to forget this isn't her life. She's so good at pretending normally that sometimes even *he's* fooled.

But no. She should be studying calculus right now. Shooting the shit with her annoying-ass cousin. She should be singing, she should be dating Jassa Singh, she should be *living* her life, not fighting for it here in the dirt with him.

He kneels at her side. The darkness makes him bolder, and he takes her face in his hand, sweeping a thumb over her fuzzy cheek. She jerks in place. "You don't have to see. Just—" *Trust me*, he wants to say, but the words get stuck in his throat.

Simran seems to hear them anyway. She exhales shakily, then presses her truck keys into his palm. "I'm ready."

So they run.

Rajan begins to relax ten minutes into their drive. He's been keeping an eye on the rearview, but nobody seems to be following. He takes plenty of random detours in case.

As he's doing yet another U-turn, Simran says, "You're not supposed to drive."

He glances at her. She's unbraided her hair, and is finger-combing the waves while staring out the window. It's the first time he's seen her hair loose and it's extremely distracting. "I think we're way past giving a shit about probation, Rapunzel."

The passing streetlights glint off the glass dust embedded in her arms. The collar of her shirt is torn. Without glasses, her eyes are huge, unguarded. But the bags under them are more pronounced, too. There's a gash on the inner corner of her nose, next to her eye.

Rajan's grip tightens on the wheel. "What happened to you before I showed up?"

She shakes her head. "He—hit me a couple times, that's all. He didn't know who I was. And it was dark. I think I'm safe."

He hit me a couple times. She says that like it's nothing. It's messed up. "You have to quit."

"I—"

"I'm not screwing around anymore," Rajan snaps. "They hit the café because they were looking for the bookkeeper. For *you.* Do you understand that? Do you understand what they wanted to do?"

Simran closes her eyes briefly. "Rajan—"

"I've watched you destroy your life for the Lions for months, and I'm done. Fuck the *end of July* thing. Do you see how dangerous this is now?"

"I'm—"

"Doesn't matter how careful you are. As long as you're with them, you're not safe, you could die, like you almost did tonight—"

"*Rajan!*" Simran shouts, loud enough that he almost crashes into the curb. She so rarely raises her voice. "I agree, okay? It's time to leave. I just don't know how. It's like you said . . . I doubt Nick will listen." Her hand trembles as she pushes up phantom glasses.

Rajan almost doesn't know what to say now that she's agreeing. "He might listen to my baseball bat," he mutters eventually. "We'll figure something out."

A foreboding silence falls. Because they both know that's not a real plan.

The closer they get to her house, the slower he drives. "Where should I park?"

"Driveway. My parents are at the gurdwara for an Akhand Paath." Simran rakes her hair back. It's so long it's spilling over her seat. No wonder she keeps it in a braid. "They won't be back until morning."

"Why didn't *you* go?"

Simran avoids his eyes. "I said I was working on Hillway stuff."

"Jesus Christ."

She ignores this. "How are *you* going to get home?"

"Don't know." Don't care. He just has to see her inside. He parks in reverse in case she needs a quick getaway. But as he twists to look behind him, his shoulder *sharply* reminds him of what happened earlier.

Simran notices. "You're hurt!"

He finishes parking. A little lopsided, but whatever, he's rusty. "Just my shoulder." He jumps when Simran reaches over and starts running her hands down his chest. "Get off me. I'm fine."

Unfortunately, right then she finds the bullet hole in his hood. Her voice hits a new pitch. "When did *this* happen?"

"Tonight. Probably."

"Probably?"

He doesn't know how to tell her he's been shot at before. "Relax, dude. It went straight through."

Simran isn't reassured. She grabs his hoodie. "Take it off. Right now."

She has no clue he's about to be psychologically tortured by those words for months to come. He pushes her hands away. "No way am I doing this here."

"Then you'll come inside." Her voice firmly indicates she won't get out of the truck until he agrees.

Rajan sighs and turns off the ignition. Only when he gets out and shuts the door does she follow suit. Then she trails him to the front door.

The two-storey house looms over him, the windows darkened. The lawn is well-trimmed. Hedges out front. Intimidatingly perfect, even when he knows the inside isn't. "Are you sure—"

"Yes." Simran unlocks the door, and his heart thuds faster than ever when she glances over her shoulder at him. He hovers on the doorstep, feeling like a goddamn vampire. Entering *her* house is . . . crossing a line.

But she holds the door open, so with a deep breath, he steps inside.

THIRTY-TWO

TJ ALWAYS ACCUSES Simran of being an adrenaline junkie, but not even Simran would've dared pull this stunt a few months ago. After all, what if her parents came home early? What if a neighbour saw her lead Rajan inside?

But, it seems the Simran of the present requires higher stakes than before to get a rush. She shuts the door behind them, encasing them in near darkness aside from the setting sun's last rays spilling in through the window. She's acutely aware of Rajan's breathing next to her, standing in her foyer. It's . . . thrilling. Intoxicatingly so.

Rajan breaks the silence, voice dry. "Should I strip now?"

"No. I need my glasses."

"Your glasses are toast."

"I have old glasses lying around somewhere." She pauses. "I think, in my bedroom."

Her words hang in the air. She holds her breath.

He stoops to pick up the vague outline of his shoes. "Well, lead the way." His voice is a little thicker than usual. Like he, too, recognizes what a bad idea this is, but can't bring himself to stop.

She turns to the staircase. Rajan follows closely, stairs creaking under their feet.

When they reach her room, illuminated only by dying sunlight, Rajan laughs softly. "Holy shit. Simran Auntie is a hoarder."

Simran doesn't need 20/20 vision to know how much clothing is strewn on the bed. That her backpack spills onto the floor. Her harmonium and rabab are still out from her last half-hearted practice, and her underwear drawer's ajar.

Heat floods her face. "It's not *that* bad." She drops her purse with a heavy thud.

"No, of course not. It's totally normal to not be able to see your carpet. Why am I not surprised?" He walks over to her desk chair, and she only remembers there's a bra slung over the back when he pauses next to it. Then he steps away. "So where are these glasses?"

Simran grabs a coat from a nearby stool and throws it over the desk chair in the least subtle move ever. "I think in the closet. Top shelf?"

She usually uses a stepping stool for that, but he easily reaches up and starts taking down boxes. They sort through the knickknacks inside. Dried-out putty. Kinder Surprise toys. Gum. A Slinky. Dollar-store jewelry her dentist handed out during childhood checkups. Each box contains more obscure things than the last.

"Why do you keep all this stuff?" Rajan examines a solved Rubik's Cube with interest. "I'm learning so much about your psyche right now, dude."

This is getting embarrassing. She takes the box from him and flings it into the depths of her closet. The Slinky *boing*s somewhere behind a suitcase. "Never mind. I'll ask my mom about it tomorrow."

Rajan grabs her wrist. "Shit, I forgot about your arms."

She looks down. There's still a fine sprinkle of glass in her arms—the sting has faded to the background, though. "I'll clean it later."

"We'll clean it *now*. Where's the bathroom?"

"I brought you in here to look at *you*—"

But he's already spotted it, right across the hall, and she lets him tug her inside. As he flicks on the bathroom light, she sinks onto the toilet seat lid and watches him. Incredibly surreal. Rajan Randhawa in her bathroom, sorting through her medicine cabinet.

He doesn't seem to notice her gawking. He sits on the edge of the tub and clacks his tweezers. "Ready?"

She offers him her arms, and he sets to picking out the glass. At one point he accidentally catches one of her long arm hairs and she winces. He lets go immediately, apologizing and running his palm over the underside of her arm.

"It's okay," she says with a little laugh, trying to distract herself from his touch. "I have a lot of hair. You can pull it out if the glass comes with it."

"I'd rather not," he says, completely serious. Her laughter dies. How much attention he pays, the care with which he tries to preserve each individual hair.

A tender feeling washes over her as he works. She longs to reach for him, to somehow articulate the feeling taking flight in her chest. It's like . . . she could tell him her most frivolous, insignificant worries, and he would take each and every one just as seriously. She feels like he cares not only about her body, or her brain, but about her *soul*.

Such a stark contrast to earlier tonight—when he was about to shoot someone in the head. In that moment, she remembered everyone's warnings about him. The ones she could never quite reconcile with the boy she knew.

But now she's seen it. She's seen his brutality, his desperation, his fear. He was going to kill that man. That wasn't what shook her. What shook her was this: She was going to let him.

After all, it made sense to tie up the loose end. What if her attacker remembered her? What if he'd gotten a good look? It would be safer that way. The cruelty of writing off his life didn't occur to her at all. What actually made her stop Rajan from doing it was the thought that she could not protect him from a murder charge.

"What's going on in your head?" Rajan dabs the last of her cuts with a Dettol-drenched cotton ball, then her bloodstained fingers.

"Have you ever killed anyone?" she asks bluntly. When his head comes up, she adds, "I know you didn't really run that guy over."

A beat. Then: "Zohra should've kept her mouth shut." He drops the cotton ball in the trash and stands to wash his hands. "I've helped put people in the hospital. I've watched people die."

"But you've never *directly*—"

"Don't get it twisted. If I were in the driver's seat, I would've killed Jai, too. Piece of shit had it coming, after what he did to Zohra."

He spits out the words, his loathing clear. Once again, Simran's left wondering what the deal is between him and Zohra.

At her silence, Rajan scoffs. "What? Does it bother you, that I think that?" He leaves the washroom, sounding irritated. "Too bad."

She catches up to him in her bedroom. "Was Zohra your girlfriend?"

He halts in the doorway. She wishes she could see his face in the silence that follows. Then: "Me and Zohra are bad for each other. We were both in a shitty place when we met. She used me and I used her, that's it."

"So you had sex," Simran says, she can't help it.

"Well, yeah." He sighs. "Are you gonna make me relive every humiliating thing I did after my mom died, or can we stop here?"

She flushes. Here she was, so enveloped in her own jealousy she didn't realize she was making him relive the darkest time in his life. "Rajan, I'm—"

"It's okay." His voice is gentle, and that makes her feel even worse. "Let me do that striptease I owe you so I can get out of here."

Simran busies herself clearing space on the bed. "Okay." She pats the space next to her.

He remains standing. "I can do it here."

"I can't see you that far away."

He sighs again, like it's a big chore, and sits on the edge of her bed with her, drawing one leg up. "Can you see me now?"

She can't make out his expression. He seems to understand that, because he brings his face closer. "How about now?"

He's a touch closer than anyone should be. She's hyperaware of his fingers spread over her comforter, nearly touching her leg. But *now* she can see every flicker on his expression. The fullness of his lips. His long, thick eyelashes. The bob of his throat as he swallows. The tiny cut on the underside of his jaw where he must've nicked himself shaving. The bruise forming on his cheekbone, despite his insistence that he didn't get injured at all. Those expressive eyes, nearly haunted tonight.

Despite everything, she feels completely at ease. She's seen every piece of him now. And she cannot help but adore the picture they create.

She looks at him straight on. "Yes," she says. "I do see you."

His breath catches. And then—then—he kisses her.

Simran freezes. His mouth is soft against hers. It reverberates down her entire body, all the way to her toes. She has no room for anything but shock—shock, and giddiness—before he abruptly pulls away.

Completely. His arms are gone. Her mattress shifts as his weight leaves, too. She's left gaping and frozen and missing his heat and he's—he's on his feet, pacing her bedroom, or at least the little of it with open floor.

He curses. Loudly. His next words are harsh and cutting. "Tell me to leave."

"Wh-what?" She touches her lips with trembling fingers. *He kissed her. Rajan kissed her.*

He runs his hands down his face and turns to face the wall. "Shit," he mutters. "Shit, shit, shit. What the *fuck* is wrong with me—the *one thing* I swore I'd never do—"

He seems to be talking to himself. Simran clutches the fabric of her comforter on either side of her. She can't draw enough breath to reply, anyway.

He finally turns her way again. "Don't look at me like that. This is the most fucked-up thing I've ever done to you. Tell me to get out."

He sounds desperate, gutted, furious. Her mouth opens and closes several times.

He doesn't appear able to wait. "Fine." He wheels away. "Don't say anything. I'm leaving."

He reaches for the doorknob. Simran stands before he can turn it. "Rajan."

It's funny, because right until then, she would've thought nothing could make him hesitate. But his whole body stills. She has power over him, she realizes. The thought makes her heady. *He kissed her.* That means something, doesn't it? Even if it was just for a moment, he wanted to do it. He wanted . . . *her*.

"Come here." She doesn't recognize her own voice.

Rajan lets go of the doorknob like it burned him. He turns back around. A thick silence falls. He doesn't come to her . . . but he's not leaving, either.

Some part of Simran reminds her this is reckless—so reckless. But she doesn't want to think about that. Just this once, she doesn't want to think at all. She wants to *feel*.

He's still not moving, so she comes to him. She puts her hands on his chest, fascinated with how unsteadily it rises and falls. She looks at his face. The hunger in his eyes thrills her.

"I still don't know how to kiss," she whispers, the confession unembarrassed. He's never made her feel ashamed for these things.

Slowly, Rajan slides his hand over the side of her neck. "Then let me teach *you* something for a change."

He leans down to her. It's a closed-mouth, simple kiss. Long enough for her to get comfortable with the press of his lips. When her hands fist the material of his hoodie, he lifts away and then comes back, head tilted the other way, his mouth coaxing hers with gentle brushes, nibbles. *Like this,* he seems to be saying, before returning from a different angle. *And this.*

A part of her she didn't know existed rises up to this challenge, matching him in counterpoint and pace. *Like this, and this, and this.* Mouths together and then apart, together and apart. Together, for longer this time. Much longer . . . His fingers sink into her hair. She wraps her arms around his neck, on her tiptoes, him bending her back slightly to accommodate their height difference. His tongue brushes hers. Heat sweeps through her, and she seeks it again, wanting to learn this part, too. And, *oh*, this is something different.

Her lungs burn, but he doesn't seem to have the same oxygen demands as her, he keeps kissing her and kissing her and *kissing her*, and eventually she has to turn her head away and gasp for air. It's a good thing he's holding her up because she's not certain she could stand otherwise.

Worry overtakes her then. Is he enjoying this as much as she is? She clutches his arms. "Am—am I doing this right?"

Rajan goes still, and for a second she fears the worst. Then he grabs the backs of her thighs and hoists her up. She squeaks as he raises her just above his eye level.

"Sahiba." His eyes are bottomless. "If *that's* what you're thinking about, *I'm* the one who's not doing it right."

And then he throws her onto the bed.

Well—he doesn't *throw* her, exactly, but it happens rather fast. He carries her over in two long strides, and then the mattress bounces as her back hits it, her hair fanning around her. She doesn't have time to process how he does it so smoothly because then he's crawling over her, her mattress bowing to accommodate the additional weight.

From above, his mouth descends on her again. His kisses take on a frantic edge, like he's on the clock. Like at any moment a bell might sound, a clanging *Wrong! Wrong! Wrong!* that makes him desperate to wring as much out of her as he can in the time they have. And it's infectious.

She wants more. He's not being daring enough for her liking—one hand cradling her jaw, the other on the pillow beside her head. Keenly aware of this unknown, terrifying clock counting down on them, she voices her urgency in the least intelligible way possible. "Touch me," she gasps between kisses. "Touch me touch me touch me—"

He pulls away to ask, "Where?"

"Anywhere," she replies, and marvels at how safe she feels saying that to him. "Anywhere you want."

However, Rajan's eyes flutter shut as if in pain. *"Simran."*

Her own name sweeps over her skin. Not *Sahiba*. Not *Auntie*. Certainly not *dude*. Just . . . *Sim-ruhn*, the syllables of her gently pried apart so he could place a kiss between them. She wonders if this is why he's never said her name by itself before. If it was always going to sound like this.

"Tell me if it's too much," he says roughly, and *then* he touches her. And she feels like she's jumped from the pot into the fire. Because she was right—his unleashed hands do absolutely scandalous things under her shirt, over her body, each touch warm and wanting and teasing and *taking*. He touches her with the certainty of someone who studied her map and plotted his route years ago. He's not exploring; he's *confirming*. And she. Could. Drown in it.

"Say my name again," she pleads, clutching the back of his neck and staring at the ceiling, feeling completely delirious. She'll probably be embarrassed with the things she's demanding of him later, but she doesn't care.

He obliges her. "Simran." He noses the collar of her shirt away to press his lips to her bare shoulder. "Simran. Simran. *Simran*."

Each utterance of her name is another kiss. Each one feels like another barrier between them that they're recklessly destroying, that can never be rebuilt. When his teeth tug down her bra strap, an involuntary noise escapes her. It's breathy and sort of embarrassing. But he stills.

"You're not playing fair, making sounds like that." His voice is ragged. "You know that shit's never gonna leave my brain."

In response, she tugs at his hoodie. "Take this *off*."

He shucks his hoodie off easy, without comment, the white under-shirt beneath momentarily rucking up with it. She can only admire how he makes even *this* thoughtless motion incredibly rewarding to her eyes.

His hoodie makes a dull thud as it joins her mess of clothes already on the floor. She hungrily takes in the acres of brown skin she's unearthed—the delicate lines of his throat and collarbones, the bolder ones of his arms and chest, and that tattoo crawling over his jugular.

While she's running her hands all over him, Rajan says, unevenly, "See? No gunshot wounds."

She pauses, remembering how he'd clutched his shoulder earlier. She prods the joint with her thumb. And there. A sharp intake of breath, subtle but noticeable without the hoodie.

Her haze of *see-want-touch* instantly washes away. She sits up, forcing him up, too. "You *are* hurt!"

"It's nothing." He smooths Simran's hair back. "Just my shoulder, that's all, I can keep going—"

"Let me see."

With a sigh, he rolls off her and onto his back. This view is surreal: Rajan in her bed, her strawberry-patterned sheets twisted around him. She swings a leg over his torso to straddle him. Funny how she suddenly feels completely comfortable doing this.

Rajan seems to think so, too, because he raises an eyebrow. Before he can comment, she prods his shoulder again, making him wince. "What happened?"

"It got dislocated."

"It *got* dislocated," she repeats. The passive voice is doing a lot of work in that sentence. "Spontaneously?"

He winks. "Exactly, Auntie."

It's clear he's not planning to discuss it. Well, at least it's back in place. Her eyes are again drawn to the black tattoo that crawls up his neck. It's jagged and bold, partially obscured by his shirt.

"Can I see?" Her fingers hover over him.

He laughs softly. "You can do anything you want." He turns his head into her pillow, baring his throat. The tattoo is a stylized crest: a lion's head silhouette, laurel leaves flaring over his collarbone, wickedly sharp lines surrounding it that flow into the base of his throat, almost touching the furious pulse usually obscured by a hoodie.

She leans down, her hair falling in a curtain around them, and presses her lips to it. He jerks a little, but she keeps going, and eventually, he settles back. She kisses up his throat, jaw, cheek—everywhere she can reach. She's wanted to do this longer than she can admit. When she pulls away, he's staring at her wide-eyed, like he doesn't know what to do with himself.

Warmth fills her chest. How does he not realize how much she adores him? He must. He *must*. She kisses his mouth again. His arm circles her waist, and he moves up so they're kissing against the headboard. The only way she can think to describe it is drunk; she feels absolutely drunk, and she's certain of this despite never having been drunk before. Her thoughts are foggy, her body out of control, and she is acting on every impulse that fires through her brain.

The door downstairs opens.

It does not sound at all like a warning bell. Just a chirp—of the security alarm system.

But they move like it was a gunshot. Suddenly they're on opposite sides of her bedroom. Rajan's flattened himself against the closet door. Simran's scrambling to hook her bra. She doesn't even know when it came undone. Her hands are shaking too much, so she gives up after wasting precious seconds.

Neither of them has to voice the obvious: They're not alone anymore. Rajan grabs his shoes and moves toward the window. Simran stops him.

"You can't go from here," she whispers, frantic. "There's nowhere to fall. Go from my sister's room. She always snuck out from there."

"Show me." His voice is urgent. No trace of anything but business. Like earlier tonight, when they were fighting for their lives.

Her knees buckle a little when she stands. She feels his hands in places he didn't even touch. He doesn't comment, just follows her to Kiran's room. Her sister's window overlooks a patch of gently sloping roof. Perfect for Kiran's midnight getaways.

Rajan slips through the door without another word. Simran leaves him and walks down the hall just as her father calls, "Simran putt?"

She leans over the staircase. "You're home early." She's amazed at how steady her voice sounds.

"We brought some dinner from the gurdwara. We're going back soon, so come eat."

"Coming." She hurries to the bathroom to look into the mirror first. The first thing she notes is how red her lips look. Then her hair; now mussed every which way, the neat middle part gone. Her eyes glitter and her skin glows as if with fever. The cut on the side of her nose is glaringly apparent. And her cheek is starting to swell.

She parts her hair in the middle with her comb and fixes her bra. After yanking on a cardigan to hide her cut-up arms, she heads downstairs.

Her parents are in the kitchen, setting plastic food containers on the table. They look up when she enters. Before they can react, she says, "I fell today. My glasses broke."

Her father tuts and comes closer, as does her mother. They force her into a chair. Her mother scolds her for being clumsy, tilting Simran's head toward the light, her fingers gentler than her words. Her father takes a bag of ice from the freezer.

"It looks worse than it is," Simran tries to say, but they won't have it. They debate whether she should go to the ER. They tell her to be more careful. Eventually, her protests ebb. It feels . . . good, to have her mother prod her face looking for soreness. It feels good to have her father wiping at the cut on her nose with a wet cloth. It feels good to be cared for. She missed her mom. She missed her dad. And *god*, she missed being a child.

Without meaning to, a tear slips out of her eye. Her father instantly wipes it away. Her mother notices, too. "Did it hurt when I pressed here?" She pokes Simran's chin.

"Or are you upset over your glasses breaking?" her father asks.

"Yes," Simran whispers, letting another tear slip out. And another. "It's my glasses." A shuddering breath ripples through her.

Her mother sighs. "Don't make a fuss, Simmi. We'll get you new ones. Why are you crying over glasses?"

"Eat, nikka putt," her dad encourages. "You'll feel better. You've been working too hard lately."

They think she's working on a Hillway proposal. They came back because they wanted to make sure she ate something tonight. *That's* why she was almost caught kissing a boy in her room. Because they love her, and believe her, and all she does is lie to them.

Silent tears stream down Simran's face while she eats the food. Soft, chewy bhaturé, thick cholé, crispy pakoré. Her dad strokes her hair, probably thinking she's still upset over her glasses. She lets him. As long as they think she's crying over something silly, it won't hurt them to watch.

Her mother announces she's going to find Simran's old glasses.

"I looked for them already," Simran says. Her mother mutters, "Yeah, right," and marches upstairs. Simran trails after her. To her surprise, her mom wrenches open Simran's dresser drawer and instantly produces a glasses case. "Did you look with your eyes closed?"

"Mom, I literally can't *see*."

Her mother ignores this and pops open the case. "How many times do I have to tell you, your life would be so much easier if you kept your room clean?"

As usual, she's right. Not that that's going to change her ways. Simran puts the glasses on. They're an old style, too small, and the prescription isn't accurate anymore, but she can now read the framed certificates on her wall.

"Simran."

"Mm-hmm." She squints at a line of text on the city volunteerism award.

"Where'd you get this?"

Simran turns, her world now in focus somewhat, only for it to fall apart when she sees her mother holding Rajan's hoodie.

It's half-turned inside out from when he took it off. Black, oversize, too big for her. Picked up off the floor.

Her mother stares at her glacially.

Terror, sheer terror, grips her. "It's a friend's." There's no point pretending it's hers.

"A friend," her mother repeats. "Or, a boyfriend?"

This horrifying question is framed casually. Almost like this would be okay. Like the consequences wouldn't blow up Simran's entire life. TJ's situation would look cute in comparison.

"No," Simran says around her dry mouth. "A classmate loaned it to me for a presentation, because I spilled tea on my shirt."

"Where was your jacket?"

"I didn't bring one."

"You always bring one. You say it's always cold at the university."

Simran *had* said that. "I forgot that day."

"I see. Why didn't you give this back after?"

"He left before I could."

"Who?"

"Jassa."

A pause. "Jassa Singh?"

"Yes." In front of her eyes, her mother relaxes slightly. Relieved, Simran extends her hand. "I'll give it back to him tomorrow."

Her mother glances down at it. "I'll wash it first."

Simran suddenly remembers the bullet hole. "Oh, I'll do it. I have lots of other things in this colour to wash."

Her mother's voice is pleasant. "No, no. I'll wash it special."

Simran hangs in limbo for a second, wanting to insist but knowing she can't. A beat passes. Then another. Finally, she drops her arm.

Her mother disappears with Rajan's hoodie. Simran closes her door softly behind her, then sinks to the carpet, lightheaded. A minute passes. Then ten. Did she get away with it?

The washer turns on downstairs. Simran awaits footsteps returning to her door. Jassa doesn't wear hoodies, really. And he's even less likely to wear a hoodie with a hole in it. Or . . . if there was blood on it . . . Simran squeezes her eyes shut. Time is limited. *Think.*

She spins every possible lie, every explanation she can think of for every scenario, poking holes into each one as she does, trying to make them bulletproof.

But, her mother doesn't return all night.

THIRTY-THREE

WHEN SIMRAN WAKES the next day, her first thought is surprise that she fell asleep. Her phone tells her it's noon. Practically early. And—she squints at her screen—she's got several missed calls from a private number. Nick.

Well, the Lions will have to wait. She rolls onto her back again and stares at the ceiling. Spreads her arms out on her bed, which feels strangely empty without . . . *him*.

Memories of last night flood back. Her. Rajan. Kissing. No—more than that. The things she asked him to do . . . in the daylight, her cheeks burn. She tugs her pillow over her face. How can she ever look him in the eye again?

The pillow makes her bruised cheek smart, and she tosses it away. Right. So much more than *that* happened yesterday. She glances at her purse on the floor. She doesn't know what possessed her to shove the last Ace ledger in her bag. Well, actually, she does. She wanted to finish decoding it. But having it in her room feels somewhat like having a grenade.

Her mom calls her name from downstairs.

"You're going to be late!"

Late? For what? Simran changes quickly, braids her hair, and puts on her old glasses. They make her look fourteen and awkward. Oh well. She grabs her purse—she's not letting that ledger leave her sight—and heads downstairs.

The smell of *cooking* wafts over, halting her on the last step. From here, she can see into the kitchen. Her mother's back is turned, and she's humming along to kirtan as she flips something on the stove. Paranthé, if the aroma is any indication. But . . . her mom hasn't cooked in months.

And Simran had thought she'd never see it again. She draws closer, drinking in the sight.

Her mother turns. "There you are."

She sounds chipper. Simran eyes her warily.

"For you." She brandishes a plate piled with paranthé. "Eggs, too. Good for your brain."

It's like the interrogation yesterday never happened. Simran sinks into a chair. The parantha is delicious: warm, crisp, filled with layers of flavour. Hadn't her mom once said she put blended daal in the dough? Simran doesn't recall exactly.

She pauses mid-chew, the enjoyment flooding away, replaced with panic. What if she never learns? What if she loses this part of her mother? "Can you show me how to make these?"

"Really?" Her mom smiles, pleased. "You've never shown interest before."

"Can you show me right *now*?"

She can't stop the desperate edge entering her voice. Her mother raises a brow. "Aren't you going to be late for Neetu?"

Neetu? Simran glances at the whiteboard. Under today's date, she'd scribbled in kirtan practice with Neetu, a re-re-rebooking. "Right." Her mom is once again paying attention to Simran's schedule—more than Simran is. "Tomorrow, then. I have to learn."

Her mother, oblivious to her inner turmoil, turns up the TV and tuts. "Look. Gangs are tearing up this city. This is the second time in two months. Almost as bad as Surrey."

Simran pauses, her spoonful of dahi halfway to her mouth. On-screen is the Lion's café. The next shot is the parking lot, surrounded by police cruisers and tape. The newscaster discusses a drug seizure. Illegal funds. Property damaged and people killed.

Simran could've been one of those people. If it wasn't for Rajan, she would've been.

The parantha turns to chalk in her mouth. She has to talk to Nick. Now.

As she's setting her spoon down, her father comes in and frowns. "Look at that bruise. You need to eat," he says, as if that's going to spontaneously clear the injury.

Her mom sniffs. "She's sitting here chewing her lip instead of her food. Even though her practice is in *fifteen minutes*." She whisks Simran's plate away. "I'll pack it."

"I don't need—"

"You'll get hungry. You'll see." She loads it with chutney and wraps it neatly. Simran accepts the package and is turning for the door when her mother speaks again.

"Aren't you forgetting something?"

Her words hang in the air. Simran pivots slowly, to find her holding out Rajan's hoodie. Newly washed and folded.

Simran accepts it. "Thanks."

"Give Jassa my hello," her mom adds.

"I will."

She holds herself stiffly as she leaves, feeling her mother's eyes on her back the whole way.

Nick picks up immediately when Simran calls on her way to the gurdwara. "Alive, are you?"

She merges onto the highway. "No thanks to the Lions."

"That was a surprise ambush. We don't know what they were looking for."

"Yes, we do. *Me.*" His silence confirms it. "So much for your security."

His voice becomes curt. "I'm not doing this over the phone. Where are you?"

"Meet me at the gurdwara in an hour." She hangs up. She has to at *least* show her face at this kirtan practice first. She's flaked on Neetu too many times.

Upon arriving at the gurdwara, she stuffs Rajan's hoodie under her seat, taking a second to run her hand down the soft material. She misses him already. But it feels vaguely incriminating to text him, especially after the near disaster last night with her mom. Her parents aren't the type to snoop through her phone, but still—with everything going on, maybe it's best to lie low for now. She'll ask Nick about him instead.

When she enters the room where practice takes place, several elementary-school-age kids are already with Neetu in the corner. Neetu's playing something in Raag Dhanasari on the harmonium but stops abruptly when she sees Simran. Her eyes widen; clearly, she hadn't expected Simran to show.

She recovers quickly, though. "Simran! You made it! Could you take them through some scales? I have to use the washroom."

Simran nods, feeling guilty. Neetu's been overseeing these kirtan practices on her own for a while, and that can't be easy with all the kids to supervise.

She takes her place in front of the harmonium and begins with the gentlest smile she can muster. The kids are rambunctious and difficult to corral at first; they interrupt her lesson to ask what happened to her face. She replies that her music instructor bashed her head into the harmonium. That gets them working.

For a while, the practice is uneventful. She's taking them through renditions of *sa-re-ga-ma-pa-dha-ni-sa* when a loud sound erupts from outside. It sounds a lot like a gunshot.

Instantly, Simran freezes. Her fingers stumble on the keys, her voice dies in her throat, and without warning, she's somewhere else.

Gunfire. In the dark, her cheek pressed against the ground. Immobilized by terror. Rajan ordering her to stay close—

"Simran Bhenji? Are you okay?"

She blinks, and she's back. The kids stare at her with concern.

She releases her white-knuckled grip on the harmonium and glances out the window. Of course it wasn't a gunshot—just someone dropping a recycling bin. Why'd she flinch? "Yes. I'm fine."

She continues the lesson. Then Neetu returns and splits the kids into groups to teach them new shabads. At some point, Simran's phone rings with a private number. She looks out the window again and spots an ice-cream truck at the curb.

Of course. She's gone ten minutes over the hour she told Nick. She turns to Neetu, a few feet away. "I have to go. Can you finish here?"

She feels terrible asking, especially when Neetu's smile dims, but it returns again. "Okay, but only if you do me a favour."

Oh no. "What do you need?"

"Gurjeevan and his family are flying in tomorrow. We're hosting a backyard party for them. I know you're busy, but it'd mean a lot if you came. Bring your family, too."

How polite of her to say Simran is *busy* instead of the truth, which is that she's flaky. "Okay."

Neetu lights up. "Really?"

Her enthusiasm makes Simran feel even worse. "Yes. I wouldn't miss it."

She leaves, telling herself she won't.

The ice-cream truck is idling one street over. Simran eats her parantha on the way; her mother was right; she *did* get hungry.

When Simran gets in, Zohra's in the driver's seat. Nick, who's lounging against one of the coolers, says, "Nice glasses."

Simran ignores this. "We need to talk."

"What, not done your tantrum yet?"

Tantrum? As if her reaction was *disproportionate*? "I almost died. I have a right to be angry."

"We got you out."

"*Rajan* got me out."

Nick scoffs. "How do you think he knew you were there? He was with me when I got the call."

Simran blinks. She hadn't . . . even thought to ask why Rajan was there yesterday.

But she won't let Nick distract her. "I've paid Rajan's debts a thousand times over. I'm leaving. For good."

"Not this again." Nick tears into a Drumstick. "How many times do I have to tell you and Rajan, I don't control that?"

She only catches one part of that answer. "You spoke to Rajan?"

"I called that little asshole like ten times last night and he only called back to bite my head off." She nods mutely, relieved. At least he's okay. Nick goes on. "I'll tell you what I told him. This is beyond us now."

"But we had an *agreement*."

Nick gives her an almost-pitying look. Zohra speaks up from the driver's seat, her eyes filling the rearview mirror.

"It's not personal, Simran. Say we let you off the hook—someone *else* will bring you back. The Lions can't afford to lose you. If you walk, a lot of money and information walks with you."

Simran shakes her head and begins pacing. She refuses to believe this. "There has to be a way. People must leave."

Nick tosses his wrapper behind him. "Yeah, people leave. All the time. Kids who move drugs for us, whose parents find out—they get their asses whooped, they don't come back, we don't care." He rolls his eyes. "Mid-tier, like Rajan, they know stuff about us. We'll try to keep them, but people still leave. They can move cities—that's what Rajan tried, by coming back here from Surrey. Might've worked if . . . ." He exhales. "Well, anyway. But people as valuable as you don't leave. They die, or go to prison."

Rajan had said the same. But . . . "Who decides I'm valuable?"

"People paid a lot more than me."

"You mean people like Manny Khullar," she says, and both Zohra and Nick shift on the spot, like a chill has picked up in the small space.

"Manny's not the biggest fish in the pond," Zohra says.

Earlier she said he was part of the crime family that built the Lions. So now she's downplaying it. Interesting. "But he's the biggest fish in Kelowna. Right?"

Nick eyes her wearily. "What are you saying, Simran?"

Simran stops pacing. "I want to meet him."

THIRTY-FOUR

IT TAKES SOME convincing, but eventually, Nick says he'll attempt to fulfill her "death wish." His wording, not hers. After securing a promise that he'll get in touch, and making it clear she won't do any bookkeeping until she meets Manny, Simran heads home. She doesn't hear from him for the rest of the day. Clearly, this could take a while.

So the following day, when her parents ask if she wants to go to the mall to buy new glasses, she happily accepts. She's in a boutique inspecting frames similar to her old ones when she hears her name called behind her.

She turns to find Chandani making a beeline into the store. And she's not alone—TJ's with her.

There's nowhere to run. Simran stands there helplessly as Chandani drags TJ in. "There's my favourite nerd!"

TJ does a double take. Simran feels self-conscious about her old glasses once again.

Chandani doesn't notice. "What're you doing here?"

"Getting new glasses." Simran jabs her thumb behind her. "With my parents."

That's a hint that she's busy, but Chandani only waves to her parents. TJ does the same. "Oh, good. I wasn't going to say anything, but the glasses you're wearing right now are godawful, worse than those other ones. What happened to them, anyway?"

"I fell."

"Thank god. I mean, not for the banged-up face. But sometimes things happen for a reason." Chandani nudges TJ. "We can find her way nicer glasses, right?"

TJ looks anywhere but at Simran. Simran's unsure what to do. They haven't seen each other since the hospital, and that feels like eons ago.

Chandani looks between them. "Oh, for god's sake. Do you bitches have some kind of drama going on? Without telling me?" She sounds more upset that she was left out of it than that there was drama in the first place.

At that moment, Simran's father returns with a pair of rectangular frames. "What about these?"

They're not Simran's type, but she reaches to try them on anyway. Chandani bats her hand away before she can. "No, Uncle ji. Let's keep looking, though." She smiles brightly. Simran's father, looking bemused, drifts away again. Chandani glances back at TJ. "Well?"

TJ examines her sharp nails. "Nothing's going on." Her voice is flat. Simran struggles to remember what exactly she said to TJ. She's burned so many bridges lately, it's hard to keep track.

"If you don't want to tell me, just say so." Chandani rolls her eyes. "I'm going to find better frames for you, Simran. We clearly can't depend on Uncle ji to solve this crisis." She disappears. Leaving Simran and TJ alone.

Simran peeks up from the price tag she's pretending to examine, only to find TJ mirroring her. They both quickly look away. This is *ridiculous*. If Simran's plan works . . . she'll be out of the Lions soon. It'll be over, and didn't she say she was going to repair those bridges when it was?

Simran sets down the frames just as TJ starts walking away. "TJ, wait." TJ stills. "Neetu's hosting a backyard party tonight. Do you want to come?"

TJ faces her. "What?"

Simran's confidence falters. "Her family is hosting Gurjeevan's—"

"I heard you. But you told me to leave you alone."

Simran winces internally. "I'm sorry about what I said. That . . ." *Wasn't me.* Except it was. She *is* this person now.

TJ doesn't wait for her to finish anyway. "I don't understand you. For months, you've avoided me, now you're inviting me to a party? Why? You just need someone to go with?"

Simran's mouth goes dry. "That's not—"

Chandani returns at that moment. "I've got the perfect frames. Jassa won't be able to keep his hands off." She cackles, shoving them into Simran's hands.

TJ makes a disinterested noise and turns for the exit. "I'm going to Sephora."

Simran watches her leave. Chandani rolls her eyes. "Bitch. Anyway, Simran, these will look *amazing* on you."

Feeling defeated, Simran puts them on and lets Chandani snap pictures. They're dark green with golden accents, the circular shape complementing her "angled face," whatever that means. Simran gets them, mostly to get Chandani off her back.

Once Chandani leaves, Simran's mom comes up to her. "So is TJ coming to the party?"

Her return from being a ghost is kind of jarring. What else did she hear? "No."

"Then her mom won't either." She sounds relieved. Simran knows the feeling—fewer lies to prepare. Maybe it's for the best, then. But her heart still feels heavy.

Simran's phone rings. Private number.

"Who's that?" her mom asks.

"Hillway. Just a second." She walks into the mall corridor, where it's crowded and busy. "Hello?"

"Manny will meet you tonight at five," Nick says without preamble.

Simran stops. The party's tonight. "So soon?"

"What can I say. Your little strike pissed him off good."

"But tonight doesn't work." She can't miss the party, she *promised* Neetu.

"Manny will meet you tonight or he'll never meet you," Nick replies. "You know where. Five, or never." He hangs up.

Her parents approach. "Everything okay?" her father asks. Simran pockets her phone.

"Paul needs my help with something at five. It'll be quick," she adds, determined. "I'll meet you at the party, Mom. Okay?"

This shouldn't take long. It can't.

At five twenty, Simran rolls through the gates of Manny's mansion. She hadn't anticipated packing her suit would take so long. It's a burnt-orange number with silver detailing, currently tucked into the back seat. For now, she's in her usual jeans and T-shirt, a thin jacket on top.

Nick and Zohra are waiting. They don't waste time when she gets out of her truck, setting for the entrance. The party is, once again, ongoing. The heavy bass sets a different tone, though.

"You're late," Nick says curtly when Simran catches up.

"Does that surprise you?"

"No. Which is why, when Manny said five thirty, I told you five."

Very tricky of him. "What else did he say?"

"Nothing. You have to be careful."

"Manny's been known to have people killed on the spot," Zohra adds. "One moment he's laughing, next thing you hear a bang, and his bodyguard just shot the guy who made him laugh."

Simran pushes her glasses up. "Well, good thing I'm not very funny then."

Nick halts at the doors. "You're not taking this seriously. You have no idea what you're walking into."

Simran swallows to work moisture into her mouth. "I don't have any other choice."

Nick shakes his head and opens the door. He and Zohra aren't smiling, aren't smoking or eating Popsicles, aren't their usual playful mocking selves. They're *anxious*. In a strange twist, Simran is the most relaxed one here.

They ascend the staircase and turn down a corridor Simran didn't notice last time. Finally, they stop at a doorway obscured by a beaded curtain. The smoke is thicker here. Tinkling laughter comes from inside.

"This is where we leave you. Last chance," Nick says. "Tell me you change your mind. You don't have to do this."

He's right. But if she pulls it off . . .

Simran squares her shoulders. "My friend's party is in thirty minutes. Don't let me miss it."

Without waiting for an answer, she pushes through the curtain.

Immediately, two Lions in all black close in to pat her down. Once they're satisfied, they shove her forward. It's a large sitting room, and at the center is a sprawling leather couch.

Simran wasn't sure what she expected of Manny Khullar. But her first thought is that he's dangerously handsome. The edges of his closely shorn beard are razor-sharp. His hair is gelled, short at the sides and long on top. He's in the kind of well-fitting, simple shirt that somehow screams money. He lounges behind a coffee table set with glittering ornaments and crystal trays of pills and powder. A blond white woman is curled up against his side in a thin bathrobe, her eyes half lidded.

Simran's eyes drift to the small, nondescript book in Manny's lap. He sets it down when she stops in front of them. Piercing gold eyes fall on her. Then he smiles.

"Simran Kaur Aujla. The refreshments are for you. Please, help yourself." He gestures to the array of drugs like they're a cheese platter. Several rings flash on his fingers.

Simran doesn't move. "You know why I'm here."

"I insist you treat yourself before we talk shop."

"I'm fine."

He drops his hand. "It wasn't a suggestion."

Nick hadn't warned her about this. Simran glances at the tray. "If you find my services valuable," she says, carefully, "why would you want me to take anything that will compromise my ability to think?"

He laughs. "No one told me you were funny, Simran."

Simran remembers Zohra's words all too vividly. "I'm not trying to be."

"That's the best part. But I have to say, the funniest thing you've done so far is this little strike." He swirls his glass. "You want better compensation, I respect that. So I'll make this easy for you—you study math at UBCO, right? We'll pay your tuition. Hell, we'll pay for you to become an accountant, and any other degree you want. Full-ride scholarship from the Lion's Share. How's that sound?"

Incredible. But Simran knows better. "How would I know you could keep that promise? The Lions couldn't even organize well enough to defend a café." His eyes flash, but she keeps going. "You can't guarantee my safety. I paid the debts I was paying. I want out."

She can't explain it, but the air in the room changes near the end of her speech. The woman at Manny's side rises, tightening the sash at her waist before padding out. The men behind Simran shift on their feet. And Manny . . .

"You know what I hate more than people who get cold feet?" His voice becomes silky. "People who think they're better than all this. Low-level, green Lions who don't understand how this works."

"I'm not—"

"I know everything about you," Manny continues. "I have eyes at the mill where your father works. I know your mother's favourite walking route. I'm glad the cancer's gone, by the way. I've also looked into your cousin, although admittedly I don't know why she looked so angry with you today at the mall. And all your musician friends, too . . . I haven't touched any of them, so maybe you think I'm bluffing."

Simran tries not to show how shaken she is.

He steeples his fingers. "Thing is, accidents happen. I have some buddies in construction who told me about one just the other day. Some young guy fell off a roof. He walked it off, though. Lucky." His eyes become brighter. "Next time, he might break his neck."

Rajan. He's got to be talking about Rajan. That dislocated shoulder of his . . . Manny's doing. A show of his power.

When she doesn't respond, Manny reclines, now looking bored. "Let me be clear. I was offering compensation to be *nice*. But I see I have to drop that shit and remind you of your place. You're a teenage girl who worked with the lowest shitheads of the Lions for a couple months. If you decide to be cute and stop working, you become a liability. So convince me right now, Simran, that you're not a liability. Convince me you're not going to walk, or do something else stupid, like talk to cops." Something cold presses against the back of Simran's head. She doesn't have to look to know one of the guards has his gun on her. "Convince me, because the only reason I allowed this ridiculous meeting was so I could personally watch a bullet go into your brain."

Simran's throat closes. Several seconds pass.

She forces herself to breathe. Manny didn't offer compensation earlier for nothing. And even now, him wanting to see her dead *personally* tells her something very interesting indeed. She *is* valuable . . . but also dangerous. He would rather not kill her, but only if he knows she can be controlled.

Her eyes flicker over the table, and the items on it. A decision settles into her chest. There was never going to be a way out, after all.

Only a way through.

She points at the lines of powder and makes the biggest gamble of her life. "I'll take my refreshments now."

THIRTY-FIVE

SIMRAN IS HAVING a fantastic time when Nick and Zohra come by later.

Seriously, *fantastic*. She's kneeling by the coffee table, paper spread everywhere, the books on the table shoved to the side. She's so busy writing that she only vaguely notes two pairs of shoes stopping next to her.

Nick taps her shoulder.

"It's time to go." His voice is low, urgent. She glances up. Nick and Zohra both look worried for some reason. Manny's just around the corner, having set her up with supplies. He gave her a green crayon instead of the pen she asked for, which was odd, especially because everyone laughed when she took it eagerly. But she could still work with it. Why are they so concerned?

"I have to write this down. Before I forget." It's so exciting, her heart races. She almost feels dizzy. Her brain, it's working in whole new *dimensions*.

Nick glances at the page. "And what, exactly, are you writing?"

"An idea to encrypt the Lions' ledgers," she says eagerly. She starts explaining it. It makes perfect sense; hard to decode, but if you're a

Lion, it's easy. It's brilliant. It's the perfect cipher. She'll call it the Simran cipher. She'll—

"You're not making a lick of sense right now," Zohra interrupts. Behind her, bricks from the fireplace come out of the wall and morph into spheres. "You realize that, right?"

Simran frowns and drops her hands, which she'd been using to illustrate her points. Of course Nick and Zohra don't understand. Manny and his friends didn't either. They let her talk for a while but they didn't listen, really. Everyone thinks she's just high. Which, fine, *yes*, but that doesn't mean she lost her brain. In fact, her neurons are firing better than ever.

Nick turns to Zohra. "Go distract Manny for a sec." He yanks Simran up. "Let's go."

Simran resists. "I need my jacket." That was important for some reason. She doesn't remember why anymore.

Nick lets her put it on. She feels her pockets to make sure she has everything, then reaches for her papers. "I need these, too."

"Fine. We'll bring your little masterpiece. But only so you can see how hard you were tripping later."

He drags her forward. She stumbles, but Nick doesn't slow down, which is rather annoying. She was having a great time until he showed up.

A soft laugh comes from around the corner. Zohra. Simran hears Manny's rumbling voice in response. She cranes her head to see what's happening, but Nick pulls her back. He tows her down the stairs, and when she pitches forward, he swings her into his arms. She spreads her hands out and makes airplane sounds. Nick sighs. She laughs, and then can't stop laughing. She laughs so hard she gets a stitch.

"Nick, you're funny, you know that?" She wipes tears as they finally reach the main level. Instead of going to the front door, Nick veers left, down another set of stairs. Then a service entrance, a set of metal double doors. "Why'd you join the Lions when you could've become a comedian?" She laughs again.

"That's right. I'm a comedian, Manny's house is the circus, and he made *you* the clown." Nick comes to a stop and sets Simran down on the floor, against a cabinet. They appear to be in an abandoned kitchen. He rummages under the sink. Her curiosity grows.

"How *did* you end up with the Lions?" she asks. "Are you like Rajan?"

"No, I'm not *like Rajan*." Nick snorts. "My family is loaded and they all love me. I'm their only son who can do no wrong. I'm not like the rest of you. I don't have a sob story. I was just bored."

She stares at his back. "Is that why you set Rajan up to fall off a roof? Because you were bored?"

"*This* again? I didn't set him up. Did he say that?"

"No, Manny did."

Nick stills. "Shit." He says it through his teeth, like he's realizing something at long last. "His PO . . . And that hammer . . ."

Simran has no clue what he's talking about. She's watching the patterns on the ceiling swirl when Zohra enters. Nick, now holding a large bucket, faces her. "Well?"

Zohra looks somewhat resigned, finger-combing her hair. "He saw you take her. He was mellow about it. Said he'd had his fun."

"Yeah, I bet." Nick's voice is dark. "This is getting out of hand, Z. Manny's doing stuff without telling me now." He lugs his bucket to the sink. "Simran, take off your jacket."

Simran hugs it closer. "No."

"Suit yourself."

While Simran's trying to figure out what he means, Zohra squats and tilts Simran's face up. "What'd you take?"

"She smells like weed," Nick says from the sink. "And I saw pills. What were they?"

"Not sure," Simran admits.

"At *least* G," Zohra says. "You know Manny loves G."

"It can't just be G. Not with the way she's acting." Nick sighs as he shakes ice into his bucket. "Rajan will use my head for swing practice if he finds out about this."

Simran hiccups. "Ooh, I'd like to see that."

Zohra's head comes up sharply. So does Nick's.

"Jesus," he says. "It really is always the quiet ones."

That's even funnier. She giggles as Zohra wipes her nose with a towel. The imagery gets to her because everything about Rajan does. Who is she kidding? She's attracted to him. So much, that sometimes if he looks at her just right her heart will flip like he kissed her. And god, the *kissing.* If they hadn't been interrupted that night, she would've—

She only realizes she's talking out loud because Zohra interrupts. "Wait, you two kissed?"

She sounds curious, not jealous. Simran nods. Zohra breaks into a grin.

"Get it, girl! Well? How was it?"

Simran fans herself. Zohra laughs.

"Sounds about right." Her smile becomes catlike. She beckons Simran closer. "If you really want him wrapped around your finger, he likes when you—"

"Okay, that's enough," Nick says, finally coming back with the water.

"Nooo," Simran cries. "Zohra, what were you going to say?"

Nick cuts her off before she can reply. "Stop encouraging this. She's gonna be so embarrassed later."

Zohra puts her hands on her hips. "I'm not trying to humiliate her. I'm just helping a girl out."

"Fucking spare me, Z." Then he dumps the bucket of water unceremoniously over Simran's head.

Simran shrieks. The icy water is a shock, drenching her hair and shoulders, and the cold seeps through her rain jacket. "What was *that* for?"

"You need to get sober. Fast." Nick drops the bucket. "*You're* the one who said you had a party to get to, remember? 'Don't let me miss it'?"

Oh. Right. Simran rubs her eyes. The buzz remains, temporarily relegated to background noise. "How long was I . . . ?"

"Over an hour," Nick says shortly. "We thought Manny killed you."

She glances at the clock. It's seven. Oh *no*. "I have to go." She can't let Neetu down. Not again. She staggers to her feet. The floor spins.

Nick doesn't move to help when she collides with the cabinet. "If this party was so important, why'd you get high with Manny Khullar? What the hell were you thinking?"

A laugh escapes her without her meaning to, and then another. What *was* she thinking?

Simran forces her giggles back with difficulty. "I had to prove my loyalty."

"The only thing you proved was that you'd be his bitch."

Simran doesn't respond. She pats herself down. Her shoulders are wet thanks to Nick's ice water, but it didn't reach her phone inside her jacket. She drops her hands and heads for the door, steadier this time.

Zohra blocks the doorway. "You're going to a party like *that*? Have you even looked in a mirror?"

The idea hadn't occurred to her. "My salwar kameez is in my truck. I'll change."

"Say 'baby hippopotamus' without slurring and we'll let you go," Nick challenges. Simran narrows her eyes.

"Baby hippopotamus."

She's quite proud of herself, really, but Nick sighs. Glances at Zohra, who shrugs.

"I mean, it's borderline?"

Nick takes his bucket and tosses more water at Simran's face.

"Stop it!" she sputters, annoyed now.

"That's better." Nick drops the bucket. "Give it one hour, *then* go."

"But I'll be so late—"

"If you go now, it'll be obvious you're tripping."

She dislikes how much sense he's making. "One hour. Then I'm going."

"Okay." Nick crosses his arms. "But for the record, it's a bad idea."

———

Sadly, Simran realizes upon arrival at Neetu's house that Nick was right.

The backyard party is in full swing; several of Neetu's and Gurjeevan's cousins flit around with mehndi-adorned hands. A seating arrangement underneath a white tent is bathed in the soft glow of fairy lights, cloth-draped tables covered with catered food. It's a warm, humid evening, and the house's screen door is slightly ajar. Inside, several aunties are on the couch having chah while little kids chase each other around.

Simran pauses at the side of the house to check her reflection in her phone screen. Zohra rebraided her hair after she put on her salwar kameez. But her nose still looks red, the blacks of her eyes too big. At least her heart has calmed somewhat, and she no longer has the urge to laugh at everything.

She clicks to her phone's photo gallery. After Manny got bored with her, and before Nick and Zohra arrived, Simran spent every moment of her time alone with the ledger on the table, photographing each page. It was just like Zohra said: Manny does drugs and counts his money at the same time. It makes sense that he would keep his ledgers close. All she had to do was get close, too.

It still wasn't easy. She had to act fast, because she had no idea when the pills she'd taken would kick in. Yet she had to pause frequently when people came to check on her. And when Manny brought another bag of cocaine, she had no choice but to accept. That was when numbers began sprouting from the page and she lost confidence in reality. Her photos became blurrier the further things went. That could've been bad. If Nick and Zohra hadn't found her . . .

"Simran putt!"

An auntie's voice makes her lower her phone immediately. She's finally been noticed.

The auntie drops her paper plate into the garbage bag next to Simran. "Did you eat anything yet? You should." She gives Simran a hug, but her embrace loosens almost immediately in surprise. Simran knows right then that despite Nick giving her a makeshift bath, she still smells like what she's been doing.

Normally, Simran could spin a lie on the spot to explain this. But at the moment, she can't think of a single thing. "Sat Sri Akaal, Auntie ji. How are you?"

The auntie, smile fading now, replies, but Simran barely hears it. Her brain feels like molasses. The longer she entertains the useless, airy conversation, the more she realizes the drugs did more than she thought. Niceties that normally come easy—such as knowing the correct responses, how to act impressed about so-and-so's son's promotion, asking after someone's health—currently feel impossible.

Her answers are one-worded and awkward. There's a small silence before the auntie says, "Well, your mother's in the house."

"Thanks. I'll get some food first," Simran says, and then they part ways. Her smile drops immediately. How could she forget her mother was here? She has to avoid her as long as possible. Her mom will *know*. Simran's stomach lurches at the thought.

Get a grip, she tells herself. She takes several deep breaths before entering the party.

The makeshift dance floor is crammed, and the buffet line long. Neetu's at a table near the front. She looks gorgeous in her plum lehenga, her hair curled loosely around her shoulders. A handsome man in a matching shirt sits beside her, his hand on her back. That must be Gurjeevan.

As if sensing her, Neetu's eyes meet hers and light up. And so Simran has no choice but to go over.

"You came! Gurjeevan, this is my friend Simran. We've been doing kirtan together for ages." She pats the seat on the other side of her.

Awkwardly, Simran sits. How had she never appreciated before the coordination it takes to maneuver into a chair? She has to consciously tuck every limb into the right place.

Neetu notices. "Are you okay?"

Simran makes a noise of confirmation before folding her hands, nodding at the others at the table. Kamaljot Uncle, Toor Auntie—Toor Uncle's wife—and someone young who looks a lot like Gurjeevan, probably a cousin. She's about to introduce herself when she spots a bunch of ants crawling over the tablecloth.

Not real. Not real . . . right? Gurjeevan would notice if there were really ants swarming on his hand. "It's nice to meet you, Gurjeevan."

"Same here." He inhales as if to ask a question, then frowns slightly.

Right. Simran gets ahead of it with a lie she prepared on the way to the table. "I'm sorry if I smell like . . . smoke. I was at Hillway before this. Someone I was working with was smoking quite heavily."

Neetu makes a sympathetic noise and reaches into her handbag for a perfume bottle. "Hold out your hands." She spritzes Simran's wrists.

"What's Hillway?" Gurjeevan asks. Neetu starts explaining, while something drops on Simran's hand.

A bright red splatter. She automatically touches her nose. Her hand comes away wet. Neetu notices at the same time, cutting off her explanation with a gasp. "Simran! You're bleeding."

Her voice is loud enough to carry. Simran takes the offered napkin to staunch her nosebleed. She only vaguely remembers the first line of cocaine. Manny showed her how to do it. She asked him to demonstrate a second time, because she hadn't understood. He laughed and did. She tried, and failed. Asked again. Manny gave her a look, and for a second, she wondered if she'd gone too far. But then, he said he'd help. Shoved her head down.

She felt the chunks in her nostrils. Her gums tingled, and she tasted it somehow all the way to her toes. Her body locked up and her thoughts slowed down. She felt tense, but in a good way.

So this is what Rajan likes, she thought, right before it hit her.

Simran lowers the napkin. There's a shocking amount of red. Everyone's staring, so Simran scrounges for a new topic. "How did you two meet again?" She knows the story, but it's the best she can think of.

Neetu indulges her for the sake of the table, though, sharing a smile with Gurjeevan. "I looked for partners through family feelers. Friends thought I was so old-school."

"As if they weren't doing the same thing on dating apps," Gurjeevan puts in. Neetu nods.

"But they'd be like, 'Why not open up to other people? That guy walking by could be your soulmate.' And I guess my answer is, I think there's multiple people, not just one, that you could be compatible with. There's eight billion people in the world, after all."

Gurjeevan says, "But none of those other soulmates are as handsome as me, right?"

The whole table laughs. Neetu elbows him before continuing. "If you follow the logic that there's plenty of people you could love, you add a couple of filters, you know? Narrow it to people who wouldn't complicate things. People who have similar goals in life, people who've had similar life experiences, so they understand you, and your families get along okay. People who make your life easier. Relationships are hard enough without adding unnecessary drama and misunderstandings."

"Well said," Kamaljot Uncle says. He nudges Simran, whose nosebleed is slowing. "TJ could learn something from these two."

Simran shifts uncomfortably. That photo of TJ and Charlie sure made the rounds.

Toor Auntie tuts. "Come now, Bhah ji. She's happy, isn't she?"

"For now," Kamaljot Uncle says ominously. "But real, long-lasting partnerships require more mature thinking. She'll see in a few years."

He sounds so confident. Even Toor Auntie shrugs, as if to say *fair enough*. It pinches at Simran. As the others move to other topics, she impulsively leans toward Neetu. "What if you met one of those other soulmates first?" she whispers. "One of the ones outside your filter, who might make your life harder? Before you met Gurjeevan. What would you do then?"

Neetu's smile fades, and Simran abruptly realizes how inappropriate this is, asking about other possible lovers in front of her fiancé. She leans back, about to say, *Never mind*, when Neetu exhales "I'm not sure. Why?"

Simran wipes her nose one last time, a bitter taste in her throat that has nothing to do with blood. "Just curious."

She can feel Neetu still looking at her oddly, but she avoids her eyes. Instead, she tries to imagine being in Neetu's place, sitting next to the perfect faceless person she specifically went looking for. Someone who ticks all the boxes. It's logical. It's the exact kind of thing she would do. The problem is, the person she imagines isn't faceless.

"Aw, dude, you wanna marry me? That's cute."

Simran jumps, whipping her head to the right. In the previously vacant seat lounges Rajan, one arm draped over the back of her chair. He's in the same black hoodie Simran has stowed in her truck. "You need to chill. We're eighteen," he goes on, taking the toothpick from his mouth, "and I don't take everything as serious as you. They're right. This was never gonna work."

Simran rubs her eyes vigorously. When she opens them, the seat next to her is vacant again.

"Simran?"

She blinks to find the whole table staring.

"You look pale," Toor Auntie notes, reaching over to press a hand to Simran's forehead. "And you're sweating! Are you sick?"

"I'm fine." Simran wishes they'd stop looking. So much concern for a person who doesn't deserve it. What would they think if they knew about her and Rajan? After her erratic behaviour these last few months, people already whisper about her, but this would be so much worse. Would they still love her? Would they still trust her as they do now?

Her nausea intensifies.

Meanwhile, Neetu jokingly says, "Maybe she inhaled too much smoke at Hillway."

"She's very brave, working there," Kamaljot Uncle says. "I don't know why she does it."

"Because she's a good person," Toor Auntie says.

"And it's wasted on them!" Kamaljot Uncle harrumphs. "They're completely disrespectful. Like that Randhawa boy, *swearing* at one of our diners at the kitchen."

Toor Auntie tuts. "Really? *That's* how they treat people?"

"Exactly!" Kamaljot Uncle exclaims. "Ungrateful—"

"You don't know him."

Simran doesn't even realize she spoke until Kamaljot Uncle blanches. The table goes quiet. She should take it back. She knows she should. But as the silence stretches, she finds that she can't.

Kamaljot Uncle says, "Simran, we've been over this. He went to jail for—"

"So what!" Simran shouts. Conversations pause. Neetu stares at her. Gurjeevan, too. "How dare you judge those people when you don't know what they've been through?" The volume of the backyard lowers even farther, and Neetu puts a hand on her arm.

"Simran—"

Simran shakes her off. "They never even get a chance to rebuild because you all keep throwing their mistakes in their faces. As if you're so angelic? Let's go through *your* dirty laundry at every party and see how *you* do. I don't want to hear another word about it. *Leave him alone!*"

Someone has actually turned down the music in the middle of Simran's rant. It feels like everyone is watching, but she can't focus enough to tell. Every face is a blur.

She gets up, chair screeching back, and strides away from the party. If anyone calls after her, she doesn't hear. Her head is filled with a roaring sound.

She darts to the side of the house, avoiding eye contact with people coming from inside. On her way she bumps into someone—a boy of about twelve, the one who asked about her face at kirtan practice yesterday. He opens his mouth.

"Get out of my way," she snaps, and his eyes widen. Even while shouldering past him, she feels awful. But she can't make herself turn back to apologize.

She slows to a stop in the driveway, breathing hard. Maybe every-thing people whisper about her is true. Maybe she's not a good person anymore. How can she set an example for kids when she literally came here after doing *cocaine*, and who knows what else? When she just ruined a good friend's celebration? When all she does is lie? And there's more, too—months of mistakes crash down on her. How can she call herself a Sikh when she's stood by while someone who might've been innocent was killed? How can she be an upstanding person when she instigated a gang war, causing an untold amount of death and misery at the play-place and beyond, all because of—she finally admits it—her ego?

That ever-present nausea rises in her throat. She's always been a gifted liar, and maybe that means she's also been lying to herself.

Simran whirls and throws up on the side of the house.

THIRTY-SIX

"YOU'RE QUIET TODAY," Kat remarks.

Rajan stares out the window. "I've had a lot going on."

"At work?"

Work *does* suck. His shoulder aches, but the foreman straight-up said he'd be fired if he took another day off. "Work's fine."

"I see." Kat watches him. "These life stressors, what are you doing to cope with them?"

Her question hangs in the air. He has a feeling she's asking about drugs. Or maybe about the drug relapse they don't talk about.

He gnaws on a toothpick. Kat can think whatever she wants. Rajan *didn't* relapse again, and no one's more surprised than him after what happened two nights ago. When he finally got home from Simran's, everyone was asleep. He'd eyed his father's bottles of whiskey. The one thing Rajan didn't have, after all, was an alcohol problem.

He was tempted. Maybe it would help him forget the bodies on the café floor, the gunfire, the heart-pounding fear, and the man he almost killed. Possibly, it would help drown his guilt about a promise he made his mother a long time ago.

However, he knew with utter certainty that alcohol could not make him forget Simran. Her hair on his skin, her body in his hands, her sounds when he kissed her. And the way she kissed *him*—he wouldn't forget that even if he was dead.

"Nothing," he says to Kat. Strangely, he currently has no desire to go do drugs. He does, however, have a desire to go find Simran. God, he resisted her for *so long*. But, as always, eventually his control failed him. Now she's all he can think about.

That counselor from juvie whispers again in his head. *You can't have one thing giving you all your happiness, whether that's a drug or something else. It'll suck the life out of everything else. Until that's all you have.*

Maybe that's why he hasn't relapsed again. He's simply found a new addiction. If that's the case, he *should* go do some coke to switch back over. At least that way, he'd only be ruining his own life.

Maybe Kat suspects his thoughts are spiraling, because she sets down her pen. "You like working with your hands, don't you? It might help to start a creative project. A way to de-stress that isn't self-destructive." A beat. "You seem . . . less settled, than the last time we met."

Rajan plucks another toothpick from his pocket. He's chewing through these faster than usual. "That's because I did something bad."

Kat goes very still. She's still smiling, but there's a slight warning in her voice. "Are you sure you want to keep talking, Rajan?"

"I kissed someone I shouldn't have."

"Oh." Kat relaxes slightly. "Well, did they not want you to?"

"No. That's the thing. She shouldn't have, either."

"Are one of you in a relationship already?"

"No."

Kat's smile becomes confused. Rajan doesn't blame her. The barriers between him and Simran are invisible to most, yet insurmountable. He almost *wishes* it were cheating. Then he could clearly explain why he's a bad person. Instead, all he can do is try to correct things the only way he knows how: avoidance. He'll talk to Simran eventually—but only once he has a solid plan to get her out of the Lions.

He flicks his toothpick into the garbage. "Are we done?"

"Almost. Didn't I tell you to put your shoulder in a sling?"

Their eyes connect. Rajan didn't think she'd mention their meeting in the ER, since she seems perfectly content ignoring everything else.

Casually, he shrugs. "For what? It works fine." While she's shaking her head, he nudges the photo on the desk. "I see you got a new frame for your kid."

"I finally found the perfect size," Kat replies. Right. "Just a few weeks of probation left, Rajan. Stay out of trouble."

Her voice is laden with meaning. It kind of pisses him off. He feels like he's fourteen again, wondering why Simran didn't rat him out to the principal. What's Kat's game? Why is she not bringing up evidence he *knows* she has?

As he leaves, Snake Tattoo loiters in the hall, waiting his turn. Despite being irritated, Rajan has the urge to turn back and tell Kat to put her photo in a drawer. But that would be stupid.

He waits until Snake Tattoo reaches him. Then he grabs him by the arm and slams him into the wall.

Before he can speak, Rajan says, "Make her cry again and I'll break both your fucking arms."

He emphasizes this with another shove, then lets go without waiting for a response. He doesn't get one, anyway. Snake Tattoo remains silent behind him.

It's a stupid move, attacking an Ace while this turf war escalates, but Rajan hasn't been thinking straight in days. He punches the down button on the elevator. Kat's right. He needs an outlet.

Rajan's shift at the construction site ends at seven, and while everyone's clocking out, he makes a show of taking off his hard hat and neon work vest. But he doesn't go home just yet. He doesn't trust himself enough not to detour. Whether that detour would be for drugs or for Simran, he can't say.

Instead, once alone, he drags out a few saws from the shed, trying to decide which would best cut that tree in his yard. He figures the trunk is big enough to make a simple outdoor bench—a nicer place to sit than that broken-down swing set. Focusing on the problem makes him feel at ease for the first time in days.

Once he's selected a chain saw, though, it changes. Staring at it, Rajan feels a strange sense of anticipation, like . . . it's becoming real. Not just a theoretical possibility, not just something he's doing to distract himself. He *could* actually make something with that maple. Something cool. And with that realization comes all sorts of other questions. Like, what size boards should he be cutting for a bench? What angle cuts? Where will the screws go?

That's how he ends up sitting on the steps of the construction trailer, sketching out bench designs on a wooden plank with a Sharpie. He's on his fourth variation when a voice sounds in the dark.

"Rajan."

His hands automatically close around the nearest two-by-four, ready to swing. But it's—*Simran.* Standing there in a pair of small glasses he recognizes from ninth grade. Wearing an orange salwar kameez. Neither of these facts register properly.

"What the— Why are *you* here?" he sputters. It's nearly nine.

"I asked your brother where you were."

"My *brother?*"

"I have Yash's number, remember? I figured if you weren't home, you might still be at work."

He sinks back to the step he was sitting on. Reluctantly. God, Simran is really testing him. At least with a drug addiction, the drugs can't literally walk up to him while he's trying to avoid them.

He can't help but notice, though, that Simran looks tired. Probably his fault. "You didn't answer my question. Why're you here?"

"Because I missed you."

Her voice is soft, a caress to his skin, which makes him remember the actual caress of her fingers, which makes him sit up to maintain vigilance against her sneak attacks on his sanity. It definitely doesn't help that she then sits beside him, smelling overpoweringly of floral perfume. Her eyes are luminous, the blacks expanded. He has to say something. Anything. Before she does—

"Do you want a relationship with me?" Simran asks.

Rajan nearly chokes on his own spit. He scrambles to his feet. So they're not ignoring it after all. *"What?"*

"Because I do," she says heedlessly. Something's off about her, but he can't tell what. "I need to know where you stand."

Oh no. *Hell* no. He starts pacing. "What about Jassa?"

She remains seated. "I don't want him. I want *you*."

His whole body wants to react to that statement. Jesus, Simran *loves* to torture him. This is exactly the nightmare he's been trying to avoid. She's giving up Jassa—the one she's been after this whole time—for *him*?

He turns back to her. "We are not doing this. You know what people would say. What our *parents* would say. And you know what? They'd be right."

"They wouldn't."

But even she doesn't sound certain. If he has to remind her of every reason they shouldn't be together, he will. "How would you know? Can you see the future?"

"Can *you*?"

He stares at her dead-on. "I know I'll fuck up, because I know myself. I've ruined people who loved me. I won't do it again." When she tries to speak, he holds up a hand. "You know how this story goes."

The uproar would be horrendous. Simran would become another cautionary tale of how far a golden girl can fall. He'll have no part in that, not when she could have someone perfect for her, like Jassa. As much as he hates to admit that. His hands ball into fists, and he gets a spontaneous rage headache at the thought of them together, of *anyone* touching her the way Rajan did.

The possessiveness surprises him. He turns away again so she won't see it on his face; his insecurities are his own problem. "Besides," he continues as evenly as he can, "I thought you were trying to make your family happy. This is the opposite. I don't have to explain that to you, do I?"

"No," Simran says, sounding miserable. They lapse into silence. Her on the step, him standing a few feet away, the moonlight their only companion.

"It's a good thing Hillway's almost over," he mutters. "We shouldn't see each other after this." Now that he knows too much about her—*intimate* things—his self-control is thin.

But when Simran sniffles, even that disintegrates. Instantly he's back at her side. She's hugging her knees, tears in her eyes, and his hands hover, wanting desperately to touch but knowing he shouldn't. "C'mon, what're you crying about? What happened today?"

She hiccups a laugh. "You just said you don't want to see me again and you're asking why I'm crying?"

"You're crying over *me*?" That's messed up. "Okay, well, we'll see each other *sometimes*, okay? Kelowna's not that big. I'll wave to you in the grocery store. As long as some uncle doesn't snipe me for looking at you. Right?" He nudges her, hoping that'll help, but instead it sets off a fresh wave of sobs. He sighs. Wanting to distract her, he picks up the hem of her kameez. "Where'd you go tonight in this pretty suit?"

Another laugh escapes her. "Neetu's. She's got an engagement party on Saturday, but she had a smaller family party tonight." Her voice becomes quieter. "I shouldn't have gone."

"Why not?" When she doesn't answer, he gives in to temptation and pushes her hair back. Strands are plastered to her temples. Why's she so sweaty? Is she nervous? There's an edge to her that's not normally there, even at her most upset. And now that he's this close, there's something sickly under her perfume, despite how much of the stuff she's doused herself in. He frowns. "Wait. Have you been throwing up? Don't tell me you're coming down with something."

Her body flinches, and then she's standing, so suddenly her kameez flutters. "I—should go. I don't know why I came here." Almost to herself, "I wasn't thinking."

"What—"

But she's already speed-walking away. He doesn't chase her. He just watches until she reaches her truck at the side of the road. Once she's driving away, he gets to his feet, too. This is probably a sign he should go home.

The house is eerily quiet when he enters. He glances down the hall and sees Yash peeking around his door. When Rajan meets his eyes, he ducks back inside.

"Yash," Rajan calls, but the door slides shut. Okay, obviously something happened. If Sukha fought him over Oreos again, Rajan swears he's putting a house-wide embargo in place.

But before he can find out, his father appears at the living room doorway. "We have a guest. Come here."

A guest? The last guests they entertained were Simran and the cops. God, if it's the cops again . . . He glances out the window, but there's no cruiser.

His father doesn't explain, just disappears back into the living room. Rajan shucks off his shoes and turns the corner, too.

Where he stops dead in his tracks.

Because the person sitting on the couch is someone he knows; very well, actually. This person has occupied a lot of his brain space lately, and caused a shit ton of grief. And yet, he hasn't ever spoken to her, or even looked her in the eye until right now. And right now . . . there's only one reason she could be here.

Simran's mother steeples her fingers. "So," she says. "You're the boy who taught my daughter to lie to me."

THIRTY-SEVEN

IT'S STUPID, BUT Rajan's automatic reflex is to mentally check his appearance. He knows he's dirty, wearing a smudged hoodie and jeans fraying at the knees. His clothes probably smell like smoke and sweat. He prays she didn't see him lugging a chain saw out back just now. His hair—he resists the urge to run his hand through it, although it's still too short to be sticking up much.

Simran's mother is wearing a brilliant green suit, clearly having come from a function. Probably Neetu's. She looks him over. He doesn't know why he's holding his breath, but when her lip curls slightly, it hits harder than it ever has with anyone else.

Rajan rallies himself. So Simran's mom hates him. Was he honestly hoping for any other outcome? "Sat Sri Akaal, Auntie ji. Can I get you something to drink? Chah, pani?"

Her expression doesn't flicker, not even slightly impressed by the offer made in his most polite Punjabi. Rajan doesn't blame her. Superficial manners don't matter when you've already insulted someone beyond belief.

"No," she replies. In *English*. Goddamn. This is worse than he thought.

His father points at the armchair. "Sit." There are a thousand threats in that word.

Slowly, Rajan obeys, not looking away from Simran's mother. Their resemblance is only there if he searches for it. The big eyes. The gentle curve of the nose. Jesus, is Simran okay? Is *this* what got her crying?

She seems to read his mind. "My daughter doesn't know I'm here. She wouldn't listen to me anyway. She's been going behind my back for so long, I don't think she can break the habit on her own. But not to worry. We will help her."

A chill runs down his back. "What are we talking about, Auntie ji?"

His father, standing beside him, smacks the back of his head. "Don't embarrass me further by lying," he snaps, and *wow*, that explains it. His father ratted him out. If Simran's mom had any suspicions at all, his father would've happily told her everything he knew.

Rajan rubs the back of his head slowly. This is still salvageable. His father doesn't have any *real* evidence. "Is this about Hillway? I'm just one of the people Simran mentored. She drove me home once, yeah, but that's it. I have nothing but respect for her."

"Yet you befriended her," Simran's mother replies. "Knowing what that would do to her reputation. What it *has* done."

He grits his teeth. "That's my fault. *She* always kept a professional boundary. I'm sorry."

She's silent for a while. "You speak such pretty, polite words now. But I don't believe you. I think you have inappropriate feelings toward my daughter. And unfortunately, I have long suspected she returns them."

His mouth goes dry. "She doesn't. I don't."

"Really?" She pins him with a stare. "Can you honestly tell me that you've never touched her?"

Heat rises up his neck. His hesitation is a second too long; her mouth tightens. His father makes a sound of disgust, again cuffing him across the head.

"Tenu sharam ni aundi? What if you got her pregnant?"

That gets him talking. "I didn't— Auntie, we never—" Rajan starts angrily, but Simran's mother cuts him off.

"It doesn't matter. We cannot reverse time, or stop you children from being such hormonal fools." Her knuckles go white on the armrests. "Whether you have already . . . ruined her life, will be known eventually."

Rajan wishes the ground would swallow him up already. "Simran would never—"

"What *matters*," Simran's mother interrupts, "is that you stop seeing her now. No, don't deny it again. I'm not interested in your lies. You claim to care about my daughter, and not just about bedding her? Then be quiet and listen."

Rajan sits back sullenly.

"Everyone knows your history," she says. "Can you honestly say you left that life behind?"

Rajan can't. She seems to know that.

"Can you honestly say your life hasn't rubbed off on her?"

He can't.

"And do you think you are her equal?"

Rajan again can't speak. It would hurt less if she shot him. Instead, she keeps going with a small nod.

"We both know she deserves someone at her level. Someone with her intelligence, a promising future, not a criminal with no career aspirations and a drug problem. She will bear all the ill will in the community from the shame you bring her. She will bear all the problems you have, and the danger. She will bear it all, and Simran has already borne too much."

He feels rooted to his armchair. Everything she's saying, he already knew, but it's worse when she lays it out like that. She's relentless. Just like her damn daughter.

"I know what you're thinking: *But I love her. Isn't that enough?* No. It's not. You children think love will erase all your problems. *Love*," she scoffs, "is a dime a dozen. Love is easy. Life is what's hard. And with you, it would be soul breaking."

"We're *friends*," he says weakly, but that's never stopped brown parents from jumping straight to marriage, and she does not even pause.

"She'll come to resent you for that, you know. She'll wish she never met you. Don't think you're so special—she will find someone better to love. Let her go now, and maybe she will be able to remember you fondly, instead of as the person who ruined her life."

Without waiting for a response, she rises, tossing her chunni over her shoulder in one dignified motion. She glances at the photo on the wall of Rajan's mother, and then at his father. "Thank you for the chah. I am very sorry about Arshdeep."

THIRTY-EIGHT

SIMRAN'S HANDS SHAKE the whole drive home. She barely pays attention to the road. A part of her knows she shouldn't be driving tonight, not when she's like this. But today has been bad decision after bad decision. What's one more?

After puking at Neetu's party, she fled. She didn't know where she was going until she stopped on the roadside to text Yash about Rajan. Somehow, she no longer cared about leaving a digital trail of her feelings for him.

Of course, once she saw Rajan in person, once he spelled out every reason they shouldn't be together, she felt stupid. But she still *wants* him. It's completely illogical, given how difficult that would make her life, given the blowup it would cause, given he didn't even answer her question about whether he wants it too . . . but there it is.

Simran's dad is waiting when she arrives home, and she gets the sense that her parents have spoken in the hour she's been MIA. She mumbles hello and is about to escape to her room when her dad suggests, of all things, that they watch a movie.

So she reluctantly sits with him on the couch, bracing herself. But he doesn't say more, just places popcorn between them. Simran barely pays attention to the animated movie.

Her dad's loving it, though. He nudges her when the characters break into song. "This guy's so funny." He offers her the popcorn again. She shakes her head, and he shrugs. "More for me."

He's being so gentle. Acting like nothing's happening. But he *must* know about the party.

"Dad," Simran ventures. "Do you believe what people are saying about me?"

He lowers the popcorn to look at her then, face serious. "I don't believe anything about you unless you tell it to me yourself."

That's an invitation. She hears it under his words.

But Simran turns back to the movie, and eventually, so does he. She wonders if she's imagining the disappointment in the silence now.

The credits are rolling when the front door opens. Simran whips around—her mom's there, taking off her shoes. Simran steels herself—time for her lecture—but her mom just says, "I brought leftovers."

Simran forces down some curry to appease her. The whole time, she's waiting for her mother to start the conversation, but she never does. In fact, she seems brighter than usual. She smiles at Simran and refills her plate. She asks if Simran's stomach is upset because she sees her clutching at it, then makes saunf water with honey. She notices Simran shivering, and puts a hand on her forehead.

"Maybe you're getting sick," she says. Simran stares into her eyes. Her mom stares back steadily. Is it not obvious to her what was obvious to everyone else? Did no one murmur their suspicions about Simran to her? Could she have gotten off scot-free?

"I'm tired," Simran says eventually.

"Yes." Her mother kisses her forehead. "Go. Sleep it off."

Sleep what off? That seems an odd thing to say about an illness. When her mom releases her and steps back, and *especially* when she smiles again, Simran can't help but feel like they're playing a game.

By morning, whatever mental fog was left from the drugs has lifted, leaving Simran painfully clear-headed. It's surreal to think back to her evening at Manny's mansion. At its best, the high was *incredible*. She can see why Rajan has a hard time staying away from it. Just the memory makes her feel almost as giddy as when they kissed.

And yet . . . . she has no desire to repeat it. Even with how good it felt, she hated being that out of control. Not to mention the consequences— her apology tour has grown by several stops after last night. She feels sick, but not in the way her mother was saying. She feels sick in her soul.

It's one in the afternoon when she finally descends the stairs. Her dad's at work. Her mom's there, though, calmly watering the plants.

"Can you help me with something?" Simran asks in a small voice. Her mother looks her up and down before nodding.

They work in the kitchen together, side by side, making small talk. Her mother is pleasant. Too pleasant. Simran goes along with it because she doesn't know what else to do. And an hour later, Simran packs their homemade semiyan and sets off for Neetu's house.

When the front door opens, Simran actually watches Neetu's mom's face fall slightly. "Oh. Simran . . . it's you."

"Sat Sri Akaal, Auntie ji." Simran attempts normalcy, as if she didn't make a scene around Neetu's future in-laws and then vomit on the side of their house. "Is Neetu home?"

"She's busy with the reception preparations, very busy . . ." She trails off. It hits Simran. Neetu doesn't want to see her. Of course she doesn't.

It was a mistake to even come. "I understand."

She's walking down the driveway when Neetu's voice calls from inside. "I'm not busy. Come in, Simran."

Simran turns back slowly. Neetu's halfway down the stairs, her hair loose, wearing sweatpants and a tie-dye T-shirt. She beckons Simran inside, expression perfectly neutral.

Simran hands the semiyan to Neetu's mom and follows Neetu up the stairs. A few of Neetu's relatives in the living room below peer up at her, which she pretends not to notice. She can imagine what they're thinking, though. *That's the girl who was inebriated last night. She insulted people at Neetu's party. Why is she imposing herself—*

Neetu leads her to her room. "Don't mind the mess," she says, despite the only thing out of place being her unmade bed and the pile of clothes on it. She starts folding her blanket. "Come sit."

Simran doesn't move from the doorway. "I'm sorry."

Neetu drops the blanket. "Simran—"

"I caused a scene last night. In front of your relatives and future in-laws. I'll apologize to your parents and Gurjeevan too, but I wanted to say it to you first. I'll do anything to fix things."

She waits, head bowed, until Neetu sighs. "Simran, look at me." Simran does, and Neetu walks forward to take her hand. "I accept your apology, okay? But you have to tell me what's going on. You haven't been yourself in months."

She doesn't feel like herself anymore, either. The secrets run so deep now, she doesn't know where to start digging them up. "You shouldn't forgive me so easily."

"Why not? You just made a mistake. You're not a bad person."

"But I *am* a bad person," she bursts, and Neetu tilts her head. "If you knew the things I've done recently, you'd say so, too. You'd say I'm not fit to wear this." Her hand drifts to her hip, where her kirpan sits under her clothes.

"Is *that* what this is about?" Neetu shakes her head. "You and I both know I can't tell you you're a bad Sikh. There's a reason we don't have priests. Why anyone can lead a congregation. No one is an authority on Sikhi, Simran. We're all equal in it. That's the point."

"But I think I *need* an authority," Simran whispers. "I can't tell the difference between right and wrong anymore. I think I need someone to tell me."

Neetu gives her a look. "You know, there's a lot up to interpretation in a book of poetry and music like ours, but there's also a rock-solid historical foundation that tells you exactly what Sikhi's about. You know what that is?" She doesn't wait for an answer. "It's about selfless service to your community. About always being willing to learn. Welcoming people from all walks of life, especially the ones everyone else has shunned. It's about being brave enough to defend them, even when you know that means everyone will start shunning you, too." Her voice softens. "Remind you of anyone?"

Simran blinks. Blinks again.

"Don't get me wrong. I think you make mistakes." Neetu frowns. "A lot of them lately, and honestly, I'm worried about you. But not for this. What you said yesterday was something a lot of us needed to hear. We've all been way too harsh on that Randhawa kid." She grins and picks up her blanket again. "I mean, he's kind of funny."

Later that afternoon, Simran heads to Hillway, courtesy of her mother's reminder text. Today's session is at an animal shelter. But when she shows up, Rajan's name isn't on the sheet of volunteers. She's assigned to someone else.

She finds Paul. "I think there's been a mistake in the assignments."

"Oh, right. I didn't have a chance to tell you. Rajan had to leave town on short notice."

Her heart drops. "What?"

"Yes, it was very quick. His PO phoned a few hours ago. He's completing his last few days of probation in Halifax."

He just up and left? *Across the country?* That can't be right. Not after last night, when he promised he'd always be around. She feels dizzy suddenly. "Why? What happened? Why Halifax?"

Paul gives her an odd look, and she clamps her jaw shut. Tries again, calmer this time. "It's just so sudden. Is he . . . okay?"

"Oh, yes. He actually came by the office earlier to fill out an eval for you. Glowing recommendation." Paul chuckles slightly. "It's probably for the best he's moving on. Don't laugh, but I'm starting to suspect he developed a slight attachment to you."

THIRTY-NINE

AFTER SIMRAN'S MOM left, Rajan knew what he had to do. He told his dad his plan, and for once, his father seemed to approve.

Rajan waited until morning before calling Kat. "I need out of Kelowna," he told her. "I've been approached by the Lions."

As Kat listened, he explained that an old friend had cornered him yesterday. Ordered him to come back to work for the Lions. If he didn't, he'd pay with his life.

By the end of his story, Kat was typing frantically. "I'm going to make some calls. I'm so glad you told me."

Once everything was arranged, he called Nick.

It's early afternoon by the time Nick rolls up in his Benz. Rajan's sure his dad sees him getting in the car, but he doesn't care. At this point, it's pretty hard to screw things up more than he already has.

"So," Nick says a few minutes into the drive. "Why'd you suddenly decide to take my advice and skip town?"

"You were right, okay?" Moodily, Rajan sinks lower in his seat. "Me staying does nothing for Simran. Actually, it makes everything worse.

I just didn't want to see that before because . . ." He sighs, finally admitting it to himself. "I didn't want to leave her."

"And what made you figure that out?"

"Simran's mom found out we kissed."

Nick brakes too hard at a red light. "What?"

"Yep." Rajan pops the *p*. "She came by our house yesterday to tell me herself."

Nick whistles, long and low. "You don't do anything halfway, man." Then, a grin creeps over his face. "So she's just your 'volunteering buddy,' huh?"

"Don't." Rajan's not in the mood.

Nick adopts an airy, exaggerated bro-drawl that does *not* sound like Rajan. "'You totally made a mistake taking her, dude. I don't give a fuck about her. That's why I completely lose my shit every time she's in trouble.'"

"Nick, I'm about to commit an actual homicide right now."

"Okay, I'm done." Nick's grin fades. "We're here, anyway."

They are; a nondescript gas station parking lot, one Rajan is very familiar with.

Nick parks, then gives him a close look. "You sure about this?"

Rajan wonders what, exactly, Nick can read on his face. "Yeah." If he's going to leave town, he's going to make damn sure Simran is taken care of first.

They go inside. Maya is sweeping the aisle, and she brightens upon seeing Rajan, which makes him feel ill.

"Haven't seen you in a while," she says. "You quit."

"I work somewhere else now," he replies. He nods at Nick, and Maya follows his gaze. "With other people."

Nick places a notebook on the counter, above the lotto tickets. Maya glances at Rajan.

"Rajan, what—"

"This is your job interview," he says shortly. "You want an accounting job? You got it."

Then he goes outside because he can't stomach watching her do it.

Eventually, Nick comes out and joins him next to his Benz. He doesn't say anything at first; just lights a cigarette. After blowing a few smoke rings, he says, "She's perfect."

Rajan knew that already. "Will it convince the godfathers?"

"If I can spin it right, maybe. She's way more qualified than Simran, that's for sure. But Simran's got something degrees can't buy. Will they be willing to make that exchange?"

"That's your problem now. I kept up my end—I got you a new bookkeeper. Now it's up to you and Zohra to use her." They're the ones with the power to make this happen. Not him. "Promise me you'll get Simran out."

"It's going to take a while."

"Then make sure she doesn't get hurt in the meantime. The Aces—"

"Won't touch her. I've got people watching her now." Before Rajan can draw breath, Nick adds, "To keep her safe. Same with your family."

Rajan narrows his eyes. "Why would you do that?"

"Because despite what you think, I actually do care," Nick says. "That's why I vouched for you, you know. When the Lions wanted to off you."

And then Nick takes another casual drag from his cigarette as if he didn't just drop a bomb. Rajan can only stare. "What the *hell*?"

"Everyone believed you killed Jai," Nick continues without looking his way. "One of *ours*. If you hadn't gotten arrested, someone would've killed you that night for sure. But me and Zohra made a deal while you were in juvie. If we got you back on the payroll, they wouldn't put out the hit. That's why we came to Kelowna." A slight smile. "Didn't count on Simran, though."

So that's why they set him up with OxyContin dude. It wasn't a game—they had to prove to the higher-ups that he was still loyal. Nick was trying to save his life.

"I know you don't trust me and Zohra," Nick adds. "We got you hooked. I get it. But you have to believe me when I say I wish I didn't do it."

Rajan finds his voice. "I'm not even close to the first person you recruited. Stop pretending you give a shit."

"You're right. I never gave a shit," Nick replies unflinchingly. "And neither did you, today." He nods at the gas station behind them, and Rajan glares. "That's right. You can make me out to be the bad guy, but for you and Simran to leave, someone else has to fall in. You don't get to walk away with your conscience intact."

"Trust me, it already wasn't."

"Then you understand. Yeah, you're right: From day one I was in this for the action. Never cared about the mess we left behind. But the guy who brought *me* into the Lions told me, before he got gunned down, that there'd be a day I'd wish I never joined. I didn't believe him. I loved this, you know? Never a boring day. What could I possibly regret?"

"This is a nice little storytime," Rajan mutters. "But I don't see your point."

"The point is, shithead, you're not the first person I recruited." Nick drops his half-smoked cigarette and grinds it under his heel. "But you were the first one I liked."

When Rajan returns home, he ignores his father, who's staring accusingly from the couch, and goes to Yash's room. Knocks. No answer, but he can hear the faint sounds of a video game.

"Yash, I know you're in there." The door is slightly ajar, so he pushes it open.

Yash is a lump under his comforter. Rajan knocks on the bedside table. "Can I come in?"

Yash lifts the corner of his comforter in response. Rajan gets under it. His feet dangle over the edge of the mattress. Yash pauses his game as Rajan props himself up on his elbows. "So—"

"I heard you talking to your probation officer," Yash says. "I know you're leaving."

There goes the gentle breaking of bad news he was going to do. Rajan sighs. "Yeah. Sorry."

"We *just* got you back."

Rajan's throat closes momentarily. "You and Sukha might be better off without me around. Like Dad said."

"No, we're *not*." With a frustrated growl, Yash buries his head into his pillow. "Why do you listen to Dad at the worst possible times?"

Rajan chooses to ignore that. "I'm only leaving for a while, okay? I'll get a job in Halifax. I'll send you money. And lobsters." He nudges Yash's foot with his own. Yash doesn't respond. "C'mon, dude. Don't be like that. You know I love you."

Yash lifts his head. "Don't say that."

"Why not?"

"Because that's what Mom said." His mouth quivers. "Before she left."

Shit. Rajan closes his eyes to the memory. Leaving home with his mom . . . her kissing his younger brothers goodbye. It feels like decades ago.

"I don't want you to die." Yash wipes his cheek. Is he *crying*?

Rajan pulls Yash close. "I'm not dying. Promise. I—"

"When will you be back?"

Rajan has no answer to that. He needs to let his name fade from the Lions' memory, however long that takes.

Yash shakes his head. "Mom didn't know either. I don't want you to go. I want everyone to be okay again. I want—" He's crying now, fully, and Rajan hugs him tight under the covers.

"Yeah, yeah, I know, me too." Yash's small body shakes against him, and Rajan embraces him tighter. *God*, he wishes they could go back. He wishes he were the kind of teenager who made *normal* mistakes, not life-shattering ones. He wishes he hadn't ruined everything.

But there's no going back.

Blinking rapidly, he kisses Yash's forehead. "If you need me, call. If you don't need me, call anyway. Cuz I'm gonna call you so much it's gonna annoy the shit out of you." He pokes him. "And if you bring Oreos into this house, I might get on a plane just to kick your ass."

Yash finally laughs, and Rajan playfully shoves his head down into his pillow, grateful they're back to this. Then he rolls out of the bed and to his feet.

Surprisingly, Sukha's door is open. Sukha is lounging on his bed, pointedly looking at his phone. Rajan's sure Sukha's heard every conversation in this house over the last few days: with Yash, with Kat, their dad, even with Simran's mom. There's nothing left to say.

However, he still feels compelled to say *something*. "I'm leaving."

Sukha yawns.

Well, if that's how it's gonna be. Rajan steps back, lingering at the door to take one last look at his bunny, and the baseball beside it. Then he walks away.

It's silent behind him. But Rajan feels a prickle in his neck telling him that only now, with his back turned, is Sukha watching him go.

Their father is waiting by the front door. "I spoke to my cousin," he says to Rajan. "The one in Halifax. She'll take you, for now."

His eyes are red-rimmed, his face expressionless. When Rajan steps forward to hug him, because that feels like the thing to do, the embrace is formal and distant. His father nods when Rajan steps away. The briefest of acknowledgements: They both agree this course of action is the best one.

Rajan picks up his bag and remembers a happier time—when his father was one of the most loving people in the world. Regularly affectionate with his sons and his wife. But that well dried up; he's stopped giving his love so easily, Rajan thinks. Because it hurt him too much.

For all that's wrong between the two of them, Rajan can't fault him for that.

Rajan has the taxi driver make one stop before the airport—the Hillway office. There, he fills out an evaluation for his mentor. He writes a glowing recommendation. He writes until he runs out of room and then he flips over the paper to finish.

When he hands it in, Paul's eyebrows are raised. Rajan doesn't care how suspicious it looks. "She's amazing," he tells Paul. "You'll never find another one like her." He doesn't wait for a response before leaving.

The taxi is idling outside. Rajan gets in, and the driver is silent, pulling out of the space before Rajan's even closed the door. Rajan leans back. Simran's going to be pissed when she hears. Honestly, if she calls him about it, he's not entirely sure he'll have the strength to ignore her.

The taxi turns onto a side street. He glances at the driver, who's reaching into his coat pocket. "Hey, are we going the right—"

The taxi driver tases him.

When Rajan comes to, he's tied to a chair.

It takes him a while to wake completely. He must've been drugged. But once he does, he registers that it's totally dark. And cold; his hoodie's gone. While waiting for his vision to adjust, he tests the bonds binding his ankles to the chair legs and his wrists behind his back. They're thin, plastic-y. Zip ties.

Fuck. He is *so* screwed. He squashes down his panic, though, because he suddenly gets the sense he's not alone.

He can see better now. The walls are metal and ridged like a tin can. The room is long and rectangular, stretching maybe forty feet ahead of him. It's a storage container.

And there's a man in here with him.

He's been standing completely still, to the side. When Rajan looks his way, he draws closer, as if he was waiting to be noticed.

Rajan doesn't recognize him. Some white guy in his thirties. Wearing Rajan's cap as if it's his. In a leather jacket and . . . steel-toed, reinforced boots. That doesn't bode well.

Hat Stealer considers him. "Word on the street is, you know who the Lions' bookkeeper is." His voice is monotone, bored.

Rajan's heart drops. He already knew deep down he got taken by the Aces, but now it's confirmed. They're still looking for Simran. Of course they are. And if that's what they want from him . . . he knows, right then, that he's spending the rest of his life in this storage container.

It's not *fair*. He promised Yash he would come back, damn it, he *promised*. And Sukha . . . he barely said anything to Sukha when he left. God, he should've said more. He should've told him he loved him, too.

He flexes his wrists, looking for any give in the ties. There isn't. "You've got the wrong guy. I'm not with the Lions anymore."

"That right?" Hat Stealer knocks on the wall before turning back to him. "Word on the street *also* says you're the one who put Axel in the hospital, during the café hit."

As he speaks, the door to the storage container opens slightly. Sunlight hits the floor. Rajan keeps his eyes on Hat Stealer. "A lot of bullshit words being said on the street, then. I'm on probation, I'm not involved."

Out of nowhere, the guy punches him in the face.

The chair tips backward, but Hat Stealer steadies it almost gently. Rajan tests his jaw. That wasn't actually too bad.

But, more than likely, it was just a teaser. Rajan's heard the horror stories. Someone you bought weed from last week gets left hanging in the rafters of some warehouse. A godfather is kidnapped and the search stretches for days before they're found, nearly unrecognizable, in the trunk of a car. Shit like that. Sometimes it's to make a point, or to get intel. Sometimes, it's just because.

But *he* was too careful to be caught, Rajan always thought. He'd fight them off. He'd do any number of things to protect his own safety. Yet here he is.

A different kind of fear grips him. The kind he doesn't like to admit to: being scared for *himself*. What right does he have to be scared for himself? What's there to protect? Nothing. But he can't help it.

Rajan steels himself. The worst thing he could do right now is show fear. "I know the LS has a bookkeeper." That, everyone knows. "But I don't *know* them. I'm not that important."

The Ace tilts his head, studying him. For a second, Rajan thinks he believes him. It's a reasonable lie, after all. But then he turns his head. "I think he needs a little help remembering, boys."

Rajan finally focuses on the group that has entered. They're clustered behind Hat Stealer, but when he moves aside, Rajan's gaze fixates on one of them. Wait. It can't be . . .

The familiar figure saunters closer, flicking a lighter on and off until he stops in front of him. And then, an amused little huff.

"Don't look so surprised, Rajan," Zach Singer says. "I've been waiting a long time for this."

FORTY

TWO DAYS AFTER Rajan leaves town, Simran has heard nothing from him. She supposes he's just doing what he said they should—cutting ties. She can practically hear him saying, *Move on.*

But it's still bitter.

When Rajan didn't answer his phone that day after Hillway, she called Nick, who confirmed it. "Yeah, he told me. Only to threaten me to get you out of the LS." His voice was wry. "I guess his PO figured he might've been in contact with the Lions? Instead of taking him to court, they moved him."

"But," Simran whispered, her mind spinning. "He didn't tell me. He's not answering his phone."

"He didn't have time to tell you."

"But he told *you*?" Silence. "Never mind." She was lowering the phone when Nick's tinny voice started talking again. She brought it back to her ear. "What?"

"I said, he hasn't picked up my calls either. You're not the only one he's ignoring."

On the third day of Rajan's absence, she tries to take her mind off him. She picks up her new glasses, which admittedly look good. She practices her rabab, then studies the ledger photos she took at Manny's mansion. She uploads them onto several USBs, and they sit on her desk, mocking her. *What are you going to do with us, huh?*

She's still trying to figure that out when her phone chimes. She grabs it lightning fast, but it's just Kiran. *I'm here.*

Right. Kiran's arrived, of course, a day before Neetu's engagement reception. She loves weddings a lot for someone who never plans to have one.

When Simran opens the door, Kiran's on the step, bag in hand. They stare at each other.

Her hair is longer, now hanging around her chin in a bob. Her face is flushed from dragging her filled-to-bursting suitcase, and she has a new dragon tattoo on the sleeve on her arm. "You should cover that up before Mom notices," Simran tells her. "She'll make a big deal of it."

All at once Kiran surges forward, dropping her bag to sweep her into a hug.

"God, I missed your righteous ass," Kiran whispers. "I'm not hiding my tattoo. It's bangin'."

Simran surprises herself by hugging back. Despite their last argument, she missed Kiran, too. And what is there to resent anymore? That Kiran's free and Simran isn't? Simran *had* freedom these last few months—and look what she did. Her family's in danger because of her. Maybe it's best they go back to how things were.

When they let go, Kiran's smile fades. "Mom's doing better, isn't she? There hasn't been more bad news?" When Simran shakes her head, she frowns. "Then why do you look . . . so sad?"

Does she? Simran tries to lift the corners of her mouth. "I'm not. Just tired." Clearly Kiran hasn't heard the gossip recently.

Kiran looks unconvinced. "You took on way too much stress with Mom's thing. Go do something fun tonight. See your friends. I'll tell Mom and Dad you're volunteering somewhere."

Friends? Simran fights a laugh. "I have to make dinner."

"I'll make it," Kiran says, shocking her into silence. Simran must look *very* tired. "You must have someone you could hang out with. It's Friday night. How are you eighteen with no Friday-night plans?'

Kiran sounds aghast. Simran, for the record, likes staying in. But Kiran's words jog her memory somewhat. It *is* Friday night, and she *does* have a standing invitation somewhere, and she *is* desperate to fill the hole in her chest.

"Fine," Simran says. "Don't burn the kitchen down."

There's quite a crowd already at the martial arts club by the time Simran arrives. Or maybe it's that the gym is small; the ring takes up most of the space, with a scarce amount of standing room surrounding it. She squeezes between several bodies to get closer to the front.

She almost doesn't recognize Jassa without his turban. His hair's tied back and covered with a bandana, but the curly ends still poke through. He's also, well, not wearing a shirt, but Simran tries not to fixate on that. He dances lightly on the balls of his feet, blocking and weaving and striking with the same ease and grace she recognizes in his everyday body language. He clashes with his opponent often, clearly on the offensive. But, from the sluggish responses of the other boy, she suspects he waited him out first.

Eventually, Jassa dives at his legs. The audience roars its approval, and even more so when the two of them grapple on the floor for the upper hand. Jassa manages to lock his legs around his opponent's neck and squeezes. The volume rises and rises until the other boy taps out, the bell rings, and then the audience *explodes.*

Jassa releases him and leaps up. Simran waits for him to gloat, to grin at the crowd the way she's seen boxers do, but he just extends his hand to the boy on the floor. His opponent takes it, and they exchange a few words that end with them cuffing each other on the back of the neck. Only after they separate does Jassa glance to the crowd. His eyes lock on hers.

Surprise glimmers through them before he smiles. A second later he ducks under the rope. With the fight over, people make way for him, the crowd loosening. He smells of sweat and something metallic underneath, almost like blood, but richer.

"Hey." He's still breathless. "You made it."

He rips at his hand wraps with his teeth, then starts unwinding them. Simran forces her brain to work. "I figured it was time."

"And here I thought you were avoiding me." His voice is teasing.

"I've been busy."

"Glad I was wrong, then." He finishes with one wrap, and thankfully, uses his now-free hand to unwrap the other one instead of his teeth. A stray curl falls from his bandana and over his eyes, and he absently flicks it out of the way. Then he does a double take. "What happened to your face?"

"My—face?"

Without warning, Jassa puts his hand on her cheek. Her breath catches in her throat; she remembers now. Her bruise has mostly faded, but there's still a mottled purple bloom if someone looks closely.

"Who hit you?" Jassa asks.

She wishes he'd put a shirt on. "Nobody. I fell."

"Simran, I know what it looks like when someone gets hit in the face." His thumb swipes across the bruise.

She tears away. This was a bad idea. The crowd roars again; two new fighters have climbed into the ring. The sound is once again deafening, but Jassa speaks at her ear. "Let's talk outside."

She doesn't want to—but she lets him lead her out. As they go, people slap him on the back. Someone catcalls him, and he blushes—she catches it just before he grabs a black T-shirt from the wall and tugs it over his head.

As soon as they're in the narrow corridor, Simran turns for the exit. "Sorry I missed most of your fight. I'll come earlier next time."

He catches her wrist. "Wait. I didn't mean to push you. I just got worried."

"It's okay." She scrounges for something else to say. His fingers wrapped around her wrist are highly distracting. "You seem really good at . . . fighting. Where'd you pick it up?"

"My brother." A smile enters his voice. "Taekwondo, wrestling, gatka . . . if I didn't learn along with him, he would've beaten me up our whole childhood."

"You know gatka, too?" He nods. She doesn't know anyone who practices the Sikh martial art. The words are out of her mouth before she can stop them. "Do you know how to fight with the smaller kirpans?"

"What, like this one?" He pulls his own kirpan out of the elastic band of his shorts, where he'd apparently kept it tied during his fight. "Yeah."

"Could you teach me sometime?" He stares at her, and she quickly shakes her head. He doesn't need to know the sequence of traumatic events that have led her to this question. "I mean . . . doesn't it make sense to know how to use it?"

"I've always thought so," he says quietly. "We should never forget the point of wearing one. It's practical, if you ever find yourself needing to defend someone. Or yourself."

His eyes flicker over her cheek. She ducks her head. "I told you, it was an accident."

He doesn't respond for a second. Then: "Remember your cousin's code? From the scavenger hunt?"

She does regret that now. "Forget it, I don't need it anym—"

"I cracked it."

Silence. Simran's sure her mouth is hanging open. Jassa, looking over her head, goes on.

"I had to do some research. It was a mash-up of a lot of different ciphers . . . but I figured it out eventually."

He's too casual about this. "Really."

"Yeah. It was kind of a weird message. Something about a playplace. Must be an inside joke?"

Simran nods. "Yeah, it's hard to explain—"

"Funny thing, though, on that *exact* date, there was a playplace in town that got shot up. Gang stuff, I heard." He meets her eyes. "Quite the coincidence."

"Quite," Simran agrees. The silence stretches. He's eyeing her bruise again. And it's like they're back to how they were a few months ago: assessing each other warily, wondering what the other knows that they don't.

He inhales, clearly on the verge of asking another question. And— she panics. She blurts the first thing that comes to mind while he's holding her wrist.

"Can I kiss you?"

Jassa's eyes widen. Instantly, Simran remembers herself. Mortified, she starts pulling away. She can come up with a lie; what was she thinking? "Never mind, I—"

"No, no," he rushes to say. "I've just never kissed anyone before."

Simran gets a rush of déjà vu.

"Have you?" he asks slowly, curiously.

"No," she replies with complete sincerity. "Do you . . . want to see what it would be like?"

In answer, his hand goes to the back of her neck. She meets him halfway. And then they're kissing in this darkened hallway.

Kissing Jassa is different. His mouth is different. The way he moves and feels and touches her—different. She's only had one experience before, so—she tells herself—it's natural to compare. He's far more hesitant, letting her lead although she hardly knows what she's doing. The scruff on his jawline startles her skin, sends unexpected sparks down her spine. And it is far too brief.

And then they're staring at each other wide-eyed. Simran tries to evaluate the feeling of it. It was . . . nice. Short and sweet; exactly how most peoples' first kisses probably are. And Rajan was right—she *can* kiss with her glasses on.

Her body suddenly feels terribly heavy.

Jassa retreats to an appropriate distance. She wonders if he wanted to kiss her again, and didn't simply out of respect. Rajan never would've held back once they got going. Not out of a lack of respect for her—no, she was all on board—but out of a lack of respect for *tradition*.

God, does she ever miss disrespecting tradition with him.

"That bad, huh," Jassa says at her silence, his mouth tilting into a self-deprecating smile.

"What? No." Simran blinks back to reality. "I . . ." Her voice fades. What is she doing, toying with Jassa? She lied to him, then kissed him so she wouldn't have to lie to him some more. "It's nothing to do with you. I'm just . . . realizing I've got a lot going on. I'm not ready for this. Not yet."

When her mom was sick, it felt like the clock was ticking on making a choice her mom would be happy about. But now . . . the hole in her chest reminds her it will not be filled easily. How people move on after loss, she doesn't understand. Right now it feels impossible. And that's not fair to either of them.

Jassa studies her for another moment before backing away. "Okay." He turns toward the room with the ring. Another round of cheers erupts, and he pauses. "But if you need help with any more . . . *scavenger hunts*, you know where to find me."

And with one last knowing glance, he slips through the door, leaving her alone in the hall.

The following afternoon, Simran is rudely awoken by a pillow hitting her face.

She pushes it aside and rolls over. The pillow bounces off her back again. This time she lifts her head to squint. "Stop—" She halts when she sees the blurry outline of Kiran, and next to her, TJ.

"Get up," Kiran says, while Simran freezes, suddenly much more awake. Why is *TJ* here? "We're doing your hair."

"I don't need my hair done."

"If we don't intervene, you're going to wake up fifteen minutes before Neetu's party and throw on a suit. Don't you ever get tired of being a slob?" Kiran picks something up from her desk. "What're these?"

Simran puts her glasses on to find Kiran examining one of the USBs. Instantly, she's on her feet to shove it in a drawer. "School project."

"On *flash drives*? You're so old-school." Kiran grins. "Well, at least it got you up."

Of course it did. The last thing Simran needs is her busybody sister plugging one in. Now that Simran's up, she notes Kiran's already fully dressed in a pink lehenga, her bangs artfully styled to frame her face. TJ's in a tank top and jeans, arms crossed tightly, avoiding Simran's gaze.

Kiran shoves Simran into the chair. "God, you look awful."

Simran yawns, leaning her face into her hand and closing her eyes. Kiran flicks her cheek.

She bolts back upright. "Would you stop that?"

"*Wake up.*" Kiran's voice is commanding, but there's a hint of worry in her eyes. "One of your closest friends is engaged and you're not even going to *pretend* you're excited?"

What's there to be excited about? Being tonight's source of gossip after the disastrous backyard party? "Just tired. From yesterday. You're the one who told me to go out on a Friday night."

"Simmi, you came home at eight p.m., I know you didn't do anything interesting." Kiran turns to TJ. "I'm going to get her something to eat. Do her hair, don't let her stop you."

And then she's gone. TJ shoves a bunch of other things off the table. "Your room is a pigsty."

"You say that—"

"Every time, I know." TJ starts brushing her hair robotically. Like it's a job she just has to get through.

Simran sighs. "TJ, I'm—"

"Don't say you're sorry." TJ's voice is tight. "That's what you always say. It doesn't mean anything if you're not going to explain."

"I understand why you're angry," Simran begins, but TJ slams down the hairbrush.

"Angry? I'm *frustrated*. Every time I see you, you're more hollowed out on the inside. I'm watching you fade away and I don't know why."

Her voice cracks slightly. That shocks Simran into silence for a moment. She thought TJ was just mad. This is almost worse. "I'm doing better now. The stuff I was dealing with . . . it's over, pretty much."

"Really? Because until now, you were doing a bang-up job pretending there wasn't *any* stuff you were dealing with."

Simran chews her trembling lip. And gives up. She can never seem to say the right thing anyway. "It's not my secret to tell, TJ. I understand why you can't forgive me. I wouldn't either." She brushes dust off the dresser. "You should go before Kiran comes back. Take the makeup, too. You spent way too much on it, and I never use it."

She keeps her gaze lowered until TJ says quietly, "See, that's the most honest you've been in a long time."

Simran raises her eyes to see TJ watching in the mirror. TJ sighs.

"But you're wrong."

Simran blinks. "About . . . ?"

"I can forgive you. I *do*." Simran's heart drops. "I can't stay mad at you. Not when I feel sad for you most of the time."

"I don't need your pity."

"I know. You don't need anything, do you?" TJ smiles humourlessly. "You spend so much time on your own, I think sometimes you forget you don't have to be."

Simran's chest aches, remembering her father's fears that she would end up isolating herself. And that's exactly what she's done. "I don't *want* to be on my own," she whispers. Tears prick at her eyes. "That's the last thing I want. But I don't know how to stop."

TJ's eyes soften. After a moment of quiet, she picks up her curling wand. Simran thinks that's it, the conversation is over, but then TJ abruptly says, "Kiran didn't ask me to come, you know. I offered. I wanted to check on you before the reception."

Simran stares at her through the mirror. "Why?"

"I heard what happened at Neetu's."

Ah. "What did you hear?"

"Oh, you know." TJ's voice lightens. "Some people think you were on drugs. Some people think you're pregnant with Rajan Randhawa's baby, which is why you threw up. And then there's the one where you've been partying a lot this year, which is why you didn't win some academic award. In other words, Simran, the usual whack rumours people always make up."

Simran releases a relieved breath. Not only because TJ's taking it as typical gossip, but because she's teasing her again. Simran doesn't know why, or how long it'll last with everything still left unsaid, but she's grateful. "I was sick and having a rough day. I said some things I shouldn't have."

"Like roasting an uncle for talking shit about your Hillway people?" When Simran grimaces, TJ claps her hands in glee. "So it's *true*? Why're you embarrassed? That's metal."

"Well, TJ, I'm not you. I don't enjoy making a scene."

"What's *that* supposed to mean?"

TJ's affronted voice almost—*almost*—brings a smile to Simran's face. "Isn't it getting late? Shouldn't you go home and get ready?"

TJ begins clipping up sections of Simran's hair. "I've got lots of time. Charlie's going to come over and curl my hair for me while I do my makeup."

"Oh." Must be nice to be able to get ready for a party with her boyfriend. Simran pushes down her jealousy as TJ starts curling, though. That's not fair. Simran's truly glad she's happy with Charlie. He's a great, trustworthy guy. Just the fact that he defended Rajan that day at TJ's makes her trust him even more.

Simran sits up straighter, struck with an idea. "TJ," she says, "is Charlie coming to the reception?"

TJ pauses with a section of her hair in hand. "I mean, secret's out, so he was going to be my plus-one . . . Why? You think I shouldn't?" She sounds uncertain, and it occurs to Simran that the whispers about her have bothered TJ more than she lets on.

Simran settles into her chair. "You absolutely *should* bring him. Give them something real to gossip about."

TJ's smile returns full force. "Now you're talking." As she gets back to work, Simran glances at the drawer holding her USBs. She now knows exactly what to do with them.

FORTY-ONE

RAJAN'S BEEN TALKING to his mother a lot lately.

This should probably alarm him, given that she's dead, but instead, it's the only comfort he's had these last few days. Some time ago—a day, maybe two? It's hard to keep track—they left him alone and shut the door. His mouth is dry. Head pounding. His ribs hurt with every breath. His nostrils are pretty much dead from the scent of gasoline.

"You should eat something," his mother says from the corner.

"They didn't exactly leave me a buffet, Mom. Also, I'm tied to a chair."

She goes on as if he hadn't spoken. "I stopped eating, too, near the end. Especially when I got more worried about you. If I'd eaten more, I would've lived longer."

He shakes his head. "You were always going to die."

"And so are you," his mother says. "As we've talked about."

He sighs. That's *all* they talk about.

She hasn't been here the whole time. But at some point, Hat Stealer got tired of kicking the shit out of him, the waterboarding, and the other stuff they tried. They tied him back into his chair. Hat Stealer turned to one of the shorter Aces and handed him a yellow gasoline can.

The Ace looked at it. "What do you want me to do?"

That broke Rajan out of his haze. The boy's voice sounded . . . young. Cracking with puberty.

"Fucking drink it. Obviously—" Hat Stealer gestured to Rajan. "He's not gonna crack."

"But . . . Zach said—"

"I don't care what Zach said," Hat Stealer snapped. "Do it."

"Do it yourself," the kid said. "I thought we were going for a drive tonight, not setting people on fire. This is fucked up." He dropped the can and started walking toward the door.

Stupid kid, Rajan thought, even before the others turned on him. He should've just done it. Now he was going to be punished for having a conscience.

While the boy's cries of pain sounded in the background, Hat Stealer poured the gasoline over Rajan's head. The smell filled his nose and made him even more lightheaded.

It was at this point, with rivulets of gasoline dripping into his vision, that his mother appeared behind Hat Stealer. Her hair was thick and shiny, cheeks rosy. She wasn't coughing, she wasn't hooked up to a dialysis machine. She was smiling. He could not take his eyes off her.

"Most of us don't get to choose when we die, sweetheart," she said to him. "Or how. But I would've wanted to die with dignity if I could. Wouldn't you?"

He nodded.

"Then keep looking at me," his mother whispered. "Only me. Don't be afraid, sweetheart. I'll be here until it's over."

The empty gasoline can clattered to the ground at Rajan's feet. The smell was sweet and cloying. The boy who'd refused the task was motionless on the floor, and the others bored with him.

"No, look at me," his mother reminded him, and he did. "Don't worry about him. He's Sukha's age, but he's not Sukha. Everything'll be okay. You left me to die alone, but I promise I won't do that to you."

He believed her. A lighter's flame illuminated the dark.

And then the door opened.

"What did I *tell* you?" Zach sounded furious.

Hat Stealer turned. There were the sounds of muffled arguments. Rajan's mother smiled and came closer when the arguing became shouting. She stroked his hair, but even with the distraction, Rajan still caught snippets of conversation—*he's mine—we need him—our only lead—don't touch him—*

Some part of him puzzled over why Zach didn't want them to hurt him. He'd thought by now he'd be missing a few fingers. At least some teeth. But, they all left. The door closed. And he's been here with his mom ever since.

She strokes his forehead and tuts. "Rajan, you look sick. You should take better care of yourself." She keeps finding new things to scold him about. "Don't worry. I'll take care of you now."

"I don't remember the last time you took care of me."

"I didn't realize you wanted that." She sounds sad. "You were always pushing me away. I thought you didn't want me around."

"Of course I did. Of course I did," he repeats. "I *wanted* you around and I *wanted* you to be proud of me and I *wanted* you to defend me when people criticized me in front of you."

"Well, why didn't you say so? You can't have expected me to know. I was sick, and in pain. You're not blaming me for that, are you?"

"No. Of course not." He squeezes his eyes shut.

"Rajan, I'm so disappointed."

"About what?" he whispers. It's hard to keep up with her. She switches the topic like this every five seconds.

"You didn't keep your promise," she says.

"What promise?"

"You don't even remember." His mother sighs. "I asked you not to poison her."

Her.

Rajan opens his eyes. "Mom, I was trying," he pleads, voice cracking, but her hand falls away. His voice gets louder, more desperate, as she steps back. "I swear I was trying. That's why I was about to leave. Mom, please believe me. Come back. I'm sorry. I'm sorry. I'm sorry."

"It's okay," she says over his apologies, in that sad voice she used when he came home holding a bad report card, or dragged in by cops. "I know you can't help it. It's just who you are."

But, she doesn't come back to stroke his hair.

He's on the cusp of begging her to when the door scrapes open. Bright sunlight hits the metal floor. He recoils, turning his head back to the darkness.

Zach claps his hands as he approaches. "How's it going, buddy? You don't look so hot." Rajan works up some saliva, spits it at his feet. Zach grins. "God, you reek."

"Whose fault is that?"

Zach ignores this. "I brought a friend. You might know him." He steps aside, and Rajan squints to look at the newcomer. Snake Tattoo.

"Oh, yeah, it's him." Snake Tattoo grins. "Little prick."

"You're breaching probation right now," Rajan responds. "Gonna tell on you, dude."

In response, Snake Tattoo grabs the back of the chair and tilts it onto the rear legs. Rajan cringes slightly, knowing what's coming—Snake Tattoo lets the chair fall backward to the metal floor. The back of Rajan's head hits, too. Pain shoots through his skull. Zach's face appears over him.

"Half dead and still so mouthy. Why can't you just cooperate, huh?"

Rajan blinks slowly at the ceiling. He has no clue what Zach's talking about. Come to think of it, there was some secret he was keeping from them, but before that . . . who knows. Has he not always been here? Where did he come from? Is there a world outside this dark place?

"No, sweetheart. It's just you and me," his mother says from the corner. He looks at her. "Focus on me, remember?"

"Yo, he's fucked *up*." Zach laughs. He rights Rajan's chair, then turns to the others. "Jon, get him some food. A change of clothes, too. He needs to look alive." Zach turns back to him. "We're split on whether or not you actually know the bookkeeper. But here's what we've agreed on over the past couple days: Even if you don't know the bookkeeper, you can give us the next best thing. You can give us the *books*."

Rajan struggles to wrap his mind around this. Retaliation, that's what they want. But how?

Zach answers his unspoken question. "You're going to run a little errand for us. You'll walk into Lion territory and pick up our ledgers, along with yours. You'll do it, because otherwise . . ."

Rajan forces himself to breathe. The Lions are protecting his family, protecting Simran. They can't touch them, they're safe—

"Your PO seems like a punctual lady," Zach comments. "Comes into work at seven o'clock every morning."

Kat.

Behind Snake Tattoo, Rajan's mother vanishes.

Snake Tattoo adds, "That bitch is in the parking garage before anyone else. Cameras, easy to loop. Understand?" He gets in close. "I'll do more than make her cry."

Rajan *knew* he shouldn't have said anything to Snake Tattoo. He shouldn't have given the slightest hint that he cared. It's the same thing that happened with Simran—he was so busy protecting one weak spot he forgot about a different one.

"We'll be following you closely," Zach says. Snake Tattoo walks behind him. A moment later, the ties around his wrists snap off. "You have one hour."

They drag him into a vehicle. When his blindfold is yanked off, he's in a dingy, windowless locker room. A towel, water bottle, sandwich, and pile of clothes await him on the bench. He's held at gunpoint while he does literally everything. Despite how degrading that is, he feels somewhat lucid once he's eaten, washed, and gotten dressed in clean jeans, hoodie, and jacket.

They blindfold him again and drive him off. During that time, Zach explains the plan. When his blindfold is lifted, they're on the corner of a familiar street, winding up a hill lined with mansions that overlook the mountains. Manny's house—the place Rajan would bet all the ledgers got moved to after the café attack—is here, and Rajan knows for a fact the surveillance cameras' range ends a few paces away. The Aces must know, too.

"If you're thinking about warning your pals, don't," Zach says conversationally. "Or Kitty is dead."

Rajan yawns pointedly before getting out of the vehicle. He's unsteady at first—four days tied to a chair will do that—but once he's gathered his bearings, he sets off up the street.

At the front gates, he's waved through easily. But he feels the eyes following him this time. It makes sense now, after what Nick told him. He's still seen as a backstabber.

He pats down the neck of his hoodie to make sure his tattoo is showing before stepping inside. As always, there are people milling around. Manny's house is more of a base than a home—rumour is he doesn't even actually live here.

He makes it up the stairs uneventfully, but someone bars him when he tries to step into the sitting room. "What are you doing?"

"Errand for Nick. He wants me to get something from the ledgers." Rajan affects a bored look. "Do you need to call him first? Is he your keeper?"

They look him up and down, then let him pass. He's been hanging around Nick enough that they believe him. But they still watch him. This will be the tricky part.

Rajan stops at the glass table. There's a crystal tray with white dust on the edges, clearly recently used. He looks away immediately, willing himself to focus, and his eyes land on something else instead.

Jackpot. Two of the ledgers are here, open, as if someone's been recently rifling through them. But isn't there one more? He scans the table. It's not there.

"What're you doing in here?"

He turns. And there's Manny Khullar himself.

Rajan hasn't seen him in years, but he looks the same. A slick, expensive snake, with rings glinting on his fingers, scotch glass in hand. His expression, currently irritated. Especially when he sees Rajan holding a ledger.

"Running an errand for Nick," Rajan repeats, and Manny's expression changes.

"Ah. *You're* the Randhawa kid." He looks him over. "You're taller than I imagined."

Rajan can't decide if that's a compliment or an insult. Manny goes on.

"You're running something for Nick? I thought you didn't work for us anymore."

"I help the bookkeeper out sometimes." Rajan tosses the ledger back on the table. Manny instantly relaxes. "She wanted to look at the Ace ledgers."

"Oh, she's folded, has she? Good. I thought I'd have to do something drastic." He circles Rajan. "You know, I swear we've met before."

"We have. When I was fourteen." Rajan glances at the clock.

"Really."

"Yeah, at one of your twisted parties. You helped me do my first line of coke. Fuck you for that."

Manny stares at him. Rajan's certain very few people talk to him that way and walk out alive. For a second, Rajan thinks he won't be an exception, but then Manny chuckles and continues circling. "If you want to blame me for your screwups, fine. I'm just here to serve the people." Although he's currently behind Rajan, a smile enters his voice. "Take Simran, for instance."

He pauses here. Deliberate. Rajan doesn't move a muscle.

Manny reenters his line of vision. "The other day, she was in here whining about her work conditions. She came to her senses eventually. Then we had a nice evening together." He nods to his crystal tray, clearly enjoying Rajan's speechlessness. "She's very different after a few lines. Talkative. Annoying, honestly."

His voice is sly. Rajan's hands curl into fists. He remembers a few days ago when Simran showed up at his worksite. Acting so damn weird. Like she was sick . . . or coming down from something. But *why?*

Manny, still grinning, picks up his phone, which is vibrating in his pocket. His smug expression fades. *"What?"*

With effort, Rajan files away the information about Simran for later. Right now, it's go time.

Manny strides to the window. "On the street? This is too far. Those fuckers—" He starts for the door. Rajan does, too, the guards so distracted by Manny's newfound distress that they don't notice Rajan casually shoving ledgers into his baggy hoodie pocket. He walks out with one of the Ace ledgers tucked under his arm, so brazenly that no one looks twice.

Rajan can't decide if it's a good or bad thing that Zach's plan goes off without a hitch. The little shootout near Manny's mansion has the Lions distracted, and Rajan barely receives any attention as he leaves. He gets picked up on the opposite end of the street, just outside the Lions' cameras, yet again. Once in the van, he tosses the books in Zach's lap.

Zach sorts through them as the van starts driving. "And where's our last ledger?"

"There weren't any more."

"Well, too bad. Kat's not off the hook until you get it."

"What? How is this *my* problem?" Zach's seemingly fighting a smile. Sick asshole is enjoying the hell out of this. Rajan takes a long breath. "What day is it?"

They tell him. Saturday. He exhales. In a different situation, he might laugh about how, somehow, all roads inevitably lead to *her*.

But if he pulls this off, it will be the last time he intrudes on her life. "Fine." He settles into his seat. "There's one other place I could look."

FORTY-TWO

SIMRAN HAS A hard time catching Charlie alone at the reception hall. TJ has latched herself to his elbow, patting down his shirt, picking invisible lint off his arm, and occasionally leaning forward to whisper in his ear. Simran would applaud TJ's little show, but it's getting in the way of her plans.

As Simran's watching, TJ gives Charlie a quick kiss before sending him off with her father, then approaches their table. She sits next to Simran, looking her up and down. "I did *such* a good job on you."

She really did. After TJ finished her makeup, she revealed an embroidered gold anarkali from a garment bag. Fancier than anything Simran has in her closet, and heavier, too. Once TJ had zipped her up, TJ and Kiran ushered her to the mirror. It had broken Simran out of her scheming when she finally saw herself. The anarkali sweeps to her feet, weighed down by layers of fabric and detailing, with equally adorned sleeves ending in gold cuffs. Matching jewelry hangs from her ears and throat, along with a gold tikka from the center part of her hair. Her knee-length hair had taken TJ the longest to style; some of it pinned and other parts loose, a waterfall of texture TJ had created down her back.

Simran knows why TJ went this far. And while it hasn't exactly cheered her up, it's certainly been a distraction. "Thank you," she says, and TJ beams. She pops a pakora in her mouth and looks to the dance floor, where Gurjeevan and Neetu are dancing. Gurjeevan is gorgeous in his off-white achkan. Neetu glows, too, in an emerald lehenga laden with jewels, a genuine blush rising in her skin.

"Gurjeevan looks so good. Maybe I'll make Charlie wear an achkan at our wedding, too," TJ muses, then stiffens, sending Simran and Kiran a sharp glance. "Don't ever tell Charlie I said that."

"Of course," Simran says. "Under no circumstances can your boyfriend know you like him."

TJ kicks her foot. Kiran snickers. And for the first time in a long time, Simran feels almost normal. Then she notices TJ's dad wandering along the edge of the crowd with a glass of whiskey in his hand. Without Charlie.

Simran stands. "I'm going to get some food."

She doesn't wait for a response before setting off into the crowd. The lights are dimmed, dance music blaring, so it's hard to make out where people are. Luckily, Charlie's wearing a bright colour—satiny pink—and she spots him at the buffet. She grabs a plate and pretends not to see an auntie in line in order to cut in next to Charlie. Toor Uncle and his wife are standing with him, pointing out various foods.

"Have the mattar paneer—"

"Oh, you *must* try the saag, Charlie —"

"Don't go without taking the tandoori—"

Simran decides to rescue him. "Take one thing at a time," she tells him. "I'd start with the saag." She smiles at Toor Uncle and Auntie, and they (tentatively) smile back. Simran will have to work a *lot* to redeem herself from the backyard party. Once they're gone, she turns to Charlie. "How's it going?"

"Good. Everyone's friendlier than TJ led me to believe." His voice is wry as they move down the buffet line.

"I didn't realize she told you anything about our family drama."

"She didn't."

It dawns on Simran that Charlie isn't a star at school politics for nothing; he's always intuited far more than he lets on. "Well, if you really understand what's going on, then you must know it didn't help that there was a photo going around of you two *kissing*."

Charlie smiles slightly. "Not my fault."

"Why do I get the feeling you actually enjoyed that part?"

His smile widens in answer. It's honestly a wonder TJ and Charlie weren't exposed sooner. Before they reach the end of the buffet table, Simran asks, "Can I ask you a favour?"

He falls back. "What is it?"

They lean against the wall. To anyone observing, it would look like they're people-watching while they eat. "You can never tell TJ. Or anyone."

The fact that he hardly blinks is testament to the strength of their high school friendship. "Name it."

She pulls a USB from her purse and presses it into his hand. He doesn't look down, but his fingers curl around it even as he gazes at her.

Casually, she looks back at the dance floor. After a moment, he does, too. "You've probably heard some rumours about me lately."

"I have," he agrees.

"TJ's probably said I've been acting strangely."

"She has," he agrees.

"I can't say anything about it or you'll be in trouble, too," she tells him. "But, hypothetically, if anything . . . suspicious, ever happened to me, I'd want you to give that to the police."

"The *police*," he repeats sharply, and she can tell she's surprised him.

"Yes."

Charlie says nothing for a long moment. Then: "What, exactly, do you think might happen to you?"

Simran lets the silence sit until there is no real question what she's thinking might happen. Charlie's poker face doesn't slip, and they both smile at an auntie who passes as if they're just making small talk.

"TJ's not the only one worried about you," Charlie says once the auntie's gone. "Am I helping or hurting you by doing this?"

From across the hall, TJ herself looks up, sees them, and stands. Simran stops being coy. "You're actually keeping me alive."

He swallows. And pockets it at once. "Okay."

As TJ approaches, Simran wonders if this was a bad idea. But she honestly couldn't think of anyone better to give it to. Most people don't associate her with Charlie at all—their quiet high school friendship is vastly overshadowed by TJ's relationship with him. Without a clear connection to Simran, he's safe from the Lions. "Don't ever plug it into a computer. Keep it somewhere safe. Secret."

"I will."

Before she can thank him, TJ reaches them. "What are you two talking about so seriously back here?"

"You," Charlie says instantly. "Simran said you can dance. I don't believe her."

"Ex-*cuse* me?" TJ's outraged voice follows Simran even as she makes her escape. Bless Charlie for his diversions.

Her mom waves her over to her table, where most seats are abandoned; people are either on the dance floor, at other tables, or taking a break from the party. Simran's thankful; her pleasantries earlier were awkward enough. The only people there now are Kiran, their mom, and TJ's mom, who's apparently drifted over for an obligatory brief conversation. By their stiff body language, Simran can tell it's going about as well as ever. She sits next to them, and her masi brightens.

"Simran. I haven't seen you in—"

"Yes, too long," Simran says quickly. She doesn't need her masi bringing up the time Simran was at their house. She turns to her mom, and the plate of gulab jaman in front of her. Simran hadn't seen any floating around the other tables. "Can I have one?"

Her mom pushes them toward her. Simran bites into a gulab jaman. It's fresh, and warm, and delicious.

"Good?" her mom says.

"*So* good."

She nods. "I got them for you."

The gulab jaman tastes even better when Simran takes her next bite. Her mom watches her eat like it gives her personal satisfaction.

Just then, Rupi Auntie returns from the dance floor, fanning herself. "Hai hai." She collapses into a chair. "Bhangra is the best exercise, no?" She glances at Simran's mom. "Tarleen! I meant to say earlier, but I'm so glad to see you here."

Her mom smiles. "Thank you. Your suit is beautiful."

Rupi Auntie leans forward and lowers her voice. "You're looking much better than you did at the hospital. Were you sick?"

Simran freezes. Rupi Auntie *saw*?

Time slows. The Diljit Dosanjh song playing over the loudspeakers seems to warp and fade. TJ's mother's eyes slide to Simran's mother, who's gone pale. Meanwhile, Rupi Auntie's guileless smile fades, as she clearly realizes her assumption that these sisters were well-versed on each other's lives was wrong.

"Hospital?" TJ's mom says quietly. "What's she talking about?"

Rupi Auntie titters. "I'm going to get some chaat. Anyone? Chaat?" When no one answers, she excuses herself.

TJ's mom instantly rounds on Simran's. "What's going on, Tarleen? Tell me, right now."

"Nothing." Simran's mother stands abruptly and without any more words, she vanishes into the crowd, too.

TJ's mother turns to Simran.

"I *knew* something was wrong. Why didn't I know— What happened to her?"

Her voice is loud. Simran's never been so glad for the deafening DJ sets at Indian weddings. She racks her brain for a believable lie. But just as she's drawing breath, a hand lands on her shoulder.

Kiran. Her face is stony as she addresses TJ's mom.

"Masi ji," she says crisply. "With respect. If you want to know what's going on with our mother, go ask her yourself."

Simran's jaw drops. TJ's mom looks taken aback, too, but then she squares her shoulders and vanishes after her sister.

Once she's gone, Simran says, "You shouldn't have said that. She'll think you're rude."

"Come on. I said 'with respect,' didn't I?" At Simran's look, Kiran shrugs. "I couldn't take it anymore. As usual you were about to take the hits for Mom. That's not *right*, Simmi. It's not your duty to protect them from their own bad behaviour." She picks up her glass of wine and downs it in one gulp as Simran stares. "And it pisses me off that I can *tell* you're sitting there feeling guilty about letting our parents down right now. And I know you think I don't care. That if I cared, I'd feel guilty, too. But did it occur to you that neither of us has to feel guilty? I know you're mad at me, and you can be—but I'm mad at *them* for making you their anchor in the world, when anyone can see what it's doing to you."

Simran has no idea what to say. She honestly never thought Kiran understood things that well, not when she's been away from home so long.

When Simran doesn't respond, Kiran shakes her head. "I'm getting more wine."

And just like that, Simran's alone again.

She doesn't want to be here if her mom and masi come back, so she takes her plate and goes back to the table she'd been at earlier with TJ. No one's there either, but she's about to sit down anyway when something gives her pause.

A toothpick is resting on her crimson napkin.

Her eyes skip to everyone else's plates. No one else has one. An odd feeling steals over her. Like she's being watched.

She scans the room. Her gaze skips to the far corners of the reception hall, the ones that are darkened, where people go to be hidden, to avoid music and eyes.

Her eyes skip over him once before her brain catches up. It's the way he stands, leaning against the wall with a glass of water, his ankles crossed. She'd recognize that careless stance anywhere.

Rajan.

Simran wonders if she took more hallucinogens without realizing. She blinks, but he's still there. It doesn't make sense. He left. Didn't he? Was Paul making it up? Did Rajan lie?

Maybe it doesn't matter. He's here, oversize navy jacket hanging open to reveal a dark orange hoodie. Very out of place among all the suits. And he's gazing at her.

Simran starts to draw toward him. She's passed several tables before she's stopped by someone at the juice bar—a family friend, cooing over her anarkali. Once Simran has disentangled herself, she glances back at Rajan. He's still there. And now that she's closer, he's looking at her differently.

He hasn't seen her dressed up before, she realizes. His gaze lowers, brushing along every fold in her anarkali, catching on every sequin. Grazing over her hip. She feels a flush following the trail he leaves. His gaze drops to her feet—her feet, hidden under the hem.

She forgets all her questions. Everything else fades. Maybe this *is* a dream—because what she does next makes no sense. Slowly, subtly, Simran gathers the fabric of her anarkali. She lifts it a few inches. Revealing her leg from the ankle down.

She pretends to adjust her shoe, in case anyone is watching. It's platformed, detailed, and matches her clothes. Of course she should show it off. When she drops her hem, the fabric falling back into place, Rajan taps his collarbone. She looks down to see her chunni is obscuring her necklace. Casually, she takes it off, under the guise of re-draping it. The exposed necklace feels cold against her collarbones. She can't stop looking at him. He can't seem to stop, either, because he tilts his head and taps his ear. She mirrors him, letting her mass of hair fall back, revealing her heavy earrings tapping against her jaw.

She sees the breath he takes from across the room. Finally, he points at the ceiling and lazily twirls his finger.

Her heart rate kicks up. She feels every sensation a million times more, the slide of fabric against her skin, the aggressive A/C blowing stray hairs against her neck. She turns on the spot. Her anarkali swishes heavily around her legs.

When she faces him again, he's downing the last of his water. He sets the glass on a table and disappears into the foyer.

Entranced, she follows. On her way she nearly bumps into somebody who's just entered, probably arriving fashionably late. "Excuse me," she mutters, but they don't seem to hear, shouldering past her roughly. She scans the large foyer. Only a few people here. There's a table near the entrance with a photo album people are signing for Neetu and Gurjeevan. But no Rajan. As she walks forward, sticking close to the wall, she starts thinking she *did* hallucinate him. Why, after all, would he be—

Someone pulls her into the dim service hallway. She stiffens until she hears his voice.

"Hey, Auntie. Miss me?"

And that voice, that *voice* melts four days of tension. It fills her chest instantly, relieving the ache so fast she could cry. "Rajan," she breathes, as he lets her go. "I thought you left."

"I'm going to." He looks at the wall behind her head. Despite his lighthearted greeting, he's not smiling. There's something off about him. "But there were a few loose ends to tie up first. Where's the last Ace ledger?"

The question is so out of left field that she's thrown. "The Ace ledger? How do you know about that?"

"Because Nick needs it. He knows you have it."

It's in her purse, of course, where it's been since the night she took it. But this isn't how she pictured their reunion going. "Why come here to ask that? Why not wait? Why—"

"*Simran,*" he interrupts. Her questions die on her lips. He tugs on one of her curls. As it bounces back into place, he puts his hand on the side of her neck, fingers sliding under her mass of hair to the nape. His thumb strokes the sensitive skin right behind her ear. "Simran, tell me where that ledger is, and I'll go."

She can hardly think when he's touching her like that, when he's saying her name like that. "I don't *want* you to go."

He braces his free hand on the wall behind her, and she notes that he's holding himself differently. Leaning a bit to one side. That hand on the wall doesn't seem to be for her benefit, but for his own.

Suspicion overtakes her. She reaches into his unzipped jacket and takes a fistful of his hoodie, hauling him closer.

She only notices because she's watching his face—he winces. He *definitely* winces.

"What happened?" She starts patting him down. "Where does it hurt?" When her hand goes to his ribs, he pushes it away. There's sweat beading on his temple. She touches it. His skin is clammy, and he smells very faintly of gasoline. "Rajan, what's going on?"

He twists his head away from her touch. "It's from when I hurt my shoulder, that's all. Just . . . tell me where the ledger is. Please, Simran."

She clutches onto his hoodie, feeling lightheaded. She doesn't want to give it to him. If she does, he leaves. That's the last thing she wants. She half thinks if he tries, she'll drag him back, make him press her into the wall exactly like this again.

Rajan's expression changes, like he's following the direction of her thoughts. He bends down to her. His hands settle on her hips, nose grazing her necklace. He inhales, then quite suddenly presses his face fully against the side of her neck, lips on her pulse. She squeaks, unable to think, to do anything. She doesn't remember what he was asking her, not when he's found the shape of her leg under the layers of fabric, running one hand down the back of her thigh.

"You," he breathes, lips brushing against her earring, "dressed like this," he draws a fistful of her anarkali into his hand, pulling it up, "is driving me up the *wall*, let me tell you."

She loves his hands on her. Reverent. Yet deliciously disrespectful. "Dressed like what?"

He looks at her straight on, the blacks of his eyes swallowing her up. "Like a bride."

Her lungs cease to work. But just then, a stifled gasp has her pushing away instinctively.

It's TJ.

TJ, staring wide-eyed from the end of the hallway. Simran smooths down her anarkali. "TJ—"

TJ marches toward them. "Get away from her!"

Her glare is fixed on Rajan, who has already stepped back, hands now in jacket pockets. "TJ," he says with a lazy grin. "I see you haven't learned how to relax."

"I cannot believe this." TJ looks furious. "I'm going to—"

"*TJ,*" Simran says, louder. TJ halts in her tracks, focusing on Simran for the first time. Uncertainty flits over her face.

Distantly, in the foyer, there's a scuffle of shoes on tile, a commotion that seems to be brewing. It wouldn't be the first time an altercation broke out at a wedding, but Rajan glances in that direction immediately, his smile fading. He backs away. "Don't worry," he says to Simran. "I'm gonna take care of everything."

He disappears down the hall before she can ask what he means. TJ blocks her path before she can follow.

"Holy shit," TJ is saying. "Holy shit."

"TJ, I have to—"

"There are tons of people in the foyer now," TJ says harshly. "You can't go out a second after him looking like—the way you do right now."

"What—"

TJ grabs her hand and drags her farther down the hall to a private washroom. Simran glances over her shoulder, but Rajan's gone.

TJ tows her inside. "You need to take a minute."

Simran glances into the mirror as TJ locks the door behind them.

Her eyes are too bright, tendrils of hair falling over her cheeks, her cheeks burning—flushing all the way into her neckline.

Simran flushes even more. She can't look her cousin in the eye.

"God," TJ says. "So much is starting to make sense. So. Much."

"Please don't lecture me."

TJ pauses. *"Why?"*

She sounds so baffled, so hurt, so frustrated.

Simran braces her hands against the sink. TJ's question could mean so many things. *Why him? Why didn't you tell me? Why didn't you see how badly this was going to end?*

"Actually, you know what?" TJ says after several seconds of silence. "Let's just drop that messed-up topic for now. Why don't we talk about how your mom has cancer."

Simran closes her eyes. The washroom is beginning to spin. "Who told you?"

"I overheard." TJ's voice is flat. "Your mom and mine were talking. Loudly. My mom was pissed."

Simran keeps her eyes closed. "I'm sorry."

Silence. Then, all at once, she finds herself crushed into a hug. Simran's eyes fly open. "You're . . . not mad?"

"I'm *so* mad, Simran." TJ's voice cracks a little. "But I understand now. God, I finally, *finally* understand."

Simran sniffles. Before she can help it, she's sobbing, sobbing into her cousin's beautiful embroidered suit, clutching onto the fabric for dear life. "I'm sorry. I'm sorry," she babbles, but TJ only holds her tighter.

"I know. I know."

Her voice is exceedingly gentle. TJ *knows*. The secret is out. And Simran can finally breathe. "My mom had her surgery," she tells TJ. "We . . . have an appointment with the oncologist coming up, to talk about next steps, but it's not as bad as it was."

"My mom knows all the oncologists here. She can help." TJ grabs a paper towel and delicately dabs the makeup under Simran's glasses.

"You should see them out there now. My mom is holding your mom's hand. Weirdest thing I'd ever seen, at least until I came here and saw you letting Rajan Randhawa hike up your skirt."

Simran pulls away from TJ at the mention of his name. Right, there was that whole thing a second ago. Why did he show up here, anyway? He said he came for the ledger, but he left in a hurry without it, as soon as he heard those men in the lobby . . .

It hits her.

Meanwhile, TJ is still talking. "How long have you two been a thing? *Please* don't tell me you were hooking up in high school and I just didn't notice— What are you looking for?"

Simran's desperately ripping open her purse. The zipper of the largest compartment is undone. She unzips it all the way.

Empty.

Her face burns. All those touches . . . just a distraction. He must've suspected she had the ledger on her. But it doesn't make sense that he took it for Nick. Didn't Nick say Rajan was ignoring his calls?

She's getting a bad feeling about this. With fumbling fingers, she texts Yash to ask if he's heard from Rajan. Then she calls Nick.

He picks up first ring. "Simran, tell me why Rajan thought it'd be a good idea to steal all the ledgers. Because Manny's putting a hit out on him right now."

Simran shuts her eyes. Her worst fears, confirmed. "He didn't talk to you either?"

"Simran, I haven't spoken to Rajan since he left. And I definitely can't help him *or* you when he does shit like this! You don't have anything to do with it?"

"No." Her phone buzzes; she briefly pulls it away to see Yash's reply: He hasn't called me back either . . .

There's no way Rajan would ignore his youngest brother. Simran's fingers tighten around the phone. "Nick, I think Rajan's in trouble."

Rajan pays for his detour. He's doubled over on the floor of this shithole they brought him to, still coughing, when Snake Tattoo hauls him back upright.

"I'll ask one more time. Where were you those minutes you were gone?"

"Who cares? I got you your last ledger, didn't I?" He braces for another blow, but then the door opens.

Zach. "Stop."

Snake Tattoo shoves him into a chair. Rajan attempts not to breathe too deeply as they loom over him.

It wasn't a good plan, but he had no choice. He told them to drop him off at the place right *next* to the banquet hall. A large fabric store, which he explained had a back room the Lions used. It was just absurd enough to be true. He finally succeeded in losing his tail in the lace section—they were hesitant following him, which might've been funny in another situation—and slipped into the banquet hall through the inside corridor. But they caught on too quickly and followed him there. He'd heard them, when he was with Simran. That was when he knew he'd stayed longer than he should've.

Snake Tattoo turns to Zach. "He's still not answering our questions. We should kill him now, cut our losses and go. We have the ledgers, that's enough."

But Zach shakes his head. "We got this far. Just imagine the looks on everyone's faces when we bring back our ledgers *and* the Lions' book-keeper. Not those other assholes they have on the job—*us*. Let's not lose focus here."

Hat Stealer nods slowly, and after a moment, Snake Tattoo does, too. Rajan understands something right then. Nobody, outside of the people who've been interrogating him the past few days, knows Rajan is here. These Aces are operating on their own.

While he's processing that, Zach comes up to him. "Last chance, buddy. Because honestly, I think you know who the bookkeeper is. Axel's concussion is so bad he doesn't remember much from that night, but it's got you written all over it. Tell us and maybe we let you die quickly. Maybe we don't hurt Kitty after all."

Several pieces click into place, and once Rajan gets it—well, he's sort of impressed.

Only Zach knew him from high school, when Rajan brought his bat to fights; so only Zach would've recognized the rolling pin move as his. And he'd connected the dots—if Rajan was at the café attack, Rajan also knew the bookkeeper. But Zach hadn't told his higher-ups. No, he'd wanted to pursue his lead without any interference. He knew if he let his idea get out, others would take over the operation. *And* the glory for any success.

Unfortunately, this also means Zach is very invested in his lead working out. Rajan blinks sweat away. "I would've given them up already if I knew who they were. You think I give two shits about the Lions? Come on." Zach just stands there, eyes bright, and Rajan adds, "*Please.*"

Zach grins then. Snake Tattoo huffs a little laugh and points his gun at Rajan's head. He stares down the barrel, unable to muster a reaction. His life is over. Fine. He accepted that days ago.

But . . . Simran is alive. He can practically still feel her pulse pounding against his lips. And he can either die here wondering if they'll eventually find her and kill her too, or he can go knowing he saved her.

And so the decision comes to him easily, settling into his bones with a calm he didn't know he was still capable of.

"It's me," Rajan says. "I'm the bookkeeper."

FORTY-THREE

HIS WORDS ARE met with laughter.

"And I'm the Easter Bunny," Zach says once he's done wheezing. "Seriously, buddy, you were so stupid in high school you needed tutoring just to graduate. You expect me to believe *you're* keeping the Lions' books? That you cracked ours?"

"As if your books are hard to crack? Internet Explorer's got better security."

Snake Tattoo wrenches him forward by the hoodie, but Zach holds a hand up.

"Don't."

With a frustrated sigh, Snake Tattoo shoves him back. Rajan steadies himself. Why does Zach keep defending him? The dude should be first in line to rock his shit.

"Your bookkeeper must be pretty important," Zach says. "For you to protect them like this."

"The only reason I'm telling you now is for *Kat*," Rajan retorts. "She's a shit PO, but that doesn't mean I want her dead." But he can tell they're growing restless. Time to change tactics. But how? He can't even sell it to himself. How many times did he sit in the Northridge library, watching Simran command numbers into order and privately wishing he could do the same? She so easily dismantled equations into simple parts and, just as easily, combined them into something more complicated. Even now it's as frustrating as it is awe-inspiring. Math is a whole different language, and if you miss even *one* part, you're lost . . .

"I can prove I'm the bookkeeper," Rajan says after a moment.

Zach scoffs. "How?"

He nods at the ledgers in Zach's hands and channels Simran. "Give me a pen."

"He can't be far," Nick says once Simran explains her suspicions. "If you just saw him, we have a radius."

"How many people can you get on the search?"

"Dunno." He's zipping things in the background. Loading a gun. "Most people looking for him want the reward for killing him."

Simran swallows. "But Rajan has the ledgers. Doesn't Manny want those back?"

"If you're right, the ledgers are already in Ace hands. They'll just spray the scene with bullets, and Rajan, too. *If* he's still alive."

"Of course he's alive." TJ leans in, clearly hanging on to every word, but Simran doesn't care. "They kept him this long. He's valuable."

A pause. "Simran," Nick says softly, "I need you to prepare yourself. If we're too late . . . well, the Aces can be—"

"No." Simran hangs up. Not *no* in the sense that she's denying Nick's claim. Not an answer to anything he said. Just a refusal to listen to more. She doesn't like feeling helpless.

She pushes through the washroom door and heads to the main lobby in search of her mom. She needs the car keys. Stupidly, she didn't bring her own truck.

TJ trots after her. "What was *that* about? Rajan was just here. And who're the Aces? Like, the Silver Aces? The gang?" She laughs.

Simran marches for the doorway back into the banquet hall. Is it her imagination, or are the people in the lobby giving her strange looks?

"Simran," TJ says.

"What."

"I . . . don't think I was the only one who saw you in the hallway."

Simran focuses on the phone screen TJ is holding up. A text from Kiran. You didn't know about her and Rajan. Right??

Simran now looks more closely at the people watching her. Their gazes are wary. A few girls her age whisper around their hands.

She reaches for her own phone. There are several messages and missed calls. The first she sees is Kiran's text: WHERE ARE YOU??

Despite her worst-case scenario coming to pass, Simran feels very little. She feels calmer, actually. The secrets are all out. But she can't go back into the banquet hall. If she does, she'll never leave. This situation is going nuclear, and she doesn't have time for it.

She spins back for the parking lot. "Give me your keys."

"Are you serious?" TJ huffs. "I don't even know what's going on—"

"*Give them to me!*"

TJ flinches.

Simran takes several deep breaths. Every second spent here is a wasted one. "TJ," she says more calmly. "Either help me, or get out of my way."

TJ stares at her like she's never seen her before.

"I'm not giving you my keys," she says slowly. "I'm coming with you."

The room is silent as Rajan is handed a pen and the ledger. For a second, his brain stalls, like he's taking a math test and a teacher is watching him work.

The muzzle of a gun juts into his forehead. "I'm waiting," Zach says.

Rajan bats it away. "I'm trying to remember. It's been a while."

He's not lying. He *is* trying to remember something. How many times has he seen Simran work on the ledgers? The times she explained what she was doing?

The room falls silent again, but this time, he imagines a different kind of silence. Silence like the Northridge library, or an empty classroom with Simran. She never made him nervous when she watched. She'd already seen him screw up in the worst ways possible. There was nothing more to hide.

He puts pen to paper.

Simran's voice echoes in his head as he explains what he's writing. "Like I said, your books are easy. The Caesar cipher of i is i plus three. The most frequent number translates into the most common letter in the alphabet, e. The rest comes from there." He circles the end formula and throws in a few confusing buzzwords. "The inverse of the function is how you decrypt it."

This is the hard part. Using the formula to translate the numbers into letters. He plugs it in. Double-checks his work. He scrawls the message he's decoded across the page. It's an inventory of supplies—outdated, but correct.

Everyone peers over his work. He can tell by their blank stares they're not following his thought process. Thank god math is so confusing.

But, it seems to sway Snake Tattoo. He cracks his knuckles.

"It's our lucky day."

Zach, however, shakes his head. "I'm not buying it."

Rajan twirls the pen between his fingers. "You want me to decode your whole ledger to prove even *I* could do it? Are you sure you wanna go through that kind of embarrassment?"

Zach doesn't answer. Instead, he sorts through the ledgers. "There's one thing I'd like to know." He comes back with a piece of paper. "How you decoded *this*."

Rajan recognizes it immediately. It's an exact copy of the message Simran had found in the Aces' book.

Confusing, convoluted, and mind-numbing is what he'd call that decryption process, but not to Simran. It so clearly thrilled her. So much that, despite himself, he had to know why.

He's glad he paid attention during that dinner conversation now. He takes the note from Zach. "It took a while to realize these were coordinates," he begins, and then starts drawing out the process as best he can remember. The grid. The sentence at the top being the password to decode it. The transposition of letters . . . Ironically, it was easier to understand than the other ciphers Simran cracked. This one didn't require fancy equations or formulas, x or y, the sorts of things that mess with his brain. No, this was math only in its purest form: a creative way of looking at numbers.

And when he thought of it like that, for just a moment he understood why Simran loved it.

He's halfway through the last grid when Zach rubs his face. "Shut up."

Rajan falls silent. Thank god—he barely remembers any of the other ciphers.

"It's him," Zach mutters, almost to himself. "Shit, it's really him."

"Can we off him now?" Hat Stealer asks. Dude knows his priorities.

"No," Zach snaps. "We have to bring him to our people first. They have to hear it from him. They're not going to believe us if we just kill him here."

Hat Stealer frowns. So does Rajan, but thankfully nobody's looking at him. This is the tricky part. He cannot, under any circumstances, let these clowns take him to the Aces' godfathers. Because those guys will *really* cross-fucking-examine him on the bookkeeping, and his entire ruse will fall apart. He can't afford that. No, Zach and his friends have to go back to their superiors with Rajan's body in a bag. They'll have to accept the story at face value—and the search for the bookkeeper will end.

Zach is the leader. Zach is the person Rajan has to convince to kill him.

"If we try to take him anywhere, that's another chance for him to try to escape," Snake Tattoo argues. "He almost lost us back there. They'll have to believe us at our word. We'll bring those calculations he did for us."

Finally, someone on Rajan's side. But Zach shakes his head.

"We'll keep an eye on him. We're so close."

Rajan speaks up. "Close to what? Getting shot? Because that's what'll happen when your godfathers realize you tried to pull this operation without their green light."

Snake Tattoo prowls closer. "Nobody will care about that. They only care about results. And we'll have 'em."

"Hate to break it to you, but they'll take all the credit and leave you losers fighting over scraps."

The others shift, as if that hadn't occurred to them. Zach, however, doesn't. "You don't know what you're talking about. Bring the truck around," he tells one of his buddies, who disappears from the room.

Zach's way too calm right now. New strategy, then. Rajan takes a deep breath and recalls what he remembers from when he was fourteen, reading Zach's personal files on the principal's desk. It's a nasty play, what he's about to do. But fuck it.

"I hope for your sake it works, Zach," he says. "Still not a full member after all these years, huh? Kind of stunning."

"Run your mouth, it won't save you," Zach says, bored. Rajan is undeterred.

"I guess, knowing your background, they don't trust you to handle a lot of money."

Zach goes still.

Rajan keeps going. "They probably think you'd steal some. You're a little too desperate. Desperation is good in the low-level jobs, because you'll do anything for a bit of money." He knows that intimately. "But when you're the one *handling* the money, you actually gotta use your head. You've never had much experience with that."

"Shut up," Zach says, and Rajan knows he's on the right track.

Hat Stealer doesn't, though. "What're you even talking about?" he says to Rajan. "Zach's rolling in money. He doesn't need it."

Rajan grins with all his teeth, still looking at Zach. "Really?"

"Well, yeah." Hat Stealer glances between Rajan and Zach, finally clued in that something else is going on. Zach hasn't moved a muscle in like a minute. "Zach, your dad is a hotshot lawyer. Isn't he?"

Rajan's eyebrows rise. Zach really went all the way with this ruse. It's sad, really. He had to pretend his family was rich to become respected as a leader among his friends. He probably feels like he's so close to gaining that full membership. It would be *terrible* if someone came around and ruined his progress.

"You know what," Rajan says thoughtfully, "now that you mention it, I remember reading that."

Zach speaks then, his jaw clenched. "Where the fuck would you have read that?"

"Mr. Kerr," Rajan replies offhandedly. "He used to leave student files out on his desk all the time. I read some of them. Like yours."

Zach turns white so fast, Rajan has the impression that poverty isn't the only secret he's hiding.

But Rajan's certain whatever else was in that file is no big insult. It's probably just sad. And if Zach wasn't such a dick, Rajan might even feel sorry for him. But since Zach *is* a dick, and has also been torturing him for four days straight, Rajan will use it to his advantage.

"Why don't *you* tell them, Zach?" Rajan suggests. Zach says nothing. "There was a lot of interesting stuff in your file. You always acted like you had big money, but the truth is, you and your family are—"

"Hold him down," Zach barks at Snake Tattoo, and Rajan settles back. *Finally.*

Snake Tattoo, however, looks confused. "I thought you said—"

"I changed my mind," Zach snaps. "We'll bring the notes back. And the ledgers. That'll be enough proof. You're right, I don't trust him to not escape."

More like, he doesn't trust Rajan to not be a loudmouth about his family's exact circumstances the whole way there. But Snake Tattoo, appearing pleased that Zach's agreeing, doesn't question him further.

They all look at Rajan, and the energy in the room changes slightly. Rajan knows what this means. He feels strangely calm, though. Whatever they do to him, it will be over eventually. He just has to ride it out.

Then Zach produces a syringe from his pocket.

"Wait," Rajan says slowly. "What's that?"

Zach examines the syringe. "Remember when Perry threatened me with a needle?"

Of course Rajan remembers. There are some things he can never forget.

"He gave me an idea," Zach continues, nodding at the guys around him, and the circle tightens around the chair. The foreboding feeling intensifies. "Ever done the IV stuff, buddy?"

It all clicks. The needle Zach's uncapping. The reason Zach didn't want anyone giving him obvious injuries—it wasn't just because they needed him for a mission. It was because Zach had always planned to kill him like this.

It's the *one* way he doesn't want to die.

Rajan launches himself out of the chair.

They clearly didn't expect that, because he gets halfway across the room before there's a blow to the back of his head. He staggers. They grab at him, voices everywhere.

"Careful with the face—"

"Grab his legs—"

"The jacket—"

He's slammed back to the floor. His already injured ribs and shoulder explode in pain. That's all they need to roll him over. Dazed, he barely registers the flash of scissors. His jacket and hoodie are being cut off, leaving him in his T-shirt.

He claws at them with his fingernails, and when they force his arms to his sides, he surges toward the pointed part of the scissors. He's yanked back instantly, someone putting him in a choke hold. Snake Tattoo gives him a disbelieving look. "What are you doing, you freak?"

Zach answers for him. "He's trying to get his face carved up so they can't write him off as an OD." He lights a cigarette, a smile twitching on his lips. "But you know what, buddy, that just isn't gonna happen."

Rajan pants, immobilized. Zach sinks to his haunches to speak in his ear. "To answer your question, this is heroin. And fentanyl. Everyone knows you prefer"—he mimes snorting a line—"but tonight it wasn't enough, was it? You wanted something new, but you took it too far. Open-close case, when they find you. No one gives a shit about a junkie."

Rajan finds he has only one word in his vocabulary. "No," he whispers. "No—no—"

Zach blows smoke into his face. "Goodbye, Rajan."

His arm is forcibly extended as Zach gets up. The voices around him become almost soothing. Mockingly so.

"Relax, man."

"Yeah, take it easy."

"You'll enjoy this."

"OD'ing is a nice way to go."

No, it's not. It will confirm what everyone thinks about him. The words on his medical records—*substance use disorder*—will be his legacy. Everyone—his dad, his brothers, Kat, Simran—will believe it. He's already relapsed once. The bruising on his arm will damn him. So what if he's a tiny bit scuffed up? Junkies usually are. His sobriety before all this will mean nothing, his struggles will mean nothing. Everything he tried to do for himself, meant nothing in the end.

The needle comes down, flashing in the dim light. He's still saying *No*, but now it's a long breathless stream, *nonononononononono*—

There's a pinch in the crook of his elbow. Then it burns. Right before it lights him up from the inside.

A head rush, so unbelievably beautiful. The voices distort into a buzz, and Rajan's *no* dies in his chest. They let go of him. Someone pats his cheek roughly. His head lolls to the side, vision focusing long enough to see several sets of legs walking out of the room. The light turns off.

He waits to see his mother. But this time, when the door swings shut, he is alone in the dark.

FORTY-FOUR

ON THE WAY to Manny's, Simran fills TJ in. On everything. As long as she's explaining the last few months to her cousin, she doesn't have to think about what could be happening right now.

TJ, to her credit, doesn't interrupt, but she's quite pale by the end. "So it's bad. Really bad." Simran doesn't answer. TJ grips the steering wheel harder. "These people . . . they could kill you, Simran. Oh my god. How did this happen?" She shakes her head, a horrified laugh escaping her. "How did any of this *happen* to you?"

Simran glances out the window. They're two streets away from the Khullar mansion. "You can wait here."

TJ pulls over and reaches for her seat belt. "Screw that. I'm coming with you."

"No, you're not. The last thing I need is you on the Lions' radar. I can't be distracted trying to protect you. It has to just be me." TJ's staring again. "What?"

"I've learned more about you in the past hour than I have our whole lives," TJ says.

—

Tonight, Manny is waiting for her.

Tonight, there's no smoke. No partying, no girls draped on his arm, no ledgers in sight. He's in an office this time. Simran's escorted in silently, and then they're alone. There's no smirk on his face, just focus. And when he speaks, there's none of his earlier condescension.

"Give me one reason why I shouldn't kill you right now."

She swallows. "The Aces took Rajan. They forced him to steal the ledgers. You need to stop the hit on him."

He laughs, a hint of mockery breaking through. "Simran, don't test my patience. I *just* got the police out of my hair for that fiasco outside. Even if what you're saying is true, I don't care. He's been a dead man walking ever since he killed one of us."

"Maybe you should rethink that." She tosses a USB on the desk. Manny stares at it for several seconds.

"What's—"

"I think you know." He's silent, so she goes on. "I've learned a lot, working for the Lions. About your inventory, your cash flow, who you pay off and who you cheat, your distribution methods . . . Look at the numbers long enough, and you start seeing the people behind them. Foot soldiers, runners, dealers, buyers. You also see the people who are higher up, because they *always* get a cut. And that leaves a footprint."

A muscle in Manny's jaw ticks.

"That last ledger was particularly interesting. The one with the names." Every four-digit code has a name attached. Of course, they have to keep track somewhere. And of course, Manny kept such important information close. So Simran had to *get* close. "Some of those names surprised me."

Manny's silent.

"Police have been trying to connect your family to the Lion's Share for years," Simran continues quietly. "This information might be useful for prosecution. And sentencing."

Manny finally moves. He reaches for his drawer and retrieves a small silver gun. "Or I could blow your brains out."

Simran doesn't flinch. Somehow, she finds the barrel of a gun less intimidating now than she used to. Her plan either works or it doesn't.

She nods at the USB. "Shoot me and you'll find out exactly how many copies I made."

She can practically see the calculations running behind Manny's eyes. Gauging the probability that she's bluffing . . . or that she's not. For all he knows, she handed the USBs out like candy. He could try and torture it out of her, but by that time, the information would be public. Theoretically.

He seems to arrive at that conclusion, too. He flicks the safety off. "Maybe I put a bullet in your head anyway."

"Then what? You go to prison to spite me?" His jaw tightens. "There's no need for that. As long as Rajan doesn't die tonight, you don't have to worry about this getting out."

"If the Aces have him, he's probably already dead."

"Then you'd better pray he isn't." She holds his gaze. "Because if all goes well, after this, we can leave each other alone. Rajan and I walk, and you conduct your business in peace. Simple."

Manny keeps his gun trained on her.

"I'd start by taking back that hit you have out on him." Very slowly, Simran turns on the spot. "I'm going to leave now."

She takes a cautious step toward the door. He doesn't shoot. No one stops her from leaving the room. Not a peep as she walks down the glass staircase and through the front doors. It's like she's invisible.

Or, protected.

FORTY-FIVE

THE SHIT MOVIE THAT PLAYS IN YOUR HEAD RIGHT BEFORE YOU DIE

SCENE I

(A random shithole—night. Gunshots outside. Sounds like a real party out there. It's dark and quiet in this room, though. At least until a door opens and light floods in.)

> SOME DUDE WITH A GOATEE:
> Fuck.

(A YOUNGER KID in a hoodie enters too and stops dead. GOATEE DUDE skids over to you and pats you down.)

> YOUNGER KID:
> He's not—shot, is he?

> GOATEE DUDE:
> I don't see anything. But he's not breathing right for some reason. *(to*

you) Get up, asshole! It's me, Nick.
I didn't go through all this shit so
you could die on me. *(to YOUNGER KID)*
Don't just stand there! *You* insisted
on coming. Now help.

*(YOUNGER KID sinks down at your side. He pries open
one of your eyes and sucks in a breath.)*

                    YOUNGER KID:
I think he took something. His pupils
are tiny.

                    NICK:
Seriously? The Aces are sick. Shit.
Shit.

                    YOUNGER KID:
I—have a Narcan kit. In the truck.

                    NICK:
Why the fuck do you have— Never mind.
Get it, if you want your brother to
live.

*(YOUNGER KID exits the room. The gunshots start
dying down; sirens replace them. NICK shakes you
again.)*

                    NICK:
Wake up. Tell me to go to hell. Punch
me in the face. *Breathe.* Holy shit, why
aren't you breathing?

*(The scene begins fading to black as YOUNGER KID
reenters the room, this time holding a grey bag.*

NICK dumps the contents on the ground. The scene becomes so dark you can't see what he's doing, at least until he plunges a needle into your arm. The scene brightens suddenly. Brighter than before. A blond girl enters, pale and tight-lipped.)

> BLOND CHICK:
> Is he—

> NICK:
> No. Do we have an exit strategy?

> BLOND CHICK:
> Only through the cops. You know what's gonna happen if they find him here. And we're toast, too.

(There's a long pause as they all digest that. Then, suddenly, BLOND CHICK moves back to the door.)

> NICK:
> What're you doing?

> BLOND CHICK:
> I'm gonna distract them. Get him out.

> NICK:
> Zohra! Wait!

(But she's gone. After a moment, NICK turns back to you. The scene begins fading again.)

> NICK:
> He's going again. Do you have another dose?

(YOUNGER KID gives it to him. NICK fumbles with the packaging.)

> NICK:
> You know, your brother said he'd kill me if I ever came near you. Let's hope he gets the chance.

> YOUNGER KID:
> You're the one who put out a call for people to look for him.

> NICK:
> Well, I didn't mean *you*. I never even wanted to know you existed. God, is fucking up in your genes or something? You should walk away from all this. Now I have to blacklist your name to everybody I know, so you never get a job with us. And hope he never asks me about you ever again.

(YOUNGER KID doesn't reply. He just cradles your head in his arms. There are shouts from outside, the squealing of tires.)

> YOUNGER KID:
> Do—do you think that's our people—

> NICK:
> Guess we're about to find out. Let's go.

(You don't hear anything else.)

FORTY-SIX

THE FOLLOWING AFTERNOON, Simran comes downstairs fully dressed to find Kiran happily munching leftover chaat next to their mother. And if *that's* not a strange enough sight, their masi stands at the stove, stirring a pot and talking to her mom.

". . . I'll speak to your oncologist. I don't think you need further treatment. With negative lymph nodes, the chances of recurrence are low."

Simran reaches the foot of the stairs. Kiran and her mom look up and freeze. Her masi, who has her back to Simran, keeps going as she shuts off the stove. "Don't worry, I'll take care of—" She halts as she spots Simran, too.

Simran sighs inwardly. After her chat with Manny, she'd asked TJ to take her home. They spent the rest of the evening in her bedroom, Simran ignoring her buzzing phone except for when Nick called to tell her Rajan was alive. Then she sank to the floor in her beautiful anarkali and cried so hard not even TJ could have salvaged her makeup. TJ left shortly after, and when Simran's family came home, she simply pretended to be asleep.

So, now's her first time showing her face with all the secrets out. Is it too much to hope she'll walk away unscathed? She gives them all a bland smile and heads for the door. One, two, three—

Surprisingly, it's her masi who speaks.

"Simran putt, where are you off to?"

Her words are polite, but firm. Simran stops. When did *she* become the nuclear daughter? That used to be Kiran.

Simran faces them. "I'm visiting my friend Rajan in the hospital."

Spoons clack on plates. Kiran's eyes are round. She probably didn't think Simran would announce it so boldly. Her masi glances quickly at her mom, and Simran's gaze unwillingly goes there, too.

Her mom looks at the ceiling instead of her. Simran almost thinks she's going to ignore her, which is probably the best outcome. But then she says, "Go if you must."

Simran waits. The silence stretches. When she starts for the door again, her mother adds, "But I won't speak to you anymore."

Simran freezes.

"Tarleen," Simran's masi admonishes, in similar horror. "Don't you think that's harsh?"

Kiran interjects. "Don't worry, Masi ji, that's just Mom for you." She rolls her eyes, apparently over her shock. "She loves being dramatic. Remember when I said I'd never get married? Mom said she wouldn't talk to me again. But here we are." She laughs. Bitterly.

Simran remembers that day vividly. It's true that, eventually, they started talking again—out of necessity. But Simran's seen how they interact now. Shallowly. No warmth, no meaning.

Simran knows she's hanging from the same precipice. If she goes, it will be the final straw. She has to, though. She *needs* to see that Rajan's okay.

But she *wants* her mother's blessing. "Mom, please—"

"You think I'm trying to hurt you?" Her mother's eyes are bright. "I'm trying to stop you from *being* hurt. You think I don't know, while I've been sick, what you've been up to? Where you've been? Who you've been with?" Each of these questions hits Simran in the gut. "I've seen your grades this semester, left out on your desk. I've heard the voicemails from Hillway, wondering where you are when you're not answering your phone. I watched you at Neetu's party, acting like you were drunk or worse. I've noticed you disappear at odd hours, without telling anyone where you're going."

Simran's face heats. Her mother's been paying attention this whole time? "None of that has to do with Rajan."

"It has *everything* to do with him. He came into your life and it immediately began falling apart. If he hadn't been there, would you have done any of those things?"

Simran's eyes burn. The kitchen is silent.

"Listen to me." Her mother folds her hands on the tabletop. "When I leave this world one day—"

"Mom, you're not *dying*—"

"—the only thing I want is to know you'll be safe and settled and happy."

An ache builds in Simran's chest. *Happy.*

Historically, her mom has always known what's best for her before she does. Like, *Stop biting your hangnail or it'll bleed. You'll get hungry, take a parantha. Clean your room or you'll never be able to find anything.* The list goes on; her mother can see, ten steps ahead, what will hurt her, while Simran ignores the warning signs and plows forward.

Is her mom seeing this before it happens, too? Simran had scoffed at TJ for how she avoided the big questions of life posed by her parents, but maybe Simran's doing the same. Maybe she's a silly, inexperienced girl making a mistake.

Her masi speaks. "This is ridiculous, Tarleen." She bangs the pot down, voice rising. "Children make their own choices. Accept it. You say your piece and let them learn for themselves. Or who knows, maybe you'll be proven wrong."

This seems to irritate Simran's mother quite a bit. "I don't need lessons on parenting from *you*. She's *my* daughter—"

"And *you will lose her!*" her masi shouts. "*Just* like you lost me."

Silence. They glare at each other, more openly than ever. Simran glances between them. The awkwardness is gone. Maybe this is what was always underneath.

"I lost you?" Simran's mom says quietly. "You left."

"Because you are *infuriating*," Simran's masi seethes. "You're stubborn and smothering and you believe what you say is right and there's no other way—"

Simran's mom makes an unimpressed sound. "So I'm a terrible mother, am I?"

"No! That's the thing!" Her voice is heated. This conversation is definitely not just about Simran anymore. "If you were completely terrible, it'd be *easy* for Simran to walk away. But you've devoted your life to making hers better, you'd cut off your arm for her without a second thought— and look at the girl you've raised Simran to be. Clearly you're doing something right. But you're also doing something wrong. You think it's a coincidence Kiran and I both left you?"

"Whoomp, there it is," Kiran mumbles into her bowl.

Simran's mother looks at Simran. Her anger has faltered. In her brown eyes, the same ones Simran sees in the mirror every morning, there's fear. Real fear.

Simran wonders what would happen if she said, *Yes, you will lose me, too*. If that would break her.

But she's done with threats. What kind of healthy relationship can come out of an ultimatum? Tiredly, she takes another step toward the door. "I'll be back soon."

Her mother speaks again, softly. "You're making a mistake with him. And you'll have to live with it forever."

Simran pauses again.

She knows what some people would say. *Follow your heart, not your parents*. But that makes it seem so simple. As if her parents won't always influence her heart. They are, after all, a part of it. And everything her mom has ever done, including this, has come from a place of love. A misguided love, maybe. An overwhelming love that she lacks the words to explain in all its complexity. But love. Simran's never doubted that.

However, they're arguing two fundamentally different debates. To her mother, stability is happiness. And Rajan is the opposite of stability. He's a risk; he said it himself.

But, in a different way her mother doesn't understand, he *is* stability. He is a shelter in the storm. A reliable comfort even on bad days. A listening ear whenever she needs it. He is stability . . . to her soul. And when she almost lost him last night, she felt a part of herself drift, the same as when she first heard her mom's diagnosis. She doesn't want to lose either of them.

But that's not up to her, is it?

"You're right," Simran says finally, and her mother exhales, at least until Simran goes on. "For the rest of my life, I have to live with my choices. I know you're pushing me away because you're trying to stop me from making a mistake. You think I'll regret this and he'll break my heart. I don't know how I'll feel in ten years, Mom, but I know that if I don't go see Rajan right now, I'll regret it. And the only one breaking my heart right now is you."

Without waiting for a reaction, she pushes out the door.

FORTY-SEVEN

RAJAN WAKES UP to some doctor shoving a tube between his ribs.

He swears at them. A lot. Once he's been wrestled back into the stretcher, they explain that actually, he agreed to this procedure five minutes ago. He has broken ribs and fluid in his chest that needs draining.

Why are his ribs broken? His memory's a blur. They don't know, either. He was dropped off at the hospital by an unidentified driver.

It hurts enough to breathe that he lets them finish. While they do, they ask him what other drugs he took. Rajan doesn't remember taking any drugs at all. His stomach drops when they show him the bruises on his arm, and explain exactly how much Narcan he got. He relapsed *again*? And with the needle stuff? What the hell happened?

Rajan asks for something for his splitting headache. Instead of just giving him fucking Tylenol like normal people, they spend twenty extra minutes shining lights in his eyes and poking at his skull. That's how they also diagnose him with a concussion.

He's admitted to the hospital for a short stay. Overnight, he lies awake; he gets only the weakest meds for pain because everyone knows he's a user. Gradually, memories float back, in pieces. The Aces. The ledgers. Simran at Neetu's engagement party. Zach Singer. That asshole tried to OD him, didn't he? So how did Rajan end up here?

Several times during the night, he has the urge to rip out his chest tube and escape. Everything about this place reminds him of his mother. The monitors, the beeping call bells, the tubes around him. The rattling gasps of the guy one bed over. Rajan wonders if this is how his mother died: accompanied by nothing but the misery of a hospital in her final hours.

He holds it together until around three in the morning. Then the tears start. So suddenly that it surprises him—body-racking, silent sobs he smothers into the thin blanket. God, he *should have been there*. That he is glad he wasn't can only mean he was a terrible, terrible son, right? He wishes he were still delirious, if only so he could see her again and apologize. Maybe he'd be able to take her hand; the same hand that led him to his first day of kindergarten, stroked his cheek when he was upset, corrected his badly made rotis, and sewed him a bunny from scratch. Her skin would be soft and fragrant from hand cream, not sallow and cold with veins sticking out. She would hug him. He would tell her he was trying to be better. And maybe, just maybe, she would believe him.

Eventually his tears dry up. The fog in his brain starts to lift, and with each passing hour, he feels his mother drift farther away. By the time the day nurses come by, he's itching to get out of this hellhole and away from the memories.

But of course, while he's waiting to be discharged, he has a visitor. He releases a sigh when she walks through the door. "How'd you know where—?"

Simran sits on the bed next to him, drawing one leg up under her. Her expression is inscrutable. "Nick."

Of course. Nick must've been the one to find him.

Simran flips her long braid over her shoulder. Rajan watches it dangle off the bed as she says, "You almost died."

He looks up to see her staring at the chest tube running down the side of the bed. "Listen—"

"All I could think last night was, what if they didn't find you in time? And you know what? Everything I've told myself about why we shouldn't be together seemed so *pointless* suddenly." Her voice breaks.

"Stop," Rajan says, and she does, her mouth quivering, unshed tears sparkling between her lashes. He grips his blankets to keep himself from wiping them away. "You should go. You're not thinking straight."

"No. I'm thinking more clearly now than ever."

"What about your parents?"

"My parents," she says slowly. Something dawns in her eyes. "My mother came to see you, didn't she."

Rajan doesn't bother denying it. "She told you?"

"No. But she knew when we started volunteering together, although I never told her . . . She put it together by herself." Simran shakes her head. "That was out of line. She had no right to guilt you."

"Yeah, she did. All I've done is screw up her daughter's life."

"You haven't—"

"News flash, dude," he interrupts, because he's angry she hasn't given up yet. "There's going to be plenty of people lining up for you, including that Jassa guy. Give them a chance and you'll never have to settle for me. You can't just accept whatever attention's thrown your way because you don't think you'll get anything better."

That seems to piss her off. "That's rich of you to say. You let anyone who doesn't immediately run away from you use you. The Lions. Zohra. Chandani." Her voice scrapes. "Me."

He didn't know she even knew about Chandani. "I— You? You never used me."

"You're the one who pointed it out. Becoming the bookkeeper was my way of escaping my own problems."

She's getting a little *too* honest. It scares him. He keeps his voice light, stretching an arm behind his head. "You can use me anytime you want, Auntie."

She doesn't smile. "Don't flirt with me unless you're going to do something about it."

He pauses mid-stretch. Holy *fuck*. She's getting bold.

While he's speechless, she continues. "You should want *more* than being used. We both should. I don't see why we can't have that . . . with each other." She puts her hand on his cheek. His breath stalls. The memory of the last time they were on a bed together expands between them until he can't ignore it.

He pushes her hand away. "No."

His voice is louder than he intended. He turns his face away—which is how he notices another visitor at the door.

Nick coughs. "I'll come back."

"No," Rajan snaps. "We're done here."

"We're not," Simran says. Rajan shoots her a glare.

"Let me spell this out for you. If you're with me, you're always going to be in danger. It might be from me, or it might be from my past. If nothing else, someone might come around to finish me off. Because here's the thing." He taps his neck, his tattoo. "No matter how far I go, I'm always going to be a Lion."

Simran stands. She digs into her pocket and throws something at him. He catches it, confused.

"So am I," she says.

And without explaining further, she leaves. Rajan stares after her, then at the USB.

Nick drops into the chair next to his bed, a plastic bag in hand. "You know, I used to feel bad about your life always going to shit, but I'm starting to think it really is your fault."

Rajan ignores that and holds up the USB. "What's this?"

"*That's* the reason you won't get shot the minute you step out of here. Your girlfriend has the Lions by the balls," Nick informs him. "Manny wants her dead—"

"*Great.*"

"—except he can't do shit, because he's scared of the evidence she stole falling into the cops' hands." He nods to the USB.

Simran stole . . . evidence? "How'd she manage that?"

"No clue," Nick says crisply. "But it's working. As soon as we got the ledgers back, Manny locked them away. Last I heard, he was on the phone with the other godfathers, debating whether they should burn them."

Well, at least that's Manny sorted. For now. "How'd you find me?"

"We ID'd some van that was parked near the Khullar mansion earlier last night and found it where you were. There were a couple of Aces leaving the scene." Nick's voice lowers slightly. "We . . . took care of them."

"*All* of them?" Nick nods. So that's why no Aces have broken into his hospital room to off him for being the bookkeeper. All their leads died with Zach Singer. "Where's Zohra? Thought she'd want to come gloat, too." Something on Nick's face makes him sit up, ignoring the pain to his ribs. "What? What happened to her? Say something—"

Nick holds up a hand. "The cops showed up while I was trying to get you out. So Zohra distracted them."

"How?"

"How about . . . took a cop car for a joyride?" Rajan stares. Nick's lips tug into a grin. "Surprised?"

Zohra must've loved that. "But her law school—"

"We all know she owes you," Nick interrupts. "If it weren't for you, she might be in prison right now. She knew what she was doing then, and she knew now. Law school might be toast with her new criminal record, but here's the thing: She's gonna have a *criminal record*. She's not squeaky-clean anymore. The Lions can't use her. So . . . maybe she got herself out, too."

Rajan slumps back, dazed. "She shouldn't have."

"But she did. Don't waste it." Nick stands and stretches. "Well, gotta go. Flight waiting."

Rajan sits up again. This is too much information all at once. "You're *leaving*?"

"Nothing for me here anymore. I'm done babysitting Simran—Manny won't touch her now—and you're under her protection. Manny doesn't even want my help finding a new bookkeeper, so your friend Maya's safe, too. I think the Khullars wanna find some rich white accountant to blackmail." He chuckles. "Those guys are a little more predictable."

"So you're going back to Surrey?"

"Yeah. They need me back home." His expression is neutral—but Rajan wonders whether the fact that he's going back alone, without even Zohra, matters to him. Whether he cares.

Probably not—yet Rajan's struck with the urge to say he'll miss him. The words stick in his throat. How can you miss someone you met during the worst time of your life, who objectively made your life shittier? How can you miss someone when you were poison to each other?

Nick pauses halfway across the room. "Oh right, I almost forgot. We found the cab you got kidnapped in. I dropped your suitcase off at your house." At Rajan's questioning look, he adds, "I needed to make sure there wasn't any evidence lying around."

Right. "That's a nice little present."

"No, actually. Here's your present." Nick reaches into his bag and tosses something to him.

Rajan catches it. A wrapped Popsicle, sweating slightly. He rips it open and takes a bite. "Knew it," he says. "Freezer burned."

Nick chuckles. "You little asshole."

But the way he says it, Rajan can tell he's not the only one thinking of what might've been.

Rajan's discharged soon after they pull his chest tube. Kat immediately calls to set a meeting.

Seeing as he's missed a probation check-in and could be in deep shit, he goes in the same day to explain himself. It's obvious he was in the hospital, so all he has to do is tell her why: He got roughed up by people he no longer has anything to do with. That was all they wanted, he explains. To jump him out. Break some ribs, scare him . . . When they were done, that was it. He keeps his story intentionally vague, avoiding the news story of a gang shootout that conveniently happened the same night.

He suspects Kat reads between the lines anyway. By the end she says,

"I'm glad you're okay. You have a good reason for not attending your check-in in Halifax. I'll make sure that's clear."

How very neat. Unless, of course, she asks him for his medical records from the hospitalization as proof. She'd find some very interesting things. But then again, she tends to ignore interesting things.

Screw it, he *has* to ask. He can't stand this anymore. "But I *did* breach probation—I know the social worker told you. I know there's photos of me using."

Kat is silent.

He has to know. "You didn't rat me out. Why?"

"Sometimes people need more chances."

"I've had a million chances."

"What's the point of chances if your odds never change?" Kat's ever-present smile fades. She leans forward and touches the photo frame. "My son wasn't able to return to a normal life after his first incarceration. Getting a job with a criminal record is hard enough, but it's even harder when you spend much of your young life imprisoned instead of learning skills." She flips through a stack of stapled papers. "While you were . . . gone, one of the community colleges accepted you for a woodworking program. I can help you apply for funding. If you want."

She pushes the papers over. He stares at them, suddenly afraid. "Kat, I'm going to Halifax."

"I thought you said the Lion's Share wasn't going to bother you anymore."

He *did* say that. "Even if I stayed, we both know I'd flunk out."

"No. I don't know that. And neither do you." Kat's gaze drops, and he realizes he's jogging his knee up and down.

He stops immediately. "Do you remember that maple tree in our yard?" She nods slowly. "I finally cut into it, and it was rotting from the inside." He'd taken the chain saw to it after Simran's mom had left. Because suddenly, he had to know. "It's useless. I can't do anything with it, because it was already ruined. *That's* why it fell, not the storm."

She studies him. "Why are you telling me this?"

He has no clue. "Because . . . clearly, woodworking is a bust."

"I'm sure they'll supply you with materials. Nobody's going to make you chop down your own trees." Great, now even Kat's making fun of him. While he glares, her amusement fades. She says, quietly, "You are not rotten, Rajan."

All his breath leaves him in a rush. He blinks back the sudden burning in his eyes.

Kat, thankfully, doesn't appear to be looking for a response. She clasps and unclasps her hands, staring down at them. She almost looks like she's debating something. Then, out of nowhere: "Remember that evening we met in the ER?"

"No, I forgot about you shoving my arm back in its socket."

She ignores this. "Before you arrived, I was about to leave without being seen. You changed my mind. If it weren't for that, I wouldn't be talking to you right now."

He stares. "What?"

She doesn't say more. He racks his brain trying to recall their conversation that night. They talked about her son, and he told her not to blame herself. He left after she fixed his shoulder. He still doesn't know why *she* was there, she didn't have any obvious injuries—

Oh. *Oh.*

"Shit," he says at last, succinctly. That was the night her son died. "You were gonna . . ."

Kat clears her throat. "Don't ever try to tell me you're not capable of good things. I am living proof. I'm sure your brothers would agree, despite what you think. I *know* your Hillway mentor agrees." She taps a heavy stack of Hillway reports. "I may have lost my son, but you—"

"Kat, you don't have to say it—"

"You remind me of him." Her smile trembles. "Angry. Lonely. Lost. But so much more, too. And deserving of a life better than the one the system was determined to keep him in."

"Kat," he says weakly. He doesn't know what else to say.

"Goodbye, Rajan." She closes his file. "I wish you all the best."

FORTY-EIGHT

WHEN RAJAN GETS home, he opens his suitcase.

He stares inside, at T-shirts he never unrolled. A pair of shoes stuck into the side pocket. Socks that have long forgotten their partners.

A few days ago, leaving felt like the right decision. Not anymore. Now he wonders if Kat is right, and maybe he doesn't have to completely start over every time he screws up.

"You're leaving again?"

He turns to find Yash and his father in the doorway. It was Yash who spoke, and he looks afraid of the answer. The story Rajan told Yash about his hospitalization (and he knew Yash would tell Sukha and their dad) was that he overdosed, simple as that. It was hard to tell that lie. But it was better than the alternative—them worrying about people coming after him. "No. I'm here to stay."

He directs that at his father, who remains impassive. Then turns and leaves without a word.

It doesn't bother Rajan as much as it used to. Maybe Kat's right that his mom's death had nothing to do with him—maybe she's not. Either way, his dad's already made up his mind. But Rajan's done making that his problem; he's here for his brothers. He always should've been.

Yash exhales. "Really?"

The way his face lights up makes Rajan feel like a tool. How could he ever have ignored how much Yash wanted him around? "Yeah. And I'm gonna get help with the drug thing, too." That part's not a lie. Kat hooked him up with an addictions counselor. Forced OD or not, that shadow on his life isn't lifting anytime soon. He kicks his suitcase, feeling awkward. "I'm sorry for being such a shitty brother. I didn't think when I was doing it. I never wanted to leave you behind, I hope you know that."

"I know," Yash replies. "You're not a shitty brother. For that."

"For *that*?"

"Well, there was that time you ate the last Oreo—"

Rajan throws a wad of socks at his head. Yash runs away, cackling.

It doesn't take long to unpack. He doesn't have a closet, so he drags in a plastic storage bin to fold his clothes into. It's not the bedroom he had growing up, but it's something. It's a commitment.

He's zipping the empty suitcase when Sukha comes by. Maybe he heard Rajan saying he was going to stay and wants to make his disappointment known. Rajan straightens. "What's up?"

"Heard you OD'd." Sukha leans against the doorframe.

"And?"

"Just trying to put it together. You were on your way to the airport that day. You were totally sober. And, what? You just decided to go on a four-day bender instead?"

That was the last thing Rajan expected from him. "That's what addiction does to you, dude," he says blandly. "It derails your life. You do things that don't make sense."

"So nothing else happened?"

"No."

"Really?"

The continued skepticism needles him. "Why would I lie about that?

You think I'd want anyone to *believe* I overdosed if I didn't? Trust me, I wouldn't." Sukha continues to stare. Rajan feels himself getting angry— although at who, he's not sure. He just knows he *hates* that he has to lie to his brother. *Hates* that he has to mislead the one person who suspects foul play. The one family member who, if Rajan had died that night, might not have really believed he relapsed.

But better this than cause him nightmares. "Go ahead and gloat. Call me an addict. I am one, okay? *I am one.*"

Sukha's eyes flicker over him, and Rajan realizes he's standing slightly hunched. His broken ribs are bothering him. He forces himself to straighten, although it hurts.

Surprisingly, Sukha doesn't call him anything. He just says, "How much do you remember? About . . . after the OD?"

Simultaneously relieved and disappointed that he's dropping it, Rajan answers truthfully. "Nothing." It's all a blur after he cracked the Aces' ledgers. "OD'ing will do that to you. Why?"

"Just curious." Sukha picks at a thread on his sleeve. "I decided something, while you were in the hospital. I don't want to become you. So I'm done. All of it."

Rajan stares, hardly daring to believe what he's hearing. Did he finally get through his brother's thick skull? He should've tried overdosing months ago.

"I'm not doing this for you," Sukha adds. "I'm doing this for Yash. I want to be there for him. The way you weren't."

"Guess I deserve that."

"Yeah, you do. You abandoned us after Mom died," Sukha says stiffly. "I'll always hate you a little bit for that."

"I know."

"You were selfish."

"I know."

"You didn't come back. Why didn't you come back?"

Rajan's throat becomes tight. This is starting to sound suspiciously like Sukha cares. Maybe Sukha knows it too, because he turns abruptly and leaves. Rajan thinks that's it, and he's lying back on his mattress when Sukha returns holding something.

His bunny. But now, the eye is sewn back on.

Rajan blinks at his brother, the spitting image of a younger him. "Are you—giving this back to me?"

"Take it before I change my mind."

Rajan does. He hugs it close and presses his nose to its head. It no longer smells like his mother; but he can imagine her hands, carefully sewing each stitch.

He looks up at Sukha. His brother's clearly feeling softer toward him because of the OD, and this opportunity might not come again. "I've been thinking about buying a baseball glove or two. Want to help me practice sometime?" No answer. "You can aim at me when you hit the ball, if that sweetens the deal."

Sukha doesn't smile. "What's the point? I'll never be good. I never played."

"So? You can always start," Rajan says gently, and Sukha takes a very large, very deep breath.

But he only says, "There's a girl outside to see you, by the way."

A girl? Rajan opens his mouth to ask, but Sukha's already disappeared. He sets the bunny aside. A girl . . .

He shouldn't want Simran to be here as much as he does. *It's wrong*, a voice in his head warns him—a voice that sounds like his mother's.

It's not *wrong*, says another voice that sounds suspiciously like Kat's.

He rolls off his mattress, if only to shut up the angel-and-devil routine in his head.

It's sweltering out, so he doesn't bother with a hoodie on top of his tee. He pushes through the front door even though he has no idea what to say to her.

But it's not Simran at all.

TJ Powar stands on his front step with her arms crossed. She looks out of place in this beat-up neighbourhood, in a crisp white blouse, her mouth a slash of maroon lipstick.

Her narrowed eyes instantly find the uncovered tattoo on his neck. Her frown deepens. TJ didn't like him in high school. He never cared for her either. The only thing they have in common is how much they care about Simran, so he can guess what this is about.

He leans against the doorway. "Are you here to tell me to stay away from your cousin? Because I've had about enough of your family."

He waits for a comeback, but instead, TJ says, "Can we talk somewhere?"

Now curious, Rajan closes the door behind him and beckons her to the swing set next door. "What do you want?"

She perches on the swing next to him. "You're an asshole."

Not this again. Rajan stands up. "I'm not anywhere near her. Okay? Get off my case—"

"Sit down," TJ snaps. "Simran's not doing well."

Instantly, he sits. "What happened? Is her mom okay? Are people giving her a hard time because of me?"

TJ studies him. He knows he sounds completely obsessed, but he doesn't care. "Are you gonna make me beg? Because I'll beg."

TJ takes her sweet time answering. "It started after she went to see you in the hospital—"

"How do you know about that?"

"Who *doesn't*? She nearly caused World War III at her house to do it. Let me finish."

Rajan rubs his face, agonized by this information. *Why* would she make things more difficult for herself?

TJ continues. "She came back and said you told her it was over. And you know what she did next? She went right upstairs to work on some Hillway event proposal. She's barely sleeping. I think she took on, like, four new projects in the last two days. Like, what the hell?"

Rajan sighs. "That's what she does."

"Yeah. It happened when her mom got diagnosed, too. She throws herself into these unhealthy spirals when she's heartbroken."

She lets that hang in the air. Rajan's tired of the games. "Spit out whatever you want to say and go."

"Fine." TJ's nostrils flare in annoyance. "I know about the gang stuff. Her bookkeeping. The stuff *you* brought her into."

He cringes. "I never asked her to—"

TJ steamrolls over him. "But the only reason she did any of it was because of what happened to her mom. If it wasn't the Lions, she would've found some other unhealthy coping mechanism. The Lions just happened to *be* there. None of that is on you. She made her own choices, so stop acting like you turned her into a bad person. You don't have that kind of power over her, get over yourself—"

"Okay. Relax." He holds up a hand before she can really lay into him. Even if TJ's right . . . "That doesn't change the fact that I make her life complicated. I don't want to make her an outcast like me. I don't want her to wake up one day and hate me for it."

TJ laughs a little, looking down at her strappy sandals. "You didn't see her," she says, "when she thought you were dead."

His heart drops. He doesn't want to hear this. But he's also riveted.

"I've never seen her like that. *Ever.* She was unhinged. Screaming at me. Like, she was finally losing it completely. That's when I knew there was only one reason she hadn't lost it before then: you."

He can't speak.

"Look, I won't claim to get it," TJ says. "But you're special to her. I don't think the life complications really matter."

Unwillingly, he's pulled back into memories. Simran at his house— the most he'd seen her smile in ages. Her rolling her eyes and throwing a book at him in the library; that playful side he can only seem to dig out when they're alone together. And he remembers her expression when she left his hospital room—like he'd cut out her heart. Then he thinks back to a certain conversation when he was fourteen and trying to make a promise. *Don't be the reason she breaks.*

He wishes he could go back and ask his mother what exactly she meant.

But he can't. And besides, what purpose would that serve? Would it matter, what she said? When she's clearly been wrong about other things—Kat has certainly opened his eyes to that. She was *wrong* to buy things they couldn't afford and *wrong* to think those things would replace his parents being around; wrong to give up on Rajan when he acted out and wrong to stop defending him.

Rajan loves his mom, he will *always* love her, and it will always be unfair that she died. But she was human too.

TJ, to her credit, keeps her trap shut while he sorts through this in his head. Finally, he says lightly, "Are you saying you approve of me with your cousin?"

"Let's not go that far." She scuffs the gravel with her sandals. "But lately I've realized it's not my place to tell her what's good for her. Sure, people will say you and her will end up a disaster, and that you'll resent each other . . . but like, how would they know? They don't know her. They don't know who she'd resent." Her voice becomes soft. "They don't know what would make her happy."

She's staring at the ground. Rajan gets the strong sense she's not just talking about her cousin. "Well, I'm not sure Simran always knows either."

"But she should be allowed the space to figure that out herself. Are you gonna deny her that chance? After everything she's been through?" God, TJ knows exactly how to get to him. "If I thought you'd hurt her, I'd kick you to the curb myself."

Somehow, he finds himself smiling. "What did I ever do to make you hate me so much?"

"Where should we start?" She sniffs. "How about in seventh grade when you said I had a big Indian girl nose?"

Rajan's grin widens. He leans forward and tweaks her nose. TJ jerks away. "Come on, dude. It's a pretty nose, I didn't think I had to tell you that." She remains stiff, and he clasps his hands together apologetically. "Fine. I'm sorry. Happy now, Bhenji?"

She mock-gags. "Stick to 'dude,' please."

But there's the smallest smile on her lips. This is surreal. It *means* something, that someone from Simran's family is saying—in her own nasty way—that she approves. TJ has peered into the relationship between them, one they're too entangled in to see clearly, and declared there *is* something good there. Something that deserves to grow.

It just can't be the only thing going for them. While Simran's reaction to his almost-death is sort of touching, it's scary, too. Rajan doesn't *want* to be the sole reason Simran didn't lose it. And not because he thinks he sucks, or whatever, but because everyone deserves more than one thing keeping them going. *The opposite of addiction is balance.*

Luckily, Rajan has an idea on that front.

He reaches over and twists the ropes of TJ's swing. TJ, unprepared, shrieks as she's whipped around. By the time she rights herself, she's glaring daggers.

"What is your *problem?*"

She shoves him off his swing. He lets her, falling backward into the gravel-laden grass. "I change my mind," TJ announces from above, kicking pebbles onto his torso like she's planning to bury him. "I hate you again."

"Good." He grins up at the sky. "Otherwise I seriously would've thought I was dreaming."

FORTY-NINE

SIMRAN HAD PREDICTED, upon returning from the hospital, that her mother would fully ignore her. Yet, there's a cup of chah on the counter for her every day. An extra couple paranthé in the roti box every morning.

It's *very* confusing, because her mom still won't talk to her. And now that Rajan won't either, it's like she lost both of them at once.

But, if the past few months have shown her anything, it's that life goes on.

TJ's mom seems to share that mindset, because she comes by again a few days later, and she and Simran's mom are perfectly civil to each other. Simran would've thought after their big fight, things would be even worse. But instead it's like something's loosened between them. Amidst their laughter, Simran overhears them discussing the cancer: There won't be any further treatments necessary for her mom. It's really over.

For now, anyway.

And she hates that thought for digging into her head, but it does. All day, and into the evening, when she gets dressed and heads for the door.

Kiran stops her. "Can I borrow your truck?"

"I'm going to Hillway." Several people are graduating the program today, and Simran decided to set up a dinner in their honour. "Free food" was how she advertised it to them, served after their volunteering commitment that evening.

She tries to sidestep Kiran, but Kiran blocks her again. "I just," Kiran takes a deep breath, "have a job interview, okay? At a BC lifestyle magazine, and I don't want to ask Mom and Dad for their car. Can I take yours? I'll make sure you get a ride home."

"A *job* interview? Here?"

Kiran nods. "I quit my job in Ontario. It's not like my career was taking off over there anyway. I'm only going back to pick up my stuff." When Simran stares, she adds, "Don't get me wrong, I'm not planning to live in this house, but I'm coming back to BC somewhere. I want to be closer to you."

"You don't have to do that for me."

"It's for *me*. I need a reset. And . . . I want to get to know my baby sister better." She elbows Simran. "Because clearly I don't know you at all. Never would've guessed *you'd* hook up with a bad boy at a wedding reception."

Trust Kiran to make all this into a joke. "We weren't—"

"*Anyway,*" Kiran continues, grinning, "I thought you were into Jassa. You have the same interests, he's an overachiever like you, and Mom and Dad like him. Meanwhile, this Randhawa kid is the opposite of you in every way. Like, *wow*, where did my little sister's logic go?"

Simran sighs and looks at the ceiling. "Can't *one person* believe I made the right choice?"

It's more of a rhetorical question, but Kiran's smile fades.

"You know, when I moved out, I had all these big dreams. Mom and Dad thought my job was unstable and would end with me crashing and burning, and honestly . . . I wondered that, too." Her mouth twists. "Believing in myself when no one else did was the hardest thing I've ever done. It's still hard. I'm twenty-eight, I'm stuck in the same job, it's not glamorous. I haven't 'made it.' You'd think I'd finally accept that everyone was right, but I keep going anyway. You should, too."

Simran stands there, shocked. Her sister made her own decisions, and they didn't work out. And she's still admitting that to Simran. Simran could say *we told you so*, or she could say something that matters. She could give Kiran what she hopes someone will give her, in the future, if her choices end up being mistakes.

"I'm sorry I ever said your choices were illogical," Simran tells her. "I didn't know it hurt you like that. I do believe in you, you know. You're only twenty-eight. You have a whole life to make it work."

Kiran bursts into tears, surprising Simran.

"Thank you," she says. "Thank you for saying that.'

The Hillway dinner is in the gymnasium of Simran's high school. It was easy for her to book, due to her connections with the school admin. It's a convenient location, too, seeing as the afternoon's volunteering took place across the road at the indoor turf, where the group inflated bouncy castles and set up other activities for a kids' event tomorrow.

Looking up at the NORTHRIDGE SECONDARY sign, she feels a twinge of nostalgia. Her problems used to be so easily contained within these brick walls.

She shakes her head and lets herself inside.

Paul and a few other Hillway organizers are already in the gym when Simran arrives. Lights are strung over the doorway, a THANK YOU banner hanging over the stage. The caterers are bringing supplies in from their truck.

Paul spots her immediately. "Simran! I've been looking for you. The caterers were asking where we wanted the food—I was thinking the back? That way, we can leave the stage empty so the Hillway president can say a few words." He nods in the direction of a balding man in a suit, who waves from where he's talking to a volunteer nearby. "You must meet him. He's the grandson of the founder—"

A voice sounds behind Simran, so familiar she drops her water bottle. "Dude, I don't think anyone cares."

And before she can draw another breath, Rajan steps to her side, scooping up her water bottle and placing it in her hands without a second glance. While she stares at him, speechless, Paul frowns.

"Rajan, I'm glad you volunteered to help tonight, but it's an honour to have Mr. Hillway—"

"They're here to eat," Rajan interrupts. He's in a black Hillway T-shirt like everyone else. But he's finished probation—what's he doing here? "If you ask them to listen to boring speeches instead, you're just making them do more community service on their night off."

Paul glances at Simran. "What do you think?"

Simran's already on thin ice with Paul, so she chooses her words carefully. "I'm happy Mr. Hillway's here, but I agree this night should be about the volunteers. I suggest we put the food on the tables so they can eat right when they arrive."

Paul looks between them. "Well . . . it's *your* event, I suppose." He shakes his head and goes to tell the caterers.

"Damn, Simran Auntie," Rajan says when they're alone. "That was the politest fuck-off I've ever seen."

Simran faces him. "What're you doing here, Rajan?"

He doesn't miss a beat. "Volunteering. Helping humanity. Seva. Whatever you wanna call it."

He's acting too casual, but she plays along for now. "You . . . rejoined Hillway? But you're done."

He shrugs. "Paul needed extra hands tonight."

She has a feeling there's a lot more going on behind that sentence, but right then the Hillway president joins them.

"Simran. I've heard a lot about you." He shakes her hand, beaming. "I'm so impressed with what you've done for the organization. Revitalizing it with all these creative volunteering opportunities. And this dinner! It's an . . . interesting idea."

He sounds uncertain about whether it's a good one. "I don't want them to only see community service as a punishment," Simran replies. "It can be rewarding. Fun. A way to build skills. If they don't turn up, that's fine, but we should show we're genuine about it."

"Well said," he replies, and she can tell she just won him over. "Our board of governors could use some fresh minds. One of the members is retiring this year. How would you feel about joining?"

Simran blinks. "I'll—think about it."

"Excellent. So nice to meet you, Simran." He leaves her to join Paul again, and Simran glances around to find Rajan on the other side of the room draping tablecloths. She so badly wants to talk to him . . . but she doesn't want to scare him away, either. So she watches from afar. He looks worlds better than he did in the hospital, although he still holds himself differently. Probably the ribs.

It's overwhelming to see him standing there, exuding warmth and comfort and *vitality*, because if Nick had gotten to him a minute later he wouldn't be. And maybe, even if she can't be with him, she can be grateful that he's here, that he's getting the second chance he always deserved. And that can be enough.

She turns back to her work as the first Hillway mentee saunters through the door.

Surprisingly, seven volunteers turn up. Simran ordered food for twenty but would've considered the night a success if even three showed. She drifts around saying hellos and making sure everything goes smoothly— which includes ordering emergency takeout for someone with food restrictions, solving a technical issue with the sound system, and running to a classroom for an extra chair. When the night's over, she helps take down lights and wipe tables.

By the time she and Paul are wrestling the THANK YOU banner back into its much-too-small bag for future use, there's no one else left except Rajan (who's holding the bag open). When they're done, Paul takes the bag, wiping sweat off his forehead. "I'll let you lock up since you have to give the keys back anyway." He drops them into her hand. "Did you get a chance to meet John? He was hoping to recruit you to the board."

"Yes. It was nice of him to offer."

"Don't underplay it," Rajan says. "When you said you'd think about it, the dude looked ready to cream himself."

Simran hadn't realized he'd been listening. Paul, however, turns beet-red. "Rajan!" he admonishes. "We don't use that kind of crass language around our mentors." He glances anxiously at Simran, then at Rajan. "Apologize to her at once."

Rajan winks at Simran. "Sorry, Auntie."

Simran smiles at him, hoping he'll understand she doesn't need his apologies. The fact that he doesn't filter himself around her is one of her favourite things about him.

"How much of that conversation with Mr. Hillway did you hear?" she asks when Paul leaves to drag the banner bag back to his car.

"All of it. That part where you were talking about community service, though . . . you give these guys too much credit."

"How so?" She spots one last chair in the corner, the one she'd taken from a classroom. She goes over to grab it.

Rajan reaches it first. In unison they walk out into the school hallway, him dragging the chair by the backrest. "Well, you were so busy tonight you didn't notice two of them snuck out to smoke weed before dessert. Chicks were high as a kite while you were handing them cake. Does that make you regret hosting this thing?"

"No. It must've been a stressful day."

"This other dude was making fun of the way Paul talks. And someone *else* had to be seated at a different table from this other guy because they were about to get into a fight. Almost turned your little dinner into a WWE match. Does *that* make you feel stupid for hosting this?"

"No, Rajan."

"Another one was shoving the cutlery into his jacket pockets. That's why they had to keep restocking table three."

Simran is starting to enjoy this game. "They *were* fancy forks. I'll be sure to pay those compliments forward to the caterer."

"Stop fucking smiling!" While Simran unlocks the classroom door, Rajan drops the chair. "You're not getting it. You can't fix them, and they won't appreciate you trying."

"I'm not trying to fix them. I'm giving them the grace everyone should get when they make mistakes."

"They'll take advantage of it. It'll make your life miserable."

"I think I get to decide how much I'm willing to put up with."

"You're pissing me off," he says. "You're pissing me off so bad right now."

Her smile grows. She pushes the door open, flicks on the light. "Why are you here if you think it's so stupid?"

"Because it's not." He sighs and parks the chair in front of its desk. "It's *not* stupid, because it's you, and somehow when *you're* like this it's not annoying, it's . . ." He makes a frustrated sound. "It *actually* makes them want to be a better person."

Then he looks at her, gaze warmer than sunshine. She finds herself flustered, and whips off her glasses to polish them on her shirt. But the fancy, satiny material only makes the smudging worse.

Rajan watches her attempts for several seconds. "Give them to me."

She hands them over. He brings the glasses to his parted lips, nearly kissing them before he exhales, his breath sweeping over the lenses and fogging them. Heat sweeps over the back of her neck as if his mouth is there, too.

He wipes the lenses with the hem of his shirt and hands them back. She puts them on. Suddenly, her vision is crystal clear. "I missed you."

She fully expects him to recoil like last time, to suggest they go, but he doesn't. He seems unusually pensive instead. He hops onto a desk and pats the one beside him. "Sit up here for a sec. I wanna ask you something."

She obliges, heart thudding. Is this it? Is this where they acknowledge what happened and say goodbye forever? "What is it?"

He leans back on his hands. "Do I make you happy?"

Simran blinks. For several seconds, the only sound is the classroom clock ticking loudly at the front of the room. "I'm sorry, what?"

"Just answer," he says. "Not like, do I turn you on, or make you laugh at some stupid joke, but do I really make you happy?"

Her chest aches. How could he even question that? "Of course you do."

"Even if your life imploded because of me?"

"It didn't."

"Really? Because the fact that you almost died, the fact that everybody will gossip about us forever, the fact that you fought with your mom, that's because of *me*—"

"No, it's not," Simran interrupts. "That all happened because of *my* ego and *my* lying and *my* mistakes. If there's anything that happened because of you, it's that I'm here alive today. It's that even when I didn't listen, you were still there to help. It's that I know it's possible to keep going after the worst has happened. Because you've shown me that every day."

Rajan smiles dryly. "You're laying it on kinda thick, Sahiba."

"It's true. I learn from you all the time." Simran tentatively moves closer. He doesn't pull away. "You're smart in so many ways I'm not. And you're kind despite everything you've been through." After what happened with her mother, Simran appreciates that even more. His ability to maintain levity and an open heart. His *courage* to. "Of course I want to be like that."

"Nobody's ever wanted to be like me."

"Well, I do."

Rajan's quiet for a long time, his brow furrowed now. She draws a breath to say more, though she doesn't know what else she would say; she's just terrified that if she stops talking he'll leave her side.

But he speaks first. "You should go to UBC."

She blinks. "What?"

"That letter in your truck," he says. "From the math prof. You should email them back. Tell them you changed your mind. Beg them to let you transfer."

She doesn't understand. That conversation was forever ago. "You . . . You want me to leave?"

"No," he says, and repeats, sounding anguished, "*No,* Sahiba, I don't ever want you to leave. But you *should.* You should go to Vancouver and level up to the sort of math nerd you've always wanted to be, and I should stay here and go back to school like Kat has been telling me to do, and you should rejoin debate and I should teach my brothers how to play baseball. We should both . . . We should . . ." He takes a breath. "Live."

Simran's already shaking her head. These are arguments she shut down long ago. She's not sure she can bear to open them again. "I *am* living."

"Yes, but not the way you want," he argues. "I know you, Sahiba. You need a challenge. You'll be miserable here. Did your parents not let you go before?"

"I never told them," she whispers. "They would've let me. But they would be unhappy."

"Then let them be," Rajan says firmly. "Let them, and me, and whoever else, be unhappy you're not around twenty-four seven. Jesus Christ. You're not in charge of our happiness. We are. And it's better for all of us not to be dependent on you. Go, okay? Go."

His gentle urging has tears forming in her eyes and she doesn't know why. She didn't realize how much she needed it; for someone she cared about to not only tolerate her dreams but encourage them.

And why shouldn't she go? Rajan, clearly, has made the choice to hope again. She sees it now; a lightness, a *peace* about him that wasn't there before. That somehow, since the last time she saw him, he's forgiven himself for the things he couldn't control. And maybe even for some of the things he could.

If he can do that, she can do this.

Simran finds her voice. "Okay. I'll go."

His eyes clear entirely. No more words from him: he leans in and kisses her.

It's different from last time. He is gentle in a way that makes her burn—none of the desperation, all of the heat. Her chest aches in a good way, a hollow place refilling. She clutches at his Hillway shirt, and he pulls her closer, unhurried. Half on this desk, half in his arms—but she's not worried about falling. She always feels safe with him.

It's too soon when he pulls away. "Listen," he says roughly. "Just listen, okay?"

She nods, their noses nearly brushing. He takes a deep breath.

"I'm scared shitless I'll screw up, and you'll wake up one day and realize you can't take it anymore." His voice becomes raspy. "I'm even more scared that you won't. But if I can *stop* myself from screwing up, then I will. And I think this is part of it. You, me, we both need balance. I want to be part of yours. Even if I can't be someone your parents like. Or claim to understand math. Or play tabla like that prick Jassa, or— Dude, stop *laughing* at me—"

She's trying not to, truly. "Is this really what you worry about?" She cups his face. "I don't want a carbon copy of me. I want *you*."

At that, any tension remaining in his body dissipates. His hand runs down her braid, wrapping it around his wrist. "Simran."

Sim-ruhn. Again, her heart flutters. "What?"

"I'm so fuckin' glad I failed eighth-grade math." Then he takes her leg and swings it fully over his lap, and they don't talk again for a while.

Later, Simran finishes locking up and finds her dad's car waiting in the Northridge parking lot. She wonders if he saw Rajan leave through the same exit. She doesn't feel the fear she used to about that.

"Where's Kiran?" she asks when she gets in.

"She asked me to pick you up. I think she's busy." Her father sighs. "She didn't explain, as usual."

Something about his defeated tone compels Simran to speak. After all, Kiran stood up for her back at the party. It's time she does the same. "You know," she says casually, "that fight she had with you guys last year—she's not refusing to get married to spite you. It's just not in the cards for her. She's asexual."

"What does that mean?" She tells him, and he nods slowly. "Why didn't she say?"

"I think she thought you wouldn't understand things like . . ." Simran picks at a loose thread on her shirt, feeling slightly awkward. "Sexuality and stuff."

"Why wouldn't I? Kiran is by no means the first." He strokes his beard. "Not everyone from my village did things the traditional way, you know. My father's cousin lived with his best friend his whole life. They were like second parents to all the village children. Including me." Simran must look surprised because he gently adds, "Just because we don't use the same terminology as you doesn't mean we're backward."

She nods, chastised, but then points out, "You and Mom always acted like me and Kiran were going to marry men, though."

He sits back. "That is true," he acknowledges, similarly chastised. "I still have things to learn. About that, and more." He turns to face her. "I spoke to Kiran after the engagement party. She made me understand some things about you, too. We've put too much pressure on you."

"It's fine—"

"It's not. And I think I made it worse when you and I talked about how I wouldn't be here forever. I didn't mean to traumatize you. I was just trying to prepare you."

And despite herself, her chin wobbles. Because that's the crux of it, isn't it? Today her mom's news was good, but it's not really the end of the story. The end will be just that—an end. How can she ever be *prepared* for the death of her parents? How can anyone? It's overwhelming. It's unbearable.

"I don't want you to ever leave me," she whispers. It's unfair to say, it's childish, but it's the truth.

"I cannot promise you that. I would if I could," he says softly. "How long I or your mom will be here, I don't know."

That's the exact kind of straightforward response she would expect from him. She sighs, but he continues.

"But there are plenty of things I don't know. I don't know if a meteor will strike the earth before I finish my next sentence. I don't know, every night when the sun sets, whether it'll be back the next day, or if it will rain for the next two months. I don't know if the store will continue stocking my mango ice cream or if the carton I finished yesterday was the final one. Even this conversation could be the last one we ever have. Who knows? You could decide once you get out of this car that you don't want to speak to me anymore, or the continent could split in two between us and we might never find our way back to each other. Every moment in life is temporary."

"That's . . . a sad way to think about it," Simran says softly.

"On the contrary." He shrugs. "I think understanding this is a gift. We have the ability to appreciate every moment we *do* get, as it's happening. What's sad is only experiencing happiness in hindsight."

She's never thought of it that way before. She studies her father and wonders if maybe he's thought *too* much about it. Maybe that's why he's avoided confronting her screwups. Like her, he wants to cling to their relationship as is. He doesn't want to watch the peace between them die.

I don't believe anything about you unless you tell it to me yourself.

Simran makes a decision right then. If this moment between them was meant to die, she has to do it now, on her own terms. She can no longer leave their relationship as dishonest as it's become. She has to tell him the thing most likely to break them.

"Dad, I know you've heard things about me and Rajan Randhawa." She traces the dust on the dashboard. "They're true."

"Ah," he says. "I see."

There is a long, long silence.

She can't help herself. "You don't like him."

"That's not true. I don't know him."

"But?" she presses.

"But," he acknowledges, "I don't like the idea of you with him."

She knew this already, but the confirmation still feels heavy. He goes on, though, as they both stare out the windshield. "You have to understand where I'm coming from. All your mother and I want is for your life to be happy and stable. Our lives were not. We don't want you to have the problems he'll bring." He pauses. "But I didn't listen to everything my parents said, either. We cannot and should not stop you from making your own decisions."

"So you think it's a mistake."

He shrugs. "Life is about learning from your mistakes."

His casual words hit her deeply. Even he has no problem telling her he thinks she's messing up, in his own gentle way. If she keeps going regardless, does that mean she loses him? Does her relationship with her father die right here, right now, in this car?

"Dad," Simran ventures tentatively. "Do—do you still love me?"

His eyes crinkle, and a tear slips out, trickling into his beard. "What have we done to you that you have to ask that question? Of course, I will always love you."

"But will you . . . still talk to me?" Simran's voice trembles. "Can we still fly kites together in the summer? Will you still make popcorn and watch movies with me? Will you play tabla when I need you to accompany? Will you teach me—"

"Yes, nikka putt," he replies. "I will always be your father."

Her eyes blur with tears. And, earnestly, she begins to cry.

As if it's an everyday occurrence instead of something that has rarely happened before in his presence, he turns off the ignition and draws her close. Embracing her fully, flaws and mistakes and hopes and dreams and all. He sniffles a little, too.

That makes her pause. What is she doing, worrying him with the sadness that has weighed her down for months—years, really? But when she tries to pull away, he holds on tighter. And she gives in.

Maybe there's a companionship she never realized in crying with someone you love, as much as in laughing with them. And it doesn't have to weigh either of them down—but can help them both finally, finally let go of it.

EPILOGUE

AFTER NEETU'S RESPLENDENT wedding, Simran's sister moves back to Kelowna. Temporarily, anyway—her new job in Vancouver starts in the fall. In the meantime, she's living with a friend ten minutes away. And Simran's spent more time with her in a month than she has in ten years.

"I'm starting to think we're screwed on the apartments front," Kiran says one mid-August day, while they're on her childhood bed scrolling through Vancouver rental listings. "Maybe Neetu and Gurjeevan will let us live in their backyard."

Simran smiles. She's officially transferring to UBC Vancouver in January—a semester late because of her delayed acceptance, but at least she's going. "I'm sure they'd at least give us the garage."

Despite her joke, though, she *does* feel sort of anxious flipping through the rental prices. In some ways, it would've been easier to stay in Kelowna. Or at least less expensive.

"Dr. Chen told me how hard it is to get tenure as a professor," Simran admits aloud. "Now I'm afraid I'm going to finish school with a bunch of degrees but no job. Maybe everyone was right and I should've done the MCAT."

Kiran grabs a pillow and starts beating her over the head with it. "The *MCAT*? You're having a moment of weakness! Be strong! We'll get through this!"

Simran laughs, at least for a second. "Ow! You're hitting my glasses!" She shoves her off.

Kiran watches Simran adjust her frames. "You never did tell me what happened to your old ones."

Simran pauses. Without warning, dark memories rise to the surface. The rough wooden desk against her cheek. The cold metal of a gun. The crunch of glass under boots.

You're sitting on Kiran's bed, she reminds herself. *Her mattress is soft. The blankets are warm. You hear birds outside, not gunshots.*

The memories ebb slowly. She exhales. She hasn't heard from the Lions since she left Manny Khullar's mansion. Life has returned to normal. It's a relief, but also . . . it sometimes feels like she lost something. A thing she only had at the expense of every other part of her life, yes, but one that kept her afloat when she desperately needed it. "I fell."

"Stop being so clumsy, then." Kiran swings her legs off the bed. "I need a break from apartment hunting. Let's pick this up tomorrow." She opens the window.

"You're not going through the front door?"

"And deal with Mom's death glares? No thanks. I don't know how *you* handle it." She swings her leg over the windowsill. "Huh, weird."

"What?"

"There's a toothpick lodged in the shingle."

"Very weird," Simran agrees. "See you."

Once Kiran's gone, Simran heads downstairs, because she too has plans today. Her father's in the living room reading the newspaper. She's about to say hello, but he puts a finger to his lips and nods toward the kitchen.

Simran peers cautiously through the doorway. Her mom's at the counter with the laptop, scrolling through a website.

Curiosity has Simran creeping forward. It's a site for a medical office assistant program. She stops in her tracks. Her mom hasn't done more than odd jobs in decades. Why this, why now?

Simran steps on a loose floorboard, and at the faint squeak, her mother instantly slams the laptop shut. She doesn't say anything, of course. Simran knew what she was giving up, the day of their fight, but a part of her hoped somehow they'd bridge the gap. Weeks later, she's starting to see that won't happen.

But Simran still cannot see her mother as the bad guy. Not when she understands her so well now. Not when she almost *became* her.

"You should apply," Simran says quietly. "I think you might enjoy it."

Her mother speaks then. It's so surprising Simran jumps. "Enjoy? That has nothing to do with it. I would do it to make us money, to be productive. I probably won't. It would be too much time away from home."

She says this very fast, and Simran wonders if she's embarrassed. "Not everything has to be about the family. You could . . . do something *just* for yourself, too."

She thinks her mom might scoff, but instead she stares into space. It's clearly still an incomprehensible concept to her. Might always be. That's the ironic thing: It's only because of her mom's sacrifices that Simran can afford to do things for herself, to take risks, to do some things out of love rather than logic. *That* is the better life her parents made for her. But they've spent so long in survival mode they can no longer see it.

Simran exits the kitchen as quietly as she came, leaving her mother to her dreams.

Toor Uncle's workshop is loud when Simran enters, her footsteps drowned out by mechanical whirring and pistons.

Toor Uncle waves at her from a car with the hood popped open.

"Birdie, it's good to see you." She returns his hug. "Your mother's bike is over here. Finally fixed. Only took us *months!*"

He cackles, pointing. Her mother's bike is leaned against the wall, now pristine. Simran bends to examine it. "Uncle ji, you did too much." He's added a basket, a bottle cage, and a fresh coat of paint over the rust. Grey, with sunflower yellow accents. The artistry is impressive.

"Nonsense. We're family, aren't we?"

She smiles. In many ways, losing her golden-girl status has been a blessing. She no longer has to force politeness with people she doesn't like, because they don't talk to her anymore. But the people she always genuinely loved have found it in themselves to forgive her. To understand her. And . . . to try to understand someone she cares very much about.

Toor Uncle points to a corner obscured by machinery. "He's in the back."

"Thank you again for letting him work here."

"Anyone with your recommendation is welcome in my shop." He pats her shoulder. "Besides, he does good work."

Simran finds Rajan in the corner at a workbench, a drawing rolled out in front of him. He whips off his safety glasses when he sees her.

"Dude, your timing is amazing."

She peers at his drawing. It's the plans for a cabinet, the dimensions scrawled on each line. The perspective is immaculate. "Why's that?"

"Because I need a break. I can't believe I got all the way to carpentry school, and they put me in math class all over again."

Simran traces a finger over the arched top of the cabinet. His instructors can't possibly be requiring a design this ambitious. "Make this all right angles instead, and you'll have less geometry to figure out."

"That would look boring as hell."

"Ah. I see."

Rajan gives her a side-eye. "Point taken, Sahiba. But that doesn't mean I have to like it."

She blinks innocently. "Want to take a break? I need help putting my mom's bike in my truck."

"Grunt work?" He rolls the drawing up haphazardly. "That, I can do."

The sound of machinery fades as they walk behind the building, to the grassy lot where Simran's parked. Rajan lays the bike into the truck bed. In the sunlight, the paint job looks even nicer. *Too* nice. Toor Uncle doesn't seem the type to add these embellishments. Didn't he say he was busy?

It hits her. "*You* painted her bike, didn't you?"

Rajan shrugs from atop the truck bed. "Think she'll like it?"

Simran knows exactly what her mom will say. *What a waste of paint. I didn't need the bottle cage. The seat was already perfectly functional!* "Absolutely. Why yellow?"

He flicks the front wheel. It spins, stirring the loose sand in her truck bed from the sandbags. "It was my mom's favourite. The colour of sunshine, she always said. Even when she was sick, she'd sit on our porch and watch the sun rise and set."

His voice is soft by the end.

"I wish I'd met her," Simran says.

A fleeting trace of a smile. "Trust me, she knew who you were. She chewed me out for being a douchebag to you once."

"And look at you now. She'd be proud."

He lies down next to the bike, resting his head on a sandbag. "There were times," he says, "that was all I wanted. For her to be proud of me."

"And now?"

"I just want to be proud of myself."

She has no words for how proud *she* is of him for that, so she crawls into the cab on top of him and kisses him.

"Cheesy as shit, isn't it?" he says when they pull apart. "But it's true. I'm practicing being a better person. Maybe one day I'll even be able to step into the gurdwara without bursting into flames."

She laughs. "Rajan, you know Sikhism isn't about that kind of stuff."

He's grinning, too. "Yeah, fine. I'll come someday." He nods to the shop. "Uncle ji's always raving about your singing. Makes a guy curious."

He's never heard her sing. How has he never heard her sing? It's such a significant part of her, and suddenly, all she wants to do is share it with him. "In that case."

She sits up and, before he can ask what she means, begins to hum. Rajan stills. She keeps humming, though, for several lines before opening her mouth. She chooses a shabad anyone with a Sikh background would know, written by the tenth Guru when he had just lost his sons in battle and was separated from his people. It's an expression of grief, a love poem, and a spiritual declaration all in one, and that's why she likes it. There is no guilt to be felt here for being human. There's just the sand digging into her knees, the wind stirring her hair, the sun warming her skin, and the boy beneath her, all of which are, if Sikh philosophy is to be believed, ultimately the same thing.

When the last note fades, he's silent. "Well?" she asks.

"I understand now," Rajan says. "Why people believe in God."

She rolls her eyes and gets off him, although from the way he watches her, she's not entirely sure he's joking. "It sounds better with instruments accompanying, if you ever do want to come to the gurdwara."

"And have people shit-talk you even more? No thanks."

"I don't care."

"Do they? Talk shit about you?" He keeps his voice light.

"Not to my face." Her voice is equally light as she settles next to him, cross-legged. "But TJ told me an auntie asked her mom if it was true if I was dating a gangbanger."

"Fucking ridiculous," Rajan says. "*I'm* the one dating a gangbanger. Want me to pop their tires?"

"I have no idea who this person is, Rajan."

"And? That doesn't sound like a no, Sahiba." He sits up and tucks her close, his arm spanning under her ribs. Rubs his nose against the soft shell of her ear. "You know I'll do it."

Simran leans into him and closes her eyes, not caring if anyone sees. Her father's words still ring true—life's too short to waste a single moment with the people she loves. Of which there are many. It's almost funny to think that not long ago, she was certain she'd be left alone in the world.

That is, of course, still possible. But less likely, she thinks, if she stops pushing everyone away. Her cousin, her sister, her father, her friends, Rajan . . . she's slowly learning how to let them in. The rest isn't up to her.

And that, honestly, gives her a bit of peace.

Her eyes open. "What about that cabinet drawing is giving you trouble, anyway?"

Rajan smacks a kiss behind her ear before releasing her. "Don't say *I told you so*, but those arched doors are beating my ass. I've cut the wrong-size pieces twice now." He digs into his pocket with an air of defeat. "I think it has to do with the arc radius, but I can't figure out what."

Simran smiles and extends her hand. "Give me a pen."

AUTHOR'S NOTE

WHEN I FIRST started telling friends about this book, some were a bit confused about the premise: *Wait, there are Indo-Canadian gangs? Aren't gangs only in big cities? Why would teenagers be involved?*

While this is very much a work of fiction, the inspiration is real—and probably new territory for many of my readers.

A lot of us have a certain image in mind when we picture a gang, but these organizations operate everywhere and are shaped by regional context. Local policy, culture, and racial discrimination, among other factors, have historically led to marginalized diaspora communities turning to each other, rather than an officially recognized power, for governance and assistance. And to govern, you need money! And to get money . . . well . . .

This is how many ethnic gangs in British Columbia's Lower Mainland (Vancouver and the surrounding area) got their start in the 1970s and 80s. There is an extremely fascinating—and violent and tragic—history in the decades that followed that I will not rehash here, although it's certainly worth a read to understand how we got to this place. Nowadays, these organizations thrive not only in the biggest cities in Canada, but in smaller communities, where they take advantage of less surveillance to expand their operations. And just like with gangs all over the world, young people are recruited—to do the street-level dirty work, to take on the biggest risks—all while being promised grand rewards that they will never see.

However, there *is* one rather unique feature to Indo-Canadian gang culture. And it's a question that has puzzled law enforcement and community leaders for a long time: Why do a disproportionate number of young people specifically from well-to-do, "respectable" South Asian families with no gang ties, who ostensibly have everything going for them, get involved?

There's plenty of literature attempting to explain this phenomenon. But one concept that intrigued me was the idea that these kids were simply neglected in ways we don't always recognize. Their immigrant parents had to work hard to sustain their families and give their kids "a good life." So they weren't home a lot. In eastern cultures, raising kids is traditionally seen as a community endeavor. You don't *have* to always be there, as a parent, because you know your kid has others to turn to if you're busy. But this is not so much the case in North America, which tends to have a more individualistic culture. Immigrant families may not always see the implications of that difference . . . that although their kids have the things they never had, like physical safety, financial security, and opportunity for the future, they are missing out on social connection, attention, and a sense of purpose.

So those kids look for it elsewhere—and gangs do sell that image. Here there is a family, built right in . . . until it isn't. Loyalty, until it isn't. Glory, until it isn't. The young people recruited into gangs are exploited, injured, traumatized, incarcerated, or die young. And if they do live through it, it is *so* hard to claw their way back to a "normal" life once these things have happened to them. They're trapped in a cycle of crime and addiction and violence and social isolation (ironically). Not exactly the better future their elders envisioned when they moved across the world. But, of course, that's the nature of the immigrant dream: it is not always realized the way we imagined. Sometimes, it's a very different kind of story.

This novel holds many variations of that story—some told extensively, others in a passing line or two. The story's not always pretty. Or fair. But maybe we can learn from it. We can understand and empathize so we don't see these gang-involved youth in binary terms like innocent or criminal, good or bad, or as "people who never learn." but rather as people *we could have been* if we were vulnerable in just the right place at just the right time.

ACKNOWLEDGMENTS

IT FEELS SURREAL to be writing the acknowledgments for my second published novel. This book is rather special to me, and I can no longer tell if that's because of the actual story, the life I lived during the writing of it, or its journey to publication. Probably a bit of everything. So let me thank a few people who've played a part in it.

Firstly, my editor, Rachel Stark—it's a beautiful thing when your editor *gets* your book to its core. And when they constantly have you giggling in the margins of your manuscript, it's even better. Simran and Rajan's story always felt safe in your hands, Rachel, and that's not something I ever take for granted. Thank you for taking it on.

Many other folks at Disney Hyperion have breathed life into this book: In editorial, Sylvie Frank, Candice Snow, Elanna Heda, Stephanie Lurie, and Kieran Viola; in managing editorial and production, Sara Liebling, Guy Cunningham, Jill Amack, Jackie Hornberger, Jeremy Burton, and Jerry Gonzalez; in publicity, Kelly Forsythe, Daniela Escobar, and Crystal McCoy; in marketing, Dina Sherman, Maddie Hughes (special shout-out for being a huge in-house fan of this book <3), Bekka Mills, Matt

Schweitzer, Holly Nagel, Danielle DiMartino, Alex Eiserloh, Scott Myles, Enrique de la Espriella, Marina Shults, Ian Byrne, Elizabeth Tunnicliffe, and Kelly Clair; and in sales, Monique Diman, Vicki Korlishin, LeBria Casher, and the Penguin Random House sales team. In design, huge thanks to Zareen Johnson, Marci Senders, Joann Hill, and, of course, cover artist Adam Campbell, for all your hard work!

This book required a lot of research. Sometimes, I needed to consult an expert. Amy Reed was a wonderful authenticity reader, whose suggestions helped me refine my portrayals of drug use and addiction. Amanda Gates, a BC youth probation officer, took the time to answer my questions and gave me further insight into the youth justice system. All departures from reality with respect to legal timelines and logistics are creative decisions on my part.

Several folks at Azantian Literary worked on this book: Ben Baxter, Alexandra Weiss, and, of course, my agent, Jennifer Azantian. There's a reason this book is dedicated to her. This industry can be tough. When I was disheartened, she encouraged me to just write the book I wanted to write, promising we'd figure out the rest later. Thank you, Jen. Your trust in my abilities always means a lot, but I especially needed it then.

To this book's beta readers: Rachel Merritt, you were the first to read this book and present in the earliest stages of the process, always there when I needed a sober second thought—whether for pages, bouncing back and forth ideas, or just for venting. Mariel Jorgensen, you always know where I'm going, sometimes before I do; your analysis of my characters helps them come even more alive for me (plus, your *Queen of the South* episode guide was extremely high yield for this book). Meha Razdan, with your expansive literary tastes, copywriting skills, and general intellectualism hidden behind the veneer of a meme factory, I can always rely on you when I'm looking for comp titles, writing pitches, or just to check the temperature on a concept I have. I adore you all!

The nature of acknowledgments is that they get written before many people even enter the publishing process. So I'd like to briefly thank a few people who made a positive impact in my first book's publication, who I didn't get a chance to thank before: the team at Books Forward; Jessica Parra for her sweet blurb; Samantha Devotta at Penguin Random House Canada; my Queen's family (a special yoo-hoo to Sallya Aleboyeh, who almost singlehandedly ensured a decent attendance for my debut launch); the Desi KidLit Community (including Adiba Jaigirdar, who did a virtual launch with me!); the librarians and booksellers who supported my debut; and, of course, the readers. Both the new ones and the old friends who faithfully read something I warned would be different from past works. You're real ones!

Mom and Dad, thank you for your help when I ask questions like, "Hey, how would you spell this Punjabi word in English?" and for all your support, thank you so much for your work on this book! This book is, in many ways, a story about immigrants and their kids, which made me reflect on our own story. You raised me in an environment that allowed me to pursue my dreams; you were always there for me, despite how hard it all must've been for you. I'm grateful for that. And lastly, thank you to Gurbind—for the laughs, the late-night talks, and for listening. You're my best friend. I'm so lucky you also happen to be my brother.